CHASING HARRY WINSTON

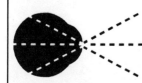

This Large Print Book carries the
Seal of Approval of N.A.V.H.

CHASING HARRY WINSTON

LAUREN WEISBERGER

THORNDIKE PRESS
A part of Gale, Cengage Learning

GALE
CENGAGE Learning

Detroit • New York • San Francisco • New Haven, Conn • Waterville, Maine • London

GALE
CENGAGE Learning

LIBRARY OF CONGRESS CATALOGING-IN-PUBLICATION DATA

Weisberger, Lauren, 1977–
    Chasing Harry Winston / by Lauren Weisberger.
      p. cm. — (Thorndike Press large print core)
    ISBN-13: 978-1-4104-0730-6 (hardcover : alk. paper)
    ISBN-10: 1-4104-0730-6 (hardcover : alk. paper)
    1. Young women — Manhattan (New York, N.Y.) — Fiction.
2. Female friendship — Fiction. 3. Manhattan (New York, N.Y.)
— Fiction. 4. Chick lit. 5. Large type books. I. Title.
    PS3623.E453C48 2008b
    813'.6—dc22

                2008018130

Published in 2008 in arrangement with Simon & Schuster, Inc.

Printed in the United States of America
1 2 3 4 5 6 7 12 11 10 09 08

for mike, with love

PANTIES IS A VILE WORD

When Leigh's doorbell rang unexpectedly at nine on a Monday night, she did not think, *Gee, I wonder who that could be.* She thought, *Shit. Go away.* Were there people who actually welcomed unannounced visitors when they just stopped by to "say hello" or "check in"? Recluses, probably. Or those friendly Midwestern folks she'd seen depicted in *Big Love* but had never actually met — yes, they probably didn't mind. But this! This was an affront. Monday nights were sacred and completely off-limits to the rest of the world, a time of No Human Contact when Leigh could veg out in sweats and watch episode after beautiful TiVo'd episode of *Project Runway.* It was her only time alone all week, and after some intensive training on her part, her friends, her family, and her boyfriend, Russell, finally abided by it.

The girls had stopped asking for Monday-night plans at the end of the nineties; Russell, who in the beginning of their relationship had openly balked, now quietly contained his resentment (and in football season relished having his own Monday nights free); her mother struggled through one night a week without picking up the phone to call, finally accepting after all these years that she wouldn't hear from Leigh until Tuesday morning no matter how many times she hit Redial. Even Leigh's publisher knew better than to assign her Monday-night reading . . . or, god forbid, knew not to log an interrupting phone call. Which is precisely why it was so incredible that her doorbell had just rung — incredible and panic-inducing.

Figuring it was her super, there to change the air-conditioning filter; or one of the delivery guys from Hot Enchiladas, leaving a menu; or, most likely of all, someone just confusing her door with one of her neighbors', she hit Mute on the TV remote and did not move a muscle. She cocked her head to the side like a Labrador, straining for any confirmation that the intruder had left, but the only thing she heard was the dull, constant thudding from above. Suffering from what her old shrink called "noise sensitivity" and everyone else described as "fucking neurotic," Leigh had, of course, thoroughly scoped out her upstairs neighbor before signing over her life savings: The apartment might have been the most perfect she'd seen in a year and a half of looking, but she hadn't wanted to take any chances.

Leigh had asked Adriana for the scoop on the woman above her, in apartment 17D, but her friend had just pursed her pouty lips and shrugged. No matter that Adriana had lived in the building's full-floor penthouse apartment from the day her parents had moved from São Paulo to New York nearly two decades before; she had completely embraced the New Yorker's I-Promise-Not-to-Acknowledge-You-If-You-Extend-Me-the-Same-Courtesy attitude toward her neighbors and could offer Leigh no info on her neighbor. And so, on a blustery December Saturday right before Christmas, Leigh had slipped the building's doorman twenty bucks, Bond-style, and waited in the lobby, pretending to read a manuscript. After Leigh spent three hours scanning the same anecdote, the doorman coughed loudly and looked at her over the top of his glasses *with meaning*. Glancing up, Leigh felt an immediate wave of relief. Before her, removing a QVC catalog from an unlocked mailbox, stood an overweight woman in a polka-dot housedress. *Not a day younger than eighty,* thought Leigh, and she breathed a sigh of relief; there would be no stilettos clacking against the hardwood floors, no late-night parties, no parade of visitors stomping around.

The very next day Leigh wrote a check for the down payment, and two months later she excitedly moved into her mint-condition one-bedroom dream apartment. It had a renovated kitchen, an oversized bathtub, and a more than decent northern view of the Empire State Building. It might have been one of the smallest units in the building — okay, *the* smallest — but it was still a dream, a beautiful, lucky dream in a building Leigh never thought she could afford, each and every obscenely priced square foot paid for with her own hard work and savings.

How could she possibly have predicted that the seemingly innocuous upstairs neighbor was a dedicated wearer of massive wooden orthopedic clogs? Still, Leigh berated herself regularly for thinking high heels were the only potential noise risk: it had been an amateur's mistake. Before she'd spotted her neighbor wearing the offending shoes, Leigh had created an elaborate explanation for the relentless upstairs racket. She decided that the woman had to be Dutch (since everyone knew Dutch people wore clogs), and the matriarch of a huge, proudly Dutch family who received constant visits from countless children, grandchildren, nieces, nephews, siblings, cousins, and general advice-seekers . . . all, most likely, Dutch clog-wearers. After spotting her neighbor wearing an air cast and feigning interest in the woman's disgusting-sounding foot ailments including (but not limited to) plantar fasciitis, ingrown toenails, neuromas, and bunions, Leigh had clucked as sympathetically as she could manage and then raced upstairs to check her copy of the co-op rules. Sure enough, they dictated that owners were required to cover eighty percent of their hardwood floors with carpet — which she realized was an entirely moot point when the very next page revealed that her upstairs neighbor was president of the board.

Leigh had already endured nearly four months of round-the-clock clogging, something that might have been funny if it was happening to someone else. Her nerves were directly tied to the volume and frequency of the steady *thump-thump-thump* that segued into a *thumpety-thump-thumpety-thump-thump* pattern when Leigh's heart began to pound right along with it. She tried to breathe slowly, but her exhales were short and raspy, punctuated by little guppy gasps. As she examined her pale complexion (which on good days she thought of as "ethereal" and all other times accepted as "sickly") in the mirrored hallway closet door, a thin sheen of perspiration dampened her forehead.

It seemed to be happening more frequently, this sweating/breathing issue — and not just when she heard the wood-on-wood banging. Sometimes Leigh would awaken from a sleep so deep it almost hurt, only to find her heart racing and her sheets drenched. Last week in the middle of an otherwise completely relaxing *shavasna* — albeit one where the instructor felt compelled to play an a capella version of "Amazing Grace" over the speakers — a sharp pain shot through Leigh's chest on each measured inhale. And just this morning as she watched the human tidal wave of commuters cram onto the N train — she forced herself to take the subway, but hated every second of it — Leigh's throat constricted and her pulse inexplicably quickened. There seemed to be only two plausible explanations, and although she could be a bit of a hypochondriac, even Leigh didn't think she was a likely candidate for a coronary: It was a panic attack, plain and simple.

In an ineffective attempt to dispel the panic, Leigh pressed her fingertips into her temples and stretched her neck from side to side, neither of which did a damn thing. It felt like her lungs could reach only ten percent capacity, and just as she considered who would find her body — and when — she heard a choked sobbing and yet another ring of her doorbell.

She tiptoed over to the door and looked through the peephole but saw only empty hallway. This was exactly how people ended up robbed and raped in New York City — getting duped by some criminal mastermind into opening their doors. *I'm not falling for this,* she thought as she stealthily dialed her doorman. Never mind that her building's security rivaled the UN's, or that in eight years of city living she didn't personally know anyone who'd been so much as pickpocketed, or that the chances of a psychopathic murderer choosing her apartment from more than two hundred other units in her building was unlikely. . . . This was how it all started.

The doorman answered after four eternally long rings.

"Gerard, it's Leigh Eisner in 16D. There's someone outside my door. I think they're trying to break in. Can you come up here right away? Should I call 911?" The words came out in a frantic jumble as Leigh paced the small foyer and popped Nicorette squares into her mouth directly from the foil wrapper.

"Miss Eisner, of course I'll send someone up immediately, but perhaps you're mistaking Miss Solomon for someone else? She arrived a few minutes ago and proceeded directly to your apartment . . . which is permissible for someone on your permanent clearance list."

"Emmy's here?" Leigh asked. She forgot all about her imminent death by disease or homicide and pulled open her door to find Emmy rocking back and forth on the hallway floor, knees pulled tight against her chest, cheeks slick with tears.

"Miss, may I be of further assistance? Shall I still —"

"Thanks for your help, Gerard. We're fine now," Leigh said, snapping shut her cell phone and shoving it into the kangaroo pocket of her sweatshirt. She dropped to her knees without thinking and wrapped her arms around Emmy.

"Honey, what's wrong?" she crooned, gathering Emmy's tear-dampened hair from her face into a ponytail. "What happened?"

The show of concern brought with it a fresh stream of tears; Emmy was sobbing so hard her tiny body trembled. Leigh ran through the possibilities of what could cause such pain, and came up with only three: a death in the family, a pending death in the family, or a man.

"Sweetie, is it your parents? Did something happen to them? To Izzie?"

Emmy shook her head.

"Talk to me, Emmy. Is everything okay with Duncan?"

This elicited a wail so plaintive it hurt Leigh to hear it. Bingo.

"Over," Emmy cried, her voice catching in her throat. "It's over for good."

Emmy had made this pronouncement no fewer than eight times in the five years she and Duncan had been dating, but something about tonight seemed different.

"Honey, I'm sure it's all just —"

"He met someone."

"He *what?*" Leigh dropped her arms and sat back on her ankles.

"I'm sorry, let me rephrase: I bought him someone."

"What on earth are you talking about?"

"Remember when I got him a membership at Clay for his thirty-first birthday because he was desperate to get back in shape? And then he never went — not one fucking time in two whole years — because, according to him, it wasn't 'an efficient use of his time' to just go and stand on the treadmill? So rather than just cancel the whole damn thing and forget about it, I, genius extraordinaire,

15

decide to buy him a series of sessions with a personal trainer so he wouldn't have to waste one precious second exercising like everyone else."

"I think I can see where this is going."

"What? You think he fucked her?" Emmy laughed mirthlessly. It sometimes surprised people to hear Emmy trash-talk with such ferocity — she was, after all, only five-one and looked no older than a teenager — but Leigh barely even noticed anymore. "I thought so, too. It's so much worse than that."

"That sounds bad enough, sweetheart." All-out loving sympathy and support were the best she could offer, but Emmy didn't appear comforted.

"You probably wonder how it could get worse, right? Well, let me tell you how. He didn't just fuck her — I could maybe deal with that. Noooo, not my Duncan. He 'fell in love' with her." Emmy jabbed out air quotes with the forefingers and middle fingers of both hands and rolled her bloodshot eyes. "He's 'waiting for her,' quote-unquote, until she's 'ready.' She's a VIRGIN, for chrissake! I've put up with five years of his cheating and lies and kinky, weird sex so he can FALL IN LOVE WITH A VIRGIN TRAINER I HIRED IN THE GYM I PAID FOR? In *love!* Leigh, what am I going to do?"

Leigh, relieved that she could finally do something tangible, took Emmy's arm and helped her to her feet. "Come in, honey. Let's go inside. I'll make us some tea and you can tell me what happened."

Emmy sniffed. "Oh, god, I forgot . . . it's Monday. I don't want to interrupt. I'll be fine. . . ."

"Don't be ridiculous. I wasn't even doing anything," Leigh lied. "Come in this minute."

Leigh led her to the couch and, after patting the overstuffed arm to indicate where Emmy should rest her head, ducked behind the wall that separated the living room from the kitchen. With its speckled granite countertops and new stainless steel appliances, the kitchen was Leigh's favorite room in the whole apartment. All of her pots and pans hung from under-cabinet hooks in order of size, and all of her utensils and spices were obsessively organized in matching glass and stainless containers. Crumbs, spills, wrappers, dirty dishes — all nonexistent. The refrigerator looked like someone had Hoovered it clean, and the countertops were entirely smudge-free. If it was possible for a room to personify its owner's neurotic personality, the kitchen and Leigh could be identical twins.

She filled the kettle (purchased just last week during a Bloomingdale's Home Sale, because who said you were entitled to new things only when you registered?), piled a tray high with cheese and Wheat Thins, and peeked through the window into the living room to make sure Emmy was resting comfortably. Seeing that she was lying flat on her back with an arm flung over her eyes, Leigh slipped out her cell phone and selected Adriana's name from her phone book. She typed: *SOS. E & D finished. Get down here ASAP.*

"Do you have Advil?" Emmy called from the couch. And then, more quietly: "Duncan always carried Advil."

Leigh opened her mouth to add that Duncan had always carried a lot of things — a business card for his favorite escort service, a wallet-sized picture of himself as a child, and, occasionally, a genital wart or two that he swore were just "skin tags" — but she controlled herself. In addition to being unnecessary since Emmy was suffering enough, it would be hypocritical: Contrary to everyone's belief, Leigh wasn't exactly in the world's most perfect relationship, either. But she pushed the thought of Russell from her mind.

"Sure, I'll get you some in a minute," she said, turning off the whistling kettle.

"Tea's ready."

The girls had just taken their first sips when the doorbell rang. Emmy looked at Leigh, who just said, "Adriana."

"It's open!" Leigh called toward the front door, but Adriana had already figured that out. She stormed into the living room and stood with her hands on her hips, surveying the scene.

"What is going on here?" she demanded. Adriana's slight Brazilian accent, little more than a soft, sexy lilting when she was calm, made her almost unintelligible when she felt, in her own words, "passionate" about someone or something. Which was pretty much always. "Where are the drinks?"

Leigh motioned to the kitchen. "Water's still hot. Check the cupboard above the microwave. I have a whole bunch of different flavors in —"

"No tea!" Adriana screeched and pointed to Emmy. "Can't you see she's miserable? We need *real* drinks. I'll make caipirinhas."

"I don't have any mint. Or limes. Actually, I'm not even sure I have the right booze," Leigh said.

"I brought everything." Adriana lifted a large paper bag over her head and grinned.

Leigh often found Adriana's abruptness irritating, sometimes a little overwhelming, but tonight she was grateful to her for taking control of the situation. It had been nearly twelve years since Leigh first saw Adriana's smile, and still it left her feeling awestruck and a little anxious. *How could someone possibly be that beautiful?* she wondered for the hundred thousandth time. *What higher power orchestrated such a perfect union of genes? Who decided that one single solitary soul deserved* skin *like that?* It was so fundamentally unfair.

It was another few minutes before the drinks were mixed and distributed and everyone had settled down; Emmy and Adriana sprawled on the couch; Leigh sat cross-legged on the floor.

"So, tell us what happened," Leigh said, placing a hand on Emmy's ankle. "Just take your time and tell us all about it."

Emmy sighed and, for the first time since she arrived, appeared cried out. "There's not that much to tell. She's absolutely adorable — like, nauseatingly cute. And young. Really, really young."

"What's really, really young?" Leigh asked.

"Twenty-three."

"That's not *so* young."

"She has a MySpace profile," Emmy said.

Leigh grimaced.

"And she's on Facebook."

"Good lord," Adriana muttered.

"Yeah, I know. Her favorite color is lavender and her favorite book is *The South Beach Diet* and she just *adores* cookie dough, campfires, and watching Saturday-morning cartoons. Oh, and she simply *must* get nine hours of sleep or else she's really, really cranky."

"What else?" Leigh asked, although she could predict the answer.

"What else do you want to know?" Adriana started the quiz show–like round. "Name?"

"Brianna Sheldon."

"College?"

"SMU, Comm major, Kappa Kappa Gamma." Emmy enunciated these last three words with a perfect Valley Girl inflection.

"Hometown?"

"Born in Richmond, raised in a suburb of Charleston."

"Music?"

"Like you even have to ask. Kenny Chesney."

"High school sport?"

"Let's just all say it in unison. . . ." Emmy said.

"Cheerleading," Adriana and Leigh simultaneously.

"Given." Emmy sighed, but then she smiled for a second. "I found some pictures of her from her sister's wedding photographer's Web site — she even manages to look good in teal taffeta. The whole thing is positively nauseating."

The girls all laughed, each accustomed to this oldest of female-bonding traditions. When your life was in the gutter because your ex-boyfriend suddenly surfaced on weddingchannel.com, nothing offered comfort like trashing the new girlfriend. It was actually how they had become friends in the first place. Leigh and Emmy met each other first in Astronomy 101, a class both were taking to fulfill the dreaded science requirement. Neither realized until it was too late that Astro was actually an aggressive mixture of chemistry, calculus, and physics — not the chance to learn all the constellations and look at the pretty stars, like they had hoped. They were the two least-competent and lowest-scoring members of their lab group, and their TA had strung together enough English words to let them know that they'd better start improving or they would fail the class, which prompted Leigh and Emmy to meet three times a week in the study lounge at Emmy's dorm, a glass-enclosed, fluorescent-lit pod wedged between the kitchen and the coed bathroom. The girls were just beginning to tackle the review notes for the upcoming midterm when they heard banging followed by distinctly female shrieks. Emmy and Leigh looked at each other and smiled as they listened to the angry words being exchanged down the hall, sure it was yet another argument between a scorned sorority girl and the drunken guy who hadn't called the next day. The yelling shifted, however, and within seconds Emmy and Leigh watched as a gorgeous honey blonde with a sexy accent took a verbal barrage from a hysterical, red-faced, significantly less pretty blonde directly outside the study lounge.

"I can't believe I voted for you!" the red-faced girl screamed. "I actually stood up in front of the whole chapter to speak on your behalf, and this is how you show your appreciation? By sleeping with my boyfriend?"

The stunner with the accent sighed. When she spoke, it was with quiet resignation. "Annie, I've said I'm sorry. I never would have done that had I known he was your boyfriend."

This was not calming to the screamer. "How could you not have known? We've been together for, like, months!"

"I didn't know, because he accosted *me* last

night, flirted with *me,* bought *me* drinks, and asked *me* to his fraternity formal. I'm sorry if it didn't occur to me that he had a girlfriend. If it had, I assure you, I wouldn't have been interested." The girl held out her hand in a gesture of reconciliation and apology. "Please. Men aren't that important. Let's forget about it, okay?"

"Forget about it?" the girl hissed, almost snarled, through closed teeth. "You're nothing more than a little freshman whore, sleeping with the seniors because you think they actually like you. Stay away from me and stay away from him, and keep your stupid freshman trampiness out of my life. Understood?" The girl's voice had gotten louder; by the time she'd asked if Adriana understood, she was shouting again.

Emmy and Leigh watched as Adriana took a long look at the girl, appeared to weigh a response in her mind, and then, deciding against it, simply said, "Understood perfectly." Immediately the angry blonde swiveled on one Puma and flounced away. Adriana finally allowed herself to smile before noticing Emmy and Leigh watching from the lounge.

"Did you just see that?" Adriana asked, moving into the doorway.

Emmy coughed and Leigh blushed and nodded. "She was really pissed," Leigh said.

Adriana laughed. "As she so kindly pointed out, I'm just some stupid freshman. How am I supposed to know who's dating who around here? Especially when the guy in question spent half the night telling me how great it is to be single again after being tied down for the last four months. Was I supposed to hook him up to a polygraph?"

Leigh leaned back in her chair and took a swig from her Diet Coke. "Maybe you should start carrying a list of every single older girl on campus and their phone numbers. That way, every time you meet a guy, you can call every one of them to make sure he's available."

Adriana's face broke into a huge smile, and Leigh was charmed: She saw immediately why the boy from the previous night had lost all memory of his girlfriend in Adriana's presence. "I'm Adriana," she said, giving first Leigh and then Emmy a little wave. "Apparently also known as Class of 2000 Queen Slut."

Leigh introduced herself. "Hey. I'm Leigh. I was thinking of rushing next semester, until I just met your 'sister.' So thanks for that informative lesson."

Emmy dog-eared her textbook page and smiled up at Adriana. "My name is Emmy. I also go by The Last Remaining Virgin in the Class of 2000, in case you haven't heard. It's a pleasure to meet you."

The girls had talked that night for three hours, and when they were finished, they had established a game plan for the next few weeks: Adriana would drop out of the sorority she had joined under duress (pressure from her mother), Leigh would withdraw her application to rush in the spring, and Emmy would lose her virginity the moment she met an appropriate candidate.

In the twelve years since that night, the girls had barely come up for air.

"And I also happened to read on her Friendster page — using Duncan's password, of course — that she dreams of having two boys and a girl and wants to be a young mom. Isn't that just precious? It doesn't seem that part bothered Duncan."

Leigh and Adriana exchanged glances then looked at Emmy, who was completely absorbed in removing a cuticle in an apparent effort not to cry.

So there it was. The new girl's age, her cheerleading, even her oh-so-adorable name might have been infuriating, but they weren't intolerable; the fact that she, too, yearned to be a mom as soon as humanly possible was the real clincher. For as long as anyone could remember, Emmy had been very vocal about her desire to have children. Obsessed. She told anyone who would listen that she wanted a huge family, and she wanted it as soon as possible. Four, five, six kids — boys, girls, a bunch of each; it didn't matter to Emmy, as long as it happened . . . soon. And while Duncan certainly knew better than anyone how badly Emmy wanted to be a mom, he had managed to wriggle free of any major discussions about the topic. The first two years of their relationship, Emmy had kept this particular desire to herself. After all, they were only twenty-five, and even she knew there was plenty of time. But as their years together started to cycle past at what felt like warp speed and Emmy grew more insistent, Duncan only got cagier. He would say things like "Statistically speaking, chances are I'll have kids one day," and Emmy would ignore the lack of enthusiasm and his telling pronoun choice, focusing instead on the fact that Duncan had uttered those three magical words: *I'll have kids.* It was because of those magical words that Emmy conceded Duncan his overnight "work" absences and once — god knows why now — an inexplicable brush with chlamydia. After all, he had agreed to be the father of her future children.

Adriana broke the silence by doing what

she always did when she got uncomfortable: changing the subject entirely.

"Leigh, *querida,* it's seventy-five degrees outside. Why are you dressed for the middle of winter?"

Leigh looked at her thick fleece pants and matching sweatshirt and shrugged.

"Do you not feel well? Are you cold?"

"I don't know; it was just what was laying around. What does it matter?"

"It's not that it matters, it's just strange that someone so, how should I say it, *temperature aware* isn't positively melting right now."

Leigh wasn't about to admit that she was actually warm — too warm — but that there were extenuating circumstances. Adriana might have asked, but she definitely didn't want to hear that Leigh swathed herself in clothing because she hated when the backs of her arms or thighs stuck to the leather couch. That of course she'd prefer to sit around in a pair of boxers and a tank top, but the skin-on-leather stickiness — not to mention the annoying ripping noises every time she shifted position — made this impossible. Leigh knew they would think her crazy if she explained that she'd actually already worn all of her lightweight, full-length pajama pants (and even all of her yoga pants) and that because she preferred to wear them without underwear, they were really only single-use pants and ended up in the wash pretty quickly. So she was really wearing the fleece sweat suit only because it was the single clean option in her closet that was capable of protecting her from the dreaded leather couch, which both her mother and Emmy had insisted would be the right choice even though Leigh had really wanted the modern fabric one that wouldn't have felt like sitting in a vat of rubber cement all the time. Not to even *mention* the fact that in a few short months (six) it would be winter, and she'd still have to dress like an Eskimo because regardless of how toasty warm she kept the apartment, the couch would feel like ice against her bare skin instead of snuggly and soft like the MicroSuede one everyone else had vetoed. No, it would be better to just leave well enough alone.

"Hmm," Leigh murmured, hoping to end the conversation by saying nothing. "I think we're ready for another round."

The second drink went down easier than the first, so easily in fact that even the increased upstairs thumping no longer made Leigh feel quite so . . . unhinged. It was time to rally for her friend.

"So, give us the top three things the cheerleader will be less than thrilled to discover about Duncan," Leigh said, placing her soles together and pushing her knees to the floor, feeling the stretch in her inner thighs.

"Yes, yes, a good idea." Adriana nodded.

A chunk of Emmy's naturally brunette hair — she was the only one among the three of them, and possibly the only woman in all of Manhattan, who had never dyed, permed, highlighted, straightened, or even so much as spritzed lemon juice on her shoulder-length mane — fell out of her ponytail, covering half of her bangs and her entire left eye. Leigh yearned to reach up and tuck it behind Emmy's ear, but she resisted. Instead she popped another piece of Nicorette in her mouth.

Emmy looked up. "What do you mean?"

"Well, what are his flaws? Disgusting habits? Deal-breakers?" Leigh asked.

Adriana threw up her hands in exasperation. "Come on, Emmy. Anything! Quirks, hang-ups, obsessions, addictions, secrets . . . It'll make you feel better. Tell us what was wrong with him."

Emmy sniffed. "There was noth—"

"Don't you dare say there was nothing wrong with him," Leigh interrupted. "Now, granted, Duncan was very" — Leigh paused here, wanting to say "manipulative" or "devious" or "deceitful," but she stopped herself just in time — "charming, but he had to have *something* you never told us about. Some sort of classified information that will have perky little Brianna hanging up her pom-poms."

"Narcissistic personality disorder?" Adriana prompted.

Leigh immediately jumped in for a back-and-forth rally. "Erectile dysfunction?"

"Gambling addiction?"

"Cried more than you did?"

"Violent drunk?"

"Mommy issues?"

"Dig deep, Emmy," Leigh urged.

"Well, there was something I always thought was a little strange . . ." Emmy said.

The girls looked at her eagerly.

"Not that it was really a big deal. He didn't do it during sex or anything," she said quickly.

"This just got a hell of a lot more interesting," Adriana said.

"Spill it, Emmy," Leigh said.

"He, uh . . ." She coughed and cleared her throat. "We didn't really talk about it, but he, uh, sometimes wore my panties to work."

This disclosure was enough to silence the two people who considered themselves

31

professional talkers. They talked their way through shrink appointments, out of traffic tickets, and into fully reserved restaurants, but for many seconds — possibly an entire minute — neither could produce a remotely logical or rational response to this new information.

Adriana recovered first. "*Panties* is a vile word," she said. She frowned and emptied the caipirinha pitcher into her glass.

Leigh stared at her. "I cannot believe you're being pedantic right now. One of your best friends just told you that her boyfriend of nearly five years liked wearing her panties, and your biggest issue is with the word?"

"I'm just pointing out its relative grossness. All women hate the word. *Panties.* Just say it — *panties.* It makes my skin crawl."

"Adriana! *He wore her underwear.*"

"I know, trust me, I heard her. I was commenting — as a side note, mind you — that in the future, I don't think we should use that word. *Panties.* Ugh. Do you not find it repulsive?"

Leigh paused for a moment. "Yeah, I guess I do. But that's not really the takeaway here."

Adriana sipped and looked pointedly at Leigh. "Well, then, what is?"

"The fact that her boyfriend" — Leigh

pointed at Emmy, who was watching the exchange with wide eyes and a blank expression — "put on a suit every day and went to the office. That under said suit he was wearing a pair of cute little lace bikinis. Doesn't *that* freak you out slightly more than the word *panties?*"

It wasn't until Emmy gasped audibly that Leigh realized she had gone too far.

"Oh my god, I'm sorry, sweetie. I didn't mean for that to sound as awful as —"

Emmy held up a hand, palm out, fingers spread. "Stop, please."

"That was so insensitive of me. I swear I wasn't even —"

"It's just that you have it all wrong. Duncan never really showed any interest in my lace bikinis. Or my hipsters or boy shorts, for that matter." Emmy smiled wickedly. "But he sure did seem to love my thongs. . . ."

"Hey, whore, I'm ready for you." Gilles swatted Adriana on the upper arm as he walked past, nearly dislodging the cell phone she had balanced between her chin and her left shoulder. "And move it along. I have better things to do than listen to you have phone sex all day."

A few of the older ladies looked up from their *Vogue*s and *Town & Country*s, eyes wide with disapproval at this breach in propriety, this complete ignorance of basic common courtesy. Looked up, actually, just in time to see Adriana place her china cup on its saucer and, now having one free hand, raise her right arm over her head and extend her middle finger. She did this without glancing up, still entirely immersed in her conversation.

"Yes, *querido,* yes, yes, yes. It will be perfect. Perfect! See you then." Her voice lowered, but just a notch. "I can't wait. Sounds delicious. Mmm. Kiss, kiss." She tapped a red lacquered nail on the iPhone's touch screen and dropped it into her wide-mouthed Bottega Veneta satchel.

"Who's this week's lucky prey?" Gilles asked as Adriana approached. He turned his swivel chair toward Adriana, who, aware that she had the entire salon's attention, bent forward the tiniest bit, allowing her silk blouse to fall a few inches from her chest and her bum — not particularly small, but rounded and tight the way men loved — before placing it, just so, on the leather.

"Oh, please, do you honestly care? He's boring to sleep with, much less talk about."

"Someone's in a good mood today." He stood behind her, working through her wavy hair with a wide-toothed comb and talking to her through the mirror. "The usual, I assume?"

"Maybe a little lighter around the face?" She finished the last of her coffee and then threw her head back into his chest. She sighed. "I'm in a rut, Gilles. I'm tired of all the men, of all the different names and faces I have to keep straight. Not to mention the products! My bathroom looks like a Rite Aid. There are so many different cans of shaving cream and bars of soap that I could go into business."

"Adi, dear" — he knew she hated that nickname, so he used it with relish every chance he got — "you sound ungrateful. Do you realize how many girls would change places with you in a heartbeat? To spend just a single night in that body of yours? Hell, just this morning I had two socialites-in-training jabbering away about how utterly *fab* your life is."

"Really?" She pouted at herself in the mirror but he could detect a hint of pleasure.

It was true that her name did regularly appear in all the gossip columns that mattered — could she help it if the society photographers flocked to her? — and of course she was on the list for just about every party, product launch, store opening, and benefit that mattered. And yes, if she was being entirely truthful, she would have to admit that she had dated some impressively wealthy, gorgeous, famous men in her time, but it drove her crazy that everyone assumed the trappings of fabulousness were enough to make her happy. Not that they weren't great — or that she'd be willing to give up a single second of it — but with her advanced age (closing in on thirty), Adriana had begun to suspect there might be something more.

"Really. So buck up, girl. You may flit around the Make-A-Wish benefit like an angel, but at core you're a dirty slut, and I love you for that. Besides, we did *you* the whole session last time. It's my turn now." Hip jutted to the side, he impatiently held his hand out while his assistant, a lanky brunette with Bambi eyes and a fearful expression, rushed to place a foil in his open palm.

Adriana sighed and motioned to the assistant for another cappuccino. "All right. How are *you* doing?"

"How lovely of you to inquire!" Gilles bent down and kissed her cheek. "Let's see. I've decided to focus my husband search on men who are already in committed relationships. Granted, it's still early, but I'm getting some positive results."

Adriana sighed. "Aren't there enough single men out there to keep you busy? Do you really need to play home-wrecker?"

"You know what they say, darling — if you can't have a happy home, wreck one."

"Who's 'they'?" she asked.

"Why, me, of course. You haven't seen a man enjoy a blowjob until you've watched a guy who hasn't gotten one in ten years."

Adriana laughed and immediately looked at her lap. Although she always feigned nonchalance and pretended to be casually cool with Gilles's comprehensive and explicit descriptions of gay sex, it actually made her a little uncomfortable, an admission that annoyed her. She blamed this bit of old-fashionedness on her parents, who, while generous with their money and exuberant in the many ways they spent it, were not what anyone would call social pioneers. Not that she was exactly conservative when it came to her own love life, granted — she had lost her virginity at thirteen and been to bed with dozens of men since then.

"I think I'm onto something, seriously," Gilles said as he artfully placed the foils in a face-framing halo, head cocked just so, forehead crinkled in concentration.

Adriana was accustomed to his ever-changing "lifestyle choices" and loved to re-tell them to the girls. Previous appointments had brought gems such as "When in doubt, wax it," "Real men use decorators," and "No weights, no dates," all rules to which he adhered with surprising dedication. He'd struggled with only one promise, made on his fortieth birthday, when he swore off prostitutes and escorts forever ("Tricks are for kids. From here on in, civilians only"), but a follow-up pledge to swear off Vegas had hoisted him back on the wagon.

Adriana's phone rang. Peering over her shoulder, Gilles saw first that it was Leigh.

"Tell her if she can't convince that Adonis boyfriend of hers to put a ring on her finger soon, I'm going to kidnap him and introduce him to the wonders of the homo lifestyle."

"Mmm, I'm sure she's terrified." To the phone: "Did you hear that, Leigh? You have to marry Russell immediately or Gilles is going to seduce him."

Gilles brushed the solution onto a lock of hair using a smooth upstroke followed by a slight wrist flick. He then swirled the ends into the roots and crisply folded the foil over the whole goopy mess with a precise tap of the comb. "What did she say?"

"That he's all yours." Gilles opened his mouth, but Adriana shook her head and held up one hand in a "stop" motion. "Splendid! Count me in. Of course I have plans tonight, but I've been desperate for a reason to cancel. Besides, if Emmy wants to go out, who are we to stand in her way? What time? Perfect, *querida,* we'll meet in the lobby at nine. Kiss!"

"What's wrong with Emmy?" Gilles asked.

"Duncan met a twenty-three-year-old who's dying to have his babies."

"Ah, but of course. How's she doing?"

"I actually don't think she's devastated," Adriana said, licking a puff of foamed milk off her lip. "She just thinks she *should* be. There's a lot of the 'I'll never meet anyone else' stuff, but not much that really has to do with missing Duncan. She should be fine."

Gilles sighed. "I dream of getting my hands on that hair. Do you even realize how rare virgin hair is these days? It's like the Holy Grail of coloring."

"I'll be sure to pass that along. Want to come tonight? We're going for dinner and drinks. Nothing major, just the girls."

"You know how much I love a girls' night, but I've got a date with the maître d' from last weekend. Hopefully he'll be leading the way directly to a quiet table in the back of his bedroom."

"I'll keep my fingers crossed for you." Adriana clearly focused on the tall, broad-shouldered man in a checked blue dress shirt and perfectly pressed slacks who had approached the reception desk.

Gilles followed her gaze to the door as he secured the last lock of hair into a foil and waved his hands in a "voilà!" motion. "I'm finished, love." The Bambi-eyed assistant grasped Adriana's arm and led her to a dryer seat. Gilles called out from his station loud enough for everyone — and certainly the newcomer — to hear, "Just sit there and concentrate on keeping your legs closed, darling. I know it isn't easy, but fifteen minutes is all I ask."

Adriana rolled her eyes dramatically and gave him another finger, this time holding it high enough for the entire salon to see. She relished the shocked looks from the society ladies, all of whom looked like her mother. She saw out of the corner of her eye that the man who had watched her and Gilles wore a small smile of amusement. *I'm too old for this,* she thought as she sneaked another look at the handsome stranger. The man walked past her and turned his smile toward her. With equal parts calculation and natural instinct, Adriana gazed up at him through wide eyes, eyes that said "Who, me?" and placed the tiniest tip of her tongue in the middle of her upper lip. She simply had to stop acting like this, there was really no question; but in the meantime, it was just too much fun.

Moving quietly around her apartment so as not to wake Otis, Emmy realized there wasn't all that much to straighten. It was a small apartment, even for a studio in Manhattan, and the bathroom was a bit grimy and the light — especially on Saturday afternoons, when you were accustomed to staying at your boyfriend's place — was virtually nonexistent, but how else could she hope to live on the best tree-lined block of the West Village for under $2,500 a month? She had decorated it as carefully as her graduate school budget would allow, which wasn't much, but at least she had managed to paint the walls a pale yellow, install a space-saving Murphy bed in the far wall, and place some comfy floor cushions around an extra-fluffy shag carpet she'd found on clearance in a remnant store. It wasn't big, but it was cozy, and so long as Emmy didn't think about the kitchens in Izzie's Miami apartment or Leigh's new one-bedroom or Adriana's palatial penthouse pad — especially Adriana's — she might have even liked it. It just seemed so fundamentally cruel that someone who loved food as much as she did, who would happily spend every free minute at either the farmers' market or the stove, should not have a kitchen. Where else on earth did $30,000 a year in rent not entitle one to an oven? Here she was forced to make do with a sink, a microwave, and a dorm-sized refrigerator, and the landlord — only after a ridiculous amount of begging and pleading — had bought Emmy a brand-new hotplate. For the first few years she'd fought valiantly to create dishes using her limited facilities, but the struggle to do anything more than reheat had worn her down. Now, like most New Yorkers, the ex–culinary student only ordered in or dined out.

She gave up on the idea of cleaning, flopped onto her unmade bed, and began to flip through the pages of the hardcover photo book she'd designed at kodakgallery.com to commemorate the first three years of her relationship with Duncan. She'd spent hours selecting the best pictures and cropping them to varying sizes and removing the red eyes. *Click, click, click* — she clicked the mouse until her fingers tingled and her hand ached, determined to make it perfect. Some of the pages were collage-style and others had only a single dramatic candid. The one she'd chosen for the cutout window on the cover had been her absolute favorite: a black-

and-white photo someone had snapped at Duncan's grandfather's eighty-fifth birthday dinner at Le Cirque; Emmy remembered the transcendent sesame-crusted cod more than anything else from that night. She hadn't even noticed until now, years later, how her arms wrapped protectively around Duncan's shoulders, or the way she looked at him, grinning, while he smiled in that controlled way of his and gazed in another direction. The body language experts at *US Weekly* would have a field day with this one! Not to mention the fact that the book, presented at a dinner celebrating their third anniversary, had elicited the kind of excitement one usually expects only from the receipt of a scarf or a pair of gloves (which, incidentally, was precisely what he had given her, a matching set, prepackaged and professionally wrapped). Duncan tore the paper and ribbons painstakingly selected for their masculinity and tossed them aside without bothering to unstick — never mind read — the card taped to the back. He thanked her and kissed her on the cheek and flipped through it while smiling that tight smile and then excused himself to answer a call from his boss. He asked her to take the photo book home with her that night so he wouldn't have to carry it back to the office, and it had remained in her living room for the next two years, opened only by the occasional visitor who inevitably commented on what a good-looking couple Duncan and Emmy made.

Otis cawed from his cage in the corner of her L-shaped studio. He hooked his beak around one of the metal bars, gave it a determined shake, and squawked, "Otis wants out. Otis wants out."

Eleven years and counting, and Otis was still going strong. She'd read somewhere that African Greys can live to be sixty, but prayed daily that it had been a misprint. She hadn't particularly liked Otis when he was squarely under the ownership of Mark, the first of Emmy's three boyfriends, but she liked him even less now that he shared her 350-square-foot apartment and had learned (with zero coaching and even less encouragement) an uncomfortably large vocabulary that focused almost exclusively on demands, criticisms, and discussions of himself in the third person. At first she had refused to watch him for the three weeks when, the July after graduation, Mark went to hone his Spanish in Guatemala. But he had pleaded and she conceded: the story of her life. Mark's two weeks became a month, and a month became three, and three became a Fulbright to study the aftereffects of civil war on a generation of Guatemalan children. Mark had long since married a Nicaraguan-born, American-educated Peace Corps volunteer and moved to Buenos Aires, but Otis remained.

Emmy unhooked the cage and waited for Otis to shove the swinging door open. He hopped ungracefully onto her proffered arm and stared her straight in the eye. "Grape!" he shrieked. She sighed and plucked one from the bowl that nestled in the puff of her down comforter. Generally Emmy preferred fruit that she could cut or peel, but Otis was fixated on grapes. The bird snatched it from her fingers, swallowed it whole, and immediately demanded another.

She was such a cliché! Dumped by her cad boyfriend, replaced by a younger woman, prepared to shred the pictorial symbol for their sham of a relationship, and kept company only by an ungrateful pet. It would be funny if it weren't her own pathetic life. Hell, it *was* funny when it was Renée Zellweger playing a sweet, chubby girl in the throes of an alcohol-fueled pity party, but it somehow wasn't so hysterical when you were that sweet, chubby girl — okay, skinny, but not attractively so — and your life had just morphed into a chick flick.

Five years down the drain. Ages twenty-four to twenty-nine had been all Duncan, all the time, and what did she have to show for it now? Not the position Chef Massey had begun offering a year ago that would give her the opportunity to travel around the world scouting new restaurant locations and overseeing openings — Duncan had begged her to keep her general manager position in New York so they could see each other more regularly. Certainly not an engagement ring. No, that would be reserved for the barely legal virgin cheerleader who would never, ever have to endure vivid nightmares involving her own shriveled ovaries. Emmy would just have to make do with the sterling silver Tiffany heart pendant Duncan had given her on her birthday, identical to the ones — she later discovered — he'd also bought for his sister and grandmother on their birthdays. Of course, were Emmy being really masochistic here, she might note that it was actually Duncan's *mother* who had selected and purchased all three in order to save her busy son the time and effort such gift-giving required.

When had she gotten so bitter? How had everything played out like this? It was no one's fault but her own; of that she was absolutely certain. Sure, Duncan had been different when they first started dating — boyish, charming, and if not exactly attentive, then at least a bit more present — but then again, so had Emmy. She had just left a waitressing job in Los Angeles to go back to culinary school, her dream since girlhood. For the first time since college she was reunited with Leigh and Adriana, and exhilarated by Manhattan, and proud of herself for taking such decisive action. Granted, culinary school wasn't exactly as she had envisioned it: The classes were often rigorous and tedious, and her classmates were shockingly competitive for externships and other restaurant opportunities. Since so many were temporary New Yorkers and knew no one but other students, the social life quickly became incestuous. Oh, and there was that small incident with the visiting Michelin-starred chef that had circulated in less time than it took to make a *croque-monsieur.* Emmy was still in love with cooking but disillusioned with culinary school when she scored an externship at Chef Massey's New York restaurant, Willow. She'd met Duncan during that externship, a crazy, sleep-deprived time in her life when she was beginning to realize that she enjoyed the front of the house more than the kitchen and was working around the clock to figure out where, if anywhere, she belonged in the food-service industry. She hated the egos of the chefs and the lack of creativity it took to merely re-create carefully dictated recipes. She hated not being able to interact with the actual people who ate the food she was helping to prepare. She hated being stuck for eight, ten hours at a time in steaming-hot, windowless kitchens with only the shouts of expediters and the clanging of pots to remind her she wasn't in hell. None of this had featured in her romantic notion of what her life would be like as a world-famous cook. What had surprised her even more was how much she loved waiting tables and tending bar, getting to chat with customers and other servers, and, later on, as assistant general manager, making sure everything was running smoothly. It was a time of turmoil for Emmy, of redefining what she really wanted from her career and her life, and she realized now that she had been ripe for picking by someone like Duncan. It was almost — almost — understandable why she'd fallen so immediately for Duncan that night at the after-party for the Young Friends of Something or Other benefit, one of the dozens that year Adriana dragged her to.

Emmy had noticed him hours before he approached her, although she still couldn't say why. It could have been his rumpled suit and loosened tie, both tastefully conservative and expertly matched, so different from the baggy polyester chef uniforms to which she'd grown so accustomed. Or maybe it was the way he seemed to know everyone and offered backslaps and cheek kisses and the occasional gallant bow to friends and friends-to-be. Who on earth was this confident? Who could move with such ease among that many people without appearing the least bit insecure? Emmy's eyes tracked him around the room, subtly at first and then with an intensity she herself didn't understand. It wasn't until most of the young professional crowd had moved on to late dinners or early bedtimes and Adriana had flitted off with her man du jour that Duncan appeared next to her.

"Hi, I'm Duncan." He slid himself sideways between her stool and the empty one next to it, leaning on his right arm against the bar.

"Oh, sorry. Here, I was just leaving." Emmy scooted backward off the stool, placing it between them.

He grinned. "I don't want your seat."

"Oh, uh, sorry."

"I want to buy you a drink."

"Thanks, but I was just, uh —"

"Leaving. Yeah, you said that. But I'm hoping I can convince you to stay just a little longer."

The bartender materialized with two martini glasses, petite compared to the fishbowl-sized ones most places served. Clear liquid in one, cloudy in the other, and both with a spear of mammoth green olives.

Duncan slid the one in his left hand toward her by the very bottom of its stem, his fingers pressing into the flattened glass base. "They're both vodka. This one's regular and this one" — as he pushed his right hand she noticed how clean and white his nails were, how soft and groomed his cuticles looked — "is extra dirty. Which do you prefer?"

Good lord! You'd think that would have been enough to activate anyone's skeeve sensor, but noooo, not Emmy. She had found him positively captivating and, when invited moments later, had happily accompanied him home. Of course, Emmy didn't sleep with Duncan that night, or the next weekend, or the one after that. She had, after all, been with only two men before him (the French chef didn't count; she had planned to have sex with him until she'd tugged down his extra-tight white briefs and discovered what, exactly, Adriana meant when she insisted Emmy would "just know" when faced with an uncircumcised situation), and both were long-term boyfriends. She was nervous. Her prudishness — something Duncan had yet to encounter from a girl — increased his determination, and Emmy stumbled, quite unwittingly, onto the concept of hard to get. The longer she held out, the more he pursued her, and in this way their interactions came to resemble a relationship. There were romantic dinners out and candlelit dinners in and big, festive Sunday brunches at trendy downtown bistros. He called just to say hi, sent her Gummi Bears and peanut butter cups at school, asked her out days in advance to ensure she wouldn't make other plans. Who could have possibly predicted that all that happiness would screech to a standstill five years later, that she would have gained such a cynical edge and Duncan would have lost half his hair and that they, the longest-lasting couple among all their friends, would collapse like a sand castle at the first sign of a tropical breeze?

Emmy posed this question to her sister the moment she picked up the phone. Izzie had been calling twice her normal amount in the week since Duncan had dumped Emmy; this was already the fourth time in twenty-four hours.

"Did you really just liken your relationship to a sand castle and the cheerleader to a *tropical breeze?*" Izzie asked.

"Come on, Izzie, be serious for a second.

Would you ever have foreseen this happening?"

There was a pause while Izzie considered her words. "Well, I'm not sure that it's exactly like that."

"Like what?"

"We're talking in circles, Em."

"Then be straight with me."

"I'm just saying that this isn't completely and totally out of left field," Izzie said softly.

"I don't know what you mean."

"It's just when you say that everything collapses at the first sign of, uh, another girl, I'm not exactly sure that would be completely accurate. Not that accurate matters, of course. He's an idiot and a fool regardless, and so not even remotely in your league."

"Okay, fine, so it wasn't exactly the *first* sign. Everyone deserves a second chance."

"That's true. But a sixth or a seventh?"

"Wow. Don't hold back now, Izzie. Seriously, tell me what you really think."

"I know it sounds harsh, Em, but it's true."

Together with Leigh and Adriana, Izzie had supported Emmy through more of Duncan's "mistakes," "poor judgment calls," "oversights," "accidents," "slip-ups," and (everyone's favorite) "relapses" than anyone cared to remember. Emmy knew her sister and friends hated Duncan for putting her through the wringer; their disapproval was palpable and, after the first year, very vocal. But what they didn't understand, couldn't possibly understand, was the feeling she got when his eyes found hers at a crowded party. Or when he invited her into the shower and scrubbed her with cucumber-scented sea salt, or got into the cab first so she wouldn't have to slide across the backseat, or knew to order her tuna rolls with spicy sauce but without crunch. Every relationship comprised such minutiae, of course, but Izzie and the girls simply couldn't know what it felt like when Duncan turned his fleeting attention toward you and actually focused, even if only for a few moments. It made all the other drama seem like insignificant noise, which is exactly what Duncan always assured her it was: innocent flirtation, nothing more.

What bullshit!

She got angry just thinking about it now. How on earth had she accepted his rationale that passing out on some girl's couch was understandable — hell, it was downright reasonable — when one drank as much whiskey as he did? What could she possibly have been thinking when she invited Duncan back to her bed without ascertaining an acceptable explanation for the rather disturbing message she'd overheard on his voice mail from "an old family friend"? And let's not even mention that whole debacle that required an emergency trip to the gynecologist where, thankfully, everything was fine except for her doctor's opinion that Duncan's "nothing little bump" was most likely a recent acquisition and not, as Duncan insisted, a flare-up from the old college days.

The sound of Izzie's voice interrupted her thoughts.

"And I'm not just saying this because I'm your sister, which I am, or because I'm obligated to — which I absolutely am — but because I sincerely believe it: Duncan is *never* going to change and you two would not, could not — not now or ever — be happy together."

The simplicity of it almost took her breath away. Izzie, younger than Emmy by twenty months and a near physical clone, once again proved to be infinitely calmer, wiser, and more mature. How long had Izzie felt this way? And why, through all the girls' endless conversations about Izzie's once-boyfriend-now-husband Kevin or their parents or Duncan, had Izzie never stated so clearly this most basic truth?

"Just because you've never heard it before doesn't mean I haven't said it. Emmy, we've all said it. *Been* saying it. It's like you went temporarily insane for five years."

"You're a real sweetheart. I bet everyone wishes they had a sister like you."

"Please. You and I both know that you're a serial monogamist and you have trouble defining yourself outside a relationship. Sound familiar? Because if you ask me, it sounds an awful lot like Mom."

"Thank you for that stellar armchair insight. Perhaps you can enlighten me as to how all of this is affecting Otis? I'm sure breakups can be devastating on parrots, too. Come to think of it, I should probably consider getting him some counseling. God, I've been so self-centered. The bird is suffering!" Although Izzie was now an ob/gyn resident at University of Miami Hospital, she'd briefly flirted with psychiatry and rarely refrained from analyzing anything — plant, person, or animal — in her path.

"Joke all you want, Em. You've always dealt with everything by making fun of it, and I'm not saying that's the worst approach. I would just urge you to spend a little time alone. Focus on yourself — do what you want, when you want, without having to consider anyone else's agenda."

"If you even start on that bullshit about two halves not making a whole or something, I'm going to puke."

"You know I'm right. Take some time just for you. Re-center your notion of self. Rediscover who *you* are."

"In other words, be single." *Easy for her to advise from the arms of her loving husband,* Emmy thought.

"Does it really sound so dreadful? You've had back-to-back relationships since you were eighteen." What she didn't say was obvious: *And* that *hasn't exactly worked out.*

Emmy sighed and glanced at the clock. "I know, I know. I appreciate the advice, Izzie, really I do, but I've got to run. Leigh and Adriana are taking me out for the big you're-better-off-without-him dinner tonight and I have to get ready. Talk to you tomorrow?"

"I'll call your cell later tonight from the hospital, sometime after midnight when things slow down. Have a few drinks tonight, okay? Go clubbing. Kiss a stranger. Just *please* don't meet your next boyfriend."

"I'll try," Emmy promised. Just then, Otis screeched the same word four times in a row.

"What's he saying?" Izzie asked.

"*Panties.* He keeps saying *panties.*"

"Should I even ask?"

56

"No, you most definitely should not."

For the very first time since Leigh had moved into her building, Adriana beat Leigh to the lobby. She did so out of necessity: Adriana had returned from a relaxing day at the salon — date with the hot stranger arranged for the following weekend — to discover that her parents had all but taken over her apartment. Technically speaking it *was* their apartment, but considering they only stopped by for a few weeks a year, she felt justified in thinking of it as exclusively her home, where they were guests. Impossible, dreaded guests. If they didn't like the authentic African zebra skins she had selected to replace their boring Oriental rugs or the way she'd arranged for all the lights, shades, and electronic equipment to work by remote control, well, that wasn't her problem. And no one, not even her parents, could claim they actually *preferred* their hand-chiseled, specially imported Italian marble shower and hot tub to the ultramodern rainfall shower, sauna, and steam room she'd replaced them with in the master bath. No sane person, at least. Which is precisely why Adriana had to dress and flee as quickly as possible: In four short hours, her sleek sanctuary had become a strife-ridden ring of hell.

Not that she didn't love them, of course. Her papa was getting older and, at this point in his life, much more mellow than he'd been when Adriana was growing up. He seemed content to let his wife call the shots, and rarely insisted on anything beyond his nightly Cuban and the tradition that each and every one of his children — three from his first wife, three from his second, and Adriana with his current, and hopefully last, wife — reunite at the Rio de Janeiro compound for the weeks before and after Christmas. The opposite had proven true for her mother. Although Mrs. de Souza had been relaxed and accepting of Adriana's teen years and all her sex-and-drug experimentation, her liberal attitude did not extend to unmarried twenty-nine-year-old daughters — especially those whose predilection for sex and drugs could no longer be called "experimental." It wasn't that she didn't understand good living; she was Brazilian, after all. Eating (low-fat, low-cal), drinking (bottle after bottle of expensive white wine), loving (when one can't conceivably feign yet another headache) — these were the very essences of life. To be conducted, of course, under the proper circumstances: as a carefree young girl and then not again until *after* one had found and claimed an

58

appropriate husband. She had traveled and modeled and partied through her own teen years — the Gisele of her generation, people still said. But Camilla de Souza had always cautioned Adriana that men were (slightly) less fleeting than looks. By the time she was twenty-three, she had secured a (fabulously) wealthy older husband and produced a beautiful baby girl. This was how it should be.

The thought of listening to her mother's spiel for another two weeks made Adriana feel woozy. She stretched out on the slightly sagging lobby sofa and thought through her strategy. Stay occupied during the day, come home late or not at all, and convince them at every possible opportunity that her energies — not to mention her substantial trust fund — were going toward securing a proper husband. If she was careful, they would never know about the grungy British rocker who lived in an East Village walk-up or the sexy surgeon with a practice in Manhattan and a wife and kids in Greenwich. If she was meticulous, they might not even catch on to the gorgeous Israeli who claimed he pushed papers at the Israeli embassy but who, Adriana was certain, worked for Mossad.

Leigh's raspy voice — one of the few naturally sexy things about the girl, Adriana was always telling her, not that she ever listened

— interrupted her thoughts. "Wow," Leigh breathed, staring at Adriana with widened eyes. I love that dress."

"Thank you, *querida*. My parents came to town, so I had to tell them I was going on a date with an Argentinean businessman. Mama was so happy to hear it that she lent me one of her Valentinos." Adriana ran her palms down the length of her short black dress and twirled around. "Isn't it fabulous?"

The dress was indeed beautiful — the silk seemed able to think, knowing where to cling to a curve and where to drape gracefully over one — but then again, Adriana could have looked lovely in a red-checked tablecloth.

"Fabulous," Leigh said.

"Come, let's leave before they come downstairs and see I'm with you and not some South American polo player."

"I thought he was supposed to be a businessman?"

"Whatever."

The cab crept across Thirteenth Street at a glacial pace, mired in the downtown Saturday-night traffic that made a few blocks feel as long as a commute from New Jersey. It would have taken the girls only ten minutes to walk from their building on University to the West Village, but neither even considered hoofing it. Adriana, especially, looked as though she would risk injury and possible paralysis if she so much as thought about walking more than a couple of carefully negotiated meters in her Christian Louboutins.

By the time they pulled up in front of the Waverly Inn, Emmy had texted each of them a half-dozen times.

"Where have you been?" Emmy hiss-whispered as the girls squeezed through the minuscule front door. She was leaning against the hostess desk and waving in their general direction. "They won't even let me sit at the bar without you."

"Mario, such a bad boy!" Adriana crooned, kissing a handsome man of indeterminate ethnicity on both cheeks. "Emmy is a friend of mine, and my dinner guest tonight. Emmy, meet Mario, the man behind the legend."

Introductions and kisses — air, cheek, and hand — were exchanged before the girls were escorted to the back room and seated at a table for three. The restaurant wasn't as jam-packed as it normally was since many of its usual revelers were in the Hamptons for Memorial Day weekend, but there was still plenty of opportunity for fantastic people-watching.

"'The man behind the legend'?" Emmy asked, rolling her eyes. "Are you serious?"

"Men need to be stroked, *querida.* I don't know how many times I've tried to teach this to both of you. They sometimes require a gentle touch. Learn when to use a firm grip and when to cover it in velvet and they are yours forever."

Leigh popped some Nicorette. "I have absolutely no idea what you're talking about." She turned to Emmy. "Is she even speaking English?"

Emmy shrugged. She was used to the secrets Adriana tried to impart year after year. They were like pretty little fairy tales: fun to hear but seemingly useless in real life.

Adriana ordered a round of vodka gimlets for the table by grasping the waiter's hand between her own and saying, "We'll have three of my favorites, Nicholas." She sat back to survey the crowd. According to Adriana, it was still a little early — it wouldn't start really buzzing until midnight or so, once all the first-timers and celeb-seekers left and the regulars could commence the night's real drinking and socializing — but so far the crowd of thirtysomething media-and-entertainment types appeared happy and attractive.

"Okay, girls, why don't we just get it out of the way so we can all enjoy our meals?" Emmy asked the moment Nicholas delivered their drinks.

Adriana returned her attention to her tablemates. "Get what out of the way?"

Emmy raised her glass. "The toast one of you will inevitably make that's intended to remind me how much better off I am without Duncan. Something about how single is fabulous. Or how I'm young and beautiful and men will be beating down my door. Come on, let's just do it and move on."

"I don't think there's anything so great about being single," Leigh said.

"And while you most certainly are beautiful, *querida,* I wouldn't say almost thirty is all that young." Adriana smiled.

"I'm sure you'll eventually meet someone wonderful, but men don't seem to beat down anyone's doors these days," Leigh added.

"At least not the unmarried ones," Adriana said.

"Are there any left who aren't married?" Leigh asked.

"The gay ones aren't."

"At least not yet. But probably soon. And then there won't be anyone at all."

Emmy sighed. "Thanks, guys. You always know just what to say. Your unending support means the world to me."

Leigh broke off a chunk of bread and swirled it around the olive oil. "What does Izzie have to say about everything?"

"She's trying not to show it, but I know she's absolutely thrilled. She and Duncan never exactly loved each other. Plus she's obsessed with the idea that I — quote — 'have trouble defining myself outside a relationship,' end quote. In other words, her usual psychobabble bullshit."

Adriana and Leigh exchanged knowing looks.

"What?" Emmy asked.

Leigh stared at her plate and Adriana arched her perfect eyebrows, but neither said a word.

"Oh, come on! Do *not* tell me you agree with Izzie. She has no idea what she's talking about."

Leigh reached across the table and patted Emmy's hand. "Yes, dear, of course. She's got a doting husband, loads of outdoor hobbies, and an MD. Did I forget anything? Oh, yes, she matched with her first choice for residency and is in the running for chief resident — a year earlier than expected. You're absolutely right . . . she sounds tremendously ill-equipped to give a little sisterly advice."

"We're getting off track," Adriana interjected. "Not to be the tactful one here, but I think Leigh was just trying to say that Izzie might have a point."

"A point?"

Adriana nodded. "It *has* been a rather long time since you've been on your own."

"Yeah, like always?" Leigh added. "Not that that's necessarily bad. But it does happen to be true."

"Wow. Anything else you two are just dying to tell me?" Emmy clasped her menu to her chest. "Don't hold back now."

"Well . . ." Adriana glanced at Leigh.

"Just say it." Leigh nodded.

"I wasn't really serious," Emmy said, her eyes wide. "There *is* something?"

"Emmy, *querida,* it's like the big white rhino in the room."

"Elephant."

Adriana waved her hand. "Whatever. The big white elephant. You are almost thirty years old —"

"Thank you for mentioning that yet again."

"— and you have only been with three men. Three! This is not to be believed, and yet it's true."

The girls quieted while Nicholas placed their shared appetizers on the table: an order of tuna tartare with avocado and a heaping plate of oysters. He appeared ready to take their order, but Emmy placed both hands atop her menu and glared. Defeated, he shuffled away.

"You two are incredible. You sit here for twenty minutes telling me that I can't be alone, and then you switch tacks — with no fair warning — and say that I haven't dated enough people. Do you hear yourselves?"

Leigh squeezed a lemon wedge over the oysters and delicately removed one from its shell. "Not dated — slept with."

"Oh, come on! What's the difference?"

Adriana gasped. "That, my darling friend, is exactly the problem. *What's the difference?* Between dating and random sex? My goodness, we have much work to do."

Emmy looked to Leigh for help but Leigh nodded in agreement. "I can't believe I'm saying this, but I have to agree with Adriana. You're a serial monogamist and as a result have only ever been with three people in any significant capacity. I think what Adi's saying" — she was able to sneak in a single use of the hated nickname here because Adriana was distracted on multiple fronts by food, drink, and sex conversation — "is that you should be single for a little while. And being single means dating different people, figuring out who and what work best for you, and, most of all, having a little fun."

"So what you're really saying — let's just be straight here — is that I should be whoring around more," Emmy said.

Leigh smiled like a proud parent. "Yes."

"And you?" Emmy turned to Adriana, who clasped her hands together and leaned forward.

"That is *exactly* what I am saying." Adriana nodded.

Emmy sighed and sat back in her chair. "I agree."

At the same time, in nearly the same disbelieving tone, Leigh and Adriana asked, "You do?"

"Of course. I've had some time to do a little self-examination, and I've arrived at the same conclusion. There's only one logical way to proceed: I am going to have sex with random men. All sorts and sizes and colors of random men. All kinds of sex, for that matter." She paused and looked at Adriana. "The level of my planned whoredom will make you proud."

Adriana gazed back and wondered if she had heard her friend correctly. She concluded that she had, but she must have missed the sarcasm somewhere along the line — this declaration was inconceivable.

She said what she always did when she had no idea what else to say. "Fabulous, *querida*. Just fabulous. I adore the whole idea."

Leigh used her knife to push a bit of tuna and a slice of cucumber onto the tip of her fork and elegantly brought it to her mouth. A quiet crunch, a couple of chews, and she swallowed. "Emmy, sweetheart. We were just kidding, you know. I think it's great you haven't been with a lot of guys. When someone asks you how many people you've slept with, you don't even have to divide by three! Now, isn't that nice? To not have to lie?"

"I'm really not kidding about this," Emmy said. She made eye contact with the waiter as he passed by their table and ordered three glasses of champagne when he approached. "This is the start of my new life, and trust me, it's long overdue. First thing I'm going to do on Monday is call up Chef Massey and tell him I'm accepting the job. What job? you might wonder. The one where they want to pay me boatloads of money and give me a huge expense account so I can travel all over the world and stay in the nicest hotels and eat in the best restaurants for inspiration. Inspiration! For new menu ideas. Have you ever heard of something so ridiculous? And who's the fucking idiot who's been saying no the last two months because she didn't want to desert her poor, lonely boyfriend? Yours truly. Didn't want poor baby Duncan to feel abandoned and unloved while I jetted off somewhere fabulous. So yes, this time I'm going to call him up and take that job, and then I'm going to fuck every single solitary appealing man I meet. Foreign, sexy, beautiful men. And I do mean *every last one.* How does that sound, girls? Acceptable?" The waiter returned with their champagne. "So please, let's toast."

Adriana made a noise that for anyone less beautiful could only be called a snort but coming from her sounded exotic and feminine. Both girls turned to look and she suddenly felt out of sorts. Her friend had just announced plans for a major life change while she herself had been coasting effortlessly along the same path for years. Was Adriana's role as the group's jet-setting partyer in jeopardy, or had she just had one too many drinks? There was something unsettling about Emmy's proclamation. And if there was one way Adriana was not accustomed to feeling, it was unsettled.

She held up her glass and forced a smile.

Emmy smiled back and said, "There's just one condition. I want company."

"Company?" Leigh asked. She gnawed her bottom lip, catching a flake of skin between her front teeth. She looked anxious. Adriana wondered why the girl always looked nervous these days, especially since everything was going so beautifully for her.

"Yes. Company. I'm willing to completely slut out if *you*" — Emmy pointed to Adriana — "agree to have a committed, monogamous relationship. With a man of your own choosing, of course."

Adriana inhaled. She incorporated one of her favorite moves, which consisted of absentmindedly touching a fingertip to her lips, letting it rest there for a moment, and then graze along to the spot right below her left ear. It prompted four men at the adjoining table to stare and Nicholas to come running. She felt that familiar thrill of being watched.

The girls ordered main courses, another round of drinks, and a plate of the truffle mac and cheese to share.

"So? What do you say?" Emmy asked.

"Did my mother put you up to this?"

"Yes, sweetheart. It was all your mom's idea for me to pledge to fall into bed with every man I meet over the course of the next year just so you'll agree to date only one person. She's a clever one," Emmy said.

"Come on, people, let's be serious for a minute," Leigh said. "Neither one of you will actually go through with this, so can we change the subject? Emmy, you made your point. If you want to dive headfirst into another five-year relationship, that's certainly your prerogative. And Adriana, it's more likely that you'll become an astronaut than date only one man. Next topic."

"It's not like I dared her to do something really drastic, like get a job. . . ." Emmy grinned.

Adriana forced a return smile even though she found it difficult to laugh at herself, especially when the jokes concerned her lack of employment. Her mother's irritating voice reverberated in her head. "Wow. Playing hardball, are we, *querida?* Well, guess what? I accept your challenge."

"You what?" Emmy asked, furiously twisting a lock of hair.

Leigh's glass halted halfway to her mouth. "You'll do it?"

"I said I'll do it. When do we start?"

Emmy bit off an asparagus end, chewed daintily, swallowed. "I say we take a little time to figure out the terms. By the end of next weekend, we'll agree to have a plan?"

Adriana nodded. "Done. And that will give you" — she waved her champagne glass in Leigh's direction — "a chance to figure out what your resolution will be."

"Me?" Leigh's recently plucked brows furrowed. "A resolution? Why? It's not even New Year's. Just because you two are crazy doesn't mean I have to be."

Emmy rolled her eyes. "Leigh? Please. What does she need to change? Perfect job, perfect boyfriend, perfect apartment, perfect nuclear family . . ." Emmy's voice became nasal and singsongy. "Marcia, Marcia, Marcia," she chanted, and dismissed Leigh's look of displeasure as momentary crankiness.

"Yes, that may be so," Adriana said, looking only at Leigh. "But she'll have to come up with something. You can do that, can't you, Leigh? Think of one single aspect of your life that you'd like to change? To work on?"

"Of course I can," Leigh said in a snippy tone. "I'm sure there are a million things."

Adriana and Emmy exchanged looks, each knowing what the other was thinking: Leigh might have all her ducks in a row, but it wouldn't kill the girl to loosen up a little and enjoy herself.

"Well, you have two weeks to choose one, *querida*," Adriana announced in her huskily authoritative voice. "In the meantime, let's toast."

Emmy hoisted her glass like it was a lead paperweight. "To us," she announced. "By next summer, I will have prostituted myself out to half of Manhattan and Adriana will have discovered the joys of monogamy. And Leigh will have . . . done something."

"Cheers!" Adriana called out, again attracting the attention of half the restaurant. "To us."

Leigh clinked her glass halfheartedly. "To us."

"We are totally, completely, royally *fucked,*" Emmy leaned in and stage-whispered.

Adriana threw her head back, half with delight and half out of habit, for effect. "One hundred percent screwed," she laughed. "Pun intended, of course."

"Can we get out of here before we begin a shame spiral the likes of which none of us has ever known? Please?" Leigh begged. The red wine Nicholas had comped them was starting to give her a headache and she knew it was only a matter of time — minutes, probably — before her friends moved from charmingly buzzed to loudly drunk.

Adriana and Emmy exchanged looks again and giggled.

"Come on, Marcia," Adriana said, shimmying her way to a standing position while pulling on Leigh's forearm. "We might just teach you to have some fun yet."

If You Think It's Too Big, You Don't Deserve It

"Come to bed, baby. It's almost one — don't you think it's time to call it a night?" Russell pulled off his T-shirt and turned on his side to face Leigh, resting his head full of black curls on his right hand. He rubbed the sheets with his left hand and patted them a little, a gesture that was meant to be tempting, appealing, but that Leigh always found a little threatening.

"I just have a few more pages. Is the light bothering you? I can move to the living room."

He sighed and picked up his book, *Strength Training Anatomy*. "It's not the light, sweetheart, and you know that. It's the fact that we haven't fallen asleep together in weeks. I just miss you."

Her first thought was that he sounded like a whiny, petulant child; this was, after all, one of the most sought-after manuscripts of the year, and it was crucial that she have it read for the next morning's acquisitions meeting. It had taken eight impossibly long years of dedicated hard work to finally — finally! — be within striking distance of senior editor (there were, after all, only six at Brook Harris, and she could potentially be the youngest one), and Russell seemed to think that after a year of dating he was entitled to commandeer her entire life. *She* wasn't the one who had asked him to stay over tonight, who had just shown up on *his* doorstep on her way from *her* weekly poker game, long lashes all a-flutter and all *Baby, I just had to see you.*

Next thought: She was the most horrid, unappreciative, ungrateful bitch alive for even thinking such things about Russell. She certainly wasn't this resentful a year ago. When he approached her at the book party Brook Harris was throwing in honor of Bill Parcells (who had just written a memoir of his years as the Cowboys' coach), she recognized him instantly. Not that she ever watched ESPN — she didn't — but with his boyish smile and dimples and reputation as one of the most desirable bachelors in Manhattan, she knew enough to be extra charming when he introduced himself. They'd talked for hours that night, first at the party and then over Amstels at Pete's Tavern. He had been almost shockingly up-front about being sick of the dating scene in New York, how he was over dating models and actresses and was ready to meet, in his words, a "real girl," implying, of course, that Leigh was a perfect candidate. Naturally, she was honored by the attention: Who wouldn't want Russell Perrin pursuing her? He fulfilled every single little box on every single checklist she'd drafted in the last ten years. He was, by all accounts, exactly the kind of man she hoped to find but never actually thought she would.

Now here she was, almost a year into a relationship with a gorgeous guy who also just happened to be sensitive, kind, caring, and madly in love with her, and all she felt was smothered. It was abundantly obvious to everyone else in Leigh's life that she had finally met The One; why wasn't it clearer to her? As if to drive this point home, Russell turned her face to his, looked into her eyes, and said, "Leigh, sweetheart. I love you so much."

"I love you, too," Leigh answered automatically, without a second's hesitation, although a third-party observer — even a perfect stranger — might have questioned the sincerity behind her declaration. What were you supposed to do when someone you liked and respected very much, someone you wanted to get to know better, announced after two months of otherwise casual dating that he was head over heels in love with you? You did what any confrontation-averse person would do and said "I love you, too" right back. Leigh figured she'd grow into those words eventually, be able to say them with more conviction once they got to know each other better. It upset her that a year later she was still waiting.

She forced herself to look up from the page and assumed a syrupy-sweet voice. "I know it's been really hectic lately, but it's like clockwork every year: The second the calendar hits June, everything turns chaotic. I promise it won't last forever."

Leigh held her breath and waited for him to explode (which so far had never happened), waited for Russell to tell her he wouldn't tolerate being patronized and that he didn't appreciate being spoken to like she was the parent and he was the toddler who had just mashed peanut butter into the carpet.

Instead, he smiled. And not a smile filled with resentment or resignation; it was genuine, full of understanding, and impossibly apologetic. "I don't mean to pressure you, baby. I know how much you love your job, and I want you to enjoy it while you can.

Take your time and come to bed whenever you're ready."

"While I can?" Leigh's head snapped up. "Are you really bringing that up again at one in the morning?"

"No, sweetheart, I'm not bringing that up again. You've made it perfectly clear that San Francisco is not in your plans for right now — but I'd really like it if you weren't so closed-minded about it. It would be an incredible opportunity, you know."

"For you," Leigh said, sulkily as a child.

"For both of us."

"Russell, we haven't even been together a year. I think it's a little early to start talking about moving across the country together." The level of annoyance in her voice surprised them both.

"It's never too early when you love someone, Leigh," he said, his own voice even and steady. This very evenness, which had appealed to her so much in the beginning, could now infuriate her; his refusal to get mad, his complete mastery of his emotions, made her wonder if he ever even heard what she was saying.

"Let's not talk about it now, okay?" she asked.

He sat up and slid to the end of the bed, closer to the corner where Leigh had placed her comfy reading chair and soft white-light reading lamp. The oversized down comforter — the one she'd spent weeks searching for, testing every brand on the market for softness and puffiness — slid to the floor and nearly knocked the bonsai tree off the nightstand. Russell didn't appear to notice. "Why don't I make you some tea?" he asked.

Again Leigh felt like she needed to harness every ounce of willpower not to scream. She didn't want to go to bed. She didn't want tea. She just wanted him to *stop talking.*

She took a deep breath, slowly, without being obvious about it. "Thanks, but I'm really fine. Just give me a few more minutes, okay?"

He gazed at her with an understanding smile before bounding out of bed and wrapping her in a bear hug. She felt her body stiffen; she couldn't help it. Russell just hugged harder and sneaked his face into the crook of her neck, wedging it in just above her shoulder and under her chin. His five o'clock shadow scratched her skin and she squirmed.

"Does it tickle?" He laughed. "My dad's always said I'd eventually have to shave twice a day, but I never wanted to believe him."

"Hmm."

"I'm going to get some water. Want some?"

"Sure," Leigh said, although she didn't. She turned her attention back to the manuscript and had worked her way through half a page when Russell called from the kitchen.

"Where do you keep the honey?"

"The what?" she yelled back.

"The honey. I'm making us tea and I want to make it with warm milk and honey. Do you have any?"

She took a deep breath. "It's in the cabinet above the microwave."

He returned moments later with a mug in each hand and a bag of Newman's Own chocolate chip cookies between his teeth. "Take a break, baby. I promise I'll leave you alone after a midnight snack."

Midnight? Leigh thought. *It's one-thirty in the morning and I have to be up in five and a half hours. Not to mention that not everyone has the naturally toned body of an elite college athlete and can afford to chow cookies at all hours.*

She bit into a cookie and remembered all the years in her early and mid-twenties that she had wanted this scene so badly: the doting boyfriend, the romantic late-night picnic, the comfortable apartment filled with all the things she loved. Back then it had felt almost impossible or, at least, very far away; now she had it all, but the reality didn't feel anything like the fantasy.

With cookies barely swallowed and tea still unfinished, Russell curled himself around a pillow and promptly fell into an intensely deep and restful sleep. Who slept like that? It never ceased to amaze Leigh. He claimed it came from a childhood surrounded by chaos, from learning to sleep through the clamor of two parents, two sisters, a live-in nanny, and three chatty beagles. Perhaps. But Leigh figured it had more to do with his clear conscience and his clean living and, if she was going to be really honest, with the fact that his life just wasn't really all that stressful. How hard would it be to sleep like a baby if your daily routine included two hours of exercise (an hour of weights and an hour of cardio) and lacked caffeine, sugar, preservatives, white flour, and trans fats? If you taped a weekly thirty-minute show on a subject (sports) you loved innately just by virtue of being male, and had a team of writers and producers who put it all together for you to read? If you had healthy and productive relationships with both family and friends, all of whom loved and admired you for just being yourself? It was enough to make a person sick, or at the very least resentful, which, if she was being perfectly frank, it often made Leigh.

Tonight it succeeded only in making Leigh desperately want a cigarette. No matter that she'd quit nearly a year ago, right when she and Russell started dating; not a day went by that she didn't desperately yearn for a nice long drag. Smokers always waxed poetic about the ritual of it, how a large part of the satisfaction was packing the box and pulling the foil wrapper and plucking an aromatic stick. They claimed they loved the lighting, the ashing, the feeling of being able to hold something between their fingers. That was all well and good, but there was nothing quite like actually smoking it: Leigh loved *inhaling*. To pull with your lips on that filter and feel the smoke drift across your tongue, down your throat, and directly into your lungs was to be transported momentarily to nirvana. She remembered — every day — how it felt after the first inhale, just as the nicotine was hitting her bloodstream. A few seconds of both tranquillity and alertness, together, in exactly the right amounts. Then the slow exhale — forceful enough so that the smoke didn't merely seep from your mouth but not so energetic that it disrupted the moment — would complete the blissful experience.

Leigh wasn't an idiot, though, and certainly knew all the nasty drawbacks of her beloved habit. Emphysema. Lung cancer. Heart disease. High blood pressure. Having to endure graphic photos of blackened lungs in magazines and terrifying commercials of gravelly voiced people with tracheotomies. The yellowed teeth and the wrinkles and the smoky hair and the stained top knuckle on her right middle finger. Her mother's constant harping. Her doctor's dire predictions. The maddening Just-in-Case-You-Haven't-Heard voice total strangers used when they sidled up to her outside her office building to enumerate smoking's many dangers. And then Russell! Mr. My Body Is a Temple would never, *ever* date a smoker, and he'd made that perfectly clear from day one. It was enough to make even the most devoted smoker call uncle, and after eight years of pack-a-day enjoyment, Leigh finally caved. It had required superhuman effort and an ability to endure torturous cravings for weeks on end, but she had persevered. So far she hadn't managed to rid herself of nicotine entirely — some might say she had succeeded only in transferring her tenacious addiction from cigarettes to nicotine gum — but that was neither here nor there. The gum wasn't going to kill her in the immediate future, she hoped, and if it did, well, so be it.

She popped an extra piece for good measure and set aside the manuscript. It usually wasn't too difficult to get engaged by a hot book that multiple publishing houses were clamoring for, but this one felt like drudgery. Would the American public really want to read *another* eight-hundred-page historical fiction tome about an ex-president from the last century? It was enough already. All she wanted to do was curl up with a good beach read and get lost in something that wasn't so deadly boring. She would've given anything for it to be a No Human Contact Monday Night. Sapped of energy and in no mood to read another word about a campaign that had taken place over a hundred years earlier, Leigh tossed aside the manuscript and pulled her MacBook onto her lap.

Often one of her friends was on IM at two in the morning, but tonight all was quiet. Leigh clicked through her favorite Web sites quickly, efficiently, her eyes scanning the pages for information. On cnn.com, an alligator attack in South Florida. On Yahoo!, a video demonstrating how to make a watermelon basket using only a chef's knife and a nontoxic marker. On gofugyourself. com a funny bit about Tom Cruise's bangs and the Flowbee. On neimanmarcus.com an announcement regarding upgraded shipping on all leather accessories. *Click, click,*

click, click. She scanned the most recent bestseller list on *Publishers Weekly,* clicked to support free mammograms at The Breast Cancer Site, and checked that her direct deposit went through at chase.com. She briefly considered checking the symptoms for obsessive-compulsive disorder at WebMD but resisted. Finally feeling weary if not entirely exhausted, Leigh carefully washed her face using the correct upward circular motions and swapped her sweats for a pair of soft cotton shorts. She watched Russell's face as she climbed in next to him, inching her way slowly under the comforter, determined not to wake him. He remained motionless. She switched off the light and managed to flip onto her side without disturbing him, but just as her mind started to slow and her limbs began to relax into the cool sheets, she felt his body press against hers. His aroused body. He enveloped her in his arms and pushed his pelvis against her lower back.

"Hey there," he whispered in her ear, his breath still smelling of cookies.

She lay there limp, simultaneously praying he would fall back to sleep and hating herself for wishing that.

"Leigh, baby, are you awake? I know I am." He gave another little push just in case she wasn't sure what he meant.

"I'm exhausted, Russ. It's so late already, and I have to be up early for the meeting tomorrow." *When did I start to sound like my mother?* she wondered.

"I promise you won't have to do a thing."

He pulled her closer and kissed her neck. She shivered, which he interpreted as delight, and ran his fingers over her goose bumps, which he took as a good sign. When they first started dating, she thought he was the best kisser on earth. She still remembered their first kiss — it had been positively transcendent. He took her home in a cab after the book party and the dive bar, and just before they reached her building, he pulled her toward him for one of the softest, most amazing kisses she'd ever experienced. He used the perfect combination of lips and tongue, the ideal pressure, the exact right amount of passion. And there was no doubt he had plenty of experience on which to draw, having been one of the most well-known and sought-after men she had ever met. Yet in the last few months, it had started to feel like she was kissing a stranger — and not in an exciting way. Instead of soft and warm, his mouth now often felt cold and damp and a little shocking on her skin. His tongue probed too voraciously; his lips always seemed either rigid or fleshy. Tonight, against the back of her neck, they felt like they were made out of papier-mâché before it properly hardened. Pulpy papier-mâché. Refrigerated, pulpy papier-mâché.

"Russ." She sighed and clenched her eyes closed.

He stroked her hair and rubbed her shoulders, trying to relax her. "What, baby? Is this so awful?"

She didn't tell him that each touch felt like a violation. Hadn't the sex once been fantastic? Back when Russell was a bit elusive and flirty and seductive, and not quite so clingy or so determined to settle down with a more serious girl than all the flighty ones from his twenties? It all seemed like so long ago.

Before she realized what was happening, he worked her shorts down to her knees and pulled her even closer. His upper arms were huge, literally bulging under her chin and inadvertently pressing against her throat. His chest threw off heat like a furnace and the hair on his thighs felt like sandpaper. And for the first time ever while in bed with Russell, she began to feel the familiar heart-attack symptoms begin.

"Stop it!" she breathed, her whisper louder than she planned. "I can't do this now."

His embrace slackened instantly and Leigh was instantly grateful that it was too dark to see his face.

"Russ, I'm sorry. It's just that —"

"No worries, Leigh. Really, I understand." His voice sounded calm but distant. He rolled away from her and within minutes his breathing steadied to its deep-sleep rate.

Leigh finally fell asleep just before six, just as the lady above donned her various foot accoutrements and commenced the day's clomping, but it wasn't until the next morning's meeting, at which she felt inarticulate and thick-tongued from exhaustion, that she remembered her final thought before drifting off. It was of dinner with the girls a couple of weeks earlier and their proclamations of change. Emmy was going to expand her experience by having lots of affairs and Adriana had made a resolution to give monogamy the old college try. For the ten days since then Leigh hadn't been able to think of anything she was willing to contribute. Until now. Wouldn't it be funny to announce that she was going to work up the nerve to end her flawed relationship even though she was utterly terrified of being alone and convinced she wouldn't meet anyone who loved her half as much as Russell so obviously did? That she kept waiting and waiting to feel the way about Russell everyone thought she should, but that so far it hadn't happened?

Ha-ha. *Hysterical,* she thought to herself. *They wouldn't believe it for a second.*

She was trying to think of something else — the weather, her upcoming trip, the fact that her parents were discussing the possibility of moving back to the States — but Adriana's mind refused to focus on anything other than the gorgeous contrast between Yani's rough, ropelike dreds and the milky texture of his skin. Each time he stretched or straightened that beautiful midsection, her pulse quickened. She watched covertly as a droplet of perspiration traveled from his forehead to his neck and tried to imagine what it tasted like. When he placed his huge hands over her hips, it was all she could do not to groan. A coarse dreadlock brushed against her shoulder; he smelled like moss, overpoweringly *green,* but it was pleasant, masculine. He placed two fingers in the small of her back and nudged her pelvis forward. "Right there," he said softly. "Just like that."

His voice got louder, but only slightly. "Gently place the left palm on the floor and rotate your body into plank position. Feel the energy flow from your hands to the earth, from the earth to your hands. Don't forget to breathe. There; hold it right there."

Adriana tried to block out the sound of his voice and, when that wasn't possible, to reconfigure his words so that they sounded slightly saner. The class moved like a choreographed dance troupe, a collection of sinewy limbs and tight torsos that made the movements appear almost effortless. She loved yoga and she lusted after Yani, but she had minimal tolerance for the touchy-feely stuff. Correction: The touchy-feely stuff was great, as long as it was Yani touching *her*. All the lecturing about energy and karma and spirit made him just a little less appealing, and that was a real shame — but nothing she couldn't overlook. She shifted her body into plank pose, her triceps quivering with effort, and glanced up to locate Yani. He was standing over Leigh with a foot positioned on each side of her extended legs, pressing the spot between her shoulder blades closer to the floor. Leigh met Adriana's gaze and rolled her eyes.

As usual, the class consisted exclusively of women. Adriana had expertly scanned the room upon entering and, after determining herself the most fit and attractive woman in attendance, laid out her mat and saved a space for Leigh. She felt proud that in this room of beautiful women — all in their twenties or early thirties, all but one at or under their ideal body weight, all groomed to within an inch of their lives despite the early Sunday morning and the physical nature of the activity — she was the most beautiful. This realization no longer surprised or delighted her the way it had when she was younger; rather, it gave her a little added confidence bump that helped smooth along the day. The fact that Yani wouldn't sleep with her most likely indicated that the problem was his and not hers, a theory she wanted her friends to confirm at a post-yoga breakfast.

"It just doesn't make any sense," Adriana said, placing her mouth delicately around a spoonful of granola. "What do you think is wrong with him?"

Leigh sipped her coffee and smiled at the waitress for more. The diner at the corner of Tenth and University wasn't the best brunch place around — the servers were always surly, the eggs were sometimes cold, and the coffee ran the gamut from watery to bitter — but it was close to the studio and both girls could be certain that they would never see anyone they knew. There weren't many places in downtown Manhattan where you could dine sporting yoga pants and sweaty ponytails without raising eyebrows, so they persevered.

"I don't know. I don't suppose you think he's gay?"

"Of course not," Adriana snapped.

"And there's no chance that he's just not that into you. . . ."

Adriana gave one of her cute mini-snorts. "Please."

"Well, then it's got to be one of the usuals. Erectile dysfunction, mid-herpes outbreak, freakishly small member. What else could it be?"

Adriana considered these options, but none of them felt quite right. Yani seemed peaceful, accepting, completely self-assured in that strong, silent way. No man had ever *not* responded to her. And it's not that she wasn't trying — it had been years since she'd needed to make an effort like this, and that time the boy's reluctance had been tied to his upcoming wedding — but it sometimes seemed like Yani didn't even *see* her. The more she swung her hair or thrust out her perfect breasts, the less he noticed.

"What else? Why, isn't it obvious? He's a total bed-wetter and he's terrified of being found out." Emmy seemed to materialize out of nowhere, and for the briefest moment Adriana was irritated to have the attention shifted away from her.

"Hey! We didn't know if you'd make it.

Here, give me your stuff," Leigh said, holding out her arms.

"What, don't you want me to sit next to you? I promise I'll sit really close, maybe rub my shoulder against yours. It'll be fun."

Leigh sighed.

Adriana patted the seat next to her; she knew Leigh had "space issues" and she tried to be understanding, but it was annoying always having to be the one who got crammed inside booths and crowded in banquettes. "How does Russell deal with the fact that you can't stand being near anyone?"

"It's not that I 'can't stand being near anyone.' I just like a little buffer zone. What's wrong with a little personal space?" Leigh asked.

"Yeah, but seriously: Does he get it? Accept it? Or does he hate it?"

Leigh sighed again. "He hates it. I feel bad. He comes from a huge, happy family of mouth-kissers! I'm an only child with parents as affectionate as ceramic statues. I'm working on it, but I can't help that all that closeness and touching seriously freaks me out."

Adriana raised her hand in defeat. "Fair enough. As long as you recognize the issue."

Leigh nodded. "Definitely aware. Constantly, neurotically, miserably aware. And working on it, I promise."

Emmy collapsed onto the bench beside Adriana; the padded vinyl heaved a bit with the extra ninety-five pounds and then settled. "How was yoga? Still no love from the Y-man?"

"Not yet. But he will succumb," Adriana said.

Leigh nodded. "They always do. For you, at least."

Emmy clapped her hand on the table. "Girls, girls! Have we forgotten so soon? Adriana is no longer seeking casual encounters. Of course, she's welcome to become Yani's girlfriend, but according to the rules, she cannot be his one-night stand."

"Ah, yes. The rules. Agreed to after one too many cocktails and, at least as of today, not settled yet. I think that still makes Yani fair game." Adriana made a point to smile cutely, not sexily, focusing on deepening the dimples that appeared when she was acting her most girlish.

Emmy blew her a kiss. "Honey, save those dimples for your future boyfriend. They're worthless at this table. And besides, I have news."

"Duncan news?" Leigh asked automatically, forgetting for a second that they'd now been broken up for nearly three weeks.

"No, not Duncan news — although I did run into his sister, who told me that he and the virgin cheerleader are going in on a Hamptons share with three other couples for July and August."

"Mmm, sounds great. They can pay twenty grand for a small bedroom and shared bathroom and bumper-to-bumper traffic, all so they can spend the summer *not* having sex. Sounds dreamy. Do I have to bring up summer of '03 again?"

Adriana shuddered. Just the thought of that summer was enough to make her feel on edge. It had been her idea — what could be so bad about a mansion in the Hamptons with a pool, a tennis court, and forty to fifty single, professional twentysomethings? — and she'd campaigned Emmy and Leigh vociferously for weeks until they finally agreed. All three had been so miserable with the 24/7 noise and partying and drinking-till-you-puke theme that they'd spent each weekend of their half-share huddled at the far end of the pool together, clinging to one another for sanity's sake. "Please, no! Don't go there. Even all these years later, it's still traumatic."

"Yeah, well, Duncan and the trainer can go hang themselves for all I care. I had a long talk with Chef Massey this week and he's still interested in having me do some work abroad. He's planning to open two new restaurants this year alone and needs people on-site to oversee the progress, help with hiring, stuff like that. And of course, menu ideas whenever possible. I start a week from Monday."

"Congratulations!" Leigh said.

Adriana squeezed Leigh's hand and tried her hardest to appear pleased. She wasn't unhappy for Emmy — after all, the girl *had* had a shitty go of it lately — but, selfishly speaking, it was hard sometimes hearing about her friends' career successes. She knew they envied her free time and would kill to have the funds and time to enjoy life a little more, but it no longer made her feel good to hear it. And of course it was not like she wanted either of their jobs; that was for sure. Emmy's tirades about egomaniacal chefs and impossible restaurant personalities were scary enough to turn anyone off a career in the food-service industry, and Leigh's hours were insane. She complained constantly of lunatic authors and oppressive reading schedules, and Adriana wondered if she wasn't just a little bit envious of those who actually got to write the books instead of edit them. But if Adriana was going to be completely honest with herself, she knew that both girls found a certain satisfaction in their jobs that she would never know from her daily schedule, however rigorous, of grooming, lunching, exercising, and socializing. It's not that she hadn't *tried* working — she'd given it a fair shot. Right after graduation she'd signed on for the buyer training program at Saks but quit as soon as she realized that she'd have to start with makeup and accessories and it would take years to work her way up to premier designer apparel. There was a brief stint at an advertising agency that she'd almost enjoyed, at least until her boss asked her to go outside *in the snow* to buy him a cup of coffee. She had even worked a few weeks for one of the famous Chelsea galleries, before realizing how naïve she'd been to think she could meet eligible straight men in the art world. Right after that job Adriana realized it just didn't make much sense to work forty hours a week and neglect so many other aspects of her life for a couple thousand dollars here or there. So while she knew from experience that she'd never trade the freedom of her situation for the drudgery of a nine-to-five, of course, there were times when she wished she was good at something besides bedding men. The exception being the current case with Yani.

". . . so I'll be traveling one to two weeks out of every four. And he's going to start looking for a new GM for Willow so I can focus even more on the new restaurants. I'll get to do a bit of everything: scouting, hiring, menu consultation, and then, once they open, stay on for a few weeks to make sure everything runs smoothly. How awesome is that?" Emmy beamed.

Adriana hadn't heard a word. "What's going on?" she asked.

Leigh glared at her. "Emmy was just saying that Chef Massey's offer is still on the table. And Emmy's going to take it."

"The salary isn't quite what I hoped for, but I'll be traveling so much that I'll barely have any living expenses. And — are you ready for this? — my first trip is to Paris. For 'training.' How amazing is that?"

Adriana tried not to resent the ebullient look on Emmy's face. *It's just Paris,* she thought to herself. *It's not like everyone hasn't been there a* thousand *times.* It took every ounce of willpower not to roll her eyes when Leigh breathed, "*So* amazing."

Emmy accidentally sipped from Adriana's coffee cup and it was all Adriana could do not to stab her hand with a fork. Why on earth was she so upset? Was she really such a jealous, petty person that she couldn't be happy for her own best friend's success? She forced herself to smile and utter some sort of congratulations in the only way she knew how. "Well, you know what that means, don't you, *querida?* Looks like your first affair will be with a Frenchman."

"Yes, I've been doing a bit of thinking about that."

"Backing out already?" Adriana said coyly. She cradled her coffee cup and pressed her lips to the edge.

Emmy cleared her throat and pretended to smooth her eyebrow with an extended middle finger. "Backing out? Hardly. I was going to clarify a few rules, is all."

"You're all about rules today, aren't you?" Adriana sniped.

"Hey, don't take it out on me that you're losing your touch. It's not my fault Yani couldn't be less interested," Emmy said.

"Come on, guys." Leigh sighed. No matter how many years passed or how much responsibility each assumed, they still managed to bicker like bitchy teenagers on a regular basis. In some way, though, each found it comforting; it reminded them how close they really were: Acquaintances were always on their best behavior, but sisters loved each other enough to say anything.

"Can I help it if I'm eager to get started?

As neither of you has been shy about pointing out, I'm way, way behind," said Emmy.

Adriana reminded herself to play nicely. She clasped her hands together and said, "Okay, let's do it. How many men are you thinking of this year?"

Leigh, desperate not to remind the girls that she hadn't agreed to any changes, anxiously chimed in. "I think three sounds fair, don't you guys?"

Adriana made a noise as though she were choking on her coffee. "Three? Please! That's a good month, not a good year."

"For once, I'm going to agree," Emmy said. "With all the traveling I'm going to be doing, I don't think three is realistic."

"So, what, are you going to screw a guy in every country you visit?" Leigh laughed. "Like, 'Here's my passport and here's my hotel key, come on in'?"

"I was actually thinking more like a guy on every continent."

"Shut up!" Leigh and Adriana said in tandem.

"What? Is that sooo impossible to imagine?"

"Yes." Leigh nodded.

"Ridiculous," Adriana agreed.

"Well, I've decided. One man for every continent I visit. Foreign, sexy men. The less American, the better. And no strings attached. No relationships, no emotional entanglements — just pure, unadulterated sex."

Adriana whistled. "*Querida!* You're making me blush!"

"What about Antarctica?" Leigh asked. "I don't think Adi has managed to sleep with a guy from Antarctica."

"I thought of that. Antarctica does seem a little unrealistic. Which is why I think Alaska can count for Antarctica." Emmy pulled a crumpled paper from her messenger bag and smoothed it flat on the table.

"Is that a chart? Please don't tell me you made a chart." Adriana laughed.

"I made a chart."

Leigh looked toward the ceiling. "She made a chart."

"I've got it all figured out. Obviously, I already have North America, so that leaves six more. And, technically speaking, Mark — Otis's daddy — was born in Moscow, so he really could count for Europe."

"I call bullshit on that," Leigh said. "It has to be within *this* year." The waitress frowned when she laid down their check.

"Seconded," Adriana said. "We'll give you America — North only — but Mark is a no-go. Why would you even want him to

101

count for Europe? You're going to Paris in a few weeks!"

Emmy nodded. "Fair enough. One down, six to go."

"What if you meet a Japanese guy in Greece, or an Australian in Thailand?" Adriana asked, looking perplexed. "Do they count as Asia and Australia, or does the sex have to take place *on* the actual continent?"

Emmy's eyebrows furrowed. "I don't know. I hadn't thought of that."

"Let's give the girl a break," Leigh said, looking to Adriana. "I think nationality or location should count. My god, it's amazing enough that she's even going to attempt this."

"I'm fine with that," Adriana agreed. "And in a demonstration of goodwill, I think you should have a free pass as well."

"Meaning?"

"Meaning that you should get to skip one continent. Otherwise, I think you're just setting yourself up for failure."

"Which one?" Emmy asked, appearing slightly relieved.

"What if Swiss guys counted as a wild card?" Leigh asked. "It's a neutral country. I think if you sleep with a Swiss guy he can count for anywhere."

The girls laughed and laughed, the kind

of laughter that happens all too rarely after college.

Adriana pulled a blue tin tub from the front pocket of her yoga bag and rubbed a bit of clear salve on her lips, aware that both her friends and nearly every patron at every surrounding table appeared transfixed by her little ritual. It made her feel a little bit better. She'd had trouble ridding herself of the thoughts that had been plaguing her lately, namely that her looks wouldn't last forever. She had known this intellectually, of course — the way a teenager knows death is inevitable — but she was completely unable to comprehend the reality. Her mother had been reminding her of this very fact since the day Adriana had, at the age of fourteen, agreed to two dates with two different boys on the same night. When asked which one she would choose to see that night, Adriana gazed at her still-beautiful mother with uncomprehending eyes.

"Why would I break plans with either one, Mama?" Adriana had asked. "There's time enough for both of them."

Her mother had smiled and cupped Adriana's cheek in a cool, open palm. "Enjoy it now, *querida*. It will not be like this always."

Of course she was right, but Adriana

hadn't counted on "always" coming so soon. It was time to utilize her beauty for something more important than attracting a steady stream of lovers. Her pledge to find a boyfriend was a step in the right direction, but it wasn't far-reaching enough.

With great flourish, Adriana held her left hand up and sighed dramatically. "Do you see this hand, girls?" Both nodded. "By this time next year, there will be a diamond on it. An extraordinarily large diamond. I hereby declare that I will be engaged to *the* perfect man within twelve months."

"Adriana!" Emmy shrieked. "You're just trying to outdo me."

Leigh choked on a piece of cantaloupe. "Engaged? To whom? Are you seeing someone?"

"No, not currently. But Emmy's commitment to making a change has inspired me. Plus, it's time to face facts, girls. We are not getting any younger, and I think we can all acknowledge that there are only a limited number of rich, handsome, successful men between the ages of thirty and forty. If we don't claim ours now" — she cupped both hands around her firm breasts and pushed them upward — "then we may as well forget it."

"Well, thank god you figured it out,"

Emmy said with amusement. "I'll just point to one of the dozens — no, hundreds — of successful, handsome, single men in their thirties I know and just make him mine. Yes, that's the plan."

Adriana smiled and tapped Emmy's hand patronizingly. "Don't forget rich, *querida.* Now, I'm not saying that's what we *all* should be doing. Clearly, you need to play a bit first, and I think your little upcoming foray into promiscuity is just what the doctor ordered. But being that I've, well, *forayed* there already —"

"If by *forayed* you mean 'completely conquered,' then I guess I'd agree," Leigh added.

"Laugh if you must," Adriana said, feeling slightly irritated that, as usual, she wasn't being taken seriously. "But there's nothing funny about a five-plus-carat round stone in a micropave setting from Harry Winston. Nothing funny at all."

"Yeah, but it's pretty funny now," Emmy said while Leigh dissolved into laughter. "Adriana engaged? It's impossible to imagine."

"No more impossible to imagine than the serial monogamist putting out for every foreign stranger who crosses her path," Adriana shot back.

Leigh wiped away a tear, taking care not to pull the delicate skin beneath her eye, skin that was probably already doomed anyway from her smoking days. She wasn't sure if it was the endorphins from a particularly strenuous yoga class or the semi-dread of having dinner with Russell's parents later that night, or just the desire to share in her friends' fun, but before she could stop it — almost before she even knew it was happening — Leigh started to talk without any forethought or awareness.

"In honor of your acts of bravery," she was saying, the words feeling as though they emerged entirely of their own volition, "I, too, would like to propose a goal. By the end of this year, I will . . ." Her words faded. She'd begun speaking without knowing what to say, assuming something would come, but she had nothing to offer. She found her job mostly rewarding, if a tad boring at times; she was perfectly comfortable with the number of men she'd slept with so far; she'd already snagged herself a boyfriend fitting all of Adriana's criteria — not just any man but a famous one, a man half of the country and the entire female population of Manhattan clamored to date; and she had finally saved enough to buy her own apartment. She was doing exactly what was expected of her. What was she supposed to change?

"Get knocked up?" Emmy offered helpfully.

"Have plastic surgery?" Adriana countered.

"Make your first million?"

"Have a threesome?"

"Get hooked on booze or drugs?"

"Learn to love the subway?" asked Adriana with a wicked smile.

Leigh shuddered. "God, no. Not *that*." She grinned.

Emmy patted her hand. "We know, honey. The dirt, the noise, the unpredictable schedule . . ."

"All those people!" Adriana added. After twelve years of friendship, she felt like she knew Leigh better than she knew herself. If there was one thing that drove the poor girl mad — even more than mess or loud, repetitive sounds or surprise — it was crowds. The girl was an anxious wreck these days, and Adriana and Emmy discussed it every chance they got.

Emmy broke the moment of silence. "Take it as a good sign that you don't have an area of your life that requires massive restructuring. I mean, how many people can really say that?"

Adriana nibbled a leftover piece of toast.

"Seriously, *querida,* all you have to do is appreciate your perfect life." She held up her coffee mug. "To changes."

Emmy reached for her nearly empty glass of grapefruit juice and turned to Leigh. "And to recognizing perfection when it's present."

Leigh rolled her eyes and forced a smile. "To gorgeous foreigners and boulder-sized diamonds," she said.

Two glasses met hers and made a wonderful clinking sound. "Cheers!" they all called in unison. "Cheers to that."

If all of her irritatingly verbose colleagues didn't shut the hell up in the next seven minutes, there was no way Leigh could make it from West Midtown to the Upper East Side by one. Didn't these people ever get sick of hearing themselves talk? Didn't they get *hungry?* Her stomach rumbled audibly as if to remind the room that it was lunch hour, but no one seemed to notice. They were discussing the upcoming publication of *The Life and Leadership of Pope John Paul II* with an intensity worthy of a presidential debate.

"Summer is a tough time for a religious biography — we knew that going in," one of the associate editors commented with some trepidation, still unaccustomed to speaking at meetings.

Someone from the sales team, a sweet-faced woman who looked far younger than her thirty-some years and whose name Leigh could never remember, addressed the table. "Of course summer isn't ideal for anything other than beach reads, but the season alone doesn't account for these disappointing numbers. Orders from everyone — B&N, Borders, the independents — are all significantly lower than forecasted. Perhaps if we could generate a little more buzz . . ."

"*Buzz?*" Patrick, the queeny head of publicity, sneered. "Just how do you propose generating 'buzz' for a book about the *pope?* Give us something even remotely appealing and maybe we could work something out. But Britney Spears could tattoo the entire contents of this book on her bare breasts and people *still* wouldn't talk about it."

Jason, the only other editor who had been promoted as quickly as Leigh and whose existence at Brook Harris was the only thing that kept her sane, sighed and looked at his watch. Leigh caught his eye and nodded. She couldn't wait any longer.

"Please excuse me," Leigh interrupted. "But I have a lunch appointment I can't miss. A business lunch, of course," she added quickly, although of course no one cared.

She quietly gathered her papers and shoved everything into the monogrammed leather folder that accompanied her everywhere and tiptoed out of the conference room.

She had just swung by her office to grab her purse when her phone rang and she saw her publisher's extension on her caller ID. Leigh had just decided to screen him when she heard her assistant's voice call out, "Henry, line one. He says it's urgent."

"He always says it's urgent," Leigh muttered to herself. She took a calming breath and picked up the receiver.

"Henry! Are you calling to apologize for missing the sales meeting?" she joked. "I'm willing to overlook it this time, but don't let it happen again."

"Ha-ha, I'm cracking up on the inside, I promise," he said. "I'm not keeping you from a lunchtime manicure or a quick jaunt to Barneys, am I?"

Leigh forced a laugh. It was positively eerie how well he knew her. Although technically it was a *blowout* and a quick jaunt to Barneys. She couldn't particularly afford either one right now, but her flakiness in both the personal hygiene and gift departments today had mandated that she splurge. "Of course not. What can I do for you?"

"There's someone in my office I'd like you

to meet. Come on over here for a minute."

Goddammit! The man had a gift for intuitively sensing the most inconvenient moments of her day and then asking for something. It was uncanny and she wondered, for the umpteenth time, if he bugged her office.

She took another calming breath and glanced at the clock. Her appointment was in fifteen minutes and the salon was a ten-minute walk away. "I'll be right there," she said with enough cheer to fell a sequoia.

She speed-walked through the cubicles and winding hallways that separated her office from Henry's. He obviously wanted her to meet a potential author or someone new they'd just signed, since he was a big believer in demonstrating how Brook Harris was run like a family and insisted on personally introducing all the editors to all the new authors. It was one of the qualities that had most impressed her when she'd first started out — and one of the main reasons so many authors signed with Brook Harris and stayed for their entire careers — but today it was really fucking annoying. Anyone less than Tom Wolfe and she wasn't interested. She ran calculations as she rounded the corner and passed the elevator bank. Her congrats-on-joining-the-family-we're-so-happy-to-have-you or some similar we'd-be-thrilled-and-honored-to-have-you-join-the-family speech would take only a couple of minutes. Another minute or two to feign interest in the new/potential author's current work, plus one more to congratulate him on the success of his previous publication, and there was a chance she'd be out in under five. At least she'd better be.

She'd been up so late the night before trying to finish her notes on the last chapter of her newest memoir acquistion that she had slept straight through her alarm and had to race, unshowered, to make the sales meeting on time. It wasn't until Leigh found a toweringly tall pale purple orchid on her desk with a note that read, "I love you and can't wait to see you tonight. Happy First Year!" that she even remembered that Russell had made reservations at Daniel to celebrate their one-year anniversary. Typical. It was the single day in her entire career — possibly her entire life — that she'd overslept and left the house looking like a homeless person, and it was the only time it mattered. Thankfully Gilles had agreed to fit her in for a last-minute blowout ("You can have Adriana's appointment at one if she doesn't mind," he'd offered. "She doesn't mind!" Leigh had screamed into the phone. "I take full responsibility!") and she planned to swing by Barneys and pick up a bottle of cologne or a tie or a dopp kit — really, whatever was closest to the register and came prewrapped — on her way back to the office. There was absolutely no time for dawdling.

"You can go right on in," Henry's perky new assistant drawled. Her spiky, pink-streaked hair didn't fit with the Southern accent — or the conservative corporate culture — but she seemed able to spell and didn't appear overtly hostile, so it was overlooked.

Leigh nodded her thanks and barreled through the open door. "Hello!" she sang to Henry. She guessed the man sitting opposite him, facing away from her, was in his early forties. Despite the early summer weather, he wore a light blue shirt and an olive corduroy blazer with patches over the elbows. His dirty-blond hair — light brown, really, now that she looked more carefully — was the perfect amount of shaggy, just grazing the top of his collar and falling slightly over the tops of his ears. Before he even turned to look at her, she knew, intuited, that he would be attractive. Perhaps even gorgeous. Which was partly why she was so taken aback when their eyes finally met.

The surprise was twofold. Her first thought was that he wasn't nearly as good-looking as she had predicted. His eyes were not the piercing shade of blue or green she'd expected, but an unremarkable grayish hazel, and his nose managed to appear flattened and protuberant at the same time. But he did have flawless teeth, straight, white, gorgeous teeth, teeth that could star in their very own Crest commercial, and it was these teeth that captured her attention. It wasn't until the man smiled, revealing deeply engraved but somehow still very appealing laugh lines, that she realized she recognized him. Sitting here, gazing at her with an easy smile and a welcoming expression, was Jesse Chapman, a man whose talents had been compared to Updike, Roth, and Bellow; McInerney, Ford, and Franzen. *Disenchantment,* the first novel he'd published, at age twenty-three, had been one of those impossibly rare books that was both a commercial and literary success, and Jesse's reputation as a bad-boy genius had only increased with every additional party attended, model dated, and book written. He had disappeared six or seven years ago, after a rumored stint in rehab and spate of brutal reviews, but no one expected him to stay hidden forever. The fact that he was here, in their offices, could mean only one thing.

"Leigh, may I introduce you to Jesse

Chapman? You're familiar with his work, of course. And Jesse, this is Leigh Eisner, my most promising editor, and my favorite, were I forced to choose."

Jesse stood to face Leigh, and although his eyes remained fixed on hers, she could feel him appraising her. She wondered if he liked girls with stringy ponytails and no makeup. She prayed he did.

"He says that about everyone," Leigh said graciously, extending her hand to meet Jesse's.

"Of course he does," Jesse said smoothly, standing to envelop her right hand between both of his. "And that's why we all adore him. Please, will you join us?" He waved his hand toward the empty space beside him on the love seat and looked at her.

"Oh, well, actually, I was just —"

"She'd love to," Henry said.

Leigh resisted the urge to glare at him while she settled into the ancient couch. *Bye-bye, blowout,* she thought. *Bye-bye, Barneys.* It would be a miracle if Russell ever spoke to her again after the disaster that tonight would surely be.

Henry cleared his throat. "Jesse and I were just discussing his last novel. I was saying how we all — really, the entire publishing industry — thought the *Times'* attack was inexcusable. Embarrassing for them, really, with its obvious agenda. Absolutely no one took it seriously. It was complete and —"

Smiling again, this time with the slightest expression of amusement, Jesse turned to Leigh. "And what did you think, dear? Did you think the review was warranted?"

Leigh was shocked by his assuredness that she had not only read but remembered both the book and this particular review. Which, irritatingly, she did. It had been the cover of the Sunday *Book Review* six years earlier, and the viciousness of it still resonated. She actually remembered wondering what it must be like for the author to read something like that about his work, had wondered where Jesse Chapman was when he first laid eyes on those brutal ten paragraphs. She would have read the book regardless — she'd studied Jesse's earlier novels in countless college lit classes — but the sheer meanness of the review had propelled her to buy it in hardcover and devour it that same week.

Leigh spoke, as she often did, without thinking. It was a habit at direct odds with her methodical personality, but she just couldn't help herself. She could meticulously organize an apartment or schedule a day or create a work plan, but she couldn't seem to master the concept that not all thoughts need to be spoken. The girls and Russell claimed they found it charming, but it could be downright mortifying sometimes. Like in a meeting with your boss, for instance. Something about Jesse's gaze — interested yet still aloof — made her forget that she was in Henry's office, talking to one of the greatest writing talents of the twenty-first century, and she barreled ahead. "The review was petty, to be sure. It was vindictive and unprofessional, a hit job if I've ever seen one. That said, I think *Rancor* was your weakest effort. It didn't deserve a review like that, but it wasn't nearly on par with *The Moon's Defeat* or, of course, *Disenchantment*."

Henry inhaled and instinctively placed his hand over his mouth.

Leigh felt faint; her heart began to race at top speed and she could feel the sweat starting to dampen her palms and feet.

Jesse grinned. "Telling it straight. No bullshit. That's rare these days, wouldn't you say?"

Not sure whether this was an actual question, Leigh stared at her hands, which she was wringing with a frightening ferocity.

"A regular charm school here, isn't it?" Henry laughed. His voice sounded hollow and more than a little nervous. "Well, thank you for sharing your opinion with Mr. Chapman, Leigh. Your *solo* opinion, of course." He smiled wanly at Jesse.

Leigh took this as her cue to leave and was positively ecstatic to oblige. "I, uh, I'm so . . . I meant no offense, of course. I'm a really huge fan and, it's just that —"

"Please don't apologize. It was a pleasure meeting you."

With tremendous effort, Leigh resisted the urge to apologize again and managed to get herself off the couch, past Jesse, and out of Henry's office without further humiliation, but one look at Henry's assistant's face and she knew she was screwed.

"Was it really that bad?" she asked, gripping the girl's desk.

"Whoa. That was ballsy."

"Ballsy? I didn't intend to be ballsy. I was trying to be diplomatic! I'm such an idiot. I can't believe I said that. Ohmigod, eight years of work and it's all down the drain because I can't keep my mouth shut. Was it really that bad?" Leigh asked again.

There was a pause. The assistant opened her mouth as if to say something, then closed it again. "It wasn't good."

Leigh checked her watch and grudgingly acknowledged to herself that there was no chance of making her appointment or getting back in time for the calls she had scheduled all afternoon with various agents. Back in her office, she began to work the phones. Her first call was to cancel with Gilles and the second was to Barneys. A pleasant-sounding salesclerk in the men's department agreed to messenger a gift to her office before six. Leigh was baffled when he asked what she'd like; unable to think clearly and not particularly caring, she instructed him to make it in the $200 range and charge her American Express.

By the time the gift-wrapped box arrived at five-thirty, Leigh was close to tears. She hadn't heard another word from Henry, who usually couldn't make it an hour without multiple phone calls or stop-ins. She'd managed to run to the gym briefly — no workout, just a quick shower — but she didn't realize until she was standing under the blessedly hot water that she'd left her gym bag in the office, the one with her cosmetics, a change of underwear, and, most important, her hairdryer. Although she would have thought it impossible, the mini-dryer attached to the gym wall with what seemed like a two-inch cord actually left her hair looking significantly worse than it had before the shower. Russell and her mother called her cell phone during the walk back to her office, but she screened both of them.

I am a vile human being, Leigh thought as she examined herself in the ladies room closest to her office. It was almost seven and she'd only just ended her final phone call with one of her least favorite agents. Her hair hung in limp, frizzy strands, its flatness accentuated by the dark bags under eyes and the angry redness of a forehead pimple that had neither hair nor foundation to conceal it. She'd forgotten that Russell had once joked that she looked "lesbian chic" in the blazer she was wearing, and although she'd always loved its shrunken fit and its chunky gold chains and the fact that it was Chanel — the only article of haute couture she owned — she had never noticed until this very moment that it made her look like a linebacker. "Don't worry," she mumbled, unaware that she was talking to herself. "Russell's a sports commentator. He works for ESPN. He dedicates his life to professional sports. Russell loves football players!" And with that, clutching the gorgeously wrapped gift box from Barneys, trying not to worry about the fact that its contents were a complete mystery, she gathered her unkempt self and hustled downstairs to hail a cab.

Russell stood outside Daniel, looking relaxed and fit and happy. Like he'd just returned from a month in the Caribbean, where he'd done nothing but treat his body like a temple. His charcoal gray suit hugged every toned muscle. His skin glowed with the health of someone who runs six miles a day; he was freshly washed and shaven. Even his shoes — a pair of black lace-ups that he'd bought on their last trip to Milan — literally shined. He was groomed to perfection, and Leigh resented him for it. Who on earth managed to work a full day and keep their tie that clean or their shirt that crisp? How was it always possible to match that well, to have coordinated cuff links with trouser socks, shoes with briefcases?

"Hi, gorgeous. I was starting to worry."

She pecked him on the lips but moved away before he could open his mouth. "Worry? Why? I'm right on time."

"Well, you know, I just hadn't heard from you all day. You did get the orchid, right? I know the purple ones are your favorite."

"I did. It was beautiful. Thank you so much." Her voice sounded strange to her own ears — it was the higher-pitched, polite tone she used with her doorman or dry cleaner.

Russell placed his hand in the small of her back and guided her through the front doors. They were immediately greeted by a tuxedoed man nearing the end of middle age who appeared to recognize Russell. They conferred momentarily in whispers, the maître d' leaning in toward Russell, the two men clapping each other on the shoulders. A moment later, he motioned for a young girl in a tight but conservative pantsuit to show them to their table.

"Football fan?" Leigh asked, more to appear interested than because she actually was.

"What? Oh, the maître d'? Yeah, he must have recognized me from the show. What else could explain this table, right?"

Only then did Leigh notice that they had easily the best table in the whole restaurant. They were facing the entire gorgeous room from their perch under one of the dramatic archways. The lighting was so soft and perfect that Leigh thought she might even look good under it, and the heavy brocade and acres of rich red velvet felt soothing after such a hellish day. The tables were adequately spaced to keep people from sitting on top of one another, the background music was unobtrusive, and there didn't appear to be a single person talking on a cell phone. From strictly an anxiety standpoint, this place was heaven on earth — a particularly good thing tonight, considering Russell would be even less thrilled than he usually was if she made a fuss over the table selection.

She relaxed even more after a glass of pinot grigio and some delicately caramelized sea scallops, but Leigh still couldn't completely switch gears from work to romantic dinner à deux. She nodded her way through Russell's description of a companywide memo he was thinking of authoring, his suggestion that they try to make it to his college buddy's Martha's Vineyard home sometime that summer, and his recap of a joke one of the show's makeup artists had told him that morning. It wasn't until the waiter delivered two flutes of champagne and something called a coconut *dacquoise* that Leigh felt alert. There, resting casually next to the plate of poached pineapples and surrounded by berries, was a black velvet box. She was surprised and a little disconcerted that her first feeling upon spying the jewelry box was one of relief: Its long, rectangular shape indicated that it wasn't — thank god — a ring. Of course she'd probably want to marry Russell someday — there wasn't a friend or family member who'd ever met him and not immediately referenced his superior husband potential, kindness, handsome looks, successful career, charisma, and obvious adoration of Leigh — but she definitely wasn't ready to marry him *now*. There didn't seem to be any harm at all in waiting another year, or maybe two. Marriage was, well, *marriage,* and she wanted to be absolutely sure.

"What's this?" she asked with genuine excitement, already envisioning an initial pendant of some sort, or perhaps a pretty gold bracelet.

"Open it and see," he said softly.

Leigh fingered the plush velvet and grinned. "You shouldn't have!"

"Open it!"

"I just know I'm going to love it."

"Leigh, open the box. You may be surprised."

The look in his eyes gave her pause, as did the way his hand tensed around his champagne glass. She snapped open the lid and, just like they do in every bad rom com she'd ever seen, she gasped. There, nestled in the very middle of the necklace-sized box, was a ring. An engagement ring. A very huge, very beautiful engagement ring.

"Leigh?" His voice shook. Gently, he took the box from her and plucked the ring out. In one swift movement, he took her left hand in his own and slid the ring onto the proper finger. It fit perfectly. "Leigh, honey? I've loved you since the moment I met you, one year ago today. I think we've both known from the very first night that this was something special — something forever. Will you marry me?"

Emmy's first meeting the next day with a local culinary staffing company wasn't until two o'clock — one of the many benefits of the hospitality industry — but she was really starting to feel the jet lag. When she'd arrived at the hotel that morning at ten, she had ordered a light room-service breakfast of coffee, croissant, and berries (after a quick conversion from euros to dollars, she realized the cost was $31, not including tip) and then bathed using the three-ounce bubble bath she found in the minibar ($50). Following a quick nap and few hours spent confirming the next day's appointments, she'd had a Niçoise salad and a Coke in the restaurant's outdoor garden ($38). None of it felt particularly extravagant, though, when compared to dinner, a simple steak-frites she had eaten alone in the hotel's lobby lounge two hours earlier. Steak, fries, and a single glass of red wine. ("House wine? What do you mean by 'house wine'?" the waiter had asked with a barely suppressed sneer. "Ah," he said after a moment of intense thought. "You mean 'inexpensive,' yes? I will bring it to you, madam.") The bill had come to a whopping $96, and the wine tasted like

Manischewitz. He hadn't even called her mademoiselle!

Occupying a prime sliver of real estate on chic Rue du Faubourg in the 1st arrondissement — just steps from the Ritz and Hermès — the Hotel Costes was legendary for its celeb-heavy clientele and ultra-chic late-night lounge scene. When the travel department asked if she had any hotel preferences, Emmy couldn't work up the nerve even to suggest the Costes. It wasn't until the agent had given her a choice between there and a gorgeous riverfront hotel on the Left Bank that she practically shrieked with excitement. What better place to get started on Tour de Whore '07?

Emmy had spent a full week anticipating her stay at the Costes. One hour after arrival she was awed by its coolness; two hours later she was intimidated; three hours after that she was ready to check out. The Costes might be the best place in town to be seen, but it seemed impossible that anyone actually *stayed* there. Either she had gotten really, really old or the Costes had a major attitude problem. The hallways were so dark that she'd taken to running her hands along the corridor walls to keep from walking into them. The music from the lounge reverberated through the rooms, and the noisy bustle of models sipping skim lattes and various nationalities of modelizers slurping Bordeaux in the central courtyard bounced off every window. Her charming claw-foot tub had no curtain, so the floor flooded when she turned on the handheld showerhead. There was no electrical outlet in the bathroom (probably because everyone brought their own stylist), so Emmy had been forced to dry her hair, sans mirror, at the desk. So far she'd been patronized, ignored, and mocked by the hotel staff. And yet, irritatingly enough, she couldn't shake the feeling that she should feel honored to stay there.

So she sat as unobtrusively as she could manage in the lounge, reading e-mails on her laptop and savoring an espresso (a flawless one, she grudgingly conceded). Her sister wrote that she and Kevin were planning to come to New York for the Fourth of July, and asked if she'd be in town. She had just written back to say that they could have her studio and she'd stay at Adriana's when her new company-provided international cell phone rang.

"This is Emmy Solomon," she said as professionally as possible.

"Emmy? Is that you?"

"Leigh? How did you get this number?"

"I called your office here and said it was an

emergency. I hope you don't mind?"

"Sweetie, is everything okay? It's two in the morning there."

"Yeah, everything's fine, I just wanted you to hear it from me before the word got out over e-mail. I'm engaged!"

"Engaged? Oh my god! Leigh, congratulations! I had no idea you guys were even thinking about it. This is so exciting! Tell me everything." Emmy saw a uniformed staffer shoot her a nasty look, but she glared right back.

"I, uh, guess I wasn't really expecting it, either," Leigh said. "It just sort of came out of nowhere."

"Well, how did he do it?"

Leigh described what was supposed to be a simple anniversary dinner, how haggish she'd looked and felt, and what each of them had ordered at Daniel in measured, factual detail. By the time she got to the dessert-time proposal, Emmy had started interrupting in a desperate attempt to get to the good stuff.

"I don't care how *you* looked — what does the ring look like? And let me remind you that now is not the time for modesty."

"It's huge."

"How huge?"

"Very huge."

"Leigh!"

"Just under four."

"Just under four! Carats? Four *carats?*"

"I'm worried it's too big. How can I wear something like that to work? I work in *book* publishing." Leigh sighed.

Emmy wanted to scream. "I won't even dignify it with a response. Did you tell Adriana that you think it's . . . I can't even bring myself to say it."

"Yes. She told me if I think it's too big I don't deserve it."

"I'll second that. Now stop being a goddamn idiot and tell me more. Have you set a date yet? When do you think you'll move into his place?"

The silence on the line was so complete that Emmy thought they'd been disconnected. "Leigh? Can you hear me?"

"Yeah, sorry about that. We haven't even come close to picking a date yet — I don't know, next summer, I guess? The summer after?"

"Leigh! You're thirty years old and not getting any younger. You think we're going to let you be engaged for two *years?* If I were you, I'd have that boy at the altar in five months. What are you waiting for?"

"I'm not *waiting* for anything," Leigh said, sounding peeved. "I just don't see what the big rush is all about. We just met, for chris-sake."

"You met a year ago, Leigh, and as you've pointed out yourself on numerous occasions, he fits every checklist of everything you've been looking for in a man. And more. You'd be insane not to lock this up at the earliest possible date. At the very least, you need to get yourself situated in his apartment. Stake your claim."

"Emmy, you're being ridiculous. 'Stake my claim'? Are you kidding? You know how I feel about living together before marriage."

Emmy shrieked a little and then, remembering where she was, slapped a hand over her mouth. "Don't tell me you're actually going to abide by that absurd idea? My god, Leigh, you sound like some religious freak!"

"Oh, Emmy, save it. You know it has nothing to do with any religious or moral reason. It's just the way I want it. It's a little old-fashioned. So what?"

"Does Russell know?"

"He certainly knows how I feel in general."

"But he doesn't know that now, even though you're engaged to be married, you're not going to move in with him?"

"We haven't gotten there yet. I'm sure he'll

be totally understanding."

"Good god, Leigh. You know you're going to have to live with him at some point, don't you? Even though he's a boy and he's gross in the bathroom and might want the TV on sometimes when you don't? You have thought about this, haven't you?"

Leigh sighed and said, "I know. In theory that all sounds okay, but in reality . . . I'm just used to living alone. I *like* living alone. The noise, and the stuff all over the place, and the always having to talk even when you just want to sit on the couch and zone out . . . it's terrifying."

Slightly relieved that Leigh had, at the very least, opened up about her fear of cohabiting, Emmy eased a little. "I know, sweetie. It's scary for everyone. Hell, Duncan and I dated for five years and never made it official. But you love him and he loves you and the two of you will figure it out. If you want to wait until you're legal, well, who am I to tell you what —"

"I'm not in love with him, Emmy." Leigh's voice was unwavering and their connection was crystal clear, but Emmy was certain she hadn't heard correctly.

"What did you say? I can't hear a goddamn thing here."

Leigh was silent on the other end.

"Leigh? Are you there? What did you just say?"

"Don't make me say it again," Leigh whispered, her throat catching on the last word.

"Sweetheart, what do you mean? You two seem so happy together! You've never uttered a negative word about Russell, only told us over and over how sweet and kind and thoughtful he is," Emmy coaxed.

"None of that changes the fact that sometimes I'm bored to tears when I'm with him. I know I shouldn't be, but it doesn't change the fact that I am. We don't have anything in common! He loves sports; I love reading. He wants to go out and network and meet people, and I just want to hole up at home. He's not the least bit interested in current events or the arts — just football, weight training, nutrition, stats. His college injury. I'm not denying that he's a terrific guy, Em, but I'm not sure he's terrific for me."

Emmy liked to think of herself as fairly intuitive, but she hadn't sensed this for a second. *Nerves,* she thought to herself. Nothing more than Leigh's inability to accept that she deserved a great guy and had actually found one. Everyone knew that crazy passion or great love affairs cooled after the first few months, maybe a year. What mattered was finding someone who would be a good partner for the long haul. Who would stay by your side, be a good husband, a good father. And if Russell wasn't that guy, she didn't know who was. She began to explain exactly this to Leigh but she was interrupted by the scowling hotel employee, who tapped her roughly on the shoulder. "Madam? Kindly remove your shoes from the furniture."

"Who's that?" Leigh asked.

"Excuse me?" Emmy peered at the man; she was momentarily intimidated, but that quickly shifted to irritation.

"I requested that you please remove your shoes from the chair. *We don't sit like that here.*" The man stood rooted to his spot and peered at Emmy.

"Emmy, what's going on? Who is that?"

Emmy, usually uncomfortable with any type of confrontation, felt a wave of anger course through her. She forgot all about Leigh and glared at the man. "*We* don't *sit* like that here? Did you really just say that to me?"

Leigh laughed. "Tell him how it is."

Emmy made a point of speaking loudly into the phone. "I'm sitting in the lounge because it's too goddamn dark to read in my own room — just sitting, mind you — and I have one of my legs tucked under me. And you want to know the type of shoes I'm putting all over the furniture? Ballet slippers. Like, not ballet-style flats but actual sole-less ballet slippers. I'm a *guest* of this hotel, and he has the nerve to *reprimand* me like a *child?*" She flashed her eyes upward to meet the man's. He shook his head as if to say *Ignorant American* and turned — pirouetted, really — away.

"Got to love French hospitality," Leigh said. "Am I to assume that you haven't snagged yourself a lover yet?"

"Nice try. Don't think you're changing the subject that easily."

"Em, I really appreciate your listening, but I don't want to talk about it anymore, okay? I'm sure everything will work out."

Now that's the spirit! Emmy thought. Leigh just needed a little time to work through her thoughts, to realize what was important. It was a mere case of overthinking, and Leigh would see she was just being silly. "Okay. Back to the ring. Tell me more."

"It's really beautiful," Leigh said softly. "So classic. I don't know how he knew I liked that — I'm not even sure I knew I liked that. We never went shopping or looking; we never even talked about it."

"That's Russell for you. What shape is it?"

"A larger emerald-cut stone in the middle

flanked by two smaller emerald-cuts on the side of a very thin platinum band."

Emmy whistled. "Sounds gorgeous. Did you really not have any idea?"

There was a long pause. For a moment Emmy again thought that they'd gotten disconnected, but then she heard Leigh breathing heavily.

"Are you okay, honey? Leigh?"

More breathing, this time in shorter, more shallow bursts.

"Oh, I'm fine. Just a little racing heart. Must be all the excitement, you know?"

Emmy pressed her cell phone to her ear, desperately wanting to hear just a little of the giggly, girly enthusiasm of someone who had just gotten engaged, but Emmy knew better. Leigh wasn't a giggly, girly girl: She was funny, she was sensible, she was loyal, and she was neurotic; giggly just wasn't her thing. Maybe Leigh was also feeling a little uncomfortable describing her ring when everyone had expected Emmy to be the first. Emmy flashed back to the dinner a few months earlier when she'd excitedly told Leigh and Adriana that Duncan had asked for her ring size. Not necessarily the most romantic gesture, she remembered thinking, but it definitely indicated good things. She felt her face redden at the memory of her excitement and decided she'd save Leigh from feeling any more pity for her.

"So what'd you get him for your anniversary?" Emmy asked with extra, perhaps excessive, cheer.

Another long pause. It sounded like Leigh was trying to moderate her breathing with measured breaths.

"Leigh?"

"Sorry, I'm, uh, I'm fine. Just a little . . . uh, I got him a laptop bag. An orange one." She took another deep breath and coughed. "From Barneys."

Emmy tried to mask her surprise. "Russell finally got a laptop? I never thought I'd see the day. How did you finally convince him?"

"He still doesn't have a laptop," Leigh sighed. "Oh, Emmy, I'm the worst person ever!"

"Honey, what's wrong? I'm so confused. Are you planning on buying him a laptop? That's cute! You couldn't have known he was going to propose that night. Don't worry about it. Russell is the last person to get upset over something like that."

There was another long pause, and when Leigh finally spoke, Emmy could tell she was crying. "I got him an orange laptop bag because I was too lazy to pick out something personal," she said, her voice filled with anger and regret. "I called the store and gave them my credit card number and that's what they sent over. A laptop bag! For someone who doesn't own a laptop. In orange." There was a sniffle. "Russell hates bright colors."

"Leigh, sweetheart, don't be so hard on yourself. Russell loves you so much that he asked you to spend the rest of your life with him. Don't let some dumb present get in the way of that. I bet he didn't mind at all, did he?"

"He laughed it off, but I could tell he was hurt."

"He's a big boy, Leigh. He can handle a little gift mix-up." Both girls knew that wasn't what had happened, but they let it slide. "So tell me, was everyone else excited?"

Leigh dutifully described her mother's reaction, and Adriana's, and Russell's family's, interjecting jokes and amusing observations in all the right places. It wasn't until the girls hung up, promising to talk in more depth the next day, that Emmy let herself feel a twinge of concern. Could there really be a problem with Leigh and Russell? Was it possible Leigh really was having serious doubts? *Absolutely not,* Emmy decided. *Just a case of nerves. Excitement and shock and nothing more sinister.* She felt confident in her analysis of the situation and certain that everything would smooth itself out as soon as the excitement settled down a bit. Turning back to her computer, Emmy braced herself to order another coffee from the hostile waiter.

"Pardon?" The male voice came from just over her right shoulder, but Emmy, convinced that another hotel employee was preparing to chastise her for something, ignored it.

"Excuse me?" the voice persisted. "Forgive me for interrupting you."

Emmy glanced up, remembering at the last minute to appear colossally bored and displeased with the interruption, but the moment she said "Yes?" in the most irritated tone she could muster, she regretted it. Peering down at her was a guy with the kind of classical good looks — thick dark hair, crinkly eyes, easy smile full of straight white teeth — that made him almost universally attractive. He wasn't drop-dead gorgeous or movie-star sexy, but his pleasing appearance combined with his confident approachability made Emmy think that there wasn't a sane woman on the planet who would find him unappealing.

"Hi," she murmured. *Bingo,* she thought. *Tour de Whore contender number one.*

138

He flashed another smile and motioned to the chair beside her with a questioning look. Emmy just nodded and stared as he sat. He was younger than she originally thought, perhaps even under thirty. Her lightning-fast appraisal — honed over so many years that it was now nearly instinctive — produced all positive points. Meticulously cut yet still casual navy cotton sweater over a white collared shirt. Good jeans that were blessedly devoid of deliberate rips, excessive fading, logos, studs, embroidery, or flap pockets. Simple but elegant brown loafers. Regular height, reasonably fit without being obsessive, well groomed but still masculine. If she had to criticize something, she might say that his jeans were a tad too tight. Then again, if one was going to seduce European men, tight jeans were an occupational hazard.

Newly emboldened by his approach, and not forgetting that the only men she'd spoken to in France so far all worked at the Costes, Emmy smiled. "I'm Emmy," she said.

He grinned and offered her a hand. No rings, no bitten nails, no clear polish — all good signs. "Paul Wyckoff. I couldn't help but overhear what that jackass said to you. . . ."

Dammit. There was no denying the obvious: Despite the painted-on jeans and the good manners and her fervent desire for it to not be so, Paul spoke English with an American accent. He was undeniably born and raised in the States, or perhaps — at the most exotic — Canada. She was bitterly disappointed.

". . . it's just incredible, isn't it?" he was saying. "It never ceases to amaze me how much people are willing to pay to be treated so poorly."

"So it's not just me?" Emmy asked, slightly relieved that the hotel hadn't singled her out.

"Definitely not," Paul assured her. "They're positively abusive to *all* of their guests. It's the only thing they're really consistent about."

"Well, thank you for that. I was starting to develop quite a complex."

"I'm glad I could help. The first time I stayed here, I was a paranoid wreck. My parents used to drag us all over the world — I practically grew up in hotels — but it only took a day here to make me feel like a bumbling idiot," he said.

Emmy laughed, already forgetting about Paul's lack of eligibility. Which was lacking, of course, for game purposes only. It had taken less than four minutes of small talk to deduce that he would make the perfect husband. But no! No, dammit; she wasn't going to fall into that trap again. *Sex good. Attachments bad.* She repeated these four words as images of her dream Monique Lhuillier wedding dress (sleeveless but not strapless, floor-length, with a dusty rose sash cinching the waist) and her perfect menu (citrus heirloom tomato salad to start, followed by a choice of grilled ahi tuna or a Matsuzake beef tenderloin) danced through her mind.

"Glad to know I'm not alone." Emmy finished her coffee and licked the spoon clean. "Why did your family travel so much?"

"This is where I should say 'army brat' or 'diplomat's son,' but really, there's not one reason. Mostly my parents are just schizophrenic about where they live, and they're both writers. So we were always on the move. I was actually born in Argentina."

It took Emmy only a split second to understand the significance of that fact. "Does that make you Argentinean?"

Paul laughed. "Among other things."

"Meaning?"

"Meaning that I'm an Argentine because I was born in Buenos Aires while my parents were both working on books. We lived there off and on for a couple of years before heading to Bali. My father is English, so I'm automatically conferred UK citizenship, and my mother is French, but their citizenship laws — like their customer service — tend to be tricky, so I've never claimed that one. It may sound interesting, but I assure you, it's a colossal mess."

"It's just that you sound so . . . American."

"Yeah, I know. I went to American schools my entire life, literally from kindergarten on, in whatever country we were in. And I went to university in Chicago. It kills my dad that I sound like a born-and-bred American."

Emmy nodded, trying to process it all. Or really to catalog every detail so that her triumphant e-mail to the girls that night would be airtight.

"You ready for something a little stronger?" Paul asked. "You might need it after listening to me talk about myself for so long."

"What were you thinking?" she responded, deliberately heavy on the eyelashes and the forward lean. *Sex good. Attachments bad.*

He laughed. "Nothing too crazy. Maybe switch from coffee to wine?"

They shared a bottle of something rich and velvety and so heavy with tannins it made Emmy's mouth pucker. A Bordeaux, she would wager, although she could no longer venture a guess to the particular vintage, as she'd been able to years ago, when she'd spent six months traveling all over France, working random restaurant jobs and visiting vineyards. Bordeaux had never been one of her personal favorites, but tonight she loved the way it tasted. They chatted effortlessly through another bottle, during which time Emmy envisioned their imminent honeymoon (an oceanfront villa in Bora Bora with an open-air sleeping pavilion and a private plunge pool, or perhaps a luxury African safari where they'd make love in their net-draped bed before a driver whisked them past elephants and lions in an imposing black Range Rover) only once. Things were quite flirtatious, actually, until Emmy asked — casually, she thought — how Paul felt about kids.

His head snapped up. "Kids? What about them?"

Was she not being as subtle as she thought? The wine must be clouding her judgment. She'd thought that asking whether he had any nieces or nephews would serve as a totally natural segue into soliciting his opinion about having his own kids one day, but perhaps this was more transparent than she had originally figured?

"Oh, nothing in particular," Emmy said. "They're just so adorable, aren't they? Although it does seem like so many people don't want them these days, doesn't it? And I just can't imagine that. I don't mean immediately, of course, but I definitely know I want them at some point, you know?"

Something about this observation seemed to remind Paul that he was late for his previously unmentioned plans.

"Yeah, I guess. Listen, Emmy, I'm actually really late meeting up with some friends," he said, staring at his watch.

"Really? Now?" It was nearly midnight, but it felt like four in the morning. She was pleasantly drunk and mellow and determined to seduce Paul like the sexually independent and freethinking woman she was. Never mind that she really just wanted to continue their conversation upstairs, tucked under a comfy duvet while they languidly talked and kissed until sunrise. She would lay her head on his chest and he would play with her hair, occasionally cupping her chin with a strong hand and gently pulling her lips to his. They would laugh at each other's silly puns and share secrets and talk about all their favorite places to visit, hoping but not yet saying — after all, it was only their first night — that they would someday travel to all of them together. They would wake in the late morning and Paul would tell Emmy how adorable she looked all sleepy and disheveled and they would order room-service breakfast (flaky croissants, fresh orange juice, coffee with full-fat milk, and a whole plate of plump, juicy berries) and work out their plan for —

"Hey there. Emmy?" Paul placed a few fingers on the top of her hand. "You still with me?"

"Sorry. What were you saying?"

"I was saying that I have to get going. I was supposed to meet some friends at ten, but I, uh, got distracted." His sheepish smile made her heart skip a beat. "Any other time I'd invite you to come — I'd insist on it — but, well, it's actually a birthday party for my ex, and I'm not sure she'd be thrilled if I brought . . . someone. You know?"

The projector in Emmy's head came to an abrupt stop; the screen showing the two of them laughing as they raided her minibar for more wine was replaced with one where she alone watched the endless loops on CNN International, clad in her holey gray T-shirt, popping those massive French *framboises* by the fistful.

She managed a smile. "No, no, no. Of course! I totally understand. It would be weird and inconsiderate to show up with another girl. Plus, I'm really feeling the jet lag right now — Christ, it's hitting me like a ton of bricks. And I have such an early meeting tomorrow, so I wouldn't be able to go, anyway." *Stop talking!* she urged herself. *You're seconds away from telling him all about the horrible ingrown on your bikini line you picked earlier today until it bled and now makes you look like you have herpes. Or the fact that all that coffee followed by all that wine is making your stomach feel a little funky, and while you're devastatingly disappointed that he's ditching you right now, you're relieved that you'll have a little time alone. Just stop speaking this moment!*

Paul motioned to the waiter for their check.

"No, please, let me," she said, reaching rather forcefully across their tiny table. A remixed Shirley Basset song thumped from the speakers behind them and Emmy was surprised to see how thoroughly the entire lobby had transformed into a dark velvety lair of magnificent people.

"I really am sorry to leave like this, but they're my oldest friends and it's been forever. . . ."

"Of course! Don't worry about a thing." She had already accepted that she was going upstairs alone. The idea of falling into bed with Paul as part of a promise she made to her friends felt ridiculous. Who was she kidding? It just wasn't in her nature. Fine for other girls — fantastic, in fact, for people like Adriana — but Emmy just wasn't made like that. She wanted to know someone, know him in every sense of the word, and sex was something that naturally followed that process, not some impulsive act that took the place of it. Besides, she was here all week. Maybe they could meet again the next day for dinner. . . . Oh, wait, she had evening meetings the next night. Well, then they'd have to meet for drinks afterward. Start at the hotel, perhaps, because it was the most convenient, and then roam some charming cobblestone streets before ducking into the perfect Parisian bistro for some late-night *frites* and Coca-Cola Lights. At that point, they would have spent hours and hours together, maybe even kissed under one of those romantic wrought-iron streetlamps — just gently, of course, a soft, whispery thing with no tongue and no pressure to take it further. Yes, that would be ideal.

He walked her to the tiny elevator tucked into a pitch-black corner of the lobby and stepped aside as an exceedingly attractive couple stepped off.

"It was nice to meet you, Em. Emmy. Which do people call you?"

"Both. But my closest friends have always used Em, so I like that." She gave him her most winning smile.

"Well, uh, I'm headed out in the morning, so I guess this is good-bye."

"Oh. Really? Where's home?" She realized she didn't even know where he lived.

"Not home yet, unfortunately. I'll be in Geneva for the next two days, and then possibly Zurich, depending."

"Sounds busy."

"Yeah, the travel schedule can be intense. But, uh, well, it really was great to meet you." He paused and grinned. "I said that already, didn't I?"

Emmy told herself that the lump in her throat was a combination of PMS and jet lag and too much wine, and had absolutely positively nothing to do with Paul. Yet she was afraid she'd cry if she tried to speak, so she merely nodded.

"Get some rest, okay? And don't let any of the Costes people push you around. Promise?"

She nodded again.

He tipped her face up toward his own and for a second she was quite certain he was going to kiss her. Instead, he looked into her eyes and smiled again. Then he kissed her cheek and turned away.

"Good night, Emmy. Take care of yourself."

"Good night, Paul. You, too."

She stepped onto the elevator, and before the doors closed, he was gone.

"Fatty! Fatty! Fatty!" the nasty bird cawed. It had awakened, like a human infant, at five-forty-five that morning — a Saturday! — and refused to go back to sleep. Adriana tried humming to it, feeding it, holding it, playing with it, and, finally, locking it in the guest bathroom with the lights off, but the little winged beast persisted in its verbal barrage.

"Big girl! Big girl! Big girl!" it screeched, its head bobbing up and down like a dashboard dog.

"Now you listen to me, you little fucker," Adriana hissed, her lips nearly touching the cage's metal bars. "I am a lot of things — a lot of lousy, crummy things — but fat is *not* one of them. Do you understand me?"

The bird cocked its head to the side as if he were considering her question. Adriana thought he may have even nodded, and she turned to go back to bed, satisfied. She hadn't even stepped through the bathroom door when the bird cawed — more quietly this time, she would swear — "Fat girl."

"You bastard!" she screamed, nearly lunging at the cage. It took every ounce of willpower not to toss the whole thing out the twenty-sixth-floor window. The bird merely looked at her curiously. "Oh my god," she muttered to herself. "I'm talking to a parrot."

Adriana had always thought Emmy was overreacting about the bird; it wasn't until this very moment — when the sleep deprivation really began to set in and her self-esteem hung by a thread — that she understood how damaging it must be to reside with the animal full-time.

She rooted through the linen closet in search of an oversized towel but eagerly grabbed a Frette fitted sheet when it was the first thing she saw. Tossing it over the cage and tucking its elasticized border snugly underneath, Adriana briefly worried that she might be suffocating it. Deciding she could live with that possible consequence, she drew the bathroom blinds and shut off the lights. Miraculously, the bird remained quiet. It wasn't until she was safely back under the covers with her cucumber eye mask resecured that she exhaled. Thank god.

She was drifting off when the phone rang, and she was so tired that she actually answered it.

"Adi? Are you still sleeping?" Gilles's voice, uncharacteristically deep for someone so slight, boomed through the phone.

"We're not meeting today until one. It's only ten. Why are you calling me?"

"Well, well, someone's not a morning person!" he sang, sounding delighted.

"Gilles . . ."

"Sorry. Look, I have to cancel lunch today. I know I'm a hideous friend, but I got a better offer."

"A better offer? First the bird calls me fat, and now you're saying you got a better offer?"

"The bird? *What?*"

"Forget it. So enlighten me, what constitutes a better offer than chopped salads and Bloody Marys and manicures?"

"Oh, I don't know. . . . Maybe, um . . . let's see . . . only the opportunity of a lifetime. Are you ready for this?"

"I'm ready," Adriana said, working hard to sound highly uninterested.

"The agency called to say that Ricardo got stuck on a shoot in Ibiza and couldn't make it back for today's booking."

"Mmm." Adriana vaguely remembered that Gilles and Ricardo were sworn competitors, although she tended to think that this vicious competition stemmed more from

151

Gilles than from Ricardo, who, much to Gilles's chagrin, seemed quite content to accept almost all of the agency's most prestigious assignments. He did most of the big names in Hollywood and his calendar was booked annually for — and a year in advance of — the awards shows. The two men had gone to beauty school together, assisted together at all the Madison Avenue salons, and then, even though both were promoted to the floor at the exact same time, Ricardo had somehow become a superstar.

"Any idea what today's booking is?" Gilles sounded ready to jump out of his skin.

"Let's see, what could it be? A photo shoot!" she said with snotty faux enthusiasm.

He ignored her. "Oh, it's nothing. I'm sure you don't want to hear what it will be like to do Angelina's hair on the set of *The City Dweller,* which just so happens to be the movie they're calling her sexiest ever. Funny, I was thinking about inviting you to come along and meet everyone, but I'm sure you'd never be into that. . . ."

"Angelina?"

"The one and only."

"Her sexiest movie ever?"

"They're saying it makes *Mr. and Mrs. Smith* look like *The Sound of Music.*"

Adriana exhaled. "Do you think Brad will be there?"

"Who knows? Anything's possible. I heard there's a good chance she'll have Maddox with her."

Maddox. An interesting development. As much as Adriana disliked children — especially the shriekers and the ones with runny noses — she'd fallen in love with the entire Brangelina brood. Granted, screams and snot didn't really come across in the pages of *US Weekly,* but Adriana was certain these children were different: composed, dignified, possibly even sophisticated. And there was no denying their style. She'd love to see that stylish Cambodian adoptee in person. Pax would be worthwhile, too, but no one — not Zahara nor even Shiloh — would be as rewarding as a Maddox sighting. She bolted upright in bed and began a frantic search through her open closet. What does one wear to a movie set?

"I'm so there!" she squealed, her usually aloof demeanor completely shattered. "Where and when?"

Gilles was kind enough not to laugh. "I thought you might be interested," he said with deliberate coolness. "Corner of Prince and Mercer in an hour. I'm not sure where the hair and makeup trailers will be parked exactly, but text me when you're there and I'll come find you."

Adriana clicked her phone shut and bolted into the shower. Hesitant to look like she'd made any effort beyond the cursory, she applied a little lemon-scented baby powder to her roots but kept her hair unwashed, resulting in a sexy tumble of waves. She used tinted moisturizer instead of her usual skin-perfecting foundation and rubbed a bit of lip gloss into her cheeks before slicking it across her lips. A quick dab of white shimmer powder in the corners of her eyes — a trick passed down from her mother's modeling days — and a single coat of brownish-black mascara completed her face. Her wall-mounted magnifying mirror confirmed that not a trace of makeup was detectable, but the outcome left her looking fresh-faced, glowing, and gorgeous.

The outfit took a bit longer. She discarded two sundresses, a belted tunic, and a pair of tight white pants before finding the winner: perfectly worn skinny Levi's that literally lifted and displayed her ass, topped with two barely-there racerback tanks layered one over the other and finished with this season's Chloe buckle flats. Her skin, permanently tan from both genes and months spent on the beaches of Rio, literally popped against the white cotton tank tops, and her hair spilled down over her shoulders. She added a mismatched bunch of gold bangles to one bronzed wrist and chose a pair of small, understated gold knot earrings to finish the look. Forty-five minutes after hanging up with Gilles, Adriana tiptoed past the guest bathroom toward the front door, loathe to wake the sleeping bird.

"Arghwahhhhhhh!"

She heard flapping and another screech — indiscernible in content but oddly mournful in nature — followed by more frantic flapping. *Christ,* she thought as she opened the bathroom door. *It sounds like he's dying in there.*

"You cannot die right now," she addressed the sheet-draped cage. "At least have the courtesy to wait until after I meet Maddox. Better yet, wait for Emmy. I have no idea what to do with a dead bird."

Silence. Then, a positively sorrowful cry. She'd never heard anything like it before, but the misery of it made her shiver with fear.

Adriana jumped forward and tore the sheet from the cage, desperate to quiet the suffering animal. "What is it, Otis?" she crooned through the bars. "Are you sick?"

It wasn't until Otis cocked his head in

that telltale — and perfectly healthy — way that Adriana knew she'd been had. She'd made it out of the bathroom and halfway through the foyer before Otis belted out "Fat Girl!" in triplicate, stopping only to cackle between calls.

"Go ahead and die, you winged rodent. I hope it's long and slow and very painful. I'll dance on your miserable birdie grave." The whole situation was enraging! Just because Emmy felt too guilty to sell or murder the damn bird should not mean that others had to endure its abuse. What are you supposed to say when your best friend calls the night before her trip, panicked that her vet no longer boards birds in his kennel? Any remotely rational person would say exactly what Adriana had said — namely, that if she couldn't wear it, eat it, or accessorize with it, she wasn't interested — but Emmy's sheer panic had eventually worn her down. She swore that Otis was relatively low maintenance and that with the exception of a few moody outbursts, Adriana probably wouldn't even notice he was there. Yeah, not notice. That's why she was standing in the elevator, wondering if her hips looked a bit wider these days. Or why she was about to trek the twenty blocks downtown rather than take a cab, because *clearly* she needed the exercise.

Fucking buzzard.

Her heart rate was elevated from a combination of physical exertion and excitement by the time she arrived, and she felt a little sticky from sweat, but the dampness gave Adriana a sheen that heightened her beauty. Not a few passing men wondered if she'd just rolled out of bed after a morning of lovemaking; the others wondered what it would be like to join her.

Gilles appeared moments after she texted him. He noticed a group of PAs standing outside one of the trailers watching them, so he grabbed Adriana's hips, pushed his pelvis against hers, and kissed her full on the mouth. "Damn, girl, you're gorgeous," he announced. "Almost makes me wish I were straight."

"Yes, *querido,* me, too. I'd marry you in a second. In fact, if I haven't found myself a husband in the next year, will you marry me?"

"Tempting, I have to say. Commit to one person for the rest of my life and a woman at that? Just castrate me now."

"Wait, I think I'm onto something. We'd have a completely open relationship, of course — you'd be welcome to sleep with anyone you like — but we could go to parties and family stuff together and still have our own separate lives. We'd be the new Will and Grace. I think it sounds fantastic."

"Yes, Adi dear, but what, may I ask, is in it for me? You forget, I do all of those things now without being married. . . ."

"What's in it for you? Hmm," Adriana pressed her forefinger to her lips and pretended to think. "Let's see. Oh, I don't know . . . unrestricted access to my unlimited trust fund, perhaps? Would that work?"

Gilles dropped to one denim-glad knee and brought her hand to his lips. "Adriana de Souza, will you marry me?"

She laughed and pulled him up. "One year, *querido*. I've got one year to find myself a proper husband — and by proper, I mean one who wants to have sex with me — and if not, you and I are getting hitched. Sound good?"

"I'm hard right now, I swear I am. Just say it again: *trust fund*."

He led her halfway down Prince Street before breaking the news that there would be no Angelina introductions that day.

"Tell me you're kidding. I got up and showered and dressed at ten A.M., for chrissake. Is Maddox at least here with a nanny?"

"Sorry, honey. But I am scheduled to do Paul Rudd in twenty minutes, and you're welcome to come sit in."

Adriana sniffed. "He's cute, I guess."

"And, if you're a good girl, I might even let you stay for the early-evening shoot —"

"Thanks, but no thanks. I'm going out with that finance guy."

"Oh, *that* finance guy. Got it. Well, as super-fun as that sounds, they're shooting a scene tonight with Tyra . . . a lingerie scene . . . and there's talk that Naomi might join her. . . ."

"Shut up."

"Not kidding."

"When?"

"It's called for seven at Sky Studios. There'll probably be drinks afterward."

Adriana slowly exhaled and looked at Gilles. "I'm in."

"Given." He pulled open the door on a Haddad's trailer and waited for Adriana to step ahead. A teenage girl she didn't recognize sat patiently in one of four chairs, back to the lit mirror, as a pudgy female stylist wrestled a round brush through the girl's thick waves. The other three chairs appeared recently vacated, still littered with Mason Pearson brushes, T3 ionic hairdryers, and every Kérastase product sold in North America.

"Gilles, they pushed up the call time by a half hour because Tobias needs to get out of here early," the stylist called out over the drone of the blowdryer. "I'm handling everything here, so why don't you head to the location for touch-ups?"

"On it," Gilles sang. He hefted a huge leather tote overflowing with supplies onto his shoulder and motioned Adriana toward the door. "To the set we go."

The scene was already under way when they arrived at the loft, and their set passes were scrutinized by no fewer than three PAs.

"This place is harder to breach than Chez Cruise," Adriana whispered when they'd finally made it inside.

Gilles smiled but remained alert, carefully sidestepping the tangle of wires and extension cords. "Right before you got here I watched them tell a mailman that he wasn't allowed to deliver the mail until they were done for the day."

The huge, classic SoHo loft had sixteen-foot ceilings and exposed brick and all sorts of very intimidating modern art sculptures. The crew had set up a king-sized bed with a metal four-poster frame — the kind that looks like a huge hollow box has been attached to the top — in the living room in front of the fireplace. With its chic brown and lime-green duvet and matching low-profile nightstands, it looked like a photo straight from the West Elm catalog. But far more interesting was the nearly nude actress splayed across it.

"Quiet on the set!" a deep male voice boomed from somewhere overhead.

Gilles held up a hand and grabbed Adriana's wrist. They both froze in midstep.

"Rolling!" another male voice called. A chorus of replies followed from all around the room.

"Rolling!"

"Rolling!"

"We are rolling!"

"And . . . action!" Adriana turned to see that these last words came from a man who sat a bit off to the side. He wore a pair of massive headphones and leaned intently forward in his chair, examining the center screen with complete concentration. Next to him, a young girl diligently took notes on a clipboard. Adriana surmised that this was the director, the god himself, and she was pleased to confirm her suspicions when she stepped a few inches to the left and was able to read the back of the man's chair. TOBIAS BARON was stitched in all caps on the black fabric. What she hadn't expected was that he'd be so young: His résumé read like that of someone in his fifties or sixties, but this man didn't look a day over forty.

Gilles and Adriana watched for a twenty-second clip while the actress, wearing an open button-down and a pair of white cotton panties that managed to be ten times sexier than most thongs, read a novel on the bed. She was just casually stroking her stomach and flipping the pages when Adriana realized the girl was Angelina's body double.

"Cut!" Tobias yelled. Within a half-second, Gilles beelined to the actress and began finger-tousling her hair. He didn't appear to notice that she was propped on her elbows with her head thrown back as if in ecstasy.

A few minutes later, with the scene set exactly the same as before, there was another round of "rolling" shouts and a call of "action!" Only this time, just as the chiseled male actor lowered himself on top of the girl, a cell phone chirped. Adriana's cell phone. Forty heads turned to stare at her as she, completely unflustered, rooted around in her bag, pulled the cell phone out, and switched it off — *after* checking the caller ID.

"And cut!" Tobias screamed. "What is this, people? Amateur hour? Lose the cell phones. Now, let's take it from Fernando's entrance. Pick it up right away and . . . action!"

This time the actors completed the scene to the director's satisfaction and Tobias grudgingly called for a break. Gilles gripped Adriana's hand so hard that his fingernails dug into her palms. She knew he was about to go berserk — he always was a screamer — but before he could drag her outside for a tongue-lashing, Tobias intercepted them. His headphones were looped around his neck; he frowned and shook his head in anger as the rest of the crew moved far enough away to avoid direct contact while remaining close enough to hear whatever went down.

"Who are you?" Tobias demanded, looking directly at Adriana.

Gilles began blathering. "I'm so sorry, Mr. Baron, you have assurance that such an incident will never —"

Tobias interrupted Gilles with an exasperated wave but didn't divert his attention from Adriana. "Who are *you*?"

He stared at her and Adriana stared back, the two of them locked in a power struggle for nearly thirty seconds without saying a word. Adriana admired his steadfastness; most men got flustered when she remained silent and defiant. She also rather liked his solidness. He was above average height for a man, probably close to six feet, but his fitted T-shirt showed off an upper body that gave him a much bigger look. As far as she could ascertain, both his tan and his thick, dark hair were real. She was close enough to smell him, and she liked that, too: a good mixture of fabric softener and a subtle, masculine cologne.

Doing her best to appear unapologetic, she looked directly into his eyes and said, "My name is Adriana de Souza."

"Ah, well, *that* certainly explains it."

"Pardon me?" And then it occurred to her — maybe this man somehow knew her mother and, as a result, wasn't surprised by Adriana's diva-like behavior. It wouldn't be the first time someone in the entertainment industry had put together Adriana's famous name and gorgeous looks.

"It explains why a young girl like you would have a João Gilberto song as her ring tone. From Rio?"

"São Paulo, actually," Adriana purred. "You do not strike me as Brazilian."

"No? Is it the name or the nose?" He finally smiled. "You don't have to be Brazilian to know bossa nova when you hear it."

"I'm sorry, I must have missed your name. You are?" Adriana asked, wide-eyed. She knew from many years of experience that if you treated the overconfident ones like dirt, they were yours forever.

His smile faded for a moment before expanding to an all-out grin, one that said, *Hey, an adversary. I like that.* And although he didn't ask for her number then and there, Adriana was one hundred percent certain that she'd be hearing from Tobias Baron.

"Why so quiet?" Russell asked as he navigated through the parking lot–like conditions on the Merritt, made even worse than usual by his steadfast refusal to work around the Trifecta of Traffic Horrors: They had left the city not only during rush hour, but during rush hour on a Friday — of a summer weekend.

Leigh sighed. Only three more days until her coveted No Human Contact Monday. "Just the usual dread."

"They're really not so bad, honey. I have to say, I don't totally understand why they get to you so much."

"Well, that's probably because you've met them all of five times in your entire life and, if anything, they know how to make good first impressions. They don't get to their real heavy-duty undermining until you've really started to know and trust them. Then . . . watch out." Annoyed that he was defending her parents, she scrolled through the iPod and turned the volume all the way up. John Mayer's "Waiting on the World to Change" blasted from the speakers.

They were in Russell's new Range Rover, which she loathed. When he'd elicited her opinion a few months earlier on what cars she liked, she'd merely shrugged.

"The beauty of living in New York is that you don't need a car. Why bother?"

"Because, darling, I want to take romantic weekend trips with you. The freedom it offers would be wonderful for us. And besides, ESPN will pay for me to garage it in the city. So, any preferences?"

"Not really."

"Leigh, come on. We'll be using it a lot together. You really have no opinion?"

"I don't know . . . the blue ones, I guess." She knew she was being impossible, but she really, honestly didn't care. Russell was going to obsess over cars regardless of what she liked or didn't, so she really didn't want to get involved.

"The 'blue ones'? You're being a bitch."

Relieved that he'd finally pushed back — an all-too-rare event — she'd relented a little. "Henry drives a blue Prius and loves it — says it gets amazing gas mileage. Someone said that the hybrid Escape is good, too — an SUV that doesn't look like a tank."

"A *hybrid*?"

"I don't know. It doesn't have to be. I also like that curvy Nissan. . . . What's it called? A Mural?"

"A Murano. Are you serious?"

"Actually, I already told you I couldn't care less, but you've forced the conversation. Get whatever one you like."

A long soliloquy ensued wherein Russell extolled the many virtues of the Range Rover. He covered its interior, exterior, horsepower, exclusivity, stylishness, and practicality in bad weather (notably leaving out any mention of gas mileage or the difficulty of getting one serviced, but Leigh refrained from pointing that out). He instinctively fell into his on-air personality and droned on and on: baritone voice animated but controlled, gaze steady, posture perfect. It was precisely what made him so charismatic and engaging on-air that could make him so grating when they were alone. She wondered what all those girls who wrote to his Web site and sent seductive pictures of themselves would think if they got to see this Russell: still gorgeous, admittedly, but also smug and not a little boring.

He had just finished telling her about some basketball player's commitment to the troops when they pulled into the driveway. Her parents had grudgingly left the city for Greenwich in the 1980s when Leigh's grandmother passed away, leaving the family home to her only son. Leigh's father was still a junior editor and her mother had only just finished law school, so the chance to live rent- and mortgage-free — even if it was, regrettably, off-island — was just too good to pass up. Leigh had lived in the beautiful old home since preschool, played tag in its surrounding woods and hosted birthday parties at its pool, and lost her virginity in the cool, cavelike basement to a boy whose name she remembered but whose face had since blurred; and yet the five-bedroom house hadn't felt like home in many years.

Leigh typed the security code (1-2-3-4, naturally) into the garage-side keypad and motioned for Russell to follow. Part of her was disappointed that her mother hadn't raced outside to grab Leigh's hand and stare at her engagement ring and wipe away tears as she kissed her only daughter and future son-in-law, but she was self-aware enough to admit that she would have been irritated and embarrassed had her mother done precisely that. Mrs. Eisner wasn't exactly the gushing, teary type, and in this way mother and daughter were similar.

"Mom? Dad? We're here!" She led Russell through the front hallway, which had long ago ceased being a mudroom and had been transformed into an elegant foyer, and walked into the kitchen. "Where is everyone?"

"Coming!" she heard her mother call from the family room. A moment later she appeared before them, looking casually elegant in one of her trillion Polo collared shirts, khaki capris, and Tod's driving moccasins.

"Leigh! Russell. Congratulations. Oh, I am so thrilled for you both." She embraced her daughter and leaned up to kiss Russell's cheek. "Now, come sit down so I can properly examine this sparkler. I can't believe I had to wait twelve full days to see this!"

Passive-aggressive comment number one, Leigh thought. *We're off and running.*

"I'm so sorry I didn't wait for you and Mr. Eisner to return, but I very much wanted to propose on our one-year anniversary," Russell rushed to explain.

Her parents had returned late the night before from their annual three-week June pilgrimage to Europe and had insisted that the happy couple join them for a celebratory dinner.

"Please," her mother waved at the air. "We understand. Besides, no one really needs their parents for these things now, do they?"

Number two. And in record time.

Russell cleared his throat and looked uncomfortable enough that Leigh felt a momentary pang of sympathy. She decided to rescue him. "Mom, how about a glass of wine? Is there some in the fridge?"

Mrs. Eisner pointed to the mahogany bar in the corner of the den. "There should be a couple bottles of chardonnay in the wine cooler. Your father likes it, but I find it a tad dry. If you would prefer red, you'll need to get it from the cellar."

"I think we'd probably rather have red," Leigh said, mostly for Russell's benefit. She knew that he hated white wine — chardonnay most of all — but would never express such a preference in front of her parents.

"You two visit for a minute," Russell said with an award-winning (an Emmy, to be precise, bestowed last year for "Outstanding Studio Show — Weekly") smile. "I'll go get the wine."

Mrs. Eisner clasped Leigh's left hand and pulled it directly under the table lamp. "My, my, he certainly did his homework, didn't he? And of course, so did you. Russell will make such a wonderful husband. You must be so pleased."

Leigh paused for a moment, uncertain of what she meant. It was implied that Leigh had been poised and ready for this moment her entire life, that this ring signified success in a way that valedictorian, Cornell, or becoming a star editor at Brook Harris never could. She loved Russell — really, she did — but it rankled that her own mother considered him Leigh's greatest achievement to date.

"It's all so exciting," Leigh offered with an extra-large smile.

Her mother sighed. "Well, I should hope so! It's so nice to see you happy for once. You've worked so hard for so long now. . . . Suffice it to say that this didn't come a moment too soon."

"Mother, do you realize that you just —" But before she could say *managed to imply that, one, I'm always negative, and two, my age is so advanced you worried I might never snag a husband,* Russell came back with Mr. Eisner in tow.

"Leigh," her father said in a voice so steady and quiet it was almost a whisper. "Leigh, Leigh, Leigh." His hair was now completely gray, although, as with many men, it made him look not so much older as more distinguished. Same with the deep lines etched in his forehead and around his mouth and eyes — they conveyed a feeling of wisdom and experience, not the air of a problem that should be dealt with at the plastic surgeon's next available appointment. Even his sweater — a three-decades-old navy cardigan with leather elbow patches and toggle buttons — seemed somehow more intelligent than the sweaters most men wore these days.

He stood in the doorway next to the piano and gazed at her in a way that always made her feel scrutinized, like he was deciding whether or not he liked her new haircut or approved of her outfit. Growing up, it was her mother who made the most immediate rules regarding their daughter — whether eyeliner was permitted, what was appropriate attire for a school dance, how late she could stay out on a school night — but it was only her father who could make her feel brilliant or idiotic, gorgeous or hideously ugly, charmed or wretched, with the most casual look or comment. Of course, while such comments could appear casual, they never were. Every word he uttered was considered, weighed, and chosen with deliberateness, and woe to the person who failed to select her words with such precision. Although Leigh couldn't recall a single occasion when her father had raised his voice, she remembered the countless times he had dissected her arguments or opinions with a quiet ruthlessness that intimidated her to this day.

"He's an editor," her mother would soothe when Leigh got upset as a child. "Words are his life. He's careful with them. He loves them, loves the language. Don't take it personally, darling." And Leigh would nod and say she understood and make a greater effort at watching what she said, while trying not to take any of it personally.

"Hi, Dad," she said almost shyly. She had seen both Emmy and Adriana call their fathers "Daddy," but it seemed impossible to imagine calling her own father something so saccharine. Even though he'd retired six years earlier, Charles Eisner would be an imposing editor-in-chief until the day he died. He'd ruled with a firm hand during the twelve years as head of Paramour Publishing — none of the "handholding warm fuzzy shit," in his words, of today's big publishing houses — and he'd remained consistently aloof and detached at home, as much as he could manage. Fall lineups, production schedules, assistant editors, pressures from corporate, even authors themselves were perfectly predictable after the first few years, which is why Leigh always thought it drove him particularly crazy that children were not. To this day Leigh tried to remain as steady and evenhanded around her father as possible, taking particular care not to blurt out whatever she was thinking.

"I've already congratulated my future son-in-law," he said, moving across the room toward Leigh. "Come here, dear. Allow me this pleasure."

After a brief embrace and a kiss on the forehead, neither particularly warm nor affectionate, Mr. Eisner ushered everyone into the dining room and began issuing quiet directives.

"Russell, would you please decant the wine? Use the stemless glasses from the bar, if you will. Carol, the salad needs to be tossed with the vinaigrette. Everything else is finished, but I didn't want that to get soggy while we waited. Leigh, dear, you may just be seated and relax. After all, tonight is your special night."

She told herself it was paranoid and neurotic to interpret this as anything other than a compliment, but she couldn't shake the feeling that it felt like a small attack. "Okay," she said. "I'll be the official relaxer."

They discussed her parents' trip over the arugula and goat cheese salad and told about their own engagement during the filet with asparagus and rosemary potatoes. Russell entertained the table with anecdotes of ring-shopping and planning the proposal, and Leigh's parents smiled and laughed far more than was usual for either of them, and everything was quite civilized, almost even enjoyable, until Leigh's cell phone rang in the middle of dessert.

She pulled her bag up from under the table and removed her phone.

"Leigh!" her mother chided. "We're *eating*."

"Yes, Mother, I know, but it's Henry. Excuse me for a minute." She took her phone and headed toward the living room but, realizing that everyone would be able to hear her, she ducked out back to the deck and heard her father say, "No publisher I ever worked with would call one of his editors at nine o'clock on a Friday night unless something was very, very wrong," right before she pulled the door closed behind her.

"Hello?" she answered, convinced her father was right and that Henry was calling to fire her. It had been ten days since the whole Jesse Chapman debacle, and although Leigh had apologized numerous times, Henry still seemed distant and distracted.

"Leigh? Henry. Sorry for the late call, but it couldn't wait until tomorrow."

Here it comes, she thought, bracing for the news. It was bad enough to get fired from the publishing house where you were on track to be the youngest senior editor in history, but having to walk inside and tell her father was going to make it unbearable.

"It's no problem. I'm at my parents' and we just finished dinner, so it's a perfect time. Is everything okay?"

Henry sighed. *Shit.* This could be worse than she thought. "You're with Charles? That's just perfect. He's going to love this."

Leigh took a deep breath and forced herself to speak. "Yes?" It sounded more like a squeak than a word.

"Are you sitting down? You're not going to believe this. God knows I barely do."

"Henry," she said quietly. "Please."

"I just hung up with Jesse Chapman . . ."

Oh, thank god, Leigh thought, her hands finally unclenching. *He's just calling to tell me that Jesse has chosen a publisher.* She knew she should probably care whether or not he chose Brook Harris, but her relief was too all-encompassing.

". . . and he has decided that he would like us to publish his next novel."

"Henry, that's wonderful! I couldn't be more thrilled. And of course you know I'll personally apologize to him again when —"

He interrupted. "I'm not finished, Leigh. He wants us to publish him, but he has a condition: He wants *you* to edit him."

Leigh was just about to say "you're kidding" when Henry spoke again.

"And this is not a joke."

Leigh tried to swallow but her mouth felt like cotton. The combination of excitement, relief, and terror was too much to endure. "Henry, please."

"Please what? Are you listening? Did you hear me? Number one *New York Times* best-selling author, winner of the Pultizer, seller of five million copies worldwide, and, up until this very moment, a complete and total vanishing act, has requested — no, excuse me, *demanded* — that you, Leigh Eisner, edit him."

"No."

"Leigh, pull it together. I don't know how else to say this. He wants you and only you. He said that once he really made it, no one would be straight with him anymore. Everyone just coddled and indulged him and told him he was brilliant, but no one — not his editor or publisher or agent — would ever give it to him straight. And apparently he loved that you weren't afraid to be honest with him. I think his exact words were 'That girl has zero bullshit tolerance and so do I. I want to work with her.' "

" 'Zero bullshit tolerance'? Henry, my entire job description is based on telling authors only what they want to hear. Hell, my whole life is. Sometimes I slip up, but —"

"Slip up?"

"Okay, so that's a slight understatement. So I've been known to talk without thinking, occasionally. But I don't think I'm capable of honesty on demand. It just sort of comes out when I'm least expecting it."

"Well, I certainly know that, but our friend Jesse does not. Nor will he." He paused. "Leigh, I have to say I was every bit as shocked as you are, probably more, but I want you to listen very carefully. You have what it takes. I wouldn't have agreed to this if I weren't absolutely certain that you could handle it. And not just handle it — make it work. You certainly don't need me to tell you how significant this will be to your career. Take some time this weekend, think this over, and come to my office when you get in Monday, okay? I'm behind you on this one, Leigh. It's going to be great."

Her family was discussing the wisdom of an engagement party when she returned to the table and quietly announced that she would be editing Jesse Chapman's new book.

"Oh, he has a new book coming out?" her mother asked while pouring herself more coffee. "How lovely. It's been a while, hasn't it?"

Russell was slightly more clued in, but not

much. He was supportive, of course, and always seemed proud to tell his friends and colleagues about her job, and he knew that Leigh had most likely offended Jesse Chapman that day in Henry's office, but authors like Jesse Chapman weren't at the top of his personal reading list.

It didn't really matter, though. The only person who understood the significance of the situation had heard her loud and clear: Her father looked as though someone had used his gut as a punching bag. "Jesse Chapman? *The* Jesse Chapman?"

Leigh just nodded, unable to trust herself to keep from gloating if she opened her mouth.

He recovered quickly and held aloft his wineglass for a toast, but Leigh could see the doubt and disbelief in his eyes. She knew he was thinking that there must be some mistake, that his daughter, so inexperienced when compared to his own illustrious career, would be editing an author bigger than any he had ever worked with. Leigh almost felt sympathetic — almost — when she saw that for the very first time in her life, her father the wordsmith, the great guru, the judge and jury extraordinaire, was speechless.

ONCE THEY'RE IN, THEY'RE REAL

While the rest of America spent the long holiday weekend watching fireworks and attending poolside barbecues, Emmy slumped with her friends on the pavement at the Curaçao airport and tried to figure out when their vacation had gone so terribly awry. She didn't even feel the sunglasses being stolen off her head. The thieves — two long-haired, pimply teenagers in a crumbling pickup truck — stopped a few hundred yards away, hung out the windows, and waved them at her while shouting gleefully in a language she didn't recognize. Still unsure, Emmy touched her head to confirm they were gone.

"Why are those kids screaming at us?" Adriana asked, looking puzzled. "Are they trying to sell us those sunglasses?"

Answering felt like an overwhelming task. Emmy's tongue was thick, unresponsive. It seemed like it should be quite simple to explain that those were *her* sunglasses, but no amount of effort on her part produced any actual sound.

Apparently Leigh didn't get it, either. "Tell them you don't need any sunglasses, that you just bought a pair," she slurred.

"But I *do* need a pair," Emmy croaked. She waved listlessly in the general direction of the boys, who had just thrown the truck into drive and were moving toward the airport exit. "Help us." She sounded like Rose from the movie *Titanic,* frozen and nearly unconscious on her raft, adrift in the Atlantic, although thankfully they were neither freezing nor afloat.

"Come on, girls, we need to get ourselves together. This is a vacation — a celebration — not a funeral," Adriana said, barely enunciating a single word.

The "vacation" was significantly less festive than the last wake Emmy had attended — not to mention that the food wasn't as good. But she said nothing. After all, they were there to celebrate Leigh's engagement, and she'd be damned if she was going to ruin it. So what if the whole thing had become a giant nightmare before it even really got started? Your best friend gets engaged only one time (hopefully . . . and if that friend was Leigh, then definitely), and she was going to show Leigh a good time if it killed her. Which it just might.

She had managed not to dwell on the irony of the whole situation, but sitting drunk and half-drugged at a Caribbean airport while local teenagers robbed her blind had prompted a bit of contemplation. Her ex-boyfriend had planned this trip to celebrate their five-year anniversary, and after said ex-boyfriend had left her for the virgin cheerleader trainer, he had offered her the tickets as some sort of consolation prize. Emmy's gut had told her to have some dignity and tell him to fuck off, once and for all, but everything was fully paid for and she'd been stressed lately with the new job and, well, it had been worth accepting just for the chance to imply that she would be going with a new boyfriend.

"Seriously, Em, go. It's all arranged and paid for. It'll be nice for you," Duncan had said when he came over to pick up his DVDs and underwear a week after she'd returned from Paris. It had been a perfect trip workwise, but she was still smarting from Paul's blatant rejection — not to mention her obvious role in driving him away with the talk about having kids. It didn't help that Duncan looked incredibly fit and happy, probably the best since she'd known him. Fucker.

"What? You and the cheerleader aren't ready for a trip together yet? Or is premarital traveling banned also?"

He had sighed, suggesting he expected nothing less from Emmy, handed her a folder with the complete itinerary, and pecked her on the cheek. "Go. Get some sun. I'd hate to see it go to waste."

"Thank you, Duncan, we'll do just that." Emphasis on the *we,* of course. He hadn't even blinked.

Bastard.

Emmy hated him for encouraging her to go, but she hated herself more for taking him up on it. She might have ditched the whole idea, but when she floated the idea of a solo trip to the Dutch Antilles to her friends, they had not been pleased.

"Solo? Why would you ever go there *alone?* Especially considering that you have two best friends sitting right here, one of whom just got engaged. I think it would be downright *negligent* not to invite us," Adriana had sniffed.

Not surprisingly, Leigh had been a bit more reserved. "Oh, please, it's not that big of a deal. And besides, things are just crazy at work right now. I'm editing my first huge author. And I don't think Russell would be thrilled if I ditched him for the Fourth."

Emmy nodded. "See? Leigh's too busy and I'm sure you've got, uh . . . stuff going on, too." No one had any clear idea what Adriana did all day, but there was an unspoken agreement never to address this. "Besides, it's only booked for two."

Post-breakup resolution or not, Emmy had little interest in spending the week scouting for men or tabletop dancing at local nightclubs. Paris and the whole Paul debacle had been a serious blow to her ego; the last thing she wanted was Adriana pushing her to hunt for men day and night.

"Two, three, what's the difference? Nothing a little phone call can't fix. And Leigh, darling, I don't give one goddamn what you have going on at work. As for Russell, he'll just have to understand that your best friends are happy for you and want to toast you." Adriana smiled expansively at both girls. "Well, that's settled. When do we leave?"

Things had rapidly deteriorated since they'd left New York, although by now the details were a little fuzzy. They'd flown on the six A.M. flight from LaGuardia to Miami and somehow, against all judgment, sense, and reason, Adriana had made a convincing case for in-flight Bloody Marys. Bloody Marys before nine in the morning. Which, although Emmy was loath to admit it, had been pretty nice. The second and third had gone down quite easily, and by the time they'd landed at the Curaçao airport, the Miami layover was little more than a hazy dream. The only solid proof that it had actually occurred — the $200 Gucci sunglasses Adriana insisted Emmy *needed* to buy at the duty-free shop — had just evaporated. Emmy's suitcase had also vanished, but the tiny pills that Adriana had insisted she and Leigh try were working their magic: suitcase, sunglasses, *whatever.* She could not care less.

In the brutal late-afternoon sun the girls sat slumped against Adriana's and Leigh's suitcases — both of which were miraculously present and intact.

"Where are we again?" Leigh asked, tugging ineffectually at the bandanna she had tied around her hair. "I can't seem to remember."

Adriana glanced up. "Jamaica?"

They giggled, both certain that Jamaica wasn't the right answer but unable to remember what was.

Emmy pulled the folder from her carry-on and began to read. "Aruba. Bonaire. Curaçao. The A-B-C islands of the Netherlands Antilles. Eighty miles off the coast of Venezuela. Population —"

Adriana held her hand up. "I'm bored."

"It's all coming back," Emmy slurred. "We are currently in Curaçao. Our flight from

185

Miami was delayed and we missed our ferry to Bonaire. We're stuck."

"Stop being so negative, girls!" Adriana sang. "We're getting great color. We're going to meet hot Dutch men." Pause. "Are Dutch men hot?"

"Dutch men? I didn't know there were Dutch men in Jamaica!" Leigh shrieked in a very un-Leigh-like way. Adriana cracked up and the two girls high-fived.

Emmy's temples throbbed with pain and her skin was on fire. "Pull yourselves together, people. We need to get out of here."

The trouble had started when the girls deplaned in Curaçao slightly buzzed but fully conscious and made their way to the ferry counter. Emmy politely requested three tickets.

"No," a fleshy black woman wearing a muumuu and sandals announced with obvious joy. "Cancel."

" 'Cancel'? What do you mean 'cancel'?" Emmy did her best to glare, but the fact that her chin barely reached the top of the counter negated the intended effect.

The woman smiled. Unkindly. "No more."

Another hour passed before they learned there once had been a ferry; there was a ferry no longer; and the only way to traverse those thirty miles now was by flying one of two local airlines, unnervingly named Bonaire Express and Divi Divi Air.

"I would rather die than fly something called 'Divi Divi,' " Adriana announced as they surveyed the airlines' side-by-side ticketing counters, each consisting of a single employee and a wheeled card table.

"You might die anyway," Leigh said. She picked up a handwritten sheet listing the current schedule. "Oh, wait, this should make you feel much better. It says here that the refurbished six-seater planes are *very* reliable."

"Refurbished? Six seats? *Reliable?* That's the best fucking adjective these people can come up with and we're entrusting our lives to them?" Emmy was about three minutes from ditching this whole godforsaken idea and getting on the next flight back to New York.

Leigh wasn't finished. "Hold on, look, here's a picture." Stapled to the back of the schedule was a surprisingly high-quality print of an airplane. A very colorful airplane. Almost fluorescent, actually. Leigh passed it to Adriana, who waved her hands in disgust and lit a cigarette. She inhaled deeply and handed the cigarette to Leigh, who reached for it instinctively before remembering she was no longer a smoker.

Adriana exhaled. "Don't show me that. Please! There is no conceivable, imaginable, acceptable excuse why a plane needs to look like a Pucci dress!" She glanced at the picture again, then inhaled and moaned simultaneously. "Oh god, it's a prop plane. I won't fly prop planes. I *can't* fly prop planes."

"Oh, you most certainly will," Leigh sang. "We're even going to let you decide which one. Divi/Pucci flies at six, and Bonaire Express — that's the one that looks like a Jackson Pollock painting, in case you were confused — has a flight at six-twenty. Which do you prefer?"

Adriana whimpered. Emmy looked at Leigh and rolled her eyes.

Adriana dug through her wallet and handed Leigh her American Express Platinum card. "Book whichever one you think gives us the best chance of surviving. I'm going to find us something to drink."

Having bought three tickets using an indecipherable combination of guilders, dollars, and traveler's checks, since the airline didn't accept credit cards, Emmy and Leigh looked for a place to sit down. Hato Airport, it seemed, didn't have much in the way of amenities, and seats were no exception. It was a dusty, open-air structure that, against all likelihood, offered not one square inch of shade from the brutal midday sun. Too exhausted to continue looking, the girls returned to the stretch of pavement where they'd sat before, an area that could have been a sidewalk or a tarmac or a parking lot. They had just collapsed atop her suitcase when Adriana, clutching a plastic bag and appearing triumphant, flopped down beside them.

Emmy grabbed the bag from her hands. "I've never needed water so bad in my life. Please say you bought more than one?" Inside the bag was only a single glass bottle of electric blue liquid. "You got Gatorade instead of water?"

"Not Gatorade, *querida*. Blue curaçao. Mmm. Doesn't that look delicious?" Adriana removed her ankle-wrap ballet flats to reveal a pale pink pedicure and tucked the bottom of her tank top under the band of her bra. Even though she'd seen Adriana's tight tummy and love handle–free sides a million times, Emmy couldn't stop staring. Adriana politely pretended not to notice. She nodded toward the bottle. "Local special. We should get started right away if we plan to be obliterated by takeoff."

Leigh took the bottle from Emmy. "It says here that blue curaçao is a sweet blue liqueur made from the dried peel of bitter oranges and that it's used to add color to cocktails," she read from the label.

"Yeah, so?" Adriana asked, massaging a dime-sized drop of Hawaiian Tropic oil onto her already golden shoulders.

"So? So it's really just food coloring with alcohol in it. We can't drink this."

"Really? I can." Adriana unscrewed the cap and took a long gulp.

Emmy sighed. "No water? I'd kill for some water."

"Of course there's no water. I covered the entire airport. The only little shop was boarded up — permanently, it appears — with a sign that says NO. I saw something that might have been a bar at one point but could've also been customs, and an area that was designated as a restaurant but looked like downtown Baghdad. There was, however, a folding card table near the Divi Divi gate staffed by a kind gentleman who claimed he was duty-free. He had about ten cartons of something called Richmond Ultra-Lights, a few crushed bars of Toblerone, and a bottle each of Jim Beam and this. I chose this." She handed Emmy the bottle. "Oh, come on, Em. Relax a little. It's a vacation!"

Emmy took the bottle, stared at it, and took a swig. It tasted like liquid Splenda with a kick. She drank again.

Adriana smiled, proud as a parent at a sixth-grade talent show. "That's the spirit! Leigh, sweetheart, take a nip. There you go. . . . Now, girls, I have a little present for you."

Leigh forced herself to swallow and shuddered. "I know that look. Please tell me you didn't smuggle in something truly illegal. If *this*" — she waved her hands expansively — "is the international airport, can you imagine what the prison looks like?"

Undeterred, Adriana pulled a red and white container shaped like a large pill capsule from her jeans pocket. She twisted off the cap and shook out three tablets. One disappeared down her throat. She handed one to each of her friends.

"Mommy's little helper," she sang.

"Valium? Since when do you take Valium?"

"When? Since we decided to fly on an aircraft that looks like a Six Flags ride."

Well, that was all the convincing Emmy needed. She swallowed the little round pill and washed it down with some blue curaçao. She watched Leigh do the same and then everything once again got soft around the edges.

An hour passed, and then another. Emmy

opened her eyes first. Her calves were a splotchy salmon color and there were six empty beer cans on the ground. Vaguely she recalled being approached by a man who wore a cooler suspended from his neck. He didn't have any water, either, but he was selling cans of beer called, suspiciously, Amstel Bright. At the time it had seemed like a good idea, but the beer and the blue curaçao and the Valium combined with hundred-plus-degree heat and no water was probably not the wisest move.

"Adriana, wake up. Leigh? I think it's time to board."

Leigh opened an eye without moving a muscle and looked up with surprising clarity. "Where are we?"

"Come on, we need to move. The only thing worse than getting on that plane is sleeping here tonight."

That seemed to motivate everyone. They managed to hobble, all together, in the right direction.

"Wow, great security here," Leigh mumbled, as the girls weaved their way toward a chalkboard that read DIVI DIVI, 6:00 P.M. "I just adore airports that don't inconvenience you with X-ray machines and metal detectors."

They boarded the six-seater with little drama, earning only one strange look from the pilot when he saw Adriana down the last of the blue curaçao and promptly pass out against the window. The flight wasn't particularly terrifying, although Emmy applauded with her fellow travelers when the wheels touched down. Naturally, their planned car and driver were nowhere to be found at Bonaire's Flamingo Airport, and Adriana's hardback cosmetic case had somehow vanished during the twenty-minute ride, but everyone seemed beyond caring.

"It makes for light traveling, this whole lose-a-bag-per-flight deal," Adriana said and shrugged.

By the time they climbed out of the taxi at the hotel, they had been awake for nearly twenty-four hours, had gotten drunk, sobered up, lost two bags, and flown an airline that sounded like a nursery rhyme from an airport that surely couldn't have passed even the most lenient FAA inspection. Blessedly, the resort looked every bit as elegant and peaceful as it did in Duncan's dossier, and Emmy thought she might kiss the check-in guy when he upgraded them to a two-bedroom suite. Leigh had already collapsed, fully dressed, on the bed in the smaller bedroom, and Adriana looked like she was about to do the same, but Emmy was determined to take a bath before passing out.

"Adi, can I borrow something to sleep in?" Emmy called from the oversized marble bathtub. She had already emptied the whole bottle of body wash under the running water and it had foamed up luxuriantly, giving the entire bathroom a eucalyptus scent.

"Take whatever you want; just save the mauve silk teddy and robe for me. It's my lucky set."

"Are you hungry?" Emmy called again.

"Starving. Room service?"

Emmy walked into Adriana's room in a hotel-provided robe and slippers and began to dig through her suitcase. She pulled out a black garter and fishnet stockings and held them up. "Don't you have just a pair of boxers or something?"

"Emmy, *querida,* in case you didn't know, boxers are for boys." She dragged herself into a sitting position and stuck a hand in her suitcase. "Here, wear these."

Emmy took the lavender silk tap pants and matching swatch of fabric and held them up. "Is this honestly what you wear when you're alone in your apartment and you just want to be comfortable?"

Adriana did her delicate femi-snort. "Hardly. They look like something my grandmother would wear. In fact, I think they're a present from her. I usually wear these." She pulled a magenta slip over her head; the silky fabric moved like liquid against her body.

Emmy sighed. "I know I shouldn't hate you for having a perfect body, but I do. I really, really do."

"Darling, these, too, can be yours" — Adriana cupped her breasts and pushed them up, causing her nightie to slide up over her hips to reveal a complete Brazilian wax — "for ten grand and a few hours under Dr. Kramer's magical hands." She glanced down and gave them each another squeeze. "I'm so glad I had them redone when they legalized silicone. It's so much more natural, don't you think?"

Emmy had admired — oh, hell, she'd *worshipped* — Adriana's implants since the moment she returned with them after Christmas break sophomore year. Granted, they didn't seem so perfect when one of them began to leak four months later and Emmy had to rush Adriana to the ER and sit with her through the night as they waited for a plastic surgeon to come rebuild her sagging left breast. But now? Swapping out the saline for silicone had been a good decision — even if it had meant another four full days and nights during which Emmy had to nurse her friend. They were flawless. So curvy and full and beautiful without looking the least bit fake . . . Well, perhaps they looked a tiny bit fake, but only to those who knew Adriana beforehand and, as Adi herself had said, with a laugh, "Once they're in, they're real." Real, fake, who really cared when they were that goddamn perfect?

Emmy had wondered a thousand times, ten thousand times, what it would be like to possess such breasts. Or, truth be told, any breasts at all. She'd always been mostly satisfied with her own slight frame, growing more pleased with her figure as she got older and realized how rare it was for a woman to stay thin naturally. Yet even though she realized how many women would kill for her metabolism, for her toothpick-thin thighs and itty-bitty bum and jiggle-free upper arms, she yearned to know how it felt to have a woman's body, with all the softness and curves that men loved so much. When faced with breasts like Adriana's, Emmy envisioned drawers full of sexy, lacy bras; halter dresses that could be filled out; a world rich with unpadded bikini tops; a total inability to shop in the children's section because her chest would never fit in a little girl's shirt. She dreamed of never hearing the "more than a handful" adage ever again, and wearing strapless dresses without stuffing them first, and having a man stare at her cleavage instead of her eyes, just once.

Of course, she'd never have the nerve to do it. Even as she examined Adriana's chest tonight, she knew she was too much of a wimp to ever go through with it. She also understood that her attractiveness to men stemmed from her delicateness, the natural gracefulness that resulted from having such a small body, the way her physical fragility made them even more aware of their own strength and masculinity, and not from anything as overtly sexual as big, beautiful breasts.

Emmy sighed. She yanked the towel off her head and threw it on the floor. "On second thought, how do you feel about skipping dinner tonight? I can't move."

Adriana held her hands to her heart. "Like you even have to ask. Less food now means better bikini bod tomorrow."

"Well put. 'Night, Adi."

"Good night, Em. I hope your dreams are filled with gorgeous foreign men. Don't think we just forgot about that. . . ."

But before she could respond, Emmy was out.

At the pool on their second day of vacation Adriana could feel Leigh watching her as she pulled a cigarette from her beach bag, lit it, and languidly inhaled. It was cruel to smoke in front of someone who missed it so much, she acknowledged this, but, hell, they were on vacation. There was no reason Leigh couldn't enjoy herself a little and quit again when she got home; after all, Adriana did it all the time.

"Want one?" Adriana asked with a wicked smile, extending her hand in the direction of Leigh's chaise.

Leigh glared and then leaned forward. "Let me just smell it," she said, sticking her face in the stream of smoke. She moaned, her raspy voice sounding even deeper than usual. "My god, that's good. If I found out I had only a year or five or ten left to live, I swear to you, the very first thing I would do is buy a pack of cigarettes."

Emmy shook her head, causing a few brown locks to come loose from her ponytail. She adjusted her bathing suit — a sporty blue two-piece that looked more like a workout outfit than a bikini — and said, "You two are disgusting with the cigarettes. Hasn't anyone told you what a vile habit it is? Fucking gross."

"Good morning, sunshine! You're a joy this morning, aren't you?" Leigh said. She drained her remaining orange juice and pulled her straw tote onto the lounge chair.

"My god, I can't wait to get some sun. Do you believe it's already July and I haven't been out once this summer?"

Adriana made a show of looking Leigh up and down. "Oh, you would never know," she said. "That translucent blue color you have going on totally works for you."

"Laugh if you must," Leigh sang, appearing genuinely happy for the first time in weeks, "but we'll see who's laughing in twenty years when you've both had huge chunks of skin cancer gouged out of your faces and massive amounts of Botox for all those wrinkles. I almost can't wait."

Adriana and Emmy watched in fascination as Leigh methodically removed two bottles and one tube of sunscreen from her tote. First she applied a thick Clarins cream, SPF 50, to every exposed inch of flesh from toe to shoulder, taking care to pull back her black bikini and work the goop into the border areas around her suit. When she finished that laborious task, she misted herself all over with an aerosol can of Neutrogena, also SPF 50, to "guarantee she didn't miss anywhere," as she explained to her captivated audience. With her body successfully coated and sprayed, she went to work on her face, massaging small puddles of some highly coveted imported French facial sunscreen into her cheeks, chin, forehead, earlobes, eyelids, and neck. She pulled her hair into a loose bun, covered it with a straw hat the circumference of an end table, and popped on a pair of oversized wraparound black sunglasses.

"Mmm," she sighed, stretching her arms over her head, taking care not to displace the hat. "This is wonderful."

Adriana glanced at Emmy and rolled her eyes. They both smiled. Leigh was particular, there was no denying it, but her ritual comforted them both with its very Leighness.

"Okay, girls, enough small talk. We have a subject that needs discussing," Adriana announced. She knew Leigh wasn't up for talking in great length about the engagement — she'd made that abundantly clear the previous beach day with her incessant anxious chatter about the new huge author she'd been assigned (just the kind of nervous chatter the girls now tuned out after so many years of hearing Leigh say "I totally failed that final" and "I'm never going to get this manuscript back on time," only to watch her score nonstop A-pluses through college and receive promotion after promotion at work) and one-word answers about her upcoming nuptials — so Adriana decided to let her off the hook. For now.

"I don't know about you, Leigh, but I know I want more details of Emmy's Paris trip," Adriana sang, looking pointedly at Emmy. "The City of Love; I'm expecting there's plenty to tell."

Emmy groaned and placed her paperback copy of *London Is the Best City in America* open-faced across her chest. "How many times do I have to say it? There's nothing to tell."

"Lies, all lies," Leigh said. "You mentioned something about a guy named Paul. Which, incidentally, does not sound like a particularly foreign name to me, but perhaps you could shed some light?"

"I don't know why you keep making me relive this," Emmy said with an imploring look. "It's sadistic. I told you the whole story: Paul the half-Argentine, half-Brit, who was well dressed, well traveled, and overall exceedingly charming and attractive, chose his ex-girlfriend's birthday party over sex with yours truly."

"I'm sure there's another explanation. Maybe he just —"

Adriana interrupted what was surely going to be Leigh's overly tactful, insanely delusional game of "maybe he." "Please! There's only one explanation for what went on that night, assuming, as we are, that Paul is both straight and male. Emmy, be honest. Did you really want to have sex with him? Did you lust after him? Really and truly *crave* his body?"

Emmy laughed uncomfortably. "Wow. I don't know how to respond. I guess? Yeah, sure. I practically threw myself at him mere hours after meeting him, didn't I?"

"And by 'threw yourself,' you mean 'nervously and subtly conveyed — or tried to — that you'd entertain the idea of another drink.' Am I right?"

"Well, maybe." Emmy sniffed. She was determined not to share the real reason for Paul's speedy departure. If she admitted to asking Paul if he wanted children one day — a perfectly reasonable question as far as she was concerned — Emmy knew her friends would never, *ever* let it go.

"So you did not actually come across to him as a carefree, wild party girl who's up for anything fun?"

"Oh, I don't know! Probably not, okay? But why do you think that is? *Because I'm not a wild party girl who's up for anything.* I'm an unremarkable girl who likes hooking up enough but would rather get to *know someone* I like than have some dirty fling with a stranger."

Adriana smiled triumphantly. "And that, my friend, is your problem."

"That's not a problem," Leigh added without opening her eyes. "It's the way she is. Not everyone can have meaningless one-night stands."

Adriana exhaled a long, frustrated sigh. "First of all, girls, 'one-night stands' are for sad little people who meet in Atlantic City casinos or Midwestern hotels. 'Hooking up' is what drunken sorority girls do after their spring formals. We have *affairs*. Fabulous, sexy, spontaneous *affairs*. Understood? Second, I think we're all losing sight of something here: I am not the one who decided Emmy should be having *affairs* in every city she visits. She made that little pronouncement all on her own. Of course, if you don't think you can handle it . . ."

The waiter, an impishly cute blond guy in a collared shirt and khaki shorts, asked if he could bring them anything. They ordered a round of margaritas and picked up the conversation as though there'd been no interruption.

"No, you're right," Emmy conceded. "This was my decision, and I'm going to do it. It'll be good for me, right? Get me less focused on the whole marriage thing. More relaxed. It's just that it sounds great in theory, but when it's midnight and you're in some strange hotel and staring at this person you barely know and thinking that he's about to see you naked when you don't know his last name . . . I, it's just . . . different."

"But done with the right attitude, it can be very freeing," Adriana said.

"Or a total disaster," Leigh added.

"Always the optimist, aren't you?"

"Look, I hear that Emmy wants to do this, and I totally understand why. I mean, if I'd only been with three guys in my entire life and they'd all been long-term boyfriends, I'd want a little taste of what else is out there. But it's important she knows that one-night stands — sorry, *affairs* — aren't always so glamorous," Leigh said.

"Speak for yourself. I've always been rather pleased," Adriana smiled. It was true, mostly. She'd been with more men than she could ever possibly count, but she'd enjoyed every one of them.

Leigh pounced. "Oh, really? Then I guess you're not remembering that surfer guy — what was his name? Pasha? — who high-fived you after sex and then called you 'dude,' as in 'Dude, just chill for a minute,' when you asked him if he wanted another glass of wine? Or the foot fetishist who wanted to lube up your feet and rub them all over his body? And who could forget the one you met at Izzie's wedding, taking a phone call from *his mother* while you were on top? Shall I go on?"

Adriana held up her right hand and summoned her most winning smile. "I think we get the idea. However, dear friend, you're being a bit misleading. A few bad apples is no reason not to visit the orchard. Those were just unfortunate exceptions. What about the Austrian baron who thought, quite rightly, that diamond shopping at Cartier was good foreplay? Or the time in Costa Rica when the surfer — the other surfer and I — made love on the beach at sunrise? Or when that architect with that amazing rooftop overlooking the Hudson —"

"Just know that it can go either way," Leigh said, looking straight at Emmy.

"You are such a killjoy!" Adriana shrieked. "I'm going for a swim." She tried to keep her tone light, but it was all starting to irritate her. What was Leigh so bitter about? The girl had an amazing job at the city's most prestigious publishing house, an adoring, sought-after sportscaster fiancé who had eyes only for her, and a put-together, sophisticated appearance that was just hot enough for men to like but not so hot that women hated her. Why was she

205

always so miserable?

"I hope that after putting me through the wringer you haven't forgotten your end of the deal?" Emmy said.

"Of course not," Adriana replied. "In fact, I think I've already met my future husband."

"Hmm," Leigh murmured, unfazed, grabbing her frozen margarita from the waiter's tray. She pressed it directly to her forehead for a moment before licking all the way around the salted rim.

"Is that so?" Emmy asked with what Adriana was irritated to hear sounded a lot like condescension.

"Yes, that's so," Adriana replied. "And although neither of you seems remotely interested, I'll have you know that he just so happens to be Tobias Baron."

Two heads snapped up to look at her in awe. *Well, that got their attention, thank god.*

"*The* Tobias Baron?" Leigh asked.

Yes, this was better. "The one and only." She nodded. "And actually, his friends call him Toby."

Leigh's eyes bulged. "Are you kidding? Spill, girl! We need to hear —"

"Of course!" Adriana smiled. "But first I'm just going to have a quick swim." She climbed out of her lounge chair like a cat unfolding from an afternoon nap and strolled toward the pool. *That'll teach them to not take me seriously.* She tested the water with her toes, then dove in, barely breaking the water with her streamlined body, and immediately began a strong yet graceful forward crawl. Although she was not a big fan of oceans (the salt water was so drying to the hair, never mind all those unpleasant stinging creatures), Adriana swam like a fish. Her mother, terrified of having young Adriana toddle into the estate's pool, had insisted she learn to swim before she could walk. This was accomplished quite efficiently in a single afternoon. Mrs. de Souza carried a squirming nine-month-old Adriana into five feet of water, pulled off the girl's water wings, and watched as the child sank. Hearing this story for the first time in her early teens, Adriana was horrified. "You just watched as I drowned?" she asked her mother.

"Please, it wasn't quite so dramatic — you were only under a moment or two. Then you figured it out and paddled your little head to the surface. A bit of water up the nose is hardly a trauma, now, is it?" Not a Dr. Phil–approved method but effective nonetheless.

She swam ten lengths of the pool and gratefully accepted a rolled beach towel from a muscled attendant, offering him a broad smile as reward. Adriana returned, and Emmy folded over the page she was reading and tossed the book aside.

"Adriana de Souza, how have you not told us this already? We've been in Aruba now for —"

"Bonaire!" Leigh and Adriana said simultaneously.

Emmy waved her arms in a silencing gesture. "Whatever. We've been in *Bonaire* for two full days already and you're just getting around to mentioning this now? What kind of friend does that?"

"It's not serious," she said, relishing her friends' expressions — she just adored withholding information until it would have the maximum effect — "but I think he has potential."

"Potential? The magazines call him an intellectual George Clooney. Handsome, accomplished, straight, unmarried —"

"Divorced," Emmy added.

Leigh swatted the air. "A mistake in his early twenties that lasted thirty-six months and produced no kids. As far as divorced men go, he barely even qualifies."

Adriana whistled. "Well, well, it seems like you're both rather informed. Does this mean you approve?"

They nodded vigorously.

"So tell us all about him," Emmy breathed, probably relieved that the focus had shifted away from her.

Adriana lifted her dripping-wet torso slightly off the chair to straighten the cushion, but it was enough to cause an audible groan from a nearby sunbather. "Well, let's see. No need to give you the biographical information — you girls clearly know that! — but, um, he really is a darling. I met him two weeks ago on the set of *The City Dweller.*"

Leigh flipped over and unhooked her bikini top across the back. "What were you doing there?"

"Gilles brought me. I was going to meet Angelina and Maddox, but instead I met Toby." Adriana proceeded to relay her conversation with Toby word for word, adding a few sentences (for color) but omitting none. When finished, she wrapped her lips seductively around her striped straw and took a long pull on her margarita. She couldn't be positive, but she thought the group of cute guys across the pool was staring at her.

"So do you think he'll call?" Emmy asked with what appeared to be genuine concern.

A little annoyed that her friend had even considered the idea that he wouldn't call, no less verbalized it, she snapped, "Of course he'll call. Why wouldn't he?"

"Oooh, sounds like someone's a little sensitive . . ." Leigh practically sang.

"What? Are you referring to Yani? I'm so over that." Adriana stretched her legs out and pointed her toes.

"Was there a development with Yani?" Emmy asked eagerly. "Why am I always the last to know everything?"

Adriana sighed. "I have no idea why we're harping on this. I gave him my number after class last week and told him to call me."

"And?"

"He gave it back." Adriana tried to sound supremely bored, but her friends knew her too well: It had been haunting her, making her even more certain that the time to find a husband was upon her. Yani's rejection — something she was sure would never have happened a couple of years ago — confirmed her window was closing.

"Did he say why?"

"No, just that he was sorry, but he wouldn't be able to use the number."

"I'm sure it was just because he —"

"Please," Adriana said with a casual wave and a deliberate smile. "I am so *not* interested. Yani the yoga instructor isn't exactly one of the most revered Hollywood directors on earth, now, is he?"

"Hi," Emmy said, sitting up and grinning

hugely in the direction of Adriana's right shoulder.

"What?" Adriana was momentarily confused until she turned around to see a man standing behind her. A rather attractive man, if she did say so. Why, yes, those Hawaiian-print board shorts sat below his hip bones, encircling an impressively toned abdomen. His sun-streaked hair was wet, and Adriana noticed his strong hands as he pushed it off his face. He could use a shave and he wasn't as tall as she usually liked, but overall he was rather delectable. And he was smiling. At *Emmy.*

"Hey there," he said. "I hope I'm not interrupting anything. . . ." An Australian! They were her absolute favorites. Her very first kiss had been with an Australian boy, age eleven, sent to São Paulo for the summer to stay with Adriana's next-door neighbors, and since then she'd been with enough of his countrymen to consider herself an honorary citizen.

"Of course not," Adriana purred, instinctively pushing her shoulders back and her chest forward.

"Well, uh, we — my mates, over there?" He pointed to the table across the pool where three guys sat, trying not to look. "We were wondering if you'd like to join us for dinner tonight?" Adriana stared at him in disbelief. It was confirmed: He was talking directly to Emmy. Unbelievable! Could this delicious little treat actually prefer Emmy to her?

"It's just that we're here for one of my mates' stag parties and, well, we've been here for three days already and are getting really tired of talking to each other. It'd, uh, be great if you girls would come with us tonight. Nothing crazy, I promise, just a cool little beachside place with good drinks and good music. Our treat. What do you say?"

By now, even Emmy had figured out that the Australian was addressing her, and Adriana, despite being shocked by the whole situation, was impressed by how quickly Emmy recovered. "Why, that's so nice of you!" she said in her best imitation of a Southern belle. "We'd love to."

The Australian, appearing pleased, trotted off to the bar in search of a pen. The moment he left, Adriana made a deliberate decision to kick it into high gear. She tried to suppress this ever-increasing panic that men no longer found her attractive and swallowed her critical thoughts of the Aussie — who was, upon further observation, quite short . . . not to mention that dirty-looking stubble; wasn't she too old for guys who didn't bother to take care of themselves? — and instead concentrated on smiling as broadly as she could manage. Leaning in conspiratorially, she whispered to her friends. "Emmy, darling, that boy has your name written all over him. Paris was Amateur Hour. You, my friend, are with the expert now. Consider yourself warned. . . ." And while Emmy blushed and Leigh gave an approving wink, Adriana focused on keeping the tears at bay.

Leigh dug around inside her purse, searching for something, anything, that she could busy herself with until Jesse arrived. She couldn't just sit there, for chrissake, staring off into space, nor did she want to be *that* girl, the one who was hunched over herself, frantically thumbing her BlackBerry. There was a hundred-page excerpt of a manuscript that her assistant had handed her as she walked out of the office, but she discarded this idea as well; pulling out a manuscript at Michael's during the lunch hour was like reading a screenplay at The Coffee Bean in Beverly Hills. Just don't. What she really wanted to do was put on her beloved noise-cancellation headphones and block out the shrill, grating voice of the man sitting behind her, screaming into his cell phone. Were she alone or with friends, she would have simply asked to move tables, but Jesse was due any second and she didn't want to be seen making a big fuss. The anxiety over the lunch combined with her upstairs neighbor's late-night clomp to the kitchen had resulted in a very deficient night's sleep, and she yearned to sneak in an earphone — just one was all she needed! — and let her trusty iPod (filled with only the most relaxing classical and mood music) soothe her jangled nerves. She was just untangling the cords when the maître d' appeared tableside, Jesse in tow.

"Good to see you again," she said smoothly, deliberately not standing to greet him but instead holding out her hand.

He leaned over to kiss her cheek. It was instinctive and totally impersonal, but Leigh nonetheless felt a little frisson of excitement. *Just nerves,* she thought.

Jesse stood next to the chair that had been pulled out for him and surveyed the scene. "Leigh, darling, could I trouble you to switch tables with me?" He stared at the two men in suits sitting behind her, one of whom was still on his cell phone, and Jesse said none-too-quietly, "I can't fucking stand people uncivilized enough to scream into their cell phones in a restaurant."

His reprimand went unnoticed by the offender, but Leigh nearly jumped from her seat and into his arms. "I loathe that guy," she said, gathering her things with great haste, but Jesse was already preoccupied with flagging down the maître d'. It wasn't until they were seated once again — this time at a perfectly situated table for two in a quiet back corner — that Leigh allowed herself to sneak a glance at Jesse.

He was wearing jeans and a blazer — perhaps the very same one he'd been wearing that day in Henry's office — and his hair was mussed. He looked well scrubbed but casually rumpled, as though he'd given not a second's thought to his appearance, and this made Leigh acutely aware of just how much time she had spent preparing.

It had been a while since she'd devoted so much time to her morning routine. She'd been so busy and sleep-deprived lately that her hour-long beauty regimen had been reduced to the basics: a quick rinse; a once-over with the hairdryer, just long enough to get the wet out; a touch of mascara; and lipstick on the go. But this morning had been different. She climbed out of bed without snoozing the alarm, carefully so as not to wake Russell, and from there her body moved through elaborate preparations as though on autopilot.

She had debated endlessly what to wear for her first official meeting with Jesse. His whole aura was informal, that much was sure, but she wanted to appear professional. Her father had never failed to remind her that older male authors would forever see her as a woman before an editor, and that if she stood any chance of gaining their respect, she should deemphasize her femininity. Or at the very least, not play it up. Leigh had always followed this prescription carefully, but today — when it should have counted most — she just couldn't bear the usual black pantsuit. Or the charcoal gray one. Or navy. Nor did her usual cotton bikinis seem sufficient; instead, she climbed into a stretchy hot pink thong and a matching mesh bra that supported little and concealed nothing. *Why not?* she thought. They were more cute than sexy, and what was wrong with changing it up a little? Over this she tied her favorite Diane von Furstenberg wrap dress, a knee-length number with three-quarter sleeves, a low neckline, and a bright yellow, white, and black abstract pattern. She blew her hair dry and applied her makeup barefoot before adding a pair of strappy sandals, going for the three-inchers instead of her more practical work kitten heels. Russell had whistled sleepily when she kissed his forehead good-bye, but the moment she stepped on the subway, she started to wonder if she was overdressed and by the time she was seated at the restaurant, she was convinced she looked more like a high-paid escort than a stylish yet serious professional.

To his credit or his obliviousness — Leigh wasn't quite sure which — Jesse kept his eyes locked firmly on her face as he said, "Where did my mousy editor go? I hope you didn't go to all this trouble on my behalf."

Leigh watched as he settled into the chair opposite hers and immediately regretted her outfit choice. She was prepared for Jesse's sexist comments — Henry had warned her of those — and judging from his literary-rock-star status, she assumed he'd be a pompous jerk, but despite all that, she wasn't ready for such a blatant insult. If she didn't set the precedent right now, their entire working relationship would be doomed. He might be a famous writer, but he was *her* famous writer now, and she had to make damn sure he understood that.

"For you?" Leigh made a show of looking herself over and laughed gaily. "Jesse, how sweet of you to notice, but it's actually for a party later." She paused, hoping she sounded more confident than she felt. "Am I to infer now that you went to all that trouble for me?"

His hands immediately went to his hair

and brushed it back off his face. "Yeah, I do look like shit, don't I?" he said a bit sheepishly. "I missed the earlier train and then the schedule was all fucked up. It was a bit of a nightmare."

"The train? I thought you lived in the city?"

"I do, but I can't concentrate here, so I've been writing in the Hamptons."

"Oh, that's —"

He interrupted with a rueful laugh. "Really fucking original, I know. Bought the place last November, just as it was starting to get cold. I was always appropriately anti-Hamptons, you won't be shocked to hear, but this was different: It was gray, isolated, the perfect place to lock down with a computer and not much else. Didn't see another soul for days at a stretch and then — *poof!* — the sun comes out for a split second in May, and the whole of the Upper East Side arrives en masse."

"So why'd you stay? It's hell on earth there in July," Leigh said.

"Sheer laziness."

"Oh, please. I don't believe that for a second."

"Believe it. I'm all set up. I just can't bring myself to leave. Besides, they're doing construction on the apartment above mine in the city and the noise is intolerable."

"Mmm," Leigh said, accepting a menu from the waiter.

Jesse shook his head and sat back in his seat with an exhale. "How do you endure so many hours with self-obsessed shits like myself?"

Leigh laughed despite herself. "Just a part of the job description," she said.

"Speaking of which, I'm sure you're curious what —"

"Jesse," she said sweetly, stopping him mid-sentence. "We're going to have plenty of time for work, so I thought it might be nice if we just got acquainted and saved the editorial discussion for next time."

He stared at her. "Are you serious?"

"Quite. If that's all right with you."

He cocked his head. "You are a strange one, aren't you? An editor who doesn't want to talk about my book. Well, well, well. What do you want to talk about, Ms. Eisner?"

Leigh was pleased. Her trip to Curaçao with the girls hadn't felt like much of an engagement celebration, but it had given her plenty of time to think through her strategy with Jesse. She knew she needed to set the tone with him early and firmly. Dictating both the pacing and the content of their conversations was the only way to do this.

He had come to this lunch expecting that his new editor at his new publishing house would be salivating to hear about his new book and so she had feigned indifference.

By the time they'd finished their entrées (the hanger steak salad for him and the herb-roasted striped bass for her), they'd talked about everything *but* writing. Leigh learned that Jesse grew up in Seattle but thought it was depressing and he spent his twenties working odd jobs around Southeast Asia but thought that was depressing, too. He told her how shocked he'd been when *Disenchantment* first hit the bestseller list and how surreal it was to make millions from what he thought of as little more than a travel diary and how crazy the party scene in New York City is when you're young, accomplished, and suddenly very, very rich. It had been a little over an hour, but Leigh felt like they were beginning to forge a connection that was unusual for them both — not romantic, of course, but somehow intimate. In passing and without the least bit of emphasis or interest, Jesse mentioned his wife.

"You have a *wife?*" Leigh asked.

He nodded.

"As in, you're *married?*"

"That is generally how people define it, yes. Are you surprised?"

"No. Well, yes. Not surprised that you would be married, just . . . uh . . . surprised that . . . well, that I didn't read it in the papers."

Jesse grinned and she thought how much better-looking he was when he smiled. Younger, somehow, and not quite as damaged. He glanced at her left hand and raised his eyebrows. "I see you, too, plan to join our *married* ranks."

She didn't know why, but she was suddenly flustered. Flustered and quite uncomfortable.

"Dessert?" she asked, picking up the menu and pretending to peruse it.

Jesse ordered espressos for both of them. Without asking. Which, naturally, Leigh found equally irritating and appealing. She would have preferred herbal mint tea had she been permitted to choose, but it was oddly nice not to make the decision.

"So tell me, Ms. Eisner. What was the last great book you edited? Before mine, of course."

"Well, I needn't remind you, Mr. Chapman, that your book's greatness remains to be seen. We're all very curious."

"As am I, about the woman who will be editing me."

"What, exactly, would you like to know?"

"Who are your other authors? Your favorites? Which of their books have pleased you?"

A bit flustered, Leigh said, "I think you probably know the answer to your own questions."

"Meaning?"

Leigh paused for a moment and considered the ramifications of complete honesty. She certainly didn't feel any moral compulsion to tell the whole truth; it just felt silly at this point to keep up the charade, so she looked him in the eye and said, "Meaning that I have no doubt you've done your homework, and you know full well that you will be my most-selling author to date — and admittedly, by a great deal — and you also must know that my boss, my colleagues, and probably the entire publishing community think I'm much too inexperienced to handle your book."

Jesse downed his espresso. "And what do *you* think, dear Leigh?" he asked, a half-smile playing at his mouth.

"I think that you're sick of all the bullshit. I don't know why you vanished the last six years, but I suspect it was something more than too much partying, or whatever else the gossip hounds claim. I think you're looking for a fresh start and an editor who has nothing to lose. Someone young and hungry and willing to take a few risks." She paused. "How am I doing?"

"Very well."

"Thank you." She felt almost high with adrenaline, anxious and on edge, but in a good way.

"And at the risk of sounding like a patronizing asshole," he said, "I am quite certain I made the right decision."

"You have," she nodded.

Jesse motioned to the waiter for their check and handed it directly to Leigh when it arrived. "This is on Brook Harris, I assume?"

"Of course." She placed her brand-new American Express Corporate Card in the little folder and sat back. "So, Jesse," she said, pulling her red leather planner from her bag, "when are we going to see each other again? I'm free for lunch Tuesday and Friday of next week, although Tuesday's probably better. Of course, you're welcome to come into the office and meet —"

"Next week isn't good for me."

"Oh. Okay, then. The week after that. How about you —"

"No, that won't work, either."

Her company had just spent three million dollars to purchase what was little more than a name and a promise, and he didn't think it enough of a priority to make himself available for a proper editorial conversation? "You didn't even let me finish," she said quietly.

"I'm sorry," he said with a barely suppressed smile. "It's just that I've no plans to come to the city again for the next few weeks. This morning's train debacle guaranteed that. Now, we can either wait until I *do* return, or if you're inclined, I'd be happy to host you in the Hamptons."

"Well, I'll have to check my schedule and get back to you," she said coolly.

"He'll tell you to come," Jesse said.

"Pardon me?"

"Henry. He'll tell you to come. Don't worry, Leigh, it's not so very far away, and I promise to take good care of you. There's even a Starbucks."

The waiter returned her card and receipt. She carefully placed each in its own compartment in her wallet and gathered her things.

"I haven't upset you, have I?" Jesse asked.

Leigh got the distinct feeling that he couldn't care less.

"Of course not. I'm just late for another appointment. I'll call you later today or tomorrow and set up our next meeting."

He grinned and stepped aside so she could walk ahead of him. "Sounds good to me. And Leigh? Try not to panic, okay? We're going to work just fine together."

It was raining when they stepped outside, and as Leigh fumbled in her gigantic tote for an umbrella, Jesse began jogging toward Sixth Avenue. "Talk later," he called without turning around.

Leigh seethed. He really *was* a conceited, pompous prick. He hadn't even bothered to ask if she needed a cab or offered to walk her back to the office — he hadn't even thanked her for lunch! She didn't know how she was going to coddle a man with such a mammoth-sized ego. She could be diplomatic and lead with the carrot, but the gentle, wide-eyed, I'm-so-impressed-with-your-brilliance-Mr. Bestseller approach just wasn't her. Not now, not ever, and certainly not for someone as obnoxious as Jesse Chapman. Hell, *Adriana* could probably do a better job with him, never having edited — or possibly even read — a single book in her entire life. This thought plagued her for the eight-block walk back to the office, a walk made even more miserable by her now-soaking-wet three-inch heels. By the time she stepped into her building, she was ready to call the entire thing off — a fact that she didn't exactly hide from Henry.

"Eisner, get in here," he called to her as she walked by his door. There was no way to get from the elevator to her office without passing Henry's, a maddening design he'd no doubt orchestrated deliberately.

Leigh would have liked a few minutes to compose herself and, truth be told, maybe tone down her outfit by adding a cardigan or a pair of flip-flops, but she knew Henry had cleared his entire afternoon in anticipation of her return.

"Hello," she said brightly and arranged herself as modestly as possible on his love seat.

"Well?" he asked. Henry looked her up and down but, blessedly, remained expressionless.

"Well, he certainly is a handful," she said before realizing how positively asinine that sounded.

"A handful?"

"He's arrogant — just like you warned — but I'm sure it's nothing we won't be able to work through. When I tried to set up our next meeting, he blatantly refused to come back to Manhattan."

Henry looked up. "Doesn't he live in the West Village?"

"Yes, but he claims he can't concentrate

here, so he bought a place in the Hamptons. He just assumed that *I'd* go *there*. . . ." Leigh trailed off with a laugh.

"Of course you will," Henry snapped, something he didn't do often.

"I will?" Leigh asked, surprised more at Henry's vehemence than anything else.

"Yes. I'll reassign your other projects if necessary. From now until his pub date, you'll make this your only priority. If that means meeting at the Bronx Zoo because he's inspired by baby lion cubs, so be it. So long as that manuscript is in by deadline and it's publishable, I don't care if you spend the next six months in Tanzania. Just make it happen."

"I understand, Henry. I really do. You can count on me. And reassigning my authors isn't necessary," Leigh said, thinking of the memoirist with chronic fatigue, the novelist whose book was out for endorsements, and the stand-up comedian turned writer who called with new jokes no fewer than three times a week.

Henry's phone rang and a moment later his assistant announced over the intercom that it was his wife. "Think about what I said, Leigh," he said, his hand over the mouthpiece.

She nodded and scurried out of his office,

barely even noticing the searing pain she felt in both heels. Her own assistant, clutching a fistful of messages and memos, pounced on Leigh the moment she collapsed into her desk chair.

"This contract needs to be signed immediately so I can FedEx it before close of business, and Pablo from the art department said he needed any cover notes for the Mathison memoir as soon as humanly possible. Oh, and —"

"Annette, can we hold off on this stuff for a minute? I need to make a call. Will you close the door on your way out? I'll only be a moment." Leigh tried to keep her voice calm and even, but she felt like screaming.

Annette, bless her heart, merely nodded and quietly pulled the door closed behind her. Not sure she would ever again have the strength to make the call if she didn't do it that second, Leigh picked up the receiver and dialed.

"Well, that was fast," Jesse answered. It sounded like a taunt. "What can I do for you, Ms. Eisner?"

"I've checked my schedule, and I'll see you in the Hamptons."

He demonstrated enough restraint not to gloat, but Leigh could *feel* him grinning. "I appreciate that, Leigh. I'll be out of town for the next couple weeks doing research. Would the second weekend in August work?"

Leigh didn't bother looking at her planner or the calendar she kept open on her computer screen. What did it matter? Henry had made it clear enough: If it worked for Jesse, it worked for her.

She took a deep breath and bit down on her thumb hard enough to leave a tooth mark. "I'll be there," she said.

MOMMY DRINKS
BECAUSE I CRY

Izzie led the way to the elevator in her building and punched the number eleven. "So you're telling me that some gorgeous Australian took you for a walk on the beach late at night after hours of drinking and dancing and that — despite your solemn pledge to yourself and your friends that you'd, pardon my French, fuck anyone in possession of a foreign passport — you *still* didn't sleep with him?"

"Yes."

"Emmy, Emmy, Emmy."

"I couldn't, okay? I just couldn't! We were rolling around in the sand, making out like crazy. He was such a good kisser. He took off his shirt, and my god —" Emmy groaned audibly and closed her eyes.

"And? I'm not hearing anything bad so far."

"And the second he went to unbutton my jeans, I freaked out. I don't know why, I just did. It was so . . . so *surreal* to see this guy on top of me, about to *enter* me, and I didn't even know his last name. I couldn't do it."

Izzie unlocked the apartment door and Emmy followed her into the small marble-floored foyer. "Did you really just say that he was about to 'enter' you?"

"Izzie," Emmy warned. "Can we stay focused here? I wanted to do it, I really did. I was *so* attracted to him. He was totally sweet and nonthreatening and *Australian,* and it would've been the perfect vacation fling. But I still made him stop."

Kevin looked up from the desk where he was sitting across the living room and smiled. "This conversation sounds significantly more interesting than my patient who just e-mailed to describe the consistency of her discharge." He closed the laptop and crossed the living room, kissing Emmy on the cheek and then enveloping Izzie in a warm, welcoming bear hug. "I missed you, baby," he murmured quietly into her ear.

Izzie pressed her lips to his and stroked his face with the back of her hand. "Mmm. I missed you, too. How was the shift?"

"Um, excuse me?" Emmy interrupted their private exchange. "I hate to break up this sweet reunion, but as you two are already married and I have no one to confide in, I'd like to focus on *me* for a little while. . . ."

Kevin laughed and patted his wife on the ass. "Fair enough. I'll throw your stuff in the second bedroom and get some drinks. You girls wait outside." He headed toward the kitchen and Izzie looked after him wistfully.

"He's nauseatingly amazing," Emmy said.

"I know." Izzie sighed with a barely suppressed smile. "He's so fucking nice. It would probably be unbearable if I didn't love him so much. Come on, let's sit on the balcony."

Emmy could envision places she'd rather sit than at the balcony's wrought-iron table in a wrought-iron chair under the blazing South Florida sun, the air thick with humidity. Like on the carpet directly in front of the air-conditioning vents, for one.

"Does one *ever* stop sweating here?" Emmy asked Izzie, who appeared completely unaffected by the swelter.

Izzie shrugged. "You get used to it after a while. Although I have to say, not many people choose August for a visit to Miami." She turned to catch the sun, but only after winking at Emmy. "Okay, so we were at the part where he was about to *enter* you. . . ."

The sliding glass door opened and Kevin, a tray full of drinks and accessories in his hands, shook his head in dismay. "I can't seem to escape this conversation. Seriously, Em, can we fast-forward a little?"

As Izzie jumped up to help Kevin, Emmy wondered where the girl found her energy. The unrelenting heat and humidity made Emmy feel like her entire body was liquefying.

"There's not much more to say," Emmy said, grabbing a handful of grapes from Kevin's tray. She plucked a bottle of water from a small ice bucket he had set down and said, "Are we not boozing? I thought neither of you was on call."

Izzie and Kevin exchanged a quick look. "Yeah, we'll open something in a minute. But first" — he handed Izzie a canvas tote bag — "we have something for you."

"For me?" Emmy asked, confused. "I should be bringing you guys something. . . . I'm the guest."

Izzie opened the canvas bag and handed Emmy a small box, festively adorned in yellow paper and rainbow-colored ribbons. "For you," she said.

"This is really very sweet, but I think it's only fair to warn you guys: If this is some sort of gift certificate for Match.com or a dating handbook or any sort of information on freezing my eggs, there's going to be trouble."

Izzie must have known she was only kidding, so Emmy was surprised to see her smile fade a little. "Just open it," she urged.

Never one to open a gift delicately — was it really worthwhile to stockpile used wrapping paper and bows? — Emmy ripped it open with relish. She was unsurprised to find a folded white T-shirt nestled among the yellow tissue paper. She and Izzie had been doing this for years, since they were old enough to earn their own money and responsible enough to post boxes on a regular basis: sending each other T-shirts with funny, obnoxious, clever, or just plain stupid sayings, always hoping to one-up the last contribution. Just a couple weeks earlier Emmy had sent Izzie a wife-beater that read TRUST ME, I'M A DOCTAH and Emmy had responded by FedExing a doggie T-shirt — intended for a cute toy breed but addressed to Otis — that read I ONLY BITE WHEN UGLY PEOPLE PET ME.

Emmy held the baby tee up. "WORLD'S BEST AUNTIE?" she read aloud. "I don't get it. What's so clever about —" The look Izzie and Kevin exchanged stopped her midsentence. "Ohmigod."

Izzie just grinned and nodded. Kevin squeezed her hand across the table.

"Ohmigod," Emmy murmured again.

"We're pregnant!" Izzie shouted, knocking over two bottles of water as she jumped up to hug Emmy.

"Ohmigod."

"Em, seriously, say something else," Kevin advised, his brow furrowing in concern for his wife.

Emmy was aware that her arms were wrapped around Izzie, that she was holding on to her sister with a fierce determination, but she was unable to formulate any words. Her mind raced to the places it always did when someone first references a pregnancy: the day, just a year or so earlier, when she'd witnessed her first live birth. Izzie had dressed Emmy in scrubs, instructed her how to behave like a med student, and brought her into the delivery room to watch a totally ordinary vaginal delivery with no complications. None of the sixth-grade health videos or gory tales she'd heard from friends or Izzie prepared her for what she witnessed that day, and now it all came rushing back. Only the stranger on the table was now her sister, and she couldn't shake the mental image of a little bald baby head emerging from her sister's private parts.

But before she could even begin to process that, her mind switched tracks entirely. Next up was a mental inventory of all the baby boutiques and Web sites she had spent so many years visiting, cooing over fuzzy booties and monogrammed burp cloths, filling her imaginary shopping cart with all the cutest things. Now she would have a real reason to shop — for her very own niece or nephew! — but how would she ever decide? Of course she would have to buy the little one onesies with clever sayings like NOBODY PUTS BABY IN THE CORNER and MOMMY DRINKS BECAUSE I CRY, but what about that darling little cashmere rollneck sweater, or the sheepskin-lined infant Uggs, or the limited-edition Bugaboo in the lime plaid print? All those little socks that look like Mary Janes were essential, as was a mini terrycloth robe. She would skip anything too functional or precious — let other people buy the Boppy nursing pillows or the bottle warmers or the engraved Tiffany spoons. She would make sure that Izzie's baby had all the Manhattan essentials. If she didn't, who would? Certainly not this baby's future parents, who would surely be too busy delivering *other* people's babies to seek out the newest, coolest, cutest stuff. Yes, there really was no choice. If ever there was a time to rise to the occasion, this was it. She would live up to the T-shirt's moniker and be the best aunt imaginable. And who knew? Perhaps she would get to use these things for her own baby one day; her kids and Izzie's kids could share their clothes and toys, just as their mothers had their whole lives. They'd be more like siblings than first cousins! In fact, now that she thought it through, she realized that Izzie could wait to time her second with Emmy's first, and then they'd both be pregnant together. They could go to prenatal yoga classes and Izzie could explain what was happening every step of the way in that calm, professional voice she used with her patients, and when it finally came time to give birth, they would do so a few weeks apart, so each sister could be there for the other. Yes, this really was a good plan, especially considering that —

"Em? Are you okay? Say something!" Izzie cried.

"Oh, Izzie, I'm so happy for you guys!" Emmy said, standing up. She hugged her sister again and then threw herself at Kevin. "I'm sorry, I was just so shocked."

"It's crazy, isn't it?" Izzie asked. "We're barely used to it ourselves. I thought it wouldn't be such a big thing since pregnancies and babies are, well, are our *life,* but it's so different when it happens to you, you know?"

Well, technically speaking, she *didn't* know. If things kept up the way they were going, she might never know. But she also knew that Izzie hadn't meant it that way at all. "How far along are you?"

Izzie reached into Emmy's lap and held both her sister's hands. "Don't be mad, Em. . . ."

"What? Are you, like, due next month? Are you one of those freaks who can be nine months pregnant and everyone thinks you've just had a few too many Krispy Kremes? Come to think of it, I had noticed your face looking a little puffier."

"I'm thirteen weeks. Just started my second trimester. Due in February."

Emmy concentrated on doing the math. Four weeks in a month, four goes into thirteen more than three times. . . . "You're already over three *months?* Didn't, like, Katie Holmes and Jennifer Garner announce it to the American *public* when they were a couple months gone? And my own *sister* waits until she's in her second trimester?"

"Em, it killed us not to say anything, but we desperately wanted to tell you in person. I wanted us all to be together, face-to-face, with the cute T-shirt. . . ." Izzie looked stricken with worry; as tears pooled in her eyes, it made Emmy want to cry herself.

"No, Izzie, don't. I'm just kidding, I promise! I love the way you told me. It wouldn't have been the same over the phone," she raced to say as the tears streamed down her sister's face. With only a moment's hesitation for Kevin's sake before remembering he was practically her brother, Emmy ripped her own tank top over her head and pulled on the new WORLD'S BEST AUNTIE top. "Look," she said, turning to show Izzie, noticing that Kevin had all-too-politely averted his gaze. "I love it. I love that you're having a baby! I love, love, love the way you told me. I love you so much, Izzie. Come here, for fuck's sake, and hug me again!"

Izzie sniffed, wiping a tear from her cheek. "It's the hormones. I'm all over the place these days."

"She is." Kevin nodded.

"Never mind about that. Let's celebrate! I'm taking you guys out tonight for the best dinner in Miami. Where should we go? Joe's Stone Crab?"

Kevin took a nap before dinner while Emmy and Izzie spent nearly two hours huddled together, hashing out every detail of this new development. Yes, they were going to find out the gender whether they wanted to or not because they'd inevitably want to see their own ultrasound and both, obviously, knew how to read them. No, they hadn't talked about any names yet, although Izzie *loved* Ezra for a boy and Riley for a girl. They discussed the adorableness of giving girls boys' names and how irritated their mother would be if the baby wasn't named after her own parents. Emmy asked Izzie to describe the baby's current developmental stage and Izzie conked out midsentence.

Emmy pulled a blanket from the hallway closet and covered her sister. Poor thing must be exhausted! Pregnant and working thirty-six-hour shifts and the excitement of telling your sister the big news. As she snuggled up to Izzie and closed her eyes, Emmy could barely contain her own thoughts. Yes, of course she was so excited Izzie was having a baby. Little Isabelle, who sucked her thumb until she was eleven and was deathly afraid of spiders and was so incredibly, brutally, undeniably tone deaf that the whole family used to beg her not to sing in the shower, was going to be someone's *mother.* The little girl who had always mimicked Emmy's mannerisms and begged to be included in her plans would soon be giving birth to her own child. It was almost too weird to comprehend. And when the thought crept in — however fleeting it was — that her younger sister was having a baby and she, Emmy, didn't have so much as a boy she liked e-mailing, well, she pushed it right out of her head. There was no place for that kind of selfish thinking, not when you wanted to support your sister and be the best aunt possible. No, she simply would not allow herself to go there, period.

Kevin gently shook them both awake. "Weren't you two supposed to wake *me?*" he asked, switching on a lamp.

Izzie buried her head under the blanket and moaned. "What time is it?"

"It's almost eleven, and I don't know about you, but there's no way I'm motivating to go out to dinner now." He leaned down and kissed Izzie on the forehead. "Sweetie? You want to come to bed?"

"Aarrgh" was all Izzie could manage.

"Ditto," moaned Emmy. She spent sixty-five hours a week in restaurants and always welcomed the idea of staying home. It just wasn't relaxing to walk into a restaurant — any restaurant — as a customer. Her brain kicked into manager mode and she couldn't help but count the staff-to-patron ratio, observe the efficiency of the bartender, determine how quickly the management was turning over the tables. It was easier just to stay in and forage for something in the fridge. But then she remembered. "Ohmigod, you're having a baby!"

Izzie laughed and kicked her sister in the ribs. "Yeah, we really weren't kidding about that."

"One look at your chipmunk cheeks and it all came rushing back," Emmy grinned.

"Bitch."

"Cow."

Kevin held up his hands in surrender. "I'm out of here. Izzie, just close down the place when you come to bed, okay?"

Izzie turned to Emmy. "Would you hate me for going to sleep now? I know it's, like, practically noon for you, but the all-nighter last night sort of killed me."

Emmy sighed dramatically and shook her head in mock disappointment. "Just because you're pregnant and working round-the-clock shifts delivering babies all night isn't an excuse, you know. Fine, I guess I'll survive on my own for the next eight hours."

Izzie poked Emmy and hugged her. "I'll be more fun tomorrow, I promise."

They tossed Emmy a couple of towels and vanished seconds after saying good night, a move Emmy didn't find entirely unwelcome. She was still a little groggy from her nap, but remembering Izzie's pregnancy made her jittery with nervous energy. Grabbing her cell phone and the latest *Elle,* she rode the elevator to the ground floor and exited the back lobby to the building's dramatically lit and landscaped pool area. Except for two guys in their twenties drinking beer and playing backgammon at one of the far tables, the place was blissfully deserted, so Emmy rolled up her capris and flopped down next to the hot tub, exhaling as she dunked her feet in the steamy water.

She dialed Leigh.

"God, I'm glad to hear from you," Leigh said after picking up on the first ring.

"Why? It's a perfectly good Friday night and you're engaged to one of the hottest guys I've seen in the flesh. Don't you have better things to be doing?"

"Russell's younger sister — the swimmer — is in New York for the weekend, so he stayed at his place with her tonight."

"Got it. That's the one you like, right?"

Leigh sighed. "Relatively speaking, yeah, I guess. She's adorably sweet and friendly and outgoing and all-around nauseatingly perfect. She's pretty much exactly like the other one."

Emmy listened to the familiar sound of Leigh popping a piece of Nicorette from its foil packet and biting into it. She could almost feel her friend's relief. "Better that than some passive-aggressive bitch who's going to make your life a living hell. You could do much worse for sisters-in-law than annoyingly friendly," she said.

"True. But I need something to complain about." Pause, chew, chew. "What'd you do tonight? Oh, wait, I forgot — aren't you in Florida?"

"I sure am. It's Africa hot here."

"How's Izzie? It's been forever since I've seen her."

"Izzie is . . ." Emmy debated how to tell Leigh. She knew she should sound more excited — hell, she *was* excited — but something about the late hour and the hot water, combined with the shock of hearing Izzie's news, had exhausted Emmy. She was genuinely thrilled for Izzie and delighted with the idea of becoming an aunt, but she couldn't shake the feeling that she was about to cry.

"Emmy, is she okay? Is everything all right?"

The sound of concern and sympathy in Leigh's voice triggered something; within moments the tears were coursing down her cheeks.

"Emmy, seriously, talk to me. What's going on with you?"

"Oh, Leigh, I'm a horrible person," she sobbed. "Disgusting. Vile. Loathsome. My only sister, my best friend on earth, is pregnant, and I can't even be happy for her."

"Izzie's *pregnant?*" Leigh asked in her serious voice.

Emmy nodded and then remembered she was on the phone. "Sure is. Due in February. They find out what it is next month."

"Oh, Emmy," Leigh said. "I want to say 'congratulations' and 'I'm sorry' at the same time, so I can only imagine how you feel."

"Of course I knew they would start a family eventually; I just didn't think it would be now. Leigh, she's my *baby* sister!"

"I know, I know," Leigh soothed her. "Just don't think for a single second that you're wrong in anything you're feeling. Of course you're happy for her, but it's understandable that you'd have mixed feelings about it. Anyone would, especially in light of everything that's happened with Duncan. . . ."

This is precisely why Emmy had called Leigh instead of Adriana or — perish the thought — her mother.

"I come down here and spend three straight hours talking about all these stupid failed flings of mine — literally, droning on and on about how I can't bring myself to sleep with strangers — and Izzie is starting a perfect family with her perfect husband at the perfect age. What's wrong with me?" The plaintiveness in her own voice made Emmy start crying all over again. This pity party felt good and, if she gave herself a little slack, deserved. She resolved to be nothing but supportive and wildly enthusiastic in front of Izzie, but that didn't mean she had to fake it for Leigh.

"Emmy, darling, there's nothing in the world wrong with you. You and Izzie are just at different stages right now. It's purely a timing thing — it has nothing to do with who you are as people. And of course I have no doubt that you're going to be a great aunt and sister, but more than that, I just know that you're going to find a great guy, too. A *perfect* guy. Okay?"

"Okay." Emmy sighed. She pulled her feet from the Jacuzzi, rolled her pants up even higher, and plunged them back in. "Distract me. Tell me what's going on with you."

It was Leigh's turn to sigh. "Not too much. Oh, wait, actually I'm lying. Guess who I met last night?"

"Give me a hint."

"Adriana has him pegged as her future husband."

"You met Tobias Baron? Oh my god! Tell me everything! I didn't even know he called her."

"I know, she's been a little weird about this one. Quiet. Almost like she's worried about jinxing it. I guess he went home to LA for a couple weeks and is now back in New York. They went out for the first time last Wednesday, and then again with Russell and me last night, and check this out — she still hasn't slept with him."

Emmy gasped. "No!"

"Really."

"So what's wrong with him? Adriana has never, *ever* gone out with a successful, famous, good-looking guy and not slept with him — and on two dates, no less. Like, *ever*."

"I know." Leigh laughed. "I think she might be taking this whole bet you two made seriously, because it didn't seem like there was anything drastically wrong with him. He was charming in that slightly smarmy Hollywood way, but not offensive. Polite, engaging, and definitely into her."

"And her?" Emmy asked.

"She appeared to worship him. We all went to a late dinner at the Odeon and I'm not sure why we bothered. The two of them couldn't stop nuzzling each other."

"That's so great," Emmy said automatically, supplying the expected response. Of course she should be happy that her commitment-phobic friend had found true love, just like she should be thrilled that her sister was having a baby. But the *shoulds* weren't translating to reality.

"Yeah, well, we'll see. She's going to LA to see him next weekend, so that'll probably be the deal-breaker. She'll screw it up then for sure."

"Leigh! That's not very best friend–like of you." Emmy feigned outrage but was actually delighted.

"Yeah, well, kill me. We both know that girl, and we know she's *nobody's* wife. Not now, and probably not ever. It's sweet that she wants to try, but I'm not sold."

"Fair enough. How are you? How's Russell?" Emmy noticed the two guys packing up their backgammon board and giving each other the not-really-touching backslap good night. The fairer one with longish hair who looked quite young gathered the two empty beer bottles and the board and walked toward the lobby. The darker-haired one, who was about five-eleven, maybe six feet, and wearing a short-sleeved white linen shirt, walked toward her.

"He's good. Not much new to report. Our mothers have gone into full wedding-planning mode, but we're both trying to stay out of it."

"Clearly a good call," Emmy murmured. She was annoyed to see the guy toss his wallet and towel on a nearby chaise and begin to remove his shirt. If the entire pool area was completely deserted, why did he have to be right next to her?

"Yeah, not so interested. Things are crazy enough at work right now, and I just found out I've got to go to Long Island next weekend."

"Hmm," Emmy said, not hearing a word. The guy stripped off his jeans to reveal navy mesh shorts beneath them, and Emmy was intrigued to see that he actually appeared much leaner without his clothes on. Some might even call him skinny, but Emmy preferred to think of him as lithe. She wondered if it was okay to describe a boy as lithe. He had a completely flat stomach and an undeveloped chest, but he was still appealing, in a John Mayer sort of way. Brooding and temperamental. Possibly even sexy, if you could get past the short-sleeved buttondown shirt.

Leigh was saying something about the Hamptons and a new author, but Emmy wasn't paying attention. She was too conscious of the guy listening to her side of the conversation, so instead she said, "Leigh, I'm just going to head inside. Can I call you in a few minutes from upstairs?"

"I'm going to sleep, so let's just talk tomorrow. Russell is —"

"Sounds good, sweetie. Sleep well." Emmy clicked the phone shut without waiting for Leigh's response.

The guy smiled at her — a nice smile, she decided, although not spectacular — and stepped onto the hot tub's top step. He lowered himself in quickly, seeming not even to notice the scalding water, and said, "Aww. Missing your boyfriend?"

She could feel herself blushing, which she hated. "No, uh, that wasn't my boyfriend. I don't have a boyfriend. It was my friend Leigh. From New York."

He grinned, and she wanted to kill him, and then herself. Why did she always talk like this? Was it any of his business who was on the phone, where she was spending the night, whether or not she had a boyfriend? She knew she had serious disclosure problems, but did he have to laugh at her for it?

"Ah, got it. How is Leigh from New York?"

Emmy couldn't tell if he was mocking her or asking seriously, and she found this unnerving. "Leigh from New York is just fine," she said, a bit more haughtily than she intended. And then, as she wiggled her toes in the warm water and watched this boy watch her, she suddenly no longer cared what he thought. "She's having a really busy week at work and doesn't sound nearly as excited about her impending marriage as I think she should be. Which is strange, because her fiancé is fantastic. She just told me that our other friend has fallen head over heels in love with a famous director — and no, I won't tell you his name, because I'm discreet like that — and it's just so unlike her because Adriana doesn't commit to men, she collects them. And to top everything off tonight, I just found out my sister — my *younger* sister — is having a baby."

"Well, it sounds like you and Leigh from New York had a lot to talk about," he said, looking amused but not surprised.

"Anything overly personal or otherwise inappropriate that you want to share with me?" Emmy asked.

He shrugged and waved his hands in a "what you see is what you get" sort of way. "Not really."

"Oh, well, that's fascinating," Emmy said. *Asshole,* Emmy thought. *She* wasn't the one who invaded someone else's personal space, interrupted a phone call, and initiated conversation, was she? Emmy pulled her feet from the water and began to stand up.

"Okay, okay. My name is George. I'm in law school at UM. That guy I was playing backgammon with is my first cousin, but he's

251

really more like a brother. And he just told me that his girlfriend has chlamydia . . . and it's not from him. Let's see, what else? I only got into UM because my father pulled strings, and he never lets me forget it. And probably the dumbest thing I ever did was get married in Vegas one night when I was really, really drunk."

Now this was more like it! He was no Paul in the intelligence department, but he was definitely amusing. Emmy laughed. "Like, Britney-style," she said.

"Like, total Britney-style, right down to the annulment. Although possibly worse, since I'd just met this girl the night before."

"Excellent." Emmy clapped her hands and dunked her legs back in the water. "So tell me, George, what do you think about —"

She stopped midsentence and stared, mouth hanging open in surprise, as George seemed to materialize in front of her. Before she had a moment to think or react, he slid his body between her legs, propped his knees up on the hot tub's bench, and placed his lips on hers. Too surprised to do much of anything, Emmy kissed him back. Instantly, she felt that long-forgotten jolt of excitement run through her, the same one she used to feel in the early days with Duncan but hadn't felt much after the first year.

It wasn't even there with the Australian she made out with in Curaçao — a perfectly nice experience if ever there was one, but she hadn't lost herself enough in the moment to shut down the constant internal monologue. Here, with George, her mind was magically, blessedly blank, with a single exception: She was vaguely aware, in some deep recess of her consciousness, that she had never been kissed like that before.

The gentleness lasted only a few minutes, just long enough for Emmy to lose herself entirely, and then George enveloped her in his arms, pressed his bare chest against her T-shirted one, and tugged her lower lip with his teeth. He buried his face in her neck and for a second — just a second — Emmy was pulled out of the moment and thought, *My god, this is straight out of a bad romance novel.* But the next minute she threw her head back in pleasure, all subtlety gone out the window, and practically begged him to keep kissing the sensitive skin on her neck and shoulders. She wrapped her legs around his waist and ran her fingers through his hair as George breathed heavily, and then, without any warning at all, lifted her butt off the cement, pulled her entire body against his, and lowered them both into the water.

This was, finally, sufficient to rouse Emmy from her dreamlike state.

"George! Oh my god. I'm fully dressed. What are you doing?"

He answered her by pressing his mouth to hers. She continued to protest until he did that thing with her lower lip again. All the moisture from their mouths and the rising steam and the unique sensation of the hot water soaking through her clothes made Emmy feel like she was melting. Floating. Which is why she noticed when George pulled her sopping wet T-shirt over her head — it was, after all, heavy with absorbed water — but didn't completely process this event. Tonight, like always, she was braless, the single perk of being boobless, so they both felt the immediate gratification of bare skin on skin, and it was this moment of intense contact that made Emmy wonder why on earth she had never felt this way before. If it weren't so goddamn fabulous, she would have been humiliated to be thirty years old and not really understand what all the fuss was about. Not that it had ever been anything less than perfectly pleasant with her previous three boyfriends, but *this?* Who needed pleasant when there was *this?*

From that moment on, George ceased to

exist as a separate person, or really as any person at all. He wasn't a law student or the guy playing backgammon or a stranger she'd met minutes earlier; he was merely the body she desperately wanted to be near. It felt like the most natural thing in the world when he expertly removed her capri pants and cotton thong and allowed them to float away, and then, using only one hand while the other held her head to his lips, slid off his own shorts. He lifted her back out of the water and laid her gently on the pavement. The cool surface and air were a relief from all the heat. Emmy forgot she was completely naked in the presence of a total stranger and in view of god knew how many apartments; she didn't worry for a single second about the state of her bikini line (just barely acceptable), the way her face flushed when she was excited (a deep wine color), or how flat her breasts looked when she lay on her back (very). She thought of absolutely nothing except how much she wanted him, and feeling him against her thigh, she maneuvered in every possible manner to get him closer, but he seemed to enjoy teasing her. It was only after what felt like an interminable amount of pressing and kissing and kneading each other that a condom materialized from his shorts pocket and George pushed into her, and Emmy knew, at that moment, she could no longer live without this.

ALL COCKY CONFIDENCE
AND KILLER SMILES

It always baffled Adriana why people hated flying so much. Really, what was so awful about a few hours spent curled under a cashmere travel blanket sipping champagne and watching movies? The food was hideous, of course, even in first class, but when you came equipped with the staples (Zone bars, a Whole Foods mixed-fruit salad, and an Evian mister), it could actually be quite enjoyable. Especially when, like today, your seatmate was a handsome, famous, unattached actor. A TV actor, admittedly, but still a star on NBC's most popular primetime series, a show even Adriana watched. He'd just gone through a very public breakup with a twenty-one-year-old trashy daytime soap star with a knockout body. Adriana had followed the whole tawdry affair in *US Weekly,* right down to reprints of the angry BlackBerry messages they'd exchanged one night from opposite coasts, and she was convinced he could do better. She'd thought it then, but now, sneaking subtle glances at his pretty profile and his sculpted biceps, she was quite positive.

Too bad *she* was taken, Adriana thought with an audible sigh. This caused her seatmate to glance up, a gesture Adriana consciously ignored. Lord knew there was no more challenging species than the ego-inflated entertainer — Adriana had dated enough actors, musicians, comedians, and professional athletes to consider herself an authority — and any girl worth her La Perlas knew that they responded to one and only one thing: a challenge. They were more like children than real people, Adriana always said, and so it stood to reason that the only thing they desperately wanted was what they couldn't have — which is precisely why Adriana pretended he didn't exist.

She had immediately recognized him when he claimed the aisle seat next to her but had provided only a "hmm" when he politely said hello. Filling the time between boarding and takeoff with as many chatty and upbeat phone calls as possible, and switching on her iPod the moment electronic devices were permitted — before *he* could make the decision to drown *her* out — Adriana felt as though she'd done an adequate job so far. And when the cheerful flight attendant asked if she'd like a drink, a request that Mr. TV Actor repeated to Adriana, she smiled only at the flight attendant, ordered another champagne, and once again donned her headphones.

Minutes later he pulled out a script and made a big show about flashing the telltale CAA cover. He began to read, although Adriana got the feeling he was really just flipping the pages for appearance's sake. For her benefit, naturally — she was supposed to be impressed. She rolled her eyes and allowed herself to smile, a gesture he picked up on immediately. Adriana wasn't the least bit surprised. He was, after all, just *waiting* for an excuse to talk to her.

"Are you listening to something funny?" he asked, flashing a pretty decent smile of his own.

Adriana wasn't actually listening to anything at all. The headphones were merely a prop, something that indicated her disinterest in talking, and as she'd predicted, they'd done their job to perfection.

She glanced at him, waited a moment, and slowly pushed the left one off her ear.

"Pardon?" she asked with wide eyes. "Did you say something?"

"I was just wondering if you were listening to something funny. You were laughing. . . ."

Adriana waited a few seconds longer than necessary to throw him off balance and then stepped in to save him. "Oh, did I? No, I was just remembering something really fun." Vague. Suggestive. Mysterious. All Adriana's specialty.

He grinned. Christ, he *was* cute. "Well, I'd love to hear about it. We've got nothing but time," he said, extending his arms. "Four and a half hours, to be precise."

"I might take a rain check," Adriana said. Slowly, she tucked a loose tendril behind her ear, making sure that he got a good look at her delicate, feminine hands, with their elegantly long fingers and pale pink lacquered nails and unblemished skin, and then offered one to him. "Adriana," she said, giving her name a little extra Brazilian inflection.

"Dean," he said, swallowing her hand in his.

Of course she already knew this, but Adriana made no sign of recognition. "So, Dean, what brings you to LA today?" she asked innocently.

"Just some meetings. With some directors and studio people, that sort of thing."

"Oh, you're an aspiring actor! I had no idea." She was laying it on thick now, but it was necessary. Of course no aspiring actor would fly first class, but he'd gotten too famous too fast; if she gave even an inch, his ego would crush them both. Plus, just a hint of recognition on her part would instantly plummet her from a sexy and sophisticated Brazilian New Yorker to a sycophantic starstruck fan, and Adriana would rather die than let *that* happen.

"Uh, no, actually, I —"

"Well, good luck with your audition! Are you nervous?"

His brow furrowed. "It's not an audition. I'm actually already —"

"Dean?" Adriana interrupted sweetly. "Would you mind flagging down the flight attendant for me? I would just adore another glass of bubbly."

He sighed, motioned for the flight attendant, and ordered a Jack and ginger in addition to Adriana's champagne. "Do you live in LA?" he asked, now even more eager to continue the conversation, in order to correct her misconceptions.

"Me? In Los Angeles? Never." Adriana laughed. "I'm just visiting a friend for the weekend." It certainly wasn't any of his business that her "friend" was actually her boyfriend, none other than Toby Baron, a name that would probably send poor Dean's head into a full spin. "Nothing as exciting as a real audition! Is it for TV or a movie?"

His expression indicated defeat. To correct her assumption, he'd basically have to announce who he was — something his ego would never allow. She had him now, she was sure. So sure, she began to count. *Five, four, three, two, one, and . . .*

"Say, Adriana, why don't you let me take you to dinner? You and your friend, if you'd like. LA's not half-bad . . . if you know where to go."

Bingo. She still had it. She might be skirting thirty, but she could still get any man — well, almost any man, but that was probably Yani's fault and not hers — to ask her out in ten minutes or less. Her work here was finished.

"Oh, I *so* wish I could, Dean, but I'm all booked up this weekend." It required superhuman effort to say the words, but she *was* in a monogamous relationship. Just last week Toby had announced he was no longer dating other people, and he expected Adriana wouldn't, either. Her first committed boyfriend — and perfect husband material to boot. Educated at all the right East Coast schools, made a name (and millions) for himself with big hits right out of USC film school, and currently one of Hollywood's most sought-after directors. It gave her great pleasure to imagine her friends' shock when, a mere few months down the road, she announced her engagement. And her mother! The woman would faint, Adriana was sure of it. Only these thoughts gave her the strength to reject this delectable treat of a man sitting next to her.

"Well, I guess we'll just have to do it in New York, then," Dean said, all cocky confidence and killer smiles.

"I guess so," Adriana shot back without a moment's hesitation. *What's a girl supposed to do?* she asked herself. A meal was just a meal, and no one could say she hadn't been the model girlfriend so far. He was just so cute.

They chatted for the rest of the flight, and by the time they deplaned, Adriana knew exactly what she'd do to him in bed. She remembered only at the last possible second that she was supposed to meet Toby in the baggage claim.

"Dean, *querido,* I've got to freshen up a bit. I must say good-bye now."

"I'll wait. I've got a car coming to pick me up, so I'll just drop you at your friend's place," he said, stopping outside a ladies room.

"No, darling, but thank you. You go

ahead." She lowered her lashes and looked up at him through half-closed eyes. "I'd rather we just wait for New York."

"Love it," he said, kissing her cheek. "I'll call you."

"You do that," she purred.

Adriana ducked into the restroom and killed five minutes freshening her makeup, after which she strode confidently to the baggage claim to meet her *boyfriend*. She wasn't distraught to find a uniformed driver holding a sign with her name instead of a smiling Toby. They were going to have the entire weekend together, after all, and she could use a few minutes' break from flirting, game-playing, and being otherwise fabulous. The driver hauled her Goyard trunk onto a luggage cart — rolling suitcases were *so* bourgeois — and handed her an envelope with the Twentieth Century Fox logo in the left corner.

"Mr. Baron sends his apologies for being unable to meet you," the driver said, leading the way to the parking lot.

"Oh, that's quite all right," Adriana said brightly. "I'm just going to nap a bit in the car, if you don't mind."

Once installed in the plush backseat of a late-model town car, however, Adriana found she was too excited to sleep. Two and a half months and she was finally going to see Toby's legendary Hollywood Hills mansion. She read and reread his letter (*Darling Adriana, I'm so sorry to have missed you at the airport, but something unexpected arose at the last minute. I promise to make it up to you. Love, T*), noted his use of *love* — probably just a Hollywood affectation, she thought, since there was no way he actually loved her already . . . was there? — and sighed with pleasure. This whole monogamy thing was a breeze. Why on earth had she resisted for so long? It might not be quite as exciting as dating half a dozen men at once, but it certainly was less exhausting. Plus, as much as she hated to admit, her mother was right. Just this morning on the plane she'd noticed her thighs spreading a touch wider on the leather seat. When she bolted to the lavatory to investigate, she noticed a tiny line near her left eye — a wrinkle. To hell with those hideous fluorescent lights and those so-called security precautions that kept a girl from bringing proper skin-care products on board! A couple more inches of thigh-spread or — god forbid — a full-fledged crow's-foot, and she wouldn't be landing successful directors or hot actors. It was time to get serious and find someone who could care for her properly, and Adriana was extremely pleased with her own progress so far. At twelve years her senior (and a teensy bit dorky, she had to admit), Toby was blessed to have someone as young and gorgeous as Adriana, and he, thankfully, seemed to realize that.

As if on cue, Toby's name flashed across her cell phone's screen. She waited for it to ring three full times and then answered.

"William?" she asked in a confused tone.

"Adriana? Is that you?" Poor Toby sounded baffled and a bit indignant.

"Oh, *Toby, querido!* How are you, sweetheart? What a lovely note you wrote!"

"Who's William?" he barked.

"William who, darling?" She sighed to herself. The whole charade was tiresome, but necessary.

"You thought I was someone named William. When you answered, you said, 'William.' I am asking you again: Who's William?"

"Toby, darling, I just made a silly little mistake! You know how forgetful I can be sometimes. I've never even met a man named William, I promise." Adriana lowered her voice and segued seamlessly from sweet schoolgirl to sexy seductress. "Now tell me, are you excited to see me? Because I am *very* excited to see you."

"I can't wait to get my hands on you," he

breathed into the phone.

Men were so easy to manipulate it was almost criminal. How could there be so many women who didn't understand that with the smallest bit of discipline and a touch of creativity, they could have any man they desired?

Her other line clicked just as the driver pulled onto the 405 and Adriana said, "Toby, I have to take that. Will you meet me at the hotel when you're free?"

"Is that William?" he asked possessively.

"No, darling, I'm sorry to report that it's nothing as exciting as a secret lover. It's actually my mother calling."

"So you admit there *is* a secret lover?"

She laughed gaily and decided to give the poor man a break; besides, it wasn't even challenging anymore. "There is absolutely no secret lover. Just a Brazilian mother in her fifties who wants to tell me all the ways I've been a horrible daughter lately."

"I'll see you soon," he said gruffly and hung up.

Adriana took a deep breath and clicked over. "Mama! So good to hear from you."

"Tell me, Adi, wherever are you these days?"

"In the figurative or the literal sense?"

"Adriana, I am not in the mood for games,"

Mrs. de Souza said.

"Is something wrong?" she asked, worrying not that her father had a heart attack or one of her hundreds of cousins had met an untimely death, only that her parents were considering an extended visit to New York.

"I just got off the phone with Gerard. He said you left this morning with a suitcase the size of a Land Rover."

"You called my doorman to spy on me?" Adriana cried, forgetting that Toby's driver could hear every word. "How dare you!"

"I called *my* doorman," Mrs. de Souza shot back. "Adriana, I thought we just discussed this. Your father did not appreciate your American Express bill last month. It was, I recall, ten thousand on clothes and shoes, and another ten on travel and entertainment. You were ordered to significantly reduce all frivolous expenses, and now you're off flitting around again."

"Mama! I am not 'flitting around' anywhere. I happen to be in Los Angeles." She lowered her voice and covered her mouth with her hand. "I'm seeing a man. A *very* eligible man." She lowered her voice even further, to a whisper. "This is not an expenditure; it's an investment."

Well, this seemed to quiet the old woman. Adriana found it humiliating that she was at her parents' mercy, since it was their apartment. They could arrive anytime, without warning, and stay for as long as they liked. They could question every dollar she spent on clothes or facials or flights simply because they were paying the bills. And now, as a thirty-year-old woman, she was being forced to justify Toby. She was glad no one else was there to witness it.

"Is that so?" her mother asked. "And who, may I ask, is this gentleman?"

"Oh, just a little movie director. You know Toby Baron, don't you?"

Adriana heard her mother gasp and was nearly delirious with pleasure.

"Tobias Baron? Didn't he win an Oscar?"

"He most certainly did. And he was nominated for two others. Yes, he's probably one of the top three most influential directors alive today," Adriana said proudly.

"What is your relationship with Mr. Baron?" her mother asked.

"Oh, he's my boyfriend." Try as she might, she couldn't mask the glee in her voice.

"Boyfriend? Adi, *querida,* you haven't had a boyfriend since seventh grade. Do you mean to tell me you are dating him exclusively?"

"That is exactly what I'm telling you, Mama," Adriana said. "In fact, this visit was all his idea. He said it felt strange not having me be a part of his life in Los Angeles, not knowing his friends and what his home looks like." Again she lowered her voice and bent her head below the driver's seat back. "Which, incidentally, I've heard is incredible."

Truth be told, she'd done more than heard: In her many hours spent researching Toby online, she'd run across an article in *InStyle* that featured a dozen or so interior shots of his bachelor pad. Adriana already knew he preferred a sparse modern look for his four bedrooms and five baths; that his home was Balinese-style with indoor/outdoor showers and gardens, plus separate pavilions for eating, living, and sleeping; that, to top it all off, there was a drop-dead gorgeous infinity pool that looked like it stretched to, well, infinity over the valley below. She had decided sight unseen that with only a few minor adjustments (surely the master bedroom would need a built-in vanity and the immediate installation of proper California Closets), she would be very, very happy living there.

"Well, *querida,* we're willing to overlook it this time. But please do show a bit of restraint in the future. I don't have to tell you that your father has been under a lot of stress lately."

"I know, Mama."

"And behave yourself with Mr. Baron," her mother warned. "Don't forget everything I've taught you."

"Mama! Of course I won't forget."

"If anything, the rules become even more important with wealthy and powerful men. They are the most accustomed to having women fall at their feet, and in turn are the most appreciative when they meet someone who refuses to do so."

"I know, Mama."

"Maintain your mystery, Adriana! I realize you go to bed with men far faster now than we did in my day, but that makes it even more important to remain a bit unattainable in other areas. Do you understand?"

"Yes, Mama. I understand perfectly."

"Because you're not setting a great precedent by flying across the country to see a man," Mrs. de Souza said.

"Mama! It's time. He's been to visit me in New York four times already." So she might have been exaggerating a touch, but her mother didn't have to know that.

"And you're staying at a hotel, I hope?"

"Of course. Even though it would be much less expensive to stay at his house . . ."

The mere suggestion of this sent her mother into a panic. "Adriana! You know better than that! Of course your father and I would appreciate your showing a bit more financial sensitivity, but this particular area is nonnegotiable."

"I was *kidding,* Mama. I have a suite reserved at the Peninsula and I plan to use it."

"And remember: no spending the night! If you absolutely must be intimate with him, then at least have the good sense to leave afterward."

"Yes, Mama." Adriana smiled to herself. Most moms warned their daughters against casual sex for fear of potential disease, disrespect, or reputation. Mrs. de Souza had none of these concerns; she feared only that a false move would irreparably damage the relationship's power balance and make the end goal — Adriana's swift betrothal to a proper man — even more difficult to achieve.

"Well, all right, dear, I'm glad we had this chat. He does sound very promising. Certainly far favorable to the men you usually date . . ."

"I'll call you when I'm back in New York on Sunday, okay?"

Her mother made a *tsk-tsk* sound and said, "Let me see here . . . I'm just checking my book. Ah, yes, we'll be in Dubai then. The cell should work, but it's always better if you just ring the apartment phone. Do you have that number?"

"I have it. I'll call you there. Wish me luck!"

"You don't need luck, *querida.* You're an absolutely stunning girl that any man — Mr. Tobias Baron certainly included — would be delighted to have. Just remember your responsibilities, Adriana."

They kissed over the phone and hung up. Adriana glanced at the driver to see how much he might have heard, but he was talking quietly into his own Bluetooth headset. There was no denying that her mother was exhausting and, judging from Leigh's and Emmy's stories, quite different from most moms, but it was hard to argue with her accomplishments. Mrs. de Souza had turned a phenomenally successful modeling career into a lifetime of luxury and leisure, all provided by a kind, hardworking man who worshipped the ground she walked on. A compound in São Paulo, an oceanfront mansion in Portugal, and gorgeous flats in both New York and Dubai . . . well, that wasn't something to sneeze at. The furs and jewels, cars and staff weren't bad, either, and naturally Mrs. de Souza made very good use of her unlimited and unquestioned spending (a clause she'd insisted upon before the wedding ceremony took place). It might be tiresome enduring the endless "lessons" from her mother, but Adriana did not question the woman's authority on all things men-related.

Adriana gazed out the window as they exited the 405 on Wilshire and weaved their way through Westwood and then Synagogue Alley. It had been a couple years since Adriana had last been in LA, but she was pretty sure the driver had just missed the turnoff to her hotel.

"Sir? Excuse me, I think we just passed the Peninsula. Wasn't that Santa Monica Boulevard?"

He coughed and looked at her through the rearview mirror. "Mr. Baron has redirected us to another location, ma'am."

"Oh, is that so? Well, I'm afraid I have to override him. I would like to go to my hotel first, please." As eager as she was to see Toby's palatial spread, i.e., her future home, she desperately needed to attend to her humidity-limpened hair and sallow travel complexion. And then there was dealing with the whole "ma'am" incident.

Much to her chagrin, and then her shock, the driver ignored her and kept driving. Was she being kidnapped? Was the driver some pervert who lost his mind the second a pretty girl got in the backseat? Should she call Toby? Her mother? The police?

"Sorry, ma'am. It's just that —"

"Can you please not call me 'ma'am'?" Adriana snapped, all thoughts of imminent death gone.

The driver looked appropriately embarrassed. "Of course. *Miss.* I was just saying that I think you'll be pleased with where we're headed."

"Are we going to Madonna's Kabbalah center?" she asked hopefully.

"No, ma'am. Uh, miss."

"Tom's Scientology center?"

"I'm afraid not." He eased the car into a left turn, a beautiful, magical, welcome left turn . . . onto Rodeo Drive.

"Paris's penitentiary?" It was easy to joke now that they were somewhere so delightful.

The driver sidled up to a curb that stated NO STANDING, turned off the car, and retrieved Adriana. He offered her his arm and said, "If you'll follow me . . ."

He led her past a Bebe store (on Rodeo!) and she panicked for a moment until she saw the sign. Adriana had to remind herself to breathe. She wanted to sing and cry and scream all at the same time. *Ohmigod, ohmi-*

god, ohmigod, she thought, forcing herself to take little sips of air. It couldn't be. Could it? A quick scan of the boutique's stunning window displays confirmed it was true: They had just entered the hallowed halls of the Oscar Adorner Extraordinaire, the guru himself: Harry Winston.

"Oh, my," she gasped audibly, forgetting momentarily that both the driver and a haughty-looking saleswoman were watching her intently.

"Yes, it can be overwhelming," the saleswoman said, nodding her head in faux understanding. "Is this your first time?"

Adriana collected herself. She'd be damned if she was going to let this woman patronize her. She flashed her most brilliant smile and reached out to touch the woman's arm. "First time?" Adriana asked with an amused little laugh. "How I wish. I was just a bit taken aback, since I thought we were headed to Bulgari."

"Ah," the woman murmured, clearly not believing a word. "Well, I'm afraid you'll just have to make do here today, now, won't you?"

Ordinarily it would take every ounce of willpower in Adriana's reserve to refrain from saying something nasty, but something about all the surrounding sparkle seemed to take the fight right out of her. Instead, she smiled. "Actually, I'm not quite sure what I'm here for. . . ."

The woman was probably in her late forties, and even Adriana had to admit that she looked pretty good for her age. Her navy suit was feminine, flattering, and professional, and her makeup was expertly applied. She extended a hand toward a little seating area and motioned to Adriana to take a seat.

The driver discreetly slipped away as Adriana settled herself onto an antique velvet divan. It was overstuffed and inviting in all its plushness, but she could only manage to perch carefully on one end if she didn't want to collapse backward. A plump woman in an old-fashioned maid's uniform set down a tray of tea and cookies.

"Thank you, Ama," the saleswoman said without a glance.

"*Gracias,* Ama," Adriana added. "*Me gustan sus aretes. ¿Son de aquí?*" I like your earrings. Are they from here?

The maid blushed, unaccustomed to being addressed by clients. "*Sí, señora, son de aquí. El señor Winston me los dió como regalo de boda hace casi veinte años.*" Yes, miss, they are. Mr. Winston gave them to me as a wedding present nearly twenty years ago.

"*Muy lindos.*" Adriana nodded approvingly

as Ama blushed again and disappeared behind a heavy velvet curtain.

"How do you speak such fluent Spanish?" the saleswoman asked, more out of politeness than any genuine curiosity.

"Portuguese is my first language, but we all learn Spanish as well. Sister languages," Adriana explained with patience, even though she could barely contain her excitement.

"Ah, how interesting."

No, it's not, Adriana thought, wondering if she was about to set some sort of time record for having a man propose to her. Toby couldn't actually be about to propose . . . could he? No, it was ridiculous; they'd only just met at the beginning of the summer. Far more likely was that he'd started feeling a bit anxious about her imaginary "secret lover" and had decided — correctly, of course — that a little bauble might swing the pendulum in his favor.

"It's unusually cool today, isn't it?" the woman was saying.

"Hmm." *Enough with the chitchat already!* Adriana wanted to scream. *I. Want. My. Present!*

"Well, dear, you're probably wondering why you're here," she said.

Understatement of the century, Adriana thought.

"Mr. Baron has asked me to present you with" — as if on cue, a sixtyish gentleman in a three-piece suit with a jeweler's loupe around his neck appeared and presented the saleswoman with a small velvet-lined tray, which she held out to Adriana — "these."

Splayed perfectly on the black velvet lay a pair of the most beautiful earrings Adriana had ever seen. More than beautiful, actually — absolutely stunning.

The saleswoman gingerly touched one of them with a manicured fingernail and said, "Lovely, aren't they?"

Adriana exhaled for the first time in over a minute. "They're exquisite. Sapphire drops, just like the ones Salma Hayek wore to the Oscars," she breathed.

The woman's head snapped up and she stared at Adriana. "My, my, you do know your jewelry, don't you?"

"Not really," Adriana said, laughing, "but I do know *your* jewelry." It was a wonder — no, it was downright astonishing — that Toby had remembered her admiring Salma's Oscar earrings in an old magazine. That alone was incredible enough, but the fact that he then saved the photo and found an identical pair, two months after the fact, was almost incomprehensible.

"Well, actually, these are the *exact* ones Ms. Hayek wore to the Oscars. They were lent to her and we've received many requests for them since then. However" — she paused for dramatic effect — "they now belong to you."

"Ohhhhhh," Adriana breathed, momentarily forgetting herself once again and fumbling to try them on.

Fifteen minutes later, with the celebworthy sapphire drop earrings firmly in place and a bottle of Evian in hand, Adriana leapt into the backseat of the Town Car. She was pleased with herself, not just for her new acquisition but for what it represented: a steady, committed boyfriend who adored her and showered her with love and affection (and Harry Winston). She finally understood why all the other girls so yearned for this kind of stability. Who needed hundreds of men and all the headaches that came with them when you could find just one who had everything? Sure, Dean the TV actor was delicious, there was no denying it, but how delicious would he be when he hadn't worked in five years and was living in some actor dorm in West Hollywood? There was no denying that she had very much enjoyed the surgeon from Greenwich and the Israeli spy and the Dartmouth fraternity boy. She had savored each and every one of them and, truth be told, countless others. But that was before, back when she was a mere child, not a grown woman with a grown woman's desires. Adriana fingered the dangly blue gems and smiled to herself. This was going to be the perfect weekend, she was sure of it.

"You don't get paid enough to make house calls," Russell murmured as he stroked Leigh's back gently, with just his fingertips.

"You're telling me," she said, praying he wouldn't stop. She snuggled in closer against his wide, warm, nearly hairless chest and buried her head in his underarm. She had always loved their cuddling, and even now it encouraged her; she might not want to have sex with Russell, but at least she wasn't repulsed by his touch. Leigh remembered Emmy going through that with Mark, the boyfriend before Duncan. She claimed the sex had never been great, not even in the beginning, but things grew steadily worse — mostly in Emmy's mind, she admitted — until she recoiled in disgust every time he tried to touch her. The story had always haunted Leigh, someone who understood perfectly what it felt like to shrink away from a boyfriend's kiss, but that was

281

precisely why she found these snuggle sessions so reassuring. She wouldn't *want* to lie naked in bed with Russell, spoon with him and enjoy his touch, if there was something wrong . . . would she? No, it was a clear indication that everything was as it should be. What woman didn't have shifts in sexual desire at times? According to the article in *Harper's Bazaar* she'd read at the nail salon the week before, a woman's libido was a tenuous thing, affected by stress, sleeping patterns, hormones, and about a million other factors she couldn't control. With a little time and a lot of patience — something Russell had exhibited in spades until very recently — *Bazaar* swore that most women would return to normal. She would simply wait it out.

"So what's he like?" Russell asked. "Is he really as crazy as everyone makes him out to be?"

Leigh wondered when Russell had Googled Jesse. "What do you mean? He seems like . . . I don't know, like an *author*. They're all nuts."

Russell rolled over on his back and slung his arm over his eyes to block out the early-morning sun that streamed in around the sides of the window shade. "Yeah, but he sold five million copies and won the Pulitzer and then vanished. For *six years*. Was it really a drug problem? Or did he just lose it?"

"I have no idea. We've only had one lunch; he hasn't exactly confided in me." Leigh tried to keep the exasperation out of her voice but it wasn't easy. "Look, I'm not dying to go out there, either."

Which was true enough. There were definitely things Leigh would rather do with two days out of the office than drive to the Hamptons right before Labor Day weekend.

"I know, sweetheart. Just don't let him push you around, okay? He may think he's some hotshot, but *you're* still *his* editor. You call the shots, right?"

"Right," she said automatically, although she was really thinking how much it rankled her when Russell sounded so much like her father. Mr. Eisner had said those exact words to her the night before in what was probably intended to be a helpful pregame pep talk, but which to Leigh had sounded like a condescending lecture from the consummate professional to the flailing amateur.

Russell kissed her forehead, pulled on a pair of boxers, and strode to the bathroom. After turning the shower to its hottest setting, he headed to the kitchen, closing the bathroom door behind him. There he'd wait for the bathroom to get all hot and steamy — just the way he liked it — while he made his daily power breakfast: soy protein shake, fat-free yogurt, and three scrambled egg whites. This ritual irritated Leigh beyond description. *What about all that wasted water?* she asked him over and over again, but he merely reminded her that water was included in the monthly maintenance fee she paid, so it didn't particularly matter. It was just one of the things about him she found utterly maddening. She completely understood the need for him to wear a full face of TV makeup once a week when he recorded the show, but she loathed watching him remove it. He used her makeup remover and pads and swabbed so delicately under his eyes and around his nose, and although she couldn't quite pinpoint why, she found it revolting. Not quite as revolting as when he forgot to remove it and she ended up with pillowcases smeared with man foundation, but still — the whole thing was just gross.

She chided herself for being so rigid and intolerant and took a deep, relaxing breath. It was only nine o'clock on a sunny Thursday morning and already she felt like she'd been awake for forty-eight hours and lived through a world war. Exhausted yet still simmering with low-level anxiety, Leigh hauled herself from bed and ducked into the steam-drenched bathroom.

She managed to throw on a pair of white jeans and pack everything else before Russell finished his own shower, so she blew him a kiss through the bathroom door and quickly left. She rolled her small suitcase to Hertz on East Thirteenth Street and, after accepting all the insurance offered — better safe than sorry! — Leigh grabbed a large iced latte from Joe, popped two pieces of Nicorette, and slid into the driver's seat of her red Ford Focus. The trip took less time than she'd planned; in a little over two hours she pulled into the parking lot of a restaurant called Estia's. It was shaped like a little clapboard cottage, just as Jesse had described it; she went inside to use the bathroom and gulp another cup of coffee before calling him.

He answered on the fourth ring.

"Jesse? It's Leigh. I'm at Estia's."

"Already? I wasn't expecting you until this afternoon."

She felt her blood pressure rise even higher. "Well, I'm not sure why, considering we spoke just yesterday and I told you that I'd be arriving between twelve and twelve-thirty."

He laughed. His voice sounded like he'd just woken up. "Yeah, but who's ever actually on time? When I say noon, I really mean three."

"Oh, really?" she asked. "Because when I say noon, I actually *mean* noon."

He laughed again. "Got it," he said. "I'm going to get dressed, and I'll be right there. Have a coffee. Try to relax. We'll get right to work, I promise."

She ordered yet another coffee and flipped to the Thursday Style section someone had left on the counter.

She heard his entrance before she saw him, since she was staring fixedly at the newspaper, pretending to be completely absorbed in an article on natural boar-bristle hairbrushes. All around her, the restaurant patrons — all locals and, from the look of it, not associates of the Billy Joel set — waved and called out their hellos. One particularly crusty-looking old guy in workman's overalls and a sewn-on name tag — the original, not one of the retro ones on sale in the Bloomingdale's young men's department — that read SMITH, raised his coffee mug and winked at Jesse.

"Morning, sir," Jesse said, clapping the man on the back.

"Chief," the man said with a nod and a swig of coffee.

"Still on for Monday night?"

The man nodded again. "Monday."

Jesse made his way down the breakfast counter, greeting each and every person along the way, before taking the empty seat next to Leigh. Although she couldn't pinpoint exactly why, Leigh thought he looked better today than he had at either of their previous meetings. Still not hot or even handsome in the conventional sense, Jesse again looked casually rumpled and, as stupid as it sounded, *cool*. It was partly the way he dressed — a slim-cut vintage plaid shirt with Levi's that looked custom-cut for his body — but it was also something more than that, something in the way he carried himself. Everything about him screamed "effortless," but unlike the self-conscious grunge of the nineties or deliberate bed-head hair, Jesse's look was genuine.

She realized she was staring.

"What's going on Monday?" she asked quickly; it was the first thing that came to mind.

"Not into the usual niceties, huh?" Jesse asked with a smile. "Me, neither. Monday is poker night and it's Smith's turn to host. He lives in a minuscule studio apartment above the village liquor store, so he arranged for all of us to meet at the East Hampton Airport — he's a flight mechanic there. We're going

287

to play in the hangar, which I'm rather looking forward to. It will be doubly festive since we'll be celebrating both the end of summer and the end of the Great Asshole Invasion — at least until next year."

Leigh shook her head. Maybe all the gossip and tabloids were right, and Jesse really had lost his mind. A few years earlier he was jet-setting on international book tours, gorging himself on the world's finest food and clothes and women, using his newfound literary fame to chase every next hot party, and now he was sequestered away in this working-class neighborhood of eastern Long Island, playing poker in deserted airplane hangars with mechanics? The new book had better be *damn* good, that's all Leigh knew.

As if reading her mind, Jesse said, "You're desperate to get started, aren't you? Just say it."

"I *am* desperate to get started. I'm only out here for two days and a night and I still haven't the first clue what you're working on."

"Let's go, then." He slid a $10 bill to the woman behind the counter and led the way outside. The instant his feet hit gravel he lit a cigarette. "I'd offer you one, but something tells me you're not a smoker."

He didn't wait for her to answer; instead,

he jumped into his Jeep.

"Follow me. The house is only a few minutes from here, but there are lots of turns."

"You sure I shouldn't check into the hotel first?" Leigh asked, twisting a piece of her ponytail around her finger. She was staying at the historic American Hotel in Sag Harbor village, a place that was just as famous for its clubby, wood-paneled, old-fashioned hospitality as it was for its mammoth martinis.

Jesse leaned out his window. "You're welcome to try, but I called on my way over here and they insist that check-in isn't until three. I'd be more than happy to wait till then, trust me. . . ."

"No, no, let's get moving. I'll take a break this afternoon to check in and then we can get back to work."

"Sounds like a dream." He rolled up the window and threw the Jeep into reverse, the back wheels kicking up dust in his wake.

Leigh rushed to her rental and pulled out behind him. He turned left onto Sagg Road and drove straight through the village and past the hotel, which he indicated to Leigh with a wave in his rearview. The main street was absolutely adorable. There were quaint boutiques, family-owned restaurants, and local fresh-food markets interspersed with the occasional art gallery and wine shop. Parents pulled kids and vegetables in red wagons. Pedestrians had the right of way. People seemed to be smiling for no reason. Everyone had a dog.

They drove through town and toward the bay, which was fronted by a marina straight out of central casting, and then over a bridge before careening back into the winding, wooded roads. Jesse's driveway was half a mile long and unpaved and the glints of light that darted through the trees gave it an ethereal feel. As they drove a bit farther, Leigh spotted what looked like a guesthouse off the side of the path. It was a small white cottage with blue shutters and a charming little porch for rocking and reading. Another five hundred yards beyond that was an elaborate — and brand-new — children's outdoor play area. It wasn't one of the brightly colored plastic Fisher-Price ones, either; rather, it appeared almost hand-carved from a rich mahogany and included a rock-climbing wall, tree house, canopied cupola, sandbox, kiddie-sized picnic table, and two slides. This left Leigh momentarily breathless. She knew Jesse had a wife (although he had given Leigh the impression that she wasn't in the Hamptons), but she had never, *ever* envisioned him as a father. Of course it made complete sense — it would almost be strange if he weren't — but something about seeing proof of this made her feel vaguely irritated and a little disappointed.

By the time they reached the house, her heart had started to beat faster and her breath began to shorten in the telltale signs of anxiety. In front of her, Jesse climbed out of his Jeep and approached her car. She felt a sweat break out on her forehead, and she wished she could be parked on her couch, reading a manuscript or chatting with Russell about his upcoming interview with Tony Romo. It'd be worth it even if he wanted to have sex *and* watch SportsCenter *and* the upstairs neighbor was hosting a dance party full of leg brace–wearing guests. Anywhere but right here, right now.

Jesse opened Leigh's car door for her and led her down a walkway to the front porch, a wide expanse of open space decorated with only a hammock and a love-seat swing. Beside the swing was an empty bottle of Chianti and a single dirty wineglass.

"Are your children here? I'd love to meet them," Leigh lied.

Jesse looked around the porch, appearing confused for a minute, and then smiled knowingly, like he could read her mind. "Oh, you mean the playground? It's for my nephews — *not* my own."

Something about the way he said this seemed definitive; even though she told herself she didn't care either way — and despite being well aware that it was rude and way too personal — she pushed it. "Does that mean you just happen not to have kids, or you don't want them ever?"

He laughed and shook his head while he opened the front door. "Jesus Christ, you say whatever you're thinking, don't you?"

In for a penny, in for a pound. "Well?" she asked.

"No, I don't want children. Not now, and not ever."

Leigh held up her hands in mock defense. "Looks like I hit a nerve."

Jesse tried to suppress his smile, but Leigh caught a glimpse of it anyway. "Anything else you'd like to know? How I'm eating, how I'm sleeping?"

"Well, then, we got the kid thing out of the way. So . . . how are you eating and sleeping?" She grinned broadly and felt her anxiety begin to dissipate. She'd forgotten how fun it was to banter with him.

His eyes were bloodshot and his face was unshaven and pale. Even his hair looked a little dull — not dirty or greasy, exactly, just uninspired. He struck an exaggerated modeling pose — hip jutted out and lips pursed — and said, "You tell me. How do you think I'm eating and sleeping?"

"Like shit," Leigh said without a moment's hesitation.

Jesse laughed and pushed the door open. "Welcome to my humble abode."

Leigh looked around. She took in the creaky floors and the gigantic, well-worn farmhouse table and the crocheted blanket flung haphazardly across the sofa and, although she had already fallen in love with the whole house based on this first room, sighed loudly for effect and said, "Jesse, Jesse, Jesse . . . did you really spend *all* your earnings on cocaine and hookers, like the tabloids claim?"

He shook his head. "Cocaine, *booze,* and hookers."

"I stand corrected."

"Okay, then, should we get started? I mostly work out back, through the living room, so why don't you get set up there and I'll bring drinks." He pulled open the fridge and bent sideways to look inside. "Let's see, I've got beer, some shitty white wine, some not-so-shitty rosé, and Bloody Mary mix. I think it's a bit early for red, don't you?"

"I think it's a bit early for any of it. I'll take a Diet Coke."

Jesse snapped his fingers and pulled a half-full bottle of Ketel from the freezer. "Excellent choice. One Bloody Mary, coming right up."

She already knew there was no point in arguing with him, and besides, he looked like he needed a drink to take the edge off last night's hangover. Leigh vaguely remembered what that was like. Back in her postcollege years in the city, when her body allowed her to drink until three and still be at work by nine, she'd occasionally had a few sips of wine with breakfast to ease the pain. She remembered all the nights out with Emmy and Adriana, traipsing across the city, from happy hour to birthday party, drinking too much, smoking too much, and kissing too many nameless, faceless boys. God, that seemed like forever ago . . . the seven, eight years felt like a lifetime. Now the heels were never quite so high (how had she ever worn something so uncomfortable?) and the packed bars had given way to more civilized restaurants (thank god) and she couldn't remember the last time she'd stayed up all night for any reason other than work or insomnia. But, Leigh reminded herself, some of those happy memories must have been revisionist history. How could they not have been? Back then there was no prestigious job, no independently owned and operated apartment, and certainly no doting fiancé.

Leigh wandered through the skylight-lit living room and opened the sliding glass door to reveal one of the most welcoming outdoor spaces she'd ever seen. It wasn't a backyard so much as an oasis in the middle of the forest. Huge towering oaks and maples created an enclosed area that was covered with inviting, but not overly manicured, green grass. A small gunite pool — so small that perhaps it was only a plunge pool or a hot tub — was flanked by two chaises, a table, and chairs, and seemed to blend into the background, allowing one's attention to focus on the real draw: a perfect little pond, maybe twenty feet by thirty, with a floating, cushioned sun dock and the simplest of wooden rowboats tethered to the shore. Behind the pond, at the very edge of the property, tucked under a cluster of leafy trees, was a Balinese-style teak daybed, the kind that easily fits two people and provides shade from a roof atop its four posts. It was all Leigh could do not to walk directly to the daybed and collapse; she wondered how, with so beautiful and relaxing a place, Jesse ever got anything done.

"Not bad, huh?" he asked, stepping onto the stone patio and handing her a Bloody Mary complete with celery stalk and lime.

"My god, this place doesn't look like much from the front — or the inside, really — but this . . . *this* is gorgeous."

"Thanks. I think."

"No, really, have you thought about having this photographed? I can so picture it in one of those design magazines, what are they called? *Dwell*. It's perfect for *Dwell*."

He ran his hands through his hair and swigged from his bottle of Budweiser. "Unlikely."

"No, really, I think it could be —"

"No reporters or photographers in my home, *ever*."

"I hear that," Leigh agreed, although she couldn't help but remember the spread of Russell's apartment she'd seen in *Elle Décor* before they'd ever even met. It was included in an article on the city's best bachelor pads and featured Russell's ultramodern TriBeCa loft as its pièce de résistance. At the time Leigh had pored over the pictures of the kitchen, which looked industrial enough to serve as a catering hall; the wenge platform bed, which was so low it may as well have been a mattress on the floor; and the bathroom, which looked like it was pulled directly from a W Hotel and plunked down in the middle of the apartment. She'd read that the place was twenty-two hundred square feet of completely open space, huge windows, and hardwood floors lacquered black, but it wasn't until their third date that Leigh saw it for herself. Since then, she'd spent as little time there as humanly possible; all that steel and black lacquer and all those sharp corners made her even more nervous than usual.

Jesse took a seat at the table and motioned for Leigh to claim the one opposite him. After another slow, deliberate pull on his beer, he took a deep breath, undid the clasp on a tatty canvas messenger bag, and pulled a phonebook-sized sheaf of paper from its center. He presented this to Leigh with both hands, the way an Asian waiter might present a check or a business card. "Be gentle," he said quietly.

"I thought you wanted honesty, not gentleness?" She took the manuscript and placed it in front of her, not sure how she could resist tearing into it for another moment. " 'No one's straight with me, I'm coddled and yessed and I just want an editor who's going to tell it like it is.' " She imitated the speech she was told he'd made in their first meeting in Henry's office.

Jesse lit a cigarette and said, "That was all bravado. Bullshit. I'm a complete baby who can barely handle constructive criticism, much less a thorough slashing."

Leigh pressed her palms into the table and smiled. "Well, that, Jesse Chapman, makes you exactly like every other author I know. I haven't had any God complexes yet, but a debilitating lack of self-confidence coupled with constant self-doubt and self-flagellation? *That* I can handle."

Jesse held up his cigarette in a "stop" motion. "Whoa, let's not get ahead of ourselves here. That" — he pointed to the manuscript — "is this year's, if not this *decade's,* finest contribution to literature — of that much I'm sure. I was just requesting a little sensitivity on the off-chance you should run across a paragraph or two that's not to your liking."

"Ah, yes, of course. A paragraph or two. I'm sure there won't even be that much." Leigh nodded in mock seriousness.

"Excellent. I'm glad we're on the same page." He paused and peered at her and then said, "Well?"

"Well what?"

"Aren't you going to read it?"

"I will once you leave me alone."

Jesse's eyes widened. "Alone? I didn't know that was standard procedure."

Leigh laughed. "You know as well as I do that nothing about this is standard procedure."

Jesse feigned a look of innocence. "I have no idea what you're talking about."

"Standard would be my boss editing your book, not me. Standard would be me having read your manuscript — or even just an outline and a sample chapter — before driving two and a half hours to meet with you. Standard would —"

Jesse held up his hands as though to block himself from the onslaught and stood up. "I'm bored," he announced. "Holler if you need anything. I'll be upstairs taking a nap." Without another word, he disappeared inside the house.

It was a moment or two before Leigh realized her fingernails were digging into her palms. Did he try to irritate her, or was it something that just came naturally for him? Was he kidding about being over-sensitive to criticism, or thinking this book — whatever it was about — really was the second coming, or was that all just a facade? He could be so charming and irreverent and witty, and then — *bam!* — a switch flipped and he reverted right back to the cocky asshole everyone reported him to be.

She checked her watch and saw that she had another hour to kill until she could check into the hotel, so with a sip of Bloody Mary and a lustful eye toward the pack of cigarettes Jesse had left behind, she began to read. The novel began at the Foreign Correspondents' Club in Phnom Penh and included a displaced, hard-drinking American narrator that Leigh couldn't help thinking felt very familiar. Not plagiarism familiar, just a bit hackneyed: *The End of the Affair, The Quiet American,* and *Acts of Faith* came immediately to mind. This alone didn't much worry her — it was easy enough to change — but as she read the next few pages, and then the pages after those, her concern increased. The story itself — about a twentysomething kid who stumbles into best-sellerdom with his very first book — was compelling in a wonderfully voyeuristic way; not surprising, considering the author's firsthand knowledge. It was the actual writing that worried her: It was flat, unoriginal, even droning at times. Totally un-Jesse-like. She took a deep breath and reminded herself it could have been far worse. Had the story itself been a disaster, she wouldn't have even known where to start.

By the time Jesse shuffled back an hour later, bleary-eyed but having traded in his beer for a bottle of water, Leigh was beginning to realize how very out of her league she was. How on earth was *she,* Leigh Eisner, junior editor and until now virgin editor of any best-selling author, supposed to tell one of the most literarily and commercially successful authors of his generation that, in its current incarnation, his newest effort wasn't going to top any bestseller lists? The answer, she realized, was simple: She wouldn't.

Jesse lit a cigarette and slid the pack to her across the table. "Live a little. You've been eyeing them all day."

"I have?"

He nodded.

So she did. Without another second's consideration and only a fleeting thought of how disappointed Russell would be if he knew, she plucked one from the pack, placed it between her lips, and leaned eagerly into the match Jesse held out. She was surprised that the first inhale burned her lungs and tasted so harsh, but the second and third were much smoother.

"A whole year down the drain," she said ruefully before inhaling again.

Jesse shrugged. "You don't strike me as someone who overindulges in booze or drugs or food or . . . anything, really. If smoking a cigarette every now and then is going to make you happy, why not just enjoy it?"

"If I could only smoke one every now and then, I would," Leigh said. "The problem is that I have one and ten minutes later I'm working my way through a pack."

"Ah, so Ms. Put Together has a weakness after all." Jesse smiled.

"Great, I'm happy my addiction struggles amuse you."

"I don't find it so much amusing as endearing." He paused and appeared to think for a moment. "But yes, I suppose it's amusing, too."

"Thanks."

Jesse motioned toward the manuscript and said, "Any thoughts so far, or is it not *standard procedure* to discuss it until you're finished?" He swigged from his water bottle.

Relieved he'd given her an out when she hadn't yet thought of one herself, Leigh said vaguely, "I'm only seventy pages in, so I'd rather wait until I've finished." She coughed.

Jesse peered at her with an intensity Leigh found discomfiting. He seemed to be studying her face for clues, and after nearly a full minute, she could feel herself start to blush. Still, he didn't say anything.

"So, I should, uh, probably get checked into the hotel," Leigh said, dropping her cigarette into the makeshift ashtray Jesse had made from his Poland Spring bottle.

"Yes."

"Should I come back here afterward, or would you rather meet somewhere else? The hotel lobby? A cafe? How does four, four-thirty sound?" The tension was palpable and unnerving; Leigh had to remind herself to stop talking.

"Come back here, but not until you've finished the manuscript."

Leigh laughed but quickly saw that Jesse wasn't kidding. "It'll take me another five, six hours minimum to read it all the way through. We could get started talking about timing, at least." When Leigh realized she sounded like she was asking his permission, she mustered up her most authoritative voice and said, "Henry made it very clear that this deadline is nonnegotiable."

"Leigh, Leigh, Leigh," he said, sounding somehow disappointed. "Every deadline is negotiable. Please read the manuscript. Come back whenever you're finished. As you may imagine, I am not early to bed."

She shrugged in a halfhearted attempt to convey casualness and gathered her things. "If you want to be up until all hours, it's fine with me."

He lit another cigarette and leaned back in his chair. "Don't be cross, Leigh. It's going to take us a little while to find our process. Be patient with it."

Leigh snorted and, without thinking, said, "'Find our process'? 'Be patient with it'?

What, did you learn that at one of your ashrams, post-rehab? Wait, are you still recovering?"

For a fleeting moment he looked as though he'd been slapped, but he recovered quickly and grinned. "Glad to hear at least you've read up on me," he said with a smoky exhale.

"I'm sorry, I didn't mean it to —"

"Please, Leigh, run along now." He waved his cigarette toward the door. "I haven't had an editor in many years, so forgive me if I'm a bit unwieldy at first, will you?"

Leigh nodded.

"Excellent. I look forward to seeing you later. No need to call first; just come whenever. Happy reading."

As she navigated her rental down Jesse's unpaved driveway, Leigh realized that she had no real idea if their first meeting had been a decent jumping-off point or an unmitigated disaster. But she suspected, with a sinking feeling in the pit of her stomach, it was probably the latter.

COUNT HIM AS
SOUTH AMERICA

Emmy removed the tray from her toaster oven and carefully flipped each of the pita chips with her fingertips, alternately delighted at their delicate crispiness and irritated that she couldn't make a bigger batch in a proper oven. Her friends were coming over for their twice-yearly visit to her apartment, and rather than whip up a feast for them (probably Italian, a good scaloppine with a side of perfectly al dente pasta), she was baking pita chips in a toaster oven that took up her entire "counter space" and mashing chickpeas in a bowl on her lap. Emmy had always comforted herself with the knowledge that she and Duncan would one day have a new place together, a place with a huge Viking stove and a Sub-Zero fridge and cabinets filled with real stainless steel pots, but that dream had vanished when he did.

She could barely believe they'd broken up

a full five months ago. Even weirder was how completely they — or, if she was going to be really honest, Duncan — had severed contact. Although Emmy hadn't told Izzie or the girls, she had called him pretty regularly during the first few months and had even showed up at his apartment, at least until he'd changed the locks. After that humiliation she managed to tone things down, and by midsummer Emmy had pretty much stopped calling, save for one little relapse after the Paris/Paul rejection. Oh, and there *was* that e-mail. It was embarrassing, but Emmy reassured herself that these things happened. She hadn't intended to write to him, but she had come home one night right before she left for Florida, slightly buzzed from a work-related wine tasting, and sat down at her computer to surf for a bit before going to sleep. Remembering it was her friend Polly's thirtieth birthday, she opened her e-mail and typed *P* in the To field, and sure enough, Duncan's e-mail address popped into place (she had him saved in her address book under "Pumpkin"). She considered this for just a moment before forging forward and crafting a fake e-mail to Paul, the guy she'd met at the Costes who had flatly rejected her and whose e-mail address she most certainly didn't have.

Hey baby,

Glad to hear you're having such a great time in St. Tropez, although I'm missing you here. Work is crazy right now, but I guess that's to be expected with a new job that requires so much traveling. It's just so hard to be away from you! Thank you so much for the gorgeous little French negligee you sent. It's so lacy and pretty and s-e-x-y. I can't WAIT to model it for you. Only one more week until I join you there . . .

xoxo E

She hit Send and felt a thrill of excitement when she saw Duncan's name in her Sent box: If that didn't elicit a response, nothing would. It had taken two full days for him to respond, and even then, it was disappointing. He'd merely replied, "I think you accidentally sent this to the wrong person," and had signed off with a smiley face. An emoticon! It was too insulting for words, and she immediately regretted the whole thing. No jealous questions about the identity of Emmy's secret lover, no reference to her new job, not even a wry acknowledgment about her sexy nightie or (supposed) upcoming trip to the South of France. That was the final straw. It had been nearly two months since that mortifying exchange and Emmy hadn't contacted him once. More to the point, she was happy to realize she hadn't so much as *thought* about him in the two weeks since she'd had hot, random sex with George. Which obviously meant one and only one thing: Much more hot, random sex was required.

Her buzzer rang at exactly eight and Emmy braced herself for Otis's imminent caw. Sure enough, he shook himself awake and squawked, "Who is it? Come on up! Who is it? Come on up!"

She sighed, slipped on her flip-flops, and headed for the stairs. The mechanism that allowed her to buzz people in was broken and although the building did have an elevator circa 1925, it had taken only one afternoon trapped inside it three years earlier to convince Emmy that the stairs were a much better option. She appreciated that Adriana and Leigh made the effort to come to her place twice a year or so — especially considering they lived in the same building and both had apartments that were significantly more comfortable than hers — but she just ended up feeling self-conscious about the size of her studio and guilty for subjecting everyone to a five-floor climb, after which they had to sit on the floor and endure a whole night of the hideous parrot's insults.

"Hi!" she called cheerfully, forgetting her reservations when she swung open the building door and saw the girls sitting on her stoop. The air was warm for October, but it was filled with smoke. "Whoa! What do I see here?"

Adriana elbowed Emmy in the side and, grinning, motioned toward Leigh. "Check this out."

Sure enough, Leigh was stamping out a cigarette as she exhaled a last plume of smoke.

"Leigh! What happened? You were doing so well!" Emmy cried.

"*Were* being the operative word."

"What happened?"

"Jesse Chapman happened," Adriana sang with obvious pleasure.

The girls began the single-file trudge upstairs.

Emmy turned around and looked at her friends. "Why is your relapse Jesse Chapman's fault?"

Leigh sighed melodramatically. "I always suspected you guys didn't listen to a word I said."

"Oh, save the drama," Adriana said. "We listen to every single Chicken Little work-related melodrama of yours. It's just lucky for us that Jesse Chapman happens to be a little more interesting than your usual lunatic authors."

"Wait! Back to the 'Jesse Chapman happened.' What does that mean?" Emmy asked. They had finally reached her apartment; Emmy was pleased to see that even though her friends were both panting and breathless, she felt perfectly fine.

"Nothing happened. You make it sound like there's something scandalous going on, which I assure you, there is not. He's just a handful."

Adriana smirked. "I'll bet he is."

Emmy motioned for the girls to claim a cushion and began pouring the red wine she had opened before their arrival. "Speaking of sex with strangers . . ."

Adriana squealed so loud that Otis began his own series of screams and caws and Leigh clamped her hands over her ears.

"Emmy! You didn't!" Adriana said.

"Oh, but I did." It felt so good to say those words, to watch the reactions on her friends' faces. Between their trips to the Hamptons and LA, the entire month of September had vanished without a single chance to tell them face-to-face, but Emmy was glad she'd waited until now.

"Noooo," Leigh breathed, looking up from her wineglass with a look of utter shock.

"Yeeeeeeees," Emmy sang gleefully.

"Fatty! Fatty! Fat girl!" Otis screeched. Adriana banged his cage with the back of her hand, which Otis immediately tried to bite.

"Tell us everything! Who was he? Where? When? How? Was it good? Is he the future father of your children?"

Emmy plopped on the floor and took a long sip of wine, savoring the attention.

"His name is George. He's a law student at Miami. Obviously, I met him when I was visiting Izzie and Kevin. And it just sort of happened," Emmy said, staring at her hands.

Adriana gave her a playful shove in the shoulder. "You are totally lying to us. Don't you think, Leigh?"

"I believe she actually did the deed," Leigh said thoughtfully, "but something's not adding up. I don't think we're getting the *real* story."

"You're in love, aren't you?" Leigh asked, leaning forward. "That's it. You fell head over heels for this guy, and you're already picturing him as your husband."

Adriana nodded her agreement. "One hundred percent. Lawyer, friend of your sis-

311

ter's, probably the nicest guy on earth. Well, I'm happy for you, honey. Not surprised, I have to say, but happy for you. However" — Adriana wagged her forefinger — "I would like us to recognize that I, as one-half of a committed relationship that I *promise* will be leading to an engagement in the next six months, have officially won our bet."

"I'm a witness," Leigh concurred. "And it's true. I, too, am happy you met the guy of your dreams, Emmy, but you are handing the contest to Adriana."

Adriana picked up a folder of take-out menus from the coffee table and began thumbing through them. "Let's order now so it gets here in time for *Grey's*. Sushi?"

"Wait just a minute," Emmy said.

"Wait! Fat girl! Wait! Fat girl!" Otis cawed.

"I don't know how you live with that repulsive creature," Adriana said.

Emmy grabbed the folder from Adriana and then snatched the remote control from Leigh. She clicked off the TV and said, "I'd like your undivided attention, please."

Leigh sighed. "Are you engaged? Please don't tell me you're marrying this guy *already*."

Adriana and Leigh cracked up laughing.

"I'll have you both know that" — Emmy

held up a finger — "one, I had completely random, attachment-free sex with someone I will never, ever see again."

Pleased to see that this had gotten her friends' attention, she continued. "And two, I liked it."

This second pronouncement was met with silence, which Adriana finally broke. "You did?"

Emmy nodded. "And when I tell you he was inappropriate, I mean it."

Emmy hadn't known herself the full extent of what she'd done until the following morning, when she'd casually mentioned George's name to her sister.

"Who?" Izzie had asked, scrambling eggs at the stove.

"A guy named George. I went down to the pool last night to call Leigh and he was there. We talked for a little while." Pause. "He seemed nice enough."

"George, George . . . I don't know a George," Izzie said.

"Maybe he's new? Whatever, it's not important." Emmy had never withheld anything from Izzie before, but she just couldn't bring herself to disclose what happened with George in light of her sister's baby announcement. It just seemed so . . . so petty, somehow. Silly.

Kevin strolled into the kitchen and poured himself a cup of coffee. "Who are we talking about?"

"Emmy met one of our neighbors last night by the pool. George. But I can't figure out who he is."

Kevin turned to Emmy and asked, "Law student?"

Emmy nodded. "Yeah, he said he was at Miami Law School."

"Tall kid, decent-looking, always wearing mesh shorts?"

"That's him," Emmy agreed.

"Jorge! I wonder when he started calling himself George. Kid's a legend around here."

Something about the way Kevin kept saying "kid" was unnerving Emmy, and the whole legend bit didn't sound so great, either.

"What do you mean?" Emmy asked, although she really didn't want to know.

"Just such an unbelievable player. Literally a different girl every night, sometimes two. That guy has been with more girls at twenty-three than most men will in their lifetimes."

Emmy froze, her OJ glass suspended in midair halfway between the table and her mouth. "Twenty-three?"

Izzie joined Emmy at the table and bit delicately into a piece of toast. "Yeah, he's a baby. But the girls do love him." She looked at Emmy with a strange look. "Why? Did something happen?"

Emmy concentrated hard on not choking and said, "Don't be ridiculous! Of course not. You know me. . . ."

Kevin drained the last of his coffee and tied his sneakers. "Izzie, honey, as beautiful as Emmy is, I imagine Jorge focuses more on the eighteen-to-twenty-five range."

Ouch.

Emmy relayed the contents of this conversation to her friends, who were literally crying tears of laughter by the time she finished.

"You. Cannot. Be. Serious!" Leigh gasped. She clutched her stomach and rolled on the floor.

"He was twenty-three, *querida?* For real?"

"It's not like I knew that! And I certainly had no idea his *hobby* was making sweet poolside love to unsuspecting women. . . ."

"Unsuspecting *older* women," Adriana added.

"Mock all you'd like," Emmy said as she tossed a towel over Otis's cage. "But it was the best sex of my old-lady life."

Leigh held up her hand. "Wait just a second here. We're not acknowledging a crucial point here. Am I to assume that Jorge is Cuban?"

Emmy shrugged. "Probably. Actually, I think Kevin mentioned later that his family are well-known anti-Castro activists."

"So . . ." Leigh bowed her head and extended her arm.

"So?" Emmy asked, confused.

"So you just had your first foreign man!" Adriana said. "Granted, he was probably born in the States, and even if he wasn't, the Caribbean doesn't really count. But I vote — in a gesture of goodwill and encouragement — that he should count."

"I second that. Count him as South America. But definitely count him."

Adriana reached over and pinched Emmy's cheek. "Congratulations, *querida.* One down — two if we're counting Duncan for North America — and five to go."

Emmy felt a frisson in the air at the sound of Duncan's name and would swear that she saw Adriana and Leigh exchange looks, but she ignored it. Emmy knew they didn't believe she was really over him, and she was growing tired of trying to convince them. "Yes, well, I am hereby cured of my monogamy addiction. And I appreciate you both being there to encourage me on my way to whoredom."

The girls clinked their wineglasses. Emmy phoned in their usual sushi order (three miso soups, two sushi entrées, one sashimi entrée, and a vat of extra-spicy sauce for dipping) and Leigh worked on setting the DVR to begin recording *Grey's* so they wouldn't have to waste time on commercials. A half-hour later, after Emmy had run the stairs again to let in the delivery guy and returned to find Adriana dangling Otis's cage out her five-story window, the girls were happily chopsticking everything in sight and working their way through wine bottle number two of Emmy's favorite gewürztraminer.

"How's Russell?" Emmy asked Leigh, hoping to draw her out a little. They'd known each other long enough that Emmy accepted her friend's fierce privacy, but she never stopped trying.

"What?" Leigh asked, clearly distracted. "Russell? Oh, he's fine. Great. He's interviewing Tony Romo this week, so he's been really preoccupied."

Adriana dunked a piece of yellowtail sushi into the soy sauce and popped it into her mouth. "Emmy said you guys were close to setting a date for the wedding, right?"

Leigh nodded. "April."

"April? Really? That's so soon!" Emmy was surprised. Considering they'd only known each other a year before getting engaged, she figured they'd wait until at least the following summer, but she was pleased to see that Leigh finally seemed to be getting into it.

"Yeah, it definitely wasn't my first choice, but it'll be fine."

"Why?"

"I don't know; I've always really liked the idea of a fall wedding, I guess. Plus, it seems a little soon. And Jesse's book is scheduled to publish right around then, so it's going to be crazy. But my parents are insisting that it's the only free weekend in the next two years at the club because someone canceled, and it works for Russell's family travel-wise, so we're going with it. Doesn't really matter." She shrugged.

"Spoken like a glowing bride," Adriana said.

Leigh shrugged again. "Why should I get all stressed out about a date? We're going to get married at some point, so does it really matter when it happens?"

"Gee, Leigh, you're making me swoon with the romance of it all," Emmy said. She'd intended it to lighten the awkwardness, but the comment had come out all wrong. She quickly moved to change the subject. "So how's everything going with Mr. Chapman? Have you met his wife yet?"

Leigh put down her chopsticks and folded her legs under herself, as though preparing to give a long talk. "You know, I haven't met her. I don't even know for sure that she exists — I've never read about her in a single newspaper or magazine — and I'd never believe it if he hadn't mentioned one time at lunch that he's married. It's strange, though, because he doesn't really even reference her — like, I don't even know her name."

"Has he hit on you yet?" Emmy asked. She wondered when Leigh was going to wake up and see what was going on here. It was obvious that she'd developed some sort of crush on this guy — who, by the way, sounded like a first-class asshole — and Emmy figured the situation could be nothing but bad news. Besides, it was irritating that Leigh had found such an amazing guy in Russell and didn't seem to appreciate him nearly as much as she should.

Leigh looked up. "Hit on me? Emmy, he's my *author*. Of course not."

"And you're engaged," Emmy added.

"Obviously! I thought that went without saying."

Adriana poured everyone another glass of

wine and said, "Girls, girls, settle down. I'm sure Mr. Jesse Chapman has his lecherous hands all over Leigh. After all, he's not exactly known for his chastity, and Leigh here is a beautiful woman. But that's certainly not her fault. Now, can we please talk about *me*? I have something to show you both."

She buried a hand inside her quilted Chanel hobo and pulled out a velvet box. "Check these out. They're from Toby. Or should I say, from Harry Winston."

Both girls leaned over to see the beautiful earrings.

"They're stunning," Leigh declared, touching them reverently with her left hand.

Emmy couldn't help but notice the juxtaposition of Leigh's sparkly engagement ring and Adriana's sapphire earrings. While her friends seemed enamored with the baubles, Emmy wondered if they even realized how lucky they were to have the loving men behind the jewelry. She would happily forsake all the diamonds in the world if she could just find the one person who was meant for her. Or, really, *keep* the one who was meant for her. If everything had gone the way they'd always discussed, she and Duncan would have been planning *their* wedding right now.

"Toby remembered how much I admired

them from an old picture of Salma Hayek at the Oscars. These are the exact ones she wore."

Emmy whistled. "He's a keeper, Adi. I hate that Leigh knows him and I don't. When do I get to meet him?"

"He's on location in Toronto for the next few weeks, but he wants to throw a big dinner party for my birthday next month. I told him thir — that age is no cause for celebration, but he insists. Where's a good place?"

The girls chatted straight through the entire *Grey's* episode, an *Entourage* rerun, and bits and pieces of Dateline's *To Catch a Predator.* They were just about to get sucked into *Notting Hill* on the Oxygen Network when Emmy announced that she was exhausted and had to be up early the next day, and as much as she appreciated everyone coming over, it might be time to wrap things up. Leigh and Adriana looked surprised but not overly concerned, and after a few minutes of gathering their things and hugging goodbye, Emmy was blessedly alone.

She just wasn't in the mood for the usual chitchat tonight. She was cranky, and a little bit sad for no good reason. *That's a total lie,* Emmy told herself as she bobby-pinned her bangs back and haphazardly washed her face. Izzie had called a couple hours earlier with the news that she and Kevin would be having a baby boy. When Emmy gushed with excitement (genuine) and asked if they were still thinking of the name Ezra, Izzie laughed and said Kevin seemed stuck on Dylan for some reason. Dylan with a D. D like Duncan. Duncan, who — if you could ever get him talking about having children — insisted that his would be only boys, and only boys named after him. She'd been *so* good for *so* long, had resisted every single previous temptation, but tonight she felt her willpower slackening. The combination of Izzie's baby announcement and that look she'd seen Leigh and Adriana exchange at the mention of Duncan's name, and Emmy couldn't stop thinking about him. She realized he could have eloped with the trainer or, worse, gotten her pregnant, and Emmy would have no idea. How had this happened? How had she ended up single at almost thirty and Adriana and Leigh — neither of whom particularly seemed to care — were both going to get married any minute now? It was so unfair. Duncan may not have been a famous director or a superstar TV anchor, but he'd been good to her, most of the time. Emmy wasn't an idiot; she knew he liked to flirt, and she heard him all those times he swore he wasn't ready to settle down, but who could have ever foreseen this?

She inched closer to the computer.

Her mind willed her not to open the laptop, screamed, *No! No! No! You'll regret this. Bad Idea! Bad Idea!* and for a moment it sounded so realistic she wondered if Otis was actually shrieking the words, but she could only hold out for so long. Four seconds later, her fingers were flying across the keyboard. Ten seconds after that, she was face-to-face with Brianna's MySpace page.

And seventeen high-definition inches' worth of pictures of Duncan and the trainer. On vacation. In bathing suits. Looking absolutely outstanding.

Emmy rapidly glanced through the pictures of the happy couple sunning on a white sand beach, lounging in what looked like a private patio pool, and smiling over heaps of devoured crab claws and empty cocktail glasses. There weren't any captions, though, which was maddening. Where were they? When? Was it a *honeymoon?* She skimmed the e-mails down the right-hand side, perky little missives from Brianna's friends, chock-full of emoticons and ellipses and too many exclamation points to count. One of the insipid messages included a link to the Kodak Gallery Web site, and Emmy sensed her torture was only beginning.

"Oh, god, no," she moaned aloud, stretching backward in her chair and staring at the computer warily, as though it might explode. She knew she shouldn't click on it, but there was no turning back. She sat up straight with her shoulders down and her chest jutted out, took a deep breath, and moved the cursor to the link. She was just about to click when, thank god, she remembered the dreaded guest book. Had she clicked the link, Kodak Gallery would've automatically remembered her from last time and saved her name in Brianna's guest book, right along with a helpful date and time stamp. Nightmare! Relieved that she had averted disaster, Emmy quickly went to the general home page, logged herself out, and logged in under the pseudonym and fake e-mail she used for such e-stalking activities. When she opened the link this time, the album greeting read, "Welcome, Lucy! Click here to see pictures from Brianna and Duncan's Mexican Adventure."

Mexican Adventure? *Please! They're lying on a fucking beach, not climbing Kilimanjaro.* With another deep breath, which was not the least bit calming, Emmy clicked.

Before the screen went into slide-show mode, Emmy saw that there were dozens, possibly hundreds, of thumbnail shots. She knew this was a very bad idea, that it was stupid from an intellectual standpoint and toxic from a sanity one, but by now it was out of her control. Frames one through six passed by in a flash; it wasn't until the seventh that Emmy collected herself enough to adjust the speed. The slower pace satisfied her for another half-dozen shots, but her compulsion to study, to *examine,* every square inch of every single photograph consumed her, and within seconds she had turned off the automatic slide show altogether. Now she could do this properly, at her own pace.

Unfortunately, the first frame that remained frozen on the screen was one that must have been taken by Duncan. It featured Brianna frolicking in knee-deep surf, leaning forward to splash the viewer and simultaneously looking up, a movement that caused her back to arch almost pornographically. Emmy moved closer to the screen. Could her ass really stand up like that, all on its own? And those breasts! Even though the girl was leaning forward in a string bikini and appeared to have solid C cups, they were barely hanging at all! Emmy peered at them for a full minute and arrived at the regretful decision that no, they weren't fake, they were just really young. Besides, twenty-two-year-old virgins don't get fake boobs, do they?

Click.

Duncan filled the screen. He was lying on a pool float, a tan, newly muscled arm draped over his forehead to shield his eyes from the sun. He was wearing an unfamiliar pair of Hawaiian-print board shorts (Emmy had pleaded with him to trade in his old-man bathing suit with the alligators stitched into it, to no avail) and, wait . . . was that a *six-pack?* She squinted. It was! Formerly doughy, pale, I-sit-at-a-desk-all-day Duncan had morphed into a goddamn beach Adonis right before her very eyes. Emmy pressed her eyes closed and rubbed them, but Duncan still looked fit — downright hot — when she opened them again.

Click.

The happy couple again . . . on a dive boat! Together they sat on a wooden bench, hands on each other's knees, looking sporty and adorable in wetsuits unzipped to their waists. They were surrounded by the debris of a recent dive, racks of tanks and regulators, discarded masks and fins, and, off to the side, a Mexican man in a white shorts uniform preparing to serve them fresh fruit and juice. Emmy had begged Duncan — literally *pleaded,* she now remembered with growing rage — to try scuba diving with her one year in the Bahamas over Christmas. He'd flatly refused, reminding her that he sure as hell wasn't going to spend his precious vacation time in a pursuit as active and challenging as scuba diving. He wouldn't even go snorkeling, that bastard, because he "wasn't into the whole floating-prey thing."

Click.

Brianna sitting atop the covers on a four-poster bed, reading a magazine, wearing very skimpy and nonvirginal boy shorts and a barely-there tank top. *Click.* The two of them in workout clothes and iPods, all sweaty and rosy-cheeked post-run. *Click.* Duncan making a silly kissing face at the camera, even though Duncan didn't make silly kissing faces *ever,* while wearing the Cornell T-shirt Emmy had bought for him at her fifth-year college reunion. *Click.* Dressed up for a candlelit dinner on the sand, where they appeared to feast on whole grilled fish, lots of fresh vegetables, and white wine. *Click. Click. Click.* Emmy finished clicking through the entire album, briefly surveyed her level of nausea, and hunkered down to start again from the beginning.

It was going to be a very long night.

FRIENDLY REALLY MEANS AVAILABLE AND DESPERATE

"Adi, the doorman just called to say your car is here," Mrs. de Souza announced from the doorway of Adriana's room.

"Okay," Adriana mumbled, summoning her reserves of patience to keep from being aggressively nasty to her mother.

"What was that, dear? Did you hear me? I said the doorman —"

"I heard you!" Adriana said more tersely than she intended.

Her mother sighed, the long, extended, dramatic sigh that almost always preceded a long, extended, dramatic conversation. "Adriana, I've tried to be understanding — really, I have — but the situation has become untenable."

Adriana felt her entire body clench, but before she could even react, the curling iron had slipped from her hand and landed on the floor, making a brief but painful stop on her thigh.

"Fuck!" she screamed, bolting to her feet and rubbing the top of her right thigh.

"Adriana! Language! I won't have you speaking like that in this house." Mrs. de Souza lowered her voice and approximated a soothing tone. "Come here now. Are you all right?"

"I burned myself. There's going to be a blister!"

"I'll bring you a little Neosporin in just a minute. But first I'd like to discuss something with you. I understand that you're —"

"Mama, please, please, *please* can we have this conversation when I get home? I'm already late, and as you can see, I'm not even close to being ready. I'm sorry for the language. Really, I am. But can this wait?"

"It's not just the language, Adi, it's that tone you've been using lately with your father and me. I don't have to remind you that this is *our* apartment, and we're welcome to use it whenever we'd like. Now, you've made it very clear that you're not happy about our presence, but have you thought how that might make us feel?"

"Mama . . ."

"And of course there's the spending. I assure you, I'm every bit as tired of this conversation as you are, but nothing changes. It's simply unacceptable."

Adriana could feel the knot in her throat begin to grow. Determined not to cry and ruin forty-five minutes' worth of careful preparation, she breathed deeply and walked toward her mother.

She had every intention of taking the older woman's hands in her own and explaining calmly why this wasn't a good time — really, she did — but the anger and frustration consumed her. Nothing on earth could inspire such rage in her as that patronizing look on her mother's face. So she did what she had done her entire life when she felt cornered by her mother: She screamed.

"WHY ARE YOU TRYING TO RUIN MY LIFE? I ASKED YOU NICELY IF WE COULD HAVE THIS DISCUSSION ANOTHER TIME AND YOU REFUSED TO LISTEN!" She moved closer to her mother, who was slowly backing into the hallway. "I AM GOING TO FINISH GETTING READY AND I'M GOING TO LEAVE AND YOU ARE GOING TO DEAL WITH IT. NOW LEAVE. ME. ALONE!"

She punctuated her diatribe with a hearty door slam and immediately felt a wave of release. Of course it was ridiculous to yell and scream and slam doors at her age; it was positively sophomoric. But that woman could be so incredibly annoying, and her sense of timing was horrific. It was unbearable that her parents had arrived yesterday out of nowhere, with no more notice than the time it took to get to the apartment from JFK, and planned to stay through Thanksgiving, a holiday they didn't even celebrate! The only solace was that Toby hadn't also arrived yesterday as planned (the horror of having them all mingling in the foyer was unspeakable), so he had adequate time to find a hotel.

"A hotel? Really?" he'd asked, sounding surprised when Adriana asked if he'd like her to make the reservation or do it himself.

"Why yes, *querido*, of course a hotel."

"I can understand why they wouldn't be comfortable with me staying in your room, per se, but do you really —"

"Toby, please!" Adriana had interrupted in frustration. "You staying here with *them* is out of the question."

He'd complied, naturally, and checked himself into the Carlyle; Adriana couldn't bring herself to explain that her beautiful apartment was really *their* beautiful apartment, a fact he would most certainly uncover were he to stay under the same roof. No, that simply was not acceptable.

Determined to calm down for the sake of

her complexion, Adriana took a seat at her vanity and brushed her cheeks and forehead with bronzer. She carefully outlined her lips with a nude pencil, filled them in with a slightly darker matte lipstick, and slicked a clear gloss for shine on top. A single tissue pucker and she was finished.

The outfit was another issue entirely. What was one supposed to wear to a business dinner? Oh, how she dreaded it! It was an unusually warm November Saturday night, and all the restaurants would surely put their tables outside, and everyone would be excited at the unexpected Indian summer, racing to hit the dance clubs and loft parties that night, and *she* was going to some stuffy apartment on the Upper East Side. It was sure to be chock-full of musty antiques and precious little collectibles, the mere thought of which was nauseating. Antiques made her sneeze. And Limoges! Just looking at those little boxes made her want to vomit. She'd complained as much as she dared when Toby announced the evening's plan, but she wasn't inclined to push it; Toby might be a tad boring in addition to being ever-so-slightly dorky, but he was her boyfriend and she planned to soldier through it like a dutiful and adoring girlfriend if it killed her.

With significantly less effort than she usually spent, Adriana quickly chose a clingy, short-sleeved cashmere wrap sweater and paired it with an extremely fitted pencil skirt. Seamed stockings — Mrs. de Souza had advocated their timeless sexiness since Adriana was a girl — and a pair of four-inch pumps completed the look.

She felt like a nun.

"I'm leaving," she called to no one in particular.

Her mother materialized out of nowhere; her eyes expertly assessed Adriana's appearance. There was a barely discernible nod of approval before the woman said, "He's not picking you up?"

"His hotel is on the Upper East Side, and so is the party. He sent a car instead." No one insisted on chivalry more than Adriana, but even she recognized the absurdity of a man riding eighty blocks downtown just to turn around and drive back again.

Mrs. de Souza did not. "Oh," she murmured vaguely, implying without a word that she disapproved.

"Don't wait up." Adriana cinched on a Burberry trench — her most conservative coat — and kissed her mother's cheek.

"What time do you think you'll be home?"

"Mama . . ."

Mrs. de Souza held up her hands. "You're right, I apologize. Go, have fun. It's just that your father and I would like to meet Mr. Baron soon. Isn't that right, Renato?"

Mr. de Souza glanced up from his *O Globo* only long enough to nod and tell Adriana that she looked beautiful and to wish her a wonderful time.

Adriana escaped the apartment without any more questions and held her breath as she waited for the elevator. It really was too much already. She was a grown woman, and still she had to endure the same parental questioning and involvement as a teenager.

She stepped out into the elegant marble lobby, so wrapped up in her anger that at first she didn't notice anyone in the lobby.

"Adi, over here," a voice called out.

Adriana turned to see Leigh standing in the building's tiny mailroom off the lobby, sorting through a pile of papers.

"Hi." Adriana sighed dramatically, sidling up next to her.

Leigh didn't look up, just tossed a Victoria's Secret catalog in the trash. "Nothing'll make you feel like shit faster than that rag," she said. "Well, not *you*, obviously, but the rest of us."

"Oh, please, you're gorgeous," Adriana said automatically, although she was pleased

— and in full agreement — with Leigh's assessment.

"Where are you headed tonight?"

Another sigh. "With Toby to some dreadful industry dinner party. Studio execs or producers or some such, in town for a reason I can't remember."

"Maybe it won't be that bad. Where is it?"

"Uptown."

Leigh crinkled her nose. "Oh. That sucks."

"What are you up to?" Adriana already knew what the answer was but felt she should ask anyway. Leigh was a lot of really wonderful things, but fun wasn't one of them.

"Me?" Leigh glanced down at her flannel pajama pants and laughed. "I've got a hot date with my TiVo and a pint of Tasti D-Lite. Shocker, I know."

Adriana shook her head. "And where's your fiancé? No, wait — let me guess. He's out somewhere like a normal person, having fun and being sociable, and you refused to go with him?"

"I didn't *refuse,* I just opted out. Besides, I have a ton of work to do."

"Okay, okay, *querida,* I must be going. If I stay here a moment longer, I'm going to get very upset with you. I'm going to sound like your mother and ask why someone as young and beautiful and charming as yourself insists on hibernating instead of flourishing."

"*Flourishing?* Did you just say that?" Leigh glanced at the cover of a Sharper Image catalog and tossed that one out, too.

"Ach!" Adriana threw her hands up in frustration. The girl was impossible. And what a waste of a perfectly good boyfriend. Poor Russell probably just wanted to go out, relax a bit, have a little fun, and his girlfriend didn't know the meaning of the word. "You should be going to this boring dinner tonight and I should be out with Russell, having fun."

Leigh rolled her eyes. "Go! Say hi to Toby for me. And behave yourself, will you? No mischief at the dinner party."

"What, are you worried we're going to have sex in the bathroom?" Adriana asked with a grin.

"I'm more worried that you'll have sex in the bathroom with someone *other* than Toby."

Adriana pretended to consider this. "Hmm. I hadn't even thought of that. Very interesting . . ."

The ride up to Seventy-fourth and Park was interminable. She was too young for formal dinner parties uptown! Too young to bury her beautiful figure under knee-length skirts and trench coats! Too young to be with only one man for the rest of her life! It was all so silly, this rush to find a husband just because she'd soon be thirty. Such pressure! From her parents, but from her friends, too: Why were they so convinced that their path was the correct one? Adriana grew angrier with every passing block; by the time they soared past the MetLife building she had resolved to end this entire farce once and for all. So she'd lose a bet — big deal.

The town car flew past Bear Stearns, and Adriana couldn't help but think of Emmy's Duncan, as she always did when she passed the building where he had once famously (in her mind, at least) claimed to "run shit." She'd never liked him, but Adriana had to admit that he was a reasonably attractive, overly confident, typical New York banker who pretty much had his pick when it came to girls. Wasn't it safe to assume that if Duncan had traded Emmy in for someone eight years younger, his friends and colleagues would do the same? Of course it was. And there was always Yani. Over the last few months she'd stepped up her efforts to flirt with him, make him notice her, until it had all ended one devastating morning when she saw him kiss another girl after class. Not one who was prettier or in better shape, mind you, but with a clear and undeniable advantage: She couldn't have been a day over twenty. And finally there was Toby. Her mother might have said it first, but Adriana didn't disagree: While there was no shortage of successful, handsome, wealthy men, not *that* many were straight or single. Of those left, how many would choose to marry a thirtysomething woman over a fresh-faced girl of twenty-two, one who looked up at them with big, adoring eyes and an expression that said, "I revere you and think every syllable you utter is the word of god"? Adriana knew she could fake it for a bit in the beginning, but her days of worshipping men were long gone — if they were worthy of her attention, they could worship *her*.

Toby was waiting for her outside the building when she arrived. Adriana almost told him he should have worn a pair of slacks with his blazer instead of jeans — Park Avenue and the Hollywood Hills didn't exactly share the same dress code — but she remembered to channel her inner twenty-two-year-old, leaned in close, and whispered in his ear, "You look so hot tonight. I can't *wait* until later."

His face lit up with unabashed joy. "Really?"

Good lord, it was too easy. Mr. Superstar Director might ooze cockiness and confidence when it came to making movies, but he clearly wasn't accustomed to this kind of compliment. Adriana did a quick calculation and figured she had probably just knocked a full month off of Ring Quest '08.

"Really," she purred.

The doorman greeted them by name and ushered them into the richly upholstered elevator. "Take it to the top," he said without a trace of irony. Adriana rolled her eyes and Toby laughed. *This isn't so bad,* she thought, allowing him to wrap his arms around her from behind as the elevator closed. *He's cuddly and sweet and he loves me. I could get used to this, if I must.*

Which lasted precisely ten more seconds, just long enough for the elevator to open directly into the penthouse apartment and for Adriana to lock eyes with the very first person she saw.

"Well, look who it is," Toby bellowed, releasing Adriana and moving forward to shake the man's hand. "Sweetheart, I'd like to introduce you to someone. Dean Decker, this is Adriana de Souza. Adriana, Dean."

Adriana's mind went into overdrive. How

did Dean and Toby know each other? Had she mentioned Toby to Dean on the plane that day? Was she about to be caught or busted by anyone for anything? She quickly concluded that no, as of this moment, she had done nothing wrong, but she was still too shocked to react in any sort of appropriate fashion. Thankfully, Dean appeared much more composed. Amused, even.

"Adriana, is it? Great name. Well, hey, it's nice to meet you." He offered his hand.

"You, too," she managed. She could feel the hair on her arms stand up when her hand touched his. His utter scrumptiousness was impossible to deny, especially since he was sporting the exact same outfit (black blazer, white shirt, and jeans) as Toby. Just moments before Toby had looked reasonably attractive, but now, standing in direct comparison to Dean, he appeared shockingly troll-like. Adriana's mind flashed to a disturbing image: photos of Toby and Dean side by side on *US Weekly*'s "Who Wore It Better" page, with a full hundred percent of those polled in Rockefeller Center voting for Dean. She'd never seen a full hundred-percent vote before — not even the time they had pitted Rosie O'Donnell against Petra Nemcova — but in her imaginary layout, the results were crystal clear.

Seeming unaware of both their matching outfits and his stunning defeat, Toby wrapped one arm possessively around Adriana's shoulders and pulled her closer to Dean, so all their three heads were inches apart. "We've just signed Dean for the lead in *Around Her*," he announced in a conspiratorial voice.

Adriana's eyes darted to Dean.

"It's true." Dean nodded and grinned.

Adriana felt herself reeling with surprise. "Really?" she squeaked. *Pull it together!* Adriana reprimanded herself. She took a deep breath and then put on a smile, the real dazzler she usually reserved for special occasions (meeting a current lover's wife, asking Papa for a new car, etc.).

"How *wonderful!* Congratulations to you both." There. That was more like it.

A tall, striking woman in a timeless Chanel suit approached them.

"Welcome to our little fete," she trilled, air-kissing the general area around the group. "We're just delighted all you California boys could make it."

"Catherine," Toby said, clasping her hands and kissing both cheeks.

Adriana wanted to puke. Puh-lease! The only thing worse than Europeans being Europeans was *Americans* being Europeans!

"I'd like to introduce you to my girlfriend, Adriana de Souza." At the sound of the g-word, Adriana stole a glance at Dean, who was already looking at her with eyebrows raised and an amused look on his face. "And also Dean Decker. Adriana, Dean, this lovely lady is your hostess for the evening."

Adriana turned to the woman, who, upon closer inspection, was older than she'd originally thought, probably closer to sixty. She forced out the usual platitudes about such a beautiful apartment, so glad to be there, love your necklace, blah, blah, blah, but the woman only stared at her. After allowing Adriana to ramble on in this manner for a bit, Catherine cupped Adriana's chin and slowly, with great gentleness, as though she were handling fine china, turned her face back and forth.

"My, my, you are lovely," Catherine said, gazing at Adriana. "Excellent cheekbones and pretty, wide eyes. But your skin!" The woman groaned. "The complexion of an angel."

Well, this was more like it. Adriana found herself flashing her second award-winning smile that night. "Thank you! How nice of you to say." She tried for an embarrassed, or at least humbled, expression, but wasn't sure of the outcome.

"Catherine . . . ," Toby said in a warning voice.

"Sorry, I know — no work at a party. I promise not to bother her tonight, although all bets are off for Monday."

The woman looked up as two more guests appeared in the foyer. "The bar is through there, in the living room." She gestured to a set of imposing French doors. "Please excuse me for just a moment."

"I think I'm going to make a beeline for the booze," Dean announced as Catherine floated to greet her new guests. "See you two later?"

"Later, man," Toby said, trying to sound cool but just sounding old.

Adriana barely knew where to begin. Did she grill Toby first about Dean or Catherine?

"You'll have to be careful, or you might just find yourself in the pages of *Marie Claire*," Toby said, grabbing two glasses of champagne from a roving waiter's tray and thrusting one toward Adriana.

"Catherine works at *Marie Claire?*" Adriana demanded.

"Catherine *used* to work at *Marie Claire*. She was the booking editor for decades and is credited with discovering loads of now-famous models. So that's quite a compliment she paid you. Not that I didn't know it already . . ." He leaned in close enough that Adriana could smell the champagne on his breath.

"Interesting," Adriana said. "Very, very interesting." She'd have to ask her mother about Catherine; if the woman really was the booking guru at *Marie Claire,* then Mrs. de Souza would certainly have known her.

"Come, darling. Let me show you off."

When it came time for dinner, Adriana located her place card, only to find that she was seated between a female editor from *Marie Claire* and Dean. Catherine had — as all good hostesses do and all their guests hate them for — split all the couples and scattered them around the table to encourage fresh conversation among strangers. Not ideal, but not a total disaster, either. She could've been seated between Dean and Toby; that would not have been fun. Adriana assessed the scene, devised a game plan, and took her seat. She nodded at Dean and then, as planned, quickly turned to her left. Adriana leaned in close to the woman, so close they nearly touched foreheads, and said, "Do you realize how lucky you are? You're seated next to the most gorgeous man in the room."

The woman, whom Toby had introduced

earlier as Mackenzie Michaels, *the* woman to know at *Marie Claire,* stared blankly at Adriana for a moment, undecided in her reaction. Adriana merely nodded, as if to say, *Well, it's true,* and Mackenzie stole a furtive glance to her left. Adriana watched as her eyes widened and she inhaled. Sitting on Mackenzie's other side was a guy even more gorgeous than Dean. He was wearing a fitted, funky pinstriped Thom Browne–esque suit with no tie. His hair was clipped tight around the back and sides, but the slightly longer top was just the right amount of spiky: cool, but not trying too hard. But best of all was how he just seemed to *gleam.* His skin looked freshly scrubbed and shaved and tan from the actual sun and not the salon; his fingernails were cut short and straight with a subtle shine that managed not to look the least bit effeminate; even his tassel-toed leather loafers glinted in the light.

Mackenzie turned back to Adriana and groaned. "You're right. He's a fucking god," she whispered.

Adriana surveyed Mackenzie's hands and, finding no rings, said, "Go for it, *querida.* Make him yours."

Mackenzie laughed, a sort of snort that wasn't nearly as delicate or as feminine as Adriana's. "Yeah, right. I'd have a better chance of going home with Matt Damon tonight."

"Is he here?" Adriana asked, forgetting her promise to herself not to look in Dean's direction. She scanned the table, carefully going over the faces of all twelve guests.

"No, he's not *here*," Mackenzie said with a laugh. "I was just making a point: There's no way in hell that gorgeous guy would go for me."

Again, Adriana assessed her new friend. Average height. Better-than-average face, with a cute button nose and a nice smile. Decent enough figure, she guessed, although it was impossible to tell *what* was happening under that babydoll dress. How she loathed babydoll dresses! Every woman on earth, herself included, looked either morbidly obese or eight months pregnant in babydoll dresses, and yet they were all the rage. Adriana suspected Mackenzie might even be hiding a pretty decent rack under that muumuu . . . a crime if there ever was one. Thankfully, the woman was somewhat saved by her flawless grooming. She sported a sleek blowout, what looked like professionally applied makeup, and a shoes-and-bag combo that most of womankind would kill for. Her appearance, combined with her success as one of the most sought-after magazine editors in New York, as Adriana would later learn, should have propelled Mackenzie into the stratosphere of confident women; her insecurity made absolutely no sense.

Before Adriana could do a thing to stop her, Mackenzie turned to the hot guy, tapped his arm insistently, and cleared her throat. She didn't seem to notice that she was interrupting his conversation with the woman to his left, nor did she catch the surprised and slightly irritated look on his face. He swiveled around and peered at Mackenzie.

"Hello," he said in a neutral voice, but Adriana could tell what he really meant was "Yes? Can I help you with something?"

Mackenzie plastered on a huge fake smile and extended her hand, a rather awkward gesture considering how tightly everyone was packed in around the table. She ended up looking slightly spastic, a fact that wasn't lost on the guy. "Hi there. I wanted to introduce myself. I'm Mackenzie Michaels, features editor at *Marie Claire.* Probably not your typical reading, since it's a women's magazine — but actually, come to think of it, we do have quite a few male readers. And surprisingly, they're not all gay, which is —"

"Mackenzie, *querida?* Would you happen to have a little breath mint, or perhaps a stick of chewing gum?" Adriana asked, gripping the woman's arm. It wasn't brilliant, but it was the best she could possibly do with this woman she barely knew. Besides, she didn't really care what was said, just so long as Mackenzie stopped talking. It was painful to see, like sitting in the front row as a comedian floundered or the best man flubbed his toast. It made *her* uncomfortable, and for this reason alone Adriana stepped in.

She looked at the hot guy and it occurred to her, for just a moment, that he was a delectable prospect. If Mackenzie was going to sabotage herself . . . But no! She had been lucky enough to find her future husband, and she wouldn't allow this dime-a-dozen playboy to tempt her. This mission was strictly one of necessity, not pleasure.

"Allo!" She turned up the Brazilian accent a few notches. "I am Adriana. Do you mind if I borrow my friend for just a moment?"

Mackenzie opened her mouth to interject, but Adriana took the liberty of pinching her forearm.

The hot guy smiled, nodded, and turned back to his original conversation.

Adriana could feel the iciness radiating from Mackenzie's whole body, but she was even more acutely aware of Dean's presence on her right. He'd watched the whole thing, and out of the corner of her eye she could see that he was smiling. Then there was Toby, who, from the other end of the table, was using her name in conversation loudly enough that she could hear every word. She should be curled up on a dark banquette with a caipirinha and a boy, and instead she was enduring one social awkwardness after another.

"If you wanted him yourself, why did you encourage me to go for him? Just to make an ass of myself?" Mackenzie hissed in Adriana's direction while staring straight ahead. Both women smiled at the waitress as she placed endive salads before them.

Adriana sighed and checked to make sure that Dean was engaged in a different conversation before continuing. "I didn't — don't — want him myself, *querida*. I just couldn't bear to watch that. It just felt so, so . . ." Adriana tried to think of another, gentler word here, but she already felt so exhausted.

"So what?" Mackenzie insisted.

Adriana met her gaze levelly. "So *desperate*."

Mackenzie inhaled sharply and Adriana felt a pang of sympathy before remembering that she was doing Mackenzie a favor. If no one had told her this already, she was pretty much doomed. So she'd hate her. Adriana had bigger things to worry about than yet another woman hating her.

"It wasn't *desperate*," Mackenzie whispered. "I was just being *friendly*."

Ah, the friendly card. Adriana was instantly transported back to her teenage years, when her mother was trying to teach her these important lessons and Adriana had raised these very same arguments. She almost smiled with the memory.

"Friendly, outgoing, engaging, charming, whatever you want to call it, it still translates into 'available and desperate' when you're the one who initiates contact."

Mackenzie appeared to mull this over, at one point opening her mouth to disagree and then changing her mind. "You think?" she asked finally.

Adriana nodded. It was boring, it was so obvious. Why didn't American women understand this? Why weren't they taught it? *The Rules* had helped a little but hadn't done nearly enough; it instructed women how to deny men, but not how seduce them. If she hadn't actually witnessed it herself over the last ten years, she never would have believed there existed grown women who thought the way to get a man was to chase him. She'd found the exact same thing with her friends

— Leigh to a slightly lesser degree because of her more reserved personality, but Emmy had been downright humiliating, initiating conversations, calling first, suggesting plans, and making herself constantly available.

"So I shouldn't have introduced myself?"

"No." Adriana sipped her wine.

"Well, how were we going to meet otherwise?"

Adriana looked at her and tried not to get frustrated; she had to remember it wasn't really Mackenzie's fault. "You would have met, probably within minutes, when *he* had introduced himself to *you.*"

"Oh, please! What's the actual difference who —"

Adriana continued as though she'd heard nothing. "At which point you would have rewarded his politeness with a smile and some smoldering eyes, and then you would have promptly dodged any of his direct questions, turned away, and become completely engaged in a conversation that did not include him."

"Even if —"

"Even if he was midsentence, even if he asked you a question, even if he seemed smitten with you. *Especially* if he seemed smitten with you. The only time it's acceptable to continue is if he's ugly, because, well, we're not really concerned with the outcome then, are we?"

Mackenzie nodded, seeming more entranced with Adriana than annoyed by her slightly patronizing tone. This was so basic it was elementary; how had this otherwise attractive, successful woman missed it?

"So basically what you're saying is that we should all be living embodiments of *The Rules?* Which, in my opinion, is totally unrealistic."

"I agree," Adriana said. "It *is* totally unrealistic. *The Rules* is a good place to start, for teenagers. But it's nothing for grown women. I mean, any book that addresses sex only as something you should avoid or withhold is not remotely relevant."

Adriana was pleased that Mackenzie appeared transfixed. She continued, "Because really, what's the point of men in the first place if you can't properly enjoy them?"

Mackenzie kept vehemently nodding her head in agreement, so Adriana kept talking. It had been a while since she'd done something out of the goodness of her heart for someone else; it was time she imparted some of her lessons to someone less fortunate.

"It's a complete myth that once a man has sex with you he'll lose interest. In fact, it should be just the opposite: If you're doing your job well, it will make him want you more. It's all about finding the balance of mysterious and unavailable and challenging with sensual and seductive and sexy. You make them work for it — not just the first time, but again and again and again — and they'll love you forever."

"You sound so sure. . . ." Mackenzie's voice trailed off, but Adriana could tell she was a believer.

"I *am* so sure. I'm Brazilian. We know men and we know sex."

Adriana began to eat her salad while Mackenzie stared at her. In almost the same moment, Adriana could see the gorgeous guy wrap up his conversation and turn to Mackenzie. "Excuse me?" he asked.

Mackenzie paused for a moment before turning to him and offering him a radiant smile. "Yes?"

"I'm afraid I didn't properly introduce myself. My name is Jack. It's nice to meet you."

Like a pro, Mackenzie peered at him for just long enough before offering another smile — only this one was slightly more teasing, with pursed, just-licked lips. "It's lovely to meet you, Jack," Mackenzie purred.

"So, how do you know Catherine?" he asked.

"Oh, who doesn't know Catherine?" She laughed confidently and turned her back to him. "Adriana, honey, you were just telling the most amusing story about that shopping disaster last week. Will you finish it for me? Please?"

Good god, Adriana thought, *the woman is a natural.* Adriana played along and crafted some fictional anecdote for the sake of conversation, just long enough for Jack to excuse himself and use the men's room.

"You were perfect," Adriana declared the moment he stood up.

"Really? I feel like I offended him. I was so rude that he left!"

"Absolutely *perfect.* You didn't offend him, and you weren't rude — you were mysterious. Keep it up for the remainder of the evening and he'll go home with you tonight. Give a little, and then ignore. Flirt, then withhold. He'll go crazy trying to pin you down."

And sure enough, when Jack returned, he spent the duration of dinner, all of dessert, and a solid hour of postdinner drinks trying to keep Mackenzie's wandering attention. The man was *working,* and Mackenzie clearly loved every minute of it. Adriana could see her confidence increasing with every passing flirtation, and she congratulated herself on a job well done. It was delightful to watch, especially since she was occupied enacting the advanced moves of what she'd just taught Mackenzie, trying to juggle with alternating cold shoulders and batted eyelashes two very different men of her own.

A little after midnight, Toby finally agreed they could leave. Dean had ducked out a bit earlier with profuse apologies that he had to get to a friend's party he simply couldn't miss (damn him!), Mackenzie was now feigning disinterest in Jack on a love seat in a dark corner, and Adriana was, once again, supremely bored. She'd already tried every trick in the book to get Toby to take her dancing, but he would have none of it. He was exhausted from the work and the travel; he was going directly back to the hotel, and he expected his girlfriend to join him.

Toby chattered on about something as he helped Adriana into her coat, but it wasn't hard to block him out. What proved more difficult was remembering that she was only thirty — a mere girl, practically! — and not the fifty-year-old woman she felt like. At least the night wasn't a total loss; it looked like Mackenzie, all touchy and laughing with Jack, was a changed woman. Adriana waited to catch her eye and offered a little wave good-bye.

Mackenzie motioned for her to wait a

minute and, like a consummate professional, lightly grazed Jack's lips with her fingertip and sashayed away from him, toward Adriana.

"You're leaving already?" Mackenzie asked, glancing at Adriana's coat.

"It's after midnight. I'm beat," Adriana lied. *Not beat, just bored,* she thought. "But it looks like you're doing great work."

"You. Are. A. Goddess!" Mackenzie whispered, leaning in and clutching Adriana's arm. "He's already invited me back to his place for a drink. I told him I'd think about it."

Adriana was impressed. Nothing worked more efficiently than a maybe. It wasn't a flat-out rejection, but it definitely sent the message that he'd have to work a little harder.

"Just remember, if you sleep with him, no staying over. I don't care if it's five in the morning; you *have* to be the one to get up and out. Stay as long as you're having sex. The moment it's time for sleep, you're out of there," Adriana advised her new pupil and tried not to think about how much she sounded like her mother.

Mackenzie nodded, hanging on every word. "What if he —"

"There are no exceptions."

Another nod.

"Enjoy!" Adriana trilled. She gave Toby's hand a little tug to pull him away from the circle of people who had entrapped him. "Honey, we really should be going. . . ."

"Oh, and one more thing," Mackenzie whispered. "I want to pitch a story idea to you, as the focus for our next issue. I'm not sure what the angle would be yet, but you have an absolute gift and I think our readers would love to know about it."

Well. This was an interesting — and unexpected — development. Adriana was accustomed to being solicited for her picture by random tourists who thought her exotically gorgeous, and tonight wasn't the first time a magazine editor had deemed her beautiful enough to be included in an issue. But a story focusing on her innate abilities with men and her talent for teaching other women how to snare them? That didn't happen every day.

She feigned indifference even though her voice shook slightly from the excitement of it all. "Oh, well, that might be nice," she said blandly.

"Oh, I do hope you'll think about it and agree. I can see a double-page spread with a full interview and lots of gorgeous glossy pictures. We'll make it phenomenal, I promise," Mackenzie gushed. She hadn't seemed like a gusher earlier in the evening, but then again, she hadn't seemed like someone who could snag a guy so expertly, either.

It was all Adriana could do not to shriek with joy. "Well, um, Catherine knows how to reach me — or, at least, how to reach Toby — so that's probably the best way. . . ."

But Mackenzie had already started back toward Jack. "I'll call you next week! Great to meet you. And thanks . . . for everything." She waved and continued her sashay back to the darkened love seat.

"I hope you had a nice time, sweetheart?" Toby asked as he hailed a cab outside the building.

"It was so much more than nice, Toby. I had a *wonderful* time," Adriana said with more honesty than she'd thought possible before Mackenzie's idea. "An amazing, splendid, wonderful time."

The knock woke Leigh out of a deep sleep, something she rarely achieved at night, never mind in the middle of the afternoon when she hadn't even intended to fall asleep. There was something about the air or the water out here, something she needed to bottle: Every time her little rental car pulled into Sag Harbor, her whole body went slack with relaxation.

"Come in," she called after a quick check to make sure she was clothed and not covered in drool. She was shocked to see that it was already dark outside.

Jesse opened the door and peeked just his head inside. "Did I wake you? Sorry, I figured you were hard at work twenty-four hours a day."

Leigh snorted. "Uh-huh. I'm learning firsthand that having two Bloody Marys before lunch isn't all that conducive to productivity."

"True enough. But how good do you feel?"

"Pretty good," she admitted. Despite the bits and pieces of her dream that were flashing back to her — something to do with walking down the aisle naked and shivering — she still felt rested and peaceful.

"Wait just a minute," Jesse said as he crossed the room in three quick strides. He sat on the edge of the bed where Leigh sat fully dressed bolstered by half a dozen pillows, on top of the quilt. "What do I see here?"

Leigh followed his eyes to the paperback that was spread open across her stomach. It sported a baby blue cover with a picture of a prettily wrapped gift and was a sequel to

Something Borrowed, a book she'd just finished and loved.

"This?" she asked, folding down a page
and handing it to him. "It's called *Something Blue.* The first one was about a girl
who falls in love with her best friend's fiancé
and doesn't know what to do. Well, they end
up together, and now in this one, we see the
story from the perspective of the best friend
who lost her fiancé. Not that she's so innocent, either, because she slept with one of
her ex-fiancé's groomsmen."

Jesse read the back cover while shaking his
head. "Incredible," he murmured.

"What?"

"The fact that *you* read *this.*"

"What is that supposed to mean?"

"Oh, come on, Leigh. You don't think
it's amusing that little Ms. Cornell-
English-major-I-only-edit-serious-works-
of-literature is reading *Something Blue* in
her free time?"

Leigh snatched the book back and pressed
it against her chest. "It's really good," she
said with a frown.

"I'm sure it is."

Leigh wanted to say that, at least as of
this moment, *Something Blue* was far better
written than the latest draft of Jesse's novel.
That it had a sensible structure and coher-

ent language. That maybe it wasn't exploring too many lofty intellectual themes, but so what? It was witty, clever, and fun to read — something Mr. Literary Hotshot could use in triplicate right about now.

But of course Leigh didn't say any of this. She merely said, "I'm not going to defend my pleasure-reading choices to you."

Jesse held up his hands in surrender. "Fair enough. But you do realize that this changes everything, don't you? I now have actual proof that the work-Nazi editor is actually a human being."

"Just because I read chick lit?"

"You got it. How tough can someone be if they read and relate to *Bridget Jones's Diary?*"

Leigh sighed. "I loved that book."

Jesse smiled. "What was that other one . . . *The Nanny Diaries?*"

"A definite classic."

"Mmm," Jesse murmured, and Leigh could tell he was rapidly losing interest. She knew his gestures now, his expressions, could decode the meaning of a furrowed eyebrow or a half-smile. She'd been to the Hamptons four times in the last three months, and with each meeting things had felt less awkward. The second time she'd again stayed at the American Hotel, although she'd spent barely a handful of hours there — a fact that said a great deal considering the visit took place on a No Human Contact Monday (she waived the rule for one night). On the third and fourth visits she accepted Jesse's offer to stay in the guesthouse he'd built for his nephews — it was so much more convenient — and it wasn't until yesterday, on this fifth visit, that Leigh had realized the wisdom of bunking in one of the main house's upstairs guest rooms. After all, they often worked late into the night, and the walk to the guesthouse was winding and dark.

It was all very innocent and, to Leigh's surprise, it felt extremely natural. She was pleased that they were able to work so well together and still maintain professional distance, even if they were sleeping in rather close quarters. Henry hadn't thought it strange when Leigh mentioned she'd stopped staying at the hotel; he had other editors who traveled to visit authors — some to places more far-flung than the Hamptons — and they often bunked down on the property somewhere. When Leigh had told her father at dinner last week that she'd taken to spending two or three days a week working with Jesse in his home, he'd said something to the effect of "It's not ideal, but if they won't come to you, you go to them." All their blasé attitudes only furthered Leigh's conviction that Russell didn't need to know.

"I wondered what you wanted for dinner," Jesse was saying. "It's almost six and it's the off-season, so if we don't motivate soon, we're going to be shit out of luck. Do you want to grab a burger somewhere, or should I make something?"

"By 'make something' do you really mean 'pour cereal in a bowl'? Because if that's the case, I'd rather a burger."

"Ah, sweet Leigh, charming as ever. Is that your way of saying 'Thanks, Jesse. I'd love a home-cooked meal, I'm just way too difficult a bitch to actually say so'?"

Leigh laughed. "Yes."

"I had a feeling. Okay, then, cooking it is. I'm going to run to Schiavoni's for some food. Any requests?"

"Lucky Charms? Or Cinnamon Toast Crunch. With two-percent milk, please."

Jesse threw up his hands in mock disgust and left the room. Leigh waited until she heard the front door close and the car start before she picked up her phone.

Russell answered on the first ring. "Hello?"

He always pretended he didn't know it was her, even though he had caller ID like the rest of the civilized world. "Hey," she said.

"It's me."

"Hi, baby, how are you? How's the lunatic these days? He staying sober enough to get any substantive work done?"

Russell had taken to putting down Jesse pretty much every chance he got, regardless of how often Leigh reassured him that Jesse was nothing like his reputation, or how many times she told him that he was just another author, alternately confident to the point of arrogance or insecure to the point of debilitation. It didn't seem to matter, and Leigh figured out the more she defended Jesse, the more it incensed Russell. He was jealous — she certainly would be if he spent so much time with another woman — but she couldn't bring herself to reassure him. Even if Jesse never mentioned his wife (and Leigh had yet to detect any actual proof of her existence), the fact remained that Jesse was married and Leigh was engaged, and they had developed a nice friendship in addition to their working relationship. A nice *platonic* friendship — something Russell claimed, much to Leigh's irritation, was an impossibility between men and women.

Leigh sighed. "He's really not like that, Russell. He's not a drunk, he's just . . . just different. He's not quite as regimented as we are."

Dammit. This was definitely not the right approach. Any conversation she allowed to veer toward Jesse would definitely end in a fight, something that, despite her very best efforts, seemed to be happening a lot lately.

"Regimented?"

"You know what I mean."

"It sounds like you think he's all chill and Zen and that I'm stressed out and . . . and . . . *regimented.*"

"*We* are different people, Russell. And in my opinion, we're the ones living like responsible adults while he's lost and directionless, okay?" Leigh didn't acknowledge to Russell that although this had been her opinion a mere month earlier, Jesse's lifestyle no longer seemed so unappealing. "Look, why are we even talking about him? Who cares? I called to see what was going on with you. How was today's postproduction meeting?"

"It was fine. Nothing out of the ordinary."

"Russell, don't sulk. It's unbecoming."

"Thank you for the etiquette lesson, *dear.* I'll remember that."

"Why are you being like this?" Leigh sighed. She had merely wanted to check in, exchange a few pleasantries, and get back to her book, but she sensed that Russell was preparing a huge State of the Relationship talk. They were his specialty and her worst nightmare.

"Leigh, what's going on with us?" His voice grew softer, gentler. "Seriously, I think we should talk about it."

Leigh took a deep breath and exhaled silently. She strove for calm although her insides were screaming, *No, no, no! I'm sick of talking about it. Let's not talk about everything. Can't we just tell each other about our days and move on? Please don't do this to me!* and said, "What do you mean, Russ? There's nothing wrong with us."

He was silent for a minute. "Do you really feel that way? Doesn't it seem like there's a lot of distance? And what am I supposed to say when people ask why we haven't had our engagement party yet? That my fiancée doesn't seem to have time, even though we've been engaged for five months?"

Oh god, please not this again. "You know what a big deal this is — why can't you be understanding?"

"Yeah, well, call me crazy, but I guess I thought that getting married would be a big deal for you, too."

"Of course it is. Which is why I want to wait until everything can be perfect."

This wasn't completely untrue. Leigh knew she was dragging her feet with all the plans. Part of it was just an overall lack of interest in all things wedding-related — she wasn't the girl who picked out her gown at age twelve — and part of it was the dread of dealing with both her mother and Russell's, but when she was completely honest with herself, Leigh knew it went beyond that.

For a while she could tell herself that everything was moving too quickly. After all, it felt like only yesterday that they were kissing for the first time on a bench in Union Square. She'd liked Russell very much then, too — she'd thought he was sweet and good-looking, and she was flattered that he was interested in her. She hoped they would date and the relationship would develop or disintegrate naturally. Either two people grow closer and thrive, or the connection slowly fizzles and it's time to break up. She'd enjoy her time with Russell and not get all stressed out about what the future held. Which had worked fairly well, until he had gone and *proposed*. And not just proposed, but slid that ring onto her finger while Leigh sat frozen in shock, and then kissed her mouth as it hung open in disbelief. She had never been less prepared for anything in her entire life, and it didn't take a genius to see that she'd been haunted by doubts these past few months. What she didn't know how to explain to Russell — or anyone else — was what, exactly, was wrong. Nothing had changed between them since they'd first met; he was still every bit as sweet and kind and understanding. The problem was that Leigh was still waiting to fall head over heels in love with him, and everyone else — her friends, her parents, and worst of all Russell — thought she was already there. In light of all this, was it really so strange that she just wanted to take her time?

It was his turn to sigh. "I understand. I just wish there was, I don't know, a little *excitement* in your voice. Do you even talk about it to the girls?"

"Of course I do," Leigh lied. Emmy and Adriana asked about the upcoming wedding plans incessantly — they desperately wanted to plan a bachelorette party — but Leigh always found herself changing the subject. Why didn't they understand that this was all going way too fast? Even thinking this, though, made her feel guilty, so she softened her voice and said, "Baby, I'm excited about everything. We'll get married, and when that's finished we'll go somewhere exotic and very, very far away, like the Maldives, and we'll just relax and enjoy each other, okay? I promise."

"Will you wear that bikini I love? The one

with the metal circles on the hips and in the middle of the top?"

"Definitely."

"And you won't bring your laptop or a single manuscript, not even just for reading on the plane?"

"Not a single one," she said with certainty, although this gave her pause. "It will be perfect."

"Deal," Russell said, sounding as though the issue had been completely resolved.

"I'll call you later to say good night, okay?"

"You're definitely back tomorrow, right? We need at least one night alone together before the big Meet the Parents Thanksgiving."

"Of course we do, baby. I'll definitely be home tomorrow night," Leigh forced herself to say. She wasn't particularly dreading Thanksgiving in Connecticut, even though she probably should be, considering Russell's entire family was flying in to spend the holiday with hers, but her desperation to hang up the phone was overtaking everything else right then.

"Mmmwah!" Russell made a loud kissing noise into the receiver, a little inside thing they'd always done when they were apart.

Leigh did it back, feeling silly and slightly

annoyed and then guilty for feeling silly and slightly annoyed. They hung up and she felt relieved, then exhausted, too tired even to reopen her book.

She awoke with the disconcerting feeling that someone was watching her. She glanced out the window and could see a few scattered snowflakes highlighted by the light above the front door. The room was nearly pitch-black, but she could feel someone else's presence.

"Jesse?"

"Hey. Sorry. Did I scare you?"

As her eyes adjusted she saw him sitting across the room in the mahogany rocking chair. His hands were crossed over his chest and his head rested against the chair back. The smell of fresh garlic and baking bread wafted in from somewhere.

"What are you doing here?"

"Just admiring your sleep."

"My sleep?"

"I came up to wake you for dinner, but you looked so peaceful. I don't really sleep, pretty much ever, so it's always nice to watch someone else. Probably creepy, but I hope you don't mind."

"It's actually ironic, because I don't sleep anywhere else but here. There's something about being out here that's better than Bambien," Leigh said.

"Isn't it Ambien? Without the *B?*"

"Bath plus Ambien equals Bambien. But even that only works some of the time."

Jesse laughed and Leigh felt a surge of happiness. And for the first time in her thirty years of life, Leigh did something without giving any thought whatsoever to any potential consequences or reactions. With a completely blank mind and absolutely no anxiety, she climbed off the bed and walked over to the rocking chair. Not even standing above him made her nervous; she extended her hand and, when he accepted it with only the slightest confusion on his face, she tugged him upward. They were face-to-face, something that felt strange because Russell was so much taller. Leigh looked down at her hands, interlaced with his, a moment of intimacy that was undeniable, unmistakable. He unhooked their hands and put them behind her neck and entangled his fingers in her hair, and their lips pressed together and opened; Jesse's tongue on her own was more surreal than exciting, strange, or foreign.

From there everything moved quickly. They fell back onto the bed and within seconds they were naked. It was a violent, needy sex Leigh had rarely experienced. Even though he played with her hair, cupped her face, kissed the tip of her nose, stroked her back — he didn't hesitate to pin her down almost roughly, hands over her head. Afterward, Jesse pulled her close, still on top of the covers, and ran his fingers lightly across Leigh's shoulders until goose bumps rose along the backs of her arms. He asked if she was okay, did she feel all right, did she want some water? When Leigh was quiet for a few minutes, he lifted her chin and kissed her with such softness she thought she might die. They kissed like that for minutes, many minutes, lazily and languidly, and when Jesse pressed the flat part of his tongue across her bottom lip, Leigh had the sensation that she could disappear entirely into his mouth. Neither lifted their head from the pillow; they turned and kissed, so warmly and softly until something snapped and the urgency became overwhelming; their teeth clashed and their nails dug and their hands again grabbed and pulled.

Afterward Leigh rested her head on his chest and through half-closed eyes peeked to see Jesse awake, looking at her. Not with curiosity or love, though; he looked as though he was trying to remember every detail. Eye contact during sex was supposed to be the ultimate intimacy, a glimpse into the soul, blah, blah, blah. But no matter how close she'd felt to Russell or to other guys before him, meeting eyes had always felt forced or contrived, as though they'd both read the same article insisting *lovemaking* included eye contact. It always made her uncomfortable, took her out of the moment, but this was different. When Jesse's eyes found hers it was hard to breathe; no one had ever looked at her like that before. It was out of a movie, and Leigh felt like a movie star. It no longer mattered that she had a small rash on her belly from an allergic reaction to a new lotion, or that Jesse's skin was a bit too pale for such dark chest hair, or that they were both red and sweaty and panting; they had become the two sexiest people on earth. They had, in a very real way, found each other.

At some point they fell asleep because when Leigh opened her eyes the sky was beginning to lighten. She eased herself out from under the throw blanket Jesse had pulled over them, and she tiptoed to the bathroom across the hall, waiting for the floods of regret, guilt, and self-flagellation. Nothing came. Instead, she peed and braced herself for the familiar stinging of a UTI, but miraculously, she felt fine. Splashing water on her face, she caught a glimpse of herself in the mirror and nearly fainted. Her chin and cheeks were raw, and patches were lightly bleeding from beard burn; her lips were swollen; the skin on her neck was splotched red with teeth marks; her hair was tangled in ratty knots; there were bruises on her inner thighs from where he'd pushed himself against her. Her head throbbed from hitting the headboard, her pelvic bone ached from grinding, and the sensitive skin between her legs felt like it had been sandpapered. Even her feet ached from curling her toes for so many hours.

Never before had she felt so awful, if by *awful* one really means *absolutely fucking fantastic*. She returned to the guest room and found Jesse sitting in bed, still naked under the blanket. Light from the bedside window illuminated his face, and Leigh could now see the clock: 7:23 A.M. He looked up and, for the first time in hours, she was overcome with self-consciousness. She was standing there completely naked in the glow of full daylight before this man she barely knew, her *author,* for chrissake. Had she really *done* this?

"Leigh."

She forced herself to look directly at him. The room was cold and she could feel the hair on her legs beginning to prickle.

"Leigh. Sweetheart. Come here." He lifted

the edge of the blanket and motioned for her to join him.

She climbed in next to him. He wrapped his arms around her and pulled the covers over them both. He kissed her on the forehead like her father used to when she was sick. And what her father would think if he could see her now . . . not just in bed with someone — bad enough for a dad — but with the man she had been assigned to edit . . . and what about Russell . . . her fiancé . . . she was still wearing the beautiful ring he'd placed on her finger only five months earlier. She was a filthy, disgusting slut, unworthy of all of them.

"You look like you're in the throes of a crushing panic attack," Jesse whispered in her ear. He pulled her even tighter against him, but it was protective, not sexual.

"I'm a filthy, disgusting, unworthy slut," she said before she could stop herself, but the second the words were out she regretted them.

Expecting a denial or, at the very least, another hug and some sympathetic clucking — Russell's specialty — Leigh was horrified, and then supremely pissed off, when Jesse started to laugh.

She wrenched her body away from his and stared, dumbstruck. "You think that's funny? You think it's *amusing* that I basically just ruined my life?"

He hugged her tighter and rather than feel suffocated like she usually did, Leigh allowed herself to relax. Jesse kissed her lips and forehead and each cheek before saying, "I'm only laughing because you remind me so much of myself."

"Oh, great," Leigh muttered.

"But we didn't do anything wrong, Leigh."

"What do you mean, we didn't do anything wrong? I wouldn't even know where to begin. Maybe with the fact that I'm engaged? Or you're married? *Or that we work together?*"

She emphasized the working together bit, but it wasn't until she'd listed everything that Leigh admitted something to herself: She'd been waiting for Jesse to offer a reasonable explanation for his marriage, something along the lines of "We're actually divorced" or "I'm not really married." She knew this was unlikely. But that hadn't stopped Leigh from hoping.

He pressed his finger to her lips and shushed her, which she was surprised to discover she found cute and not enraging. "What happened between us happened naturally. We both wanted it. What's wrong with that?"

"What's wrong with that?" she snapped, her voice taking on a mean, almost vicious tone. "What about your *wife?*"

Jesse rolled over onto an elbow so he was hovering above Leigh and looked directly into her eyes. "I'm not going to patronize you with the usual shtick about how miserable we are and how she doesn't understand me and how I'm about to leave her, because that's not true and I don't want to lie to you. But that doesn't mean there aren't extenuating circumstances. And it certainly doesn't mean that I don't want you desperately right now."

Well, *that* was definitely not what she wanted to hear. The I-hate-my-wife-she-doesn't-understand-me shtick would've been just fine as far as she was concerned. The fact that it wasn't forthcoming made her even more acutely aware of how wrong this all was, something made more confusing by the fact that it all felt so right. So *right?* What the hell was she thinking? This was lunacy. . . . There was nothing right about betraying Russell or having sex with the man she was supposed to be working with. It had been a horrible lapse in judgment, inexcusable even, and it would be a miracle if they all got through this unscathed. Of course she could no longer edit Jesse, that much was clear, but that seemed an insignificant price to pay for her overwhelming stupidity.

It was time to leave. Immediately.

"What are you doing?" Jesse asked as Leigh wrenched herself out from under him and wrapped herself in the throw blanket. She grabbed her entire overnight bag and, with one hand clutching the blanket to ensure she remained covered, she half sprinted, half hobbled to the bathroom. Only after locking the door behind her did she allow the blanket to fall, but this time she couldn't face her body in the mirror. Knowing she would only sob if she allowed herself the luxury of a shower, she pulled on a pair of clean underwear, jeans, and a button-down and wrapped her knotted, frizzy hair into a bun. She took the time only to brush her teeth and, with that single task complete, Leigh clamped her jaw shut to keep herself from crying and opened the door.

He was standing in the doorway wearing a T-shirt and boxer shorts, looking miserable. Leigh wanted nothing more than to hug him, a desire she found both repellant and appealing, but she managed to squeeze past him without so much as brushing against his arm.

"Leigh, sweetheart, don't do this," he said,

following her down the hall and then the stairs. "Sit with me for a minute. Let's talk about this."

She swept into the kitchen to gather her papers and notebooks and saw the remnants of the dinner they'd never gotten around to eating. A casserole dish of hardened lasagna rested on a hot plate between two place settings and two poured glasses of red wine; two simple silver candleholders were covered in melted ivory wax.

"I don't want to talk. I want to leave," Leigh said quietly, with no intonation.

"I know, and I'm asking you to wait." Leigh glanced at him and noticed his stubble was sprinkled with gray and the hollows around his eyes were so dark they could be mistaken for bruises.

"Jesse, please." She sighed, her back to him as she slid her files into her bag. She remembered she'd left *Something Blue* in the guest room upstairs, but there was no way she was going back for it now.

He placed his hand on her shoulder and pulled at her gently to turn her around. "Look at me, Leigh. I want you to know that I don't regret last night at all."

For the first time since she'd gotten out of bed, Leigh met his gaze. She stared at him with her iciest narrowed-eye look and said,

"Oh, I'm so relieved! Thank goodness *you* don't regret what happened. I'll sleep better tonight knowing that. In the meantime, *get your hands off me*."

He pulled away. "Leigh. I didn't mean it like that. Please, sit down with me for just a minute. . . ." Something about the way his voice trailed off let them both know that the invitation, while sincere, was not something he actually wanted. He looked tired and beaten, like a man who was exhausted by the thought of having to deal with yet another hysterical postcoital female.

She would give anything for him to say that he loved her from the moment he met her and this wasn't just another extramarital conquest for the legendary Jesse Chapman — that she, Leigh Eisner, was different — but she knew better. She slung her bag over her shoulder and walked proudly through the front door with her head held high, both surprised and saddened when Jesse didn't follow.

Three Men Do Not a Femme Fatale Make

Adriana literally could not remember the last time she'd waited so anxiously for the phone to ring. In junior high, before puberty, when, like all the other girls, she had to wonder if she would get asked to the school dance? Perhaps. She had been rather eager to hear from the campus health center a few times regarding the occasional pregnancy test, and there was that little incident in Ibiza with the smidgen of cocaine that had necessitated flying in a decent lawyer. . . . Waiting hadn't been easy then, either. But this was different: She so desperately wanted *Marie Claire* to call with good news that she could scarcely think of anything else.

Not that she was expecting anything but good news, of course — if yesterday's meeting with the editor-in-chief was any indication, she was sure she'd made a good impression — but these magazine editors were unpredictable. It wasn't Adriana's outfit that made her nervous (what sane woman wouldn't adore the contrast between a floaty Chloe dress, patent Sigerson heels, and a perfectly distressed shearling coat that nipped in just so at the waist?), or how the meeting had gone (the two had shared Pellegrinos and opinions on the city's best plastic surgeons); she just couldn't help but wonder why Elaine Tyler had wanted to meet her in the first place.

As promised, Mackenzie had called Adriana a few days after the dinner party to see if she might be interested in writing a sample advice column on sex and relationships, to which Mackenzie would then add her own pitch describing Adriana's innate talents with men. If all went as expected, Elaine would approve a trial run of the column on the magazine's Web site and they'd wait to gauge the reader reaction. It had taken Adriana only a single afternoon to compose half a dozen essays (who could ever narrow it down to just one?), missives with titles ranging from "Sex Yes, Sleep No" to "I Was Just Being Friendly and Other Idiotic Excuses." She was quite confident she'd imparted her hard-won wisdom while keeping the tone light and entertaining, so why on earth had Elaine insisted on meeting her? More to the point, why hadn't Elaine's office called yet? Dumbly, Adriana had given her home number when asked by Elaine's assistant for contact information, and when she'd tried to correct herself and provide her cell number, the girl had waved her off. It was nearing six, and on a Friday! In just a couple of hours she'd have to drag herself out from under her favorite mink throw and get ready to meet Toby. Did they really expect that she'd just sit around and wait for the phone to ring?

"Bor-ing!" Otis cawed. "Big bor-ing!" He was perched on Adriana's blanketed ankle, staring at her as she stared at the TV.

"Okay, okay, it was just a commercial. There, look. It's starting again now." Otis swiveled his head toward the television and proceeded to watch *The Hills* with rapt attention.

Adriana reached toward him and stroked his silky back. Otis pushed against her hand, loving the massage. Adriana smiled to herself, pleased with the bird's progress. After endless screaming, too many sleepless nights, and no fewer than half a dozen international phone calls to Emmy in which Adriana threatened to maim and dismember Otis were she not relieved of duty immediately, bird and girl had bonded.

Thank god for her epiphany — without it, who knows what would have become of poor

Otis. It had happened only last week and was such a welcome surprise. Adriana had just stripped off her night clothes and was sprinkling salts into her morning bath when, from his perch near the toilet, Otis screamed, "Fat girl!" Instantly Adriana's eyes darted to the mirror, seeking assurance that she hadn't ballooned overnight; when she was satisfied that her thighs looked as tight as ever, she turned to look at Otis. He was sitting on the bar of his metal cage, head hung low, beak fixed into what could only be described as a sorrowful expression. Most notably, he was staring at himself in the mirror, and just as Adriana understood the importance of this, Otis let out a long, sad sigh and croaked, "Fatty," with quiet resignation.

It was then that Adriana realized Otis thought *he* was fat, not her.

All this time Otis had been screaming "fat girl" and "fatty," and they were cries for help! He must have known Emmy always offered too much food in a desperate attempt to quiet him. Poor thing! How could he be expected to control himself with the unlimited quantities of processed pet-store birdseed constantly paraded through his cage? Adriana immediately went online and scanned a few sites on proper African Grey nutrition, and she was horrified to find that packaged commercial bird food practically guaranteed morbid obesity and early death from kidney failure. Not to mention the psychological toll it was taking on him! To look at yourself in the mirror day after day — to live your life caged in front of a mirror! — and to recognize that you're overweight but not be able to do anything about it . . . well, Adriana wasn't sure it got worse than that!

This changed everything. Once she understood that Otis's anger and insults weren't directed at her, she was overcome with sympathy for the tubby little creature. That very afternoon she'd placed a call to Irene Pepperberg, the living parrot legend herself, and asked what the woman had fed Alex, her world-famous African Grey who had a larger vocabulary than the average American eighth-grader. Mobilized with newfound knowledge and bolstered by a very foreign-feeling desire to help, Adriana immediately hit Whole Foods, the Union Square farmers' market, an upscale pet boutique, and a vet who specialized in exotic birds. It had taken nearly a week of constant work, but Otis's lifestyle makeover was nearing completion.

It was hard to say what had had the greatest effect, but Adriana guessed it was probably Otis's new digs. Banished was his rickety aluminum cage with the vile smell and nasty wire bars that looked — and sounded — like some sort of Middle Eastern torture cell. In its place was a proper avian home: an armoire-sized, handcrafted wooden chest designed by one of New York's finest architects and built by a reputable contractor who had executed the vision perfectly. The frame was made of solid oak that Adriana ordered stained an espresso color to match her living room furniture; granite made up the floor and ceiling; the sides consisted of high-grade stainless steel mesh; and the front panel was made from floor-to-ceiling unbreakable acrylic that looked just like glass. She'd ordered a lush, high-resolution jungle print from a world-renowned *National Geographic* photographer and had it laminated and mounted in the background so Otis could feel close to nature, and she'd requested a full-spectrum lighting system installed so he wouldn't struggle so much with day and night. On the advice of a parrot behaviorist, Adriana had outfitted the inside with an assortment of basking ledges, swings, shelves, feeders, and perches, although she had later removed a few accessories after worrying the space might feel too cluttered. It was undoubtedly eight grand well spent, as evidenced by the fact that Otis had literally sung upon seeing it for the very first time. Adriana swore she could see him smiling as he gazed at the jungle panorama from his bamboo perch.

She guessed Otis's new diet, which included only nutrient-rich whole grains, fruits, and vegetables, had gone a long way toward alleviating some of his body-image issues as well. Adriana purchased a bulk supply of highly nutritious quinoa and supplemented it with organic berries, carrots, and — for calcium's sake — twice-weekly servings of Greek yogurt. Once Adriana discovered that Otis preferred the taste of Fiji artesian water to both Evian and Poland Spring, she replenished his bottle three times daily to ensure he was flushing out all his toxins. A trip to the avian groomer for a bath, a conditioning mist, and a toenail clip had completed his rejuvenation regimen.

What a difference a little indulgence made! Adriana made a mental note of this, should she ever doubt the importance of pampering herself (however unlikely that was). Otis was like a new bird. He sang, he chirped, he bopped his head in rhythm to the bossa nova music constantly playing in the apartment. In just one week he'd graduated from aggressive beast banished to the bathroom to sweet-natured playmate who liked curling up on the couch. This morning he had demonstrated just how far he'd come when, finally, he responded correctly to Adriana's relentless coaching.

"Okay, Otis, now try to focus, *querido,*" she cooed as she pulled a hand mirror out from her night table. They walked into the living room and sat together on the floor, where Otis happily pecked a carrot and Adriana coached him on his new vocab words.

"Now, I'm going to show you the mirror, and you're going to tell me who you see, okay? Remember, you're a smart, beautiful bird who has nothing to be ashamed of. Are you ready?"

Otis continued to munch.

Adriana moved the mirror in front of his face and held her breath. They were close, she could feel it, but so far Otis hadn't been able to move beyond screaming "Fatty!" at the sight of his own reflection. She held the mirror very still and waited, willing him to say the right words.

He was clearly entranced with himself — a good sign if there ever was one — as his wing feathers puffed up a bit and his beak parted ever so slightly. He appeared to be pleased with what he saw, although of course there was no way to tell. *C'mon,* Adriana willed, *you can do it!* And then, sure enough, with his head cocked and his eyes gleaming, Otis cawed, "Pretty girl!"

Adriana almost fainted with excitement. "Oh, now that's a good boy!" she said in enthusiastic baby talk. "What a good boy you are! Does the good boy want a treat?"

She'd decided to give Otis a little leeway on his gender confusion — for now, at least. There was time enough for everything, and it was his crushing lack of self-esteem that had had her most worried.

"Grape!" Otis cawed, clearly delighted. "Pretty girl! Grape! Pretty girl! Grape!" He shimmied up and down Adriana's calf as he called out the words.

"One pesticide-free grape, coming right up for . . . for who? Who gets the grape? The pretty boy gets the grape!" Adriana hoisted him onto the couch arm and headed toward the kitchen. She was just reaching inside the fridge for the bowl when the phone rang.

"Hello?" Adriana said with a twinge of irritation at the interruption. She wedged the portable between her shoulder and chin while arranging a few grapes on an appetizer plate.

"Adriana?" a breathless female voice asked through the handset.

Callers who refused to identify themselves before demanding to know your name were a pet peeve of Adriana's, but she willed herself to be polite. "This is she. Who, may I ask, is calling?"

"Adriana, it's Mackenzie. Hi, sweetheart! Listen, I have some phenomenal news. Are you sitting down?"

Phenomenal news sounds good, Adriana thought with anticipation. Phenomenal news sounded like Elaine had decided to post one (or maybe more!) of her essays on the *Marie Claire* Web site. Phenomenal news might even mean that Elaine had adored Adriana so much that she planned to feature her as a regular monthly contributor on the site, complete with a splashy link on the home page and (naturally) a tastefully posed headshot of the author herself. Author! Who would've ever imagined that she, Adriana de Souza, was about to embark on a career . . . as an author! And one who would surely garner thousands, if not millions, of hits every day. Girls would be forwarding her column link to all their friends, attaching to it little notes that read, "Check this out" and "so true" and "how funny is this," while men would stealthily visit the site to gaze adoringly at Adriana's author photo and perhaps pick up a pointer or two from the enemy camp. It was almost too fabulous to fathom.

"I'm sitting, I'm sitting," she said, trying to keep the squeal out of her voice.

"Well, I just got out of a meeting with Elaine." Pause. "She was very impressed with you."

"She was?"

"Very. I've worked here for almost nine years, and I don't think I've seen her this on board with a pitch, ever."

"Really? So that means she's going to publish one of the columns on the Web site?" Clearly it was true, but Adriana needed to hear the actual words. She was already thinking ahead to whom she would tell first. The girls? Toby? Her mother?

There was another pause, just long enough to pique Adriana's anxiety before Mackenzie said, "Um, actually, that's not what she was thinking."

Not what she was thinking? But she loved it! Adriana wanted to scream. *You said so yourself! How could I have so misjudged the situation?* she wondered as she rejoined Otis on the couch and balanced the grape plate between her knees. She stroked his back as he joyfully attacked the fruit. Then she began deconstructing the whole stupid idea. American women were never going to change — hell, they'd been on this empowered-female kick for decades now — so what was the point, anyway? Besides, who needed that kind of exposure? Publicity was one thing, but Web-based exposure, what with all those tacky Web site designs and undesirable lurkers . . . yuck. It made her skin crawl just thinking of it. It was time to put an end to this silliness once and for all.

"Oh, no? How unfortunate," her voice oozed with insincerity. "Well, I do appreciate your calling to —"

"Adriana! Just shut up for a second and listen. It's true that Elaine isn't interested in the Web site articles, but that's only because — are you ready for this? — she wants to make you a regularly featured columnist! Can you believe it?"

"A what?"

"A regularly featured columnist."

"Columnist?" Adriana asked again. Her brain was refusing to process the word.

"Yes! In the print magazine."

"Which one did she choose?"

"Adriana, I'm not sure you're understanding me. She chose all of them! I think she wants to start with 'I Was Just Being Friendly,' but we're going to run them all eventually."

"All of them?"

"One a month. Every month. Depending on reader reaction, which she and I both think will be fantastic, we're going to make it a regular feature each and every month.

We're going to call it 'The Brazilian Girl's Guide to Man Handling.' "

"Ohmigod. Oh. My. God." Adriana had completely abandoned all attempts at coolness, but she didn't care.

"I know! It's phenomenal. Listen, I've got to run to a meeting, but I'm going to have my assistant call you to make all the arrangements for your photo shoot. We're closing the March issue in two weeks, so it's going to be a rush, but timing-wise it's nothing we haven't done before. Sound good?"

"Perfect," Adriana murmured.

"Oh, and Adriana? Jack called last night to ask me out for this weekend, and —"

This snapped Adriana out of her reverie. "Last night? A Thursday? Who does he think you are? Some loser who just sits around and waits for him to call? You absolutely cannot —"

Mackenzie laughed. "Can you just shut up for a minute? I told him I was completely booked all weekend even though the only thing on my entire schedule is lunch with my mother on Saturday, and" — she paused here and took a breath — "he said he wasn't hanging up until I gave him a night next week that worked. We're going out Tuesday. He already made reservations."

"*Querida!* I'm so proud of you. You're ready

to write the column yourself!" Adriana was genuinely pleased at this development. Not only did it speak volumes to her own skills and advice, but from what little she knew about Mackenzie, it seemed like she was a woman deserving of a solid, adoring man. This was all good news.

Mackenzie laughed, sounding so happy and excited that Adriana was almost a teensy bit jealous. She remembered what it was like to get that excited over a new guy.

"No, I'll still leave that up to the professional. But it might make a good introduction for your first column: a little true-story vignette about how your magic works on even the most embittered, stubbornly single magazine editor in all of Manhattan."

"Previously embittered, soon-to-be-not-single magazine editor," Adriana reminded her.

"Fair enough. Okay, I'm running. Talk later?"

"Sounds good. Thank you soooo much, *querida*. Ciao!"

Adriana collapsed into the couch and motioned for Otis to join her. He gave an obliging little chirp and hopped to Adriana's lap. He nudged her hand for a grape, but Adriana was already dialing again.

"Leigh Eisner's office," her bored-sounding assistant said.

"Hi, Annette, it's Adriana. Can you put Leigh on for me, please?"

"I don't have her right now. Can I have her return?"

Adriana was not in the mood to deal with the assistant's lingo.

"Well, my dear, you'll have to get her. It's an emergency."

"Hold, please," Annette said curtly.

Leigh's exasperated voice came on the line a moment later. "An emergency?" she asked. "Please don't tell me you're calling because everywhere is sold out of your favorite Molton Brown body wash again. Wasn't that last week's 'emergency'?"

"You are not going to believe this," Adriana sang, ignoring Leigh entirely. "You are really not going to believe this."

"Ohmigod! Are they all out of their scented candles, too? What's a girl to do?" she squealed.

"Would you please shut up? I am calling you as a friend, not a frustrated shopper. Silly me figured you might be interested to hear that I might be featured in the March issue of *Marie Claire*."

Leigh yawned audibly on the other end. "Mmm, really? Congratulations. This will make it, what, like the eleven hundredth time they pick up one of your modeling shots? Or do you mean the party pages? In that case, it must be the eleven thousandth time."

"You're being a bitch," Adriana stated. "If you would just stop talking, I'd tell you that it has nothing to do with headshots or party pictures. I'm going to be a columnist."

Leigh stopped giving whispered instructions to her assistant midsentence and was absolutely quiet for a full twenty seconds. "You're what?" she finally asked.

"You heard me. I'm going to be a columnist. A regularly featured columnist, in the print edition. It's going to be called 'The Brazilian Girl's Guide to Man Handling,' and it's going to give advice on how to deal with men."

"You mean seduce them."

"Yes, of course I mean seduce them! What else do women want to know? It's not going to be easy, and I, for one, don't think they could've found a better person for the job."

"Me, neither," Leigh murmured. She sounded not just sincere but impressed, and Adriana couldn't keep from smiling. "Adriana, honey, I don't think it's too soon to say it, and I've never been more certain of anything in my entire life: A star has been born."

■ ■ ■ ■

Emmy sighed deeply as she turned the faucet off with her foot and closed her eyes, allowing her chest and legs to submerge completely. She'd been in the hotel tub for thirty minutes already, alternately dozing and reading under a relaxing stream of hot water that she drained and refreshed every few minutes. She didn't care that her hands were pruning, or that the sheen of sweat on her forehead had begun to run down the sides of her face, or that she was being quite irresponsible, environmentally speaking. What did any of that matter when she could lie there on New Year's Day after a long, wonderful night of drinking and lovemaking, and feel this peaceful and relaxed?

His name was Rafi something or other, and he was a dream. Emmy had been shocked to see how many things had changed in the fifteen years since she'd been to Israel, but thankfully the magnificence of their men wasn't one of them. If anything, they were even more adorable now, all the young strapping soldiers in uniform and their handsome older brothers who seemed in far better shape at thirty or even forty than their American counterparts. Everywhere she turned, she was met with olive-skinned, dark-haired, beautifully muscled specimens, and among this embarrassment of riches, Rafi was one of the finest.

They'd met two days earlier, a Thursday, at a Tel Aviv restaurant called Yotvata. It was an institution in Israel, a casual, happy place right on the city's beachfront promenade that specialized in massive, creative salads and delicious fruit-and-yogurt smoothies. All of the restaurant's ingredients came directly from its namesake kibbutz on the Jordan-Israel border in the Aravah Valley.

Emmy hadn't needed to think twice when Chef Massey requested she submit a list of lesser-known areas and cuisines that might serve as inspiration for the new upscale lunch place he was opening in London. She hadn't eaten at Yotvata since the last time she'd been in Israel — at age thirteen for her own bat mitzvah, and then two years later for Izzie's — but she still remembered it as some of the freshest, tastiest food she'd ever had. She outlined the restaurant's dairy focus and the chef's insistence on using only those fruits and vegetables grown organically.

Chef Massey loved it and asked her to accompany him on a scouting trip to Israel, where they would concentrate on expanding all of his current salad menu selections beyond the usual Caesar/Greek/mixed green in balsamic vinaigrette trifecta, and also explore different kinds of Middle Eastern cuisine. As far as Emmy was concerned, anything that got her out of New York City on New Year's Eve was fine, and if her destination was Israel, it was a huge bonus. What she hadn't counted on was Chef Massey bailing on their trip at the last moment, claiming he needed to be with his family when everyone really knew he was meeting his Pakistani model girlfriend in St. Barths. Emmy had feared her own trip was in jeopardy, but he'd sent her anyway.

Emmy had walked into the restaurant, expecting to endure a late lunch with the Israeli version of a typical American PR girl: well dressed, fast-talking, irritatingly upbeat. Instead she was escorted to a window table where she was joined by a Josh Duhamel clone with green eyes and the sexy swagger common among Israeli men. It took Emmy three seconds to notice that he was not wearing a wedding ring — a mandatory check but indicative of nothing — and another five minutes to establish that he didn't have a girlfriend.

"No girlfriend?" Emmy had cooed, aware but not caring that she sounded positively cougar-like. "There must be so many pretty young things running around the kibbutz."

Rafi laughed, and Emmy knew she would sleep with him.

Which she had, that night, and the morning after that, and the evening after that. They'd had sex exactly six times in the past day and a half, so often and enthusiastically that Emmy insisted on seeing Rafi's driver's license for herself.

"My god, you're not kidding. Nineteen-seventy-eight. I have never in my life met a man over twenty-one with that kind of stamina."

He laughed again and kissed her belly. "It is a special skill," he said in an accent straight out of a movie.

"I'll say so," Emmy said, stretching out like a satisfied puppy atop the fluffy duvet, blissfully unselfconscious despite their nakedness. "Want to order breakfast in bed? I'm on an expense account."

He feigned horror and wagged his finger in reprimand. "The Dan Hotel is good for many things . . . carpets, pillows, a beautiful pool, yes? But it's a crime to order breakfast from their kitchen when Yotvata is only steps away."

"I know, but those steps require me to shower and get dressed and go out in public." Emmy stuck out her bottom lip and widened her eyes in the most dramatic pout she could manage. "Do you want me to get out of bed?"

"No, no. Just wait here." He disappeared into the bathroom.

Emmy heard the water running and couldn't help but feel a little disappointed that he hadn't invited her to join him. She had just lifted the phone to order room service when Rafi reappeared.

He held open a fluffy hotel robe and wrapped it around her with a huge hug before leading her to the bathroom.

"For you, madam," he said, waving expansively. The tub was filled to capacity with steaming water and vanilla-scented bubbles; a half-dozen lit votives encircled the marble perimeter.

Without a moment's hesitation, Emmy allowed her robe to drop from her shoulders to the floor and climbed into the tub. She let her feet acclimate and then crouched slowly until she was sitting. When she was finally able to submerge her entire body in the hot water, she closed her eyes and groaned with pleasure. "This feels amazing. Come keep me company."

"No, no." He wagged his finger and leaned over to kiss her lightly on the lips. "This is only for you. I will be back in half an hour with a feast." Another kiss, and he was gone.

And so she lounged. And soaked. And refilled. He took longer than a half-hour, but Emmy didn't mind. It gave her time to slather on some of the hotel-provided vanilla moisturizer and arrange herself prettily in the chemise she'd purchased the day before at a little lingerie boutique on Sheinken Street. She couldn't remember the last time she'd bought anything sexy or even cute, but she couldn't resist this when she'd spotted it in the window. The softness of its pink jersey material felt amazing when it clung to her body, and the sheer green lace scalloping around the neckline made it comfy, casual, and sexy all in one. *Adriana would be so proud,* she thought, smiling. She'd welcomed 2008 in the arms of a sexy stranger, and she was feeling pretty damn good about it. By the time Rafi reappeared with bags in hand, she was somehow, miraculously, ready for another round.

"Come back to bed," she purred, letting him set down the bags before she pulled him on top of her.

"Emmy, you need food," he said but kissed her back.

They had sex again, and even though they were both too exhausted to finish, it still felt wonderful. Rafi wouldn't let her get out of bed to help unpack the food, so she just fell back into the pillows — the bed was way too plush, almost like a hammock, but who was she to complain? — and watched him carefully spoon different salads, breads, and yogurts onto their plates. He set everything down on the bed and placed a mixed-fruit smoothie and a cup of coffee on the nightstand and handed Emmy silverware wrapped in a cloth napkin.

"Bon appetit," he said, holding his coffee up to Emmy's.

"*B'tayavon*," she answered with a grin.

Rafi's eyes went wide with disbelief. "We spent two full days together and you didn't tell me before that you speak *ivrit!*"

"That's because I don't speak *ivrit* — I went to Hebrew school like every other Jewish American kid and my teacher was this enormously fat woman who taught us lots of food words in addition to the prayers."

"What other words do you know?"

"Hmm, let's see. I know *m'tzi-tzah.*"

Rafi laughed and nearly spit out a mouthful of food. "Your Hebrew school teacher taught you the word for *blowjob?*"

"No, that one was all Max Rosenstein." Emmy sipped her smoothie. "How do you know English so well? And please save the

'Americans-are-the-only-ones-who-don't-learn-foreign-languages' bit, please."

"But it's true," Rafi protested.

"Of course it's true; I'm just sick of hearing it. So? How did you learn to talk like this?"

He shrugged and looked a little shy. "My mother's American. She met my father while she was studying abroad and then just stayed. Considering that, I should actually speak much better, but she almost never talked to us in English since my dad couldn't understand much and she wanted to learn Hebrew."

"Incredible," Emmy said.

"Not really. You should hear my sister. She lives in Pennsylvania now. English, Hebrew, and a Pennsylvania Dutch accent, all rolled into one . . ."

Emmy pulled the covers up around her as Rafi explained the ins and outs of his family, how he was the only one still living in Israel. She tried to pay careful attention, but with each additional word he uttered, she became more and more convinced that she liked him. He wasn't husband material, of course — she wouldn't even go there anymore — but he seemed like a pretty decent guy. And with this realization came the old creeping insecurities. Did he like her back? Would they see each other again in the States? Was

he going to change his mind about everything and vanish, like Paul had that night in
Paris?

"Very interesting," Emmy murmured. "It
all makes perfect sense, but how did you
become the resident PR person? Because I
have to say, you don't exactly fit the mold."

"English major."

"Enough said."

"And you?" Rafi asked, spearing a forkful
of shredded goat-cheese salad.

"Government."

He made a face that said "give me a break"
and poked her in the side.

"I don't know, nothing that interesting,"
Emmy said, and she meant it. She hated
when people asked her to sum up her life,
because there really wasn't that much to
tell. "Born and raised in New Jersey in a
perfectly pleasant suburb with good public
schools and soccer and the whole deal. My
dad died when I was five, so I don't really
even remember him, and after that my mom
sort of tuned out. She was always there, but
she wasn't really there, you know? She got
remarried a few years ago and moved to
Arizona, so we don't see her that much. My
younger sister, now pregnant with her first,
is a doctor in Miami. Let's see, what else?
I went to Cornell for undergrad and then

decided I wanted to be a chef, so I went to culinary school, then I decided I didn't want to be a chef at all, so I dropped out. Fascinating stuff, isn't it?"

"Of course it is."

"Liar."

"Well, it certainly seems like you have a cool job," Rafi said.

"That's true. It's only been six months, but I'm loving it so far."

"What's not to love about traveling all over the world, staying in beautiful hotels, and having affairs with foreign men?"

"I don't do that!" Emmy protested.

"Now you're the liar."

"Not all the hotels are beautiful. . . ."

Rafi laughed, a good, masculine laugh, and poked her again. "Well, I'm not complaining. I'm honored to be guy number six hundred twelve, or whatever your number is these days."

More like just plain old six, Emmy thought. Which, considering Duncan had been her third, was pretty damn respectable: Since the Tour de Whore had begun the previous June, she'd doubled the number that it had taken her nearly thirty years to reach. After a bit of effort she was over the hump, so to speak, but George had been the perfect start. Then there was last week's Australian guy, currently living in London, who had grown up in Zimbabwe because his parents owned a safari company — he was all rugged and outdoorsy and although not blond or half as cute, could definitely remind someone of Leo in *Blood Diamond* after a couple of vodka tonics. Emmy was there only for a long weekend and overbooked with work to the breaking point, but what girl on earth could possibly pass up her very own Mick Dundee? Now Rafi was a positively delicious addition to her list. All three had been completely respectful, if not downright reverent, and Emmy couldn't remember ever feeling sexier or more confident. As long as she was safe, which she was — using both the pill and condoms — and she didn't have unreasonable expectations for what would follow — generally, absolutely nothing — then there was plenty to enjoy. Which was why it bothered her so much that Leigh and Adriana were suddenly on their high horses about the kind of wild fun they had so enthusiastically encouraged.

When she'd told them about the Australian, both had laughed and applauded her adventuresome conquest. Leigh had officially declared her risk of One-Hit Wonderdom over. Adriana pressed for the usual size/position/fetish details and looked downright envious when Emmy provided them with relish. Tour de Whore was officially declared up and running. Emmy had expected the same enthusiasm, or maybe even more, about Rafi, especially when she'd answered Adriana's call the day before, but her friend had sounded more subdued.

"Hey, happy new year!" Emmy had said into her cell phone. "How is it being home?"

Adriana sighed. "São Paulo's great, and it's nice to see everyone, but I think a full week between Christmas and New Year's is a bit too ambitious."

"But I'm assuming your father's happy?"

"He's in heaven. It's the only time all year he gets all his children in one place, so what can you do? It's a command performance, but as long as we all understand that and show up and smile, it's not unbearable."

Emmy laughed to herself at Adriana's idea of unbearable: tropical weather, a massive family compound staffed with more servants than the average hotel, and a full week of doing nothing but eating, drinking, and visiting old friends. She decided to change the subject entirely before she said something unkind. "So, guess what? I may have gotten to know — in the biblical sense — a very hot Israeli guy last night. And we're spending the evening together tonight."

Adriana whistled. "Wow, *querida*. That was fast. Like lightning."

"Oh, come on, don't tell me you wouldn't leap into bed with a soldier!"

"Of course I would. But wasn't Croc Dundee just last weekend? Or am I confused? My god, Emmy, I never thought I'd have trouble keeping your men straight."

Was that annoyance Emmy was hearing in Adi's voice? Judgment? Dare she even think it might be envy?

"Rafi is cute and smart and a total sweetheart. It was so much fun."

"Let's not forget Jewish," Adriana said, and Emmy could almost see her wagging her forefinger. "We know what that means . . . husband material!"

Emmy sighed dramatically. "You and Leigh were yelling and screaming just six months ago that I have to stop husband-hunting, that I absolutely must expand my sexual repertoire. Then, when I do exactly that, all you can talk about is getting married!"

"All right, *querida,* calm down. Of course I want you to have your fun. Let's talk about something else — like me."

Emmy laughed as she scrolled through the channels on the muted hotel television. "Fair enough. How's Mr. Baron? Dreamy as always?"

"He's good. Back in Toronto filming. But I have news."

"Don't tell me that —"

"No, we're not engaged. However . . ." She paused for effect and Emmy wanted to strangle her. "*Marie Claire* is going to publish my columns!"

"Your columns?" Emmy knew she wasn't exactly being supportive, but this was the first she was hearing about this.

"Yes, can you believe it? I met one of the editors at some dinner Toby dragged me to in November, and I taught her the rules of man-catching — which, I might add, worked so beautifully that she's still dating the man she met that night — and she wants to publish my advice!"

Emmy could barely mask her shock. Adriana a columnist? Adriana getting paid by someone else for work completed? It was almost too much to comprehend. "Adi, congratulations! You'll be able to impart your wisdom to a whole new generation of young women. Incredible."

"God knows they need it. American women . . . good lord . . . but I'm going to try. Listen, I have to get ready for lunch. Papa invited the entire neighborhood over for New Year's Eve. Where are you going with the Israeli boy tonight?"

"Some restaurant in Tel Aviv, and then, if I have anything to say about it, directly back to my hotel room."

Adriana sighed. "It's like listening to a new Emmy. It warms my heart, *querida,* it really does. Just be careful, okay? No need to sleep with every guy you meet."

"Did you really just say that? What the hell did you mean by that? Do I even need to remind you —"

Adriana interrupted her with a singsongy laugh. "Must run, *querida!* Have fun tonight, and happy new year! I'll talk to you next year!"

The exchange left Emmy feeling strange, a little off-kilter, the way she used to feel in junior high when she watched her friends shoplift lipstick from Kmart: not a hundred percent guilty, but nervous and slightly ashamed. Wasn't she doing exactly as they'd ordered? She wasn't trying to make anyone her husband — not so much as a single wedding dream in months! — and still she could sense their disapproval. It seemed so unfair. Even the angel Leigh had been with twelve, maybe fifteen guys before Russell, and no one thought that was particularly noteworthy. And Adriana! Good lord. The girl had slept with men (plural) she'd met in cabs on the way home from parties at the end of the night, having never laid eyes on them before, and she had the nerve to act shocked when Emmy met a nice boy through a work-related function and made a sober, mature decision to have a fling. *Pardon me, Adi,* she thought to herself with a roll of the eyes, an *affair.* Having sex with three perfectly polite and handsome men did not a femme fatale make.

Vowing not to let the memory of her friend's newfound prudishness bother her, Emmy pushed aside her plate and snuggled into Rafi's muscular embrace.

"Do you want to see a movie tonight?" she crooned, covering his forearm with little kisses. "Or maybe just order something on Pay-Per-View?"

Rafi stroked her hair and leaned down to kiss her forehead. "I'd love to, sweetheart, but I've got to get back home." He glanced at the clock on the nightstand. "Actually, I'd better get moving now."

"Now?" Emmy shot up, almost knocking his jaw with her shoulder. Weren't they going to spend the whole afternoon in bed, making love and taking baths and drinking yogurt smoothies? She figured they'd enjoy that at least until nightfall, at which point they could pull on whatever clothes were lying around and drag themselves to some hole-in-the-wall dive with great food that was known only to locals. They'd feast on falafel and hummus and gulp cheap red wine, and then they'd stagger back to the hotel, laughing and holding hands and falling into each other the whole way back. Satiated and exhausted, they'd collapse into the cool sheets and sleep for ten straight hours, only to wake and make love some more before he drove her to the airport and kissed away her tears, vowing to come visit her in New York over the holidays, if not before. Surely she'd meet his parents then, too — normally, it would be much too soon, but considering he'd be coming all the way from Israel and they were only in Philadelphia, it would be downright silly not to meet for a meal, even if it was just a quick lunch somewhere on the —

"Emmy? Sweetheart, I told you yesterday that I'd be driving south today. Don't you remember?" His voice sounded concerned, but Emmy was convinced she detected the faintest hint of irritation.

Of course she remembered him saying that he'd have to leave, but she certainly hadn't believed it.

Emmy nuzzled into his neck. "I remember, Rafi, but that was . . . that was yesterday. You still have to leave?" She hated the sound of her voice, pleading and a little bit pathetic. She'd just finished telling anyone who would listen that she was just in it for casual, unattached fun, and here she was clinging to this near stranger like a barnacle. *Please don't pull a Paul!* she thought urgently. *Please, please, please.*

He moved away ever so slightly and gave her a strange look. "Yeah, I still have to go" were the words he actually uttered, but what Emmy heard was something closer to "The last twenty-four hours were great, but not so great that I'm going to change my plans and stay with you."

Stung, Emmy tucked the sheet under her arms and rolled, making sure to keep as much skin covered as possible. She felt exposed and vulnerable, yes, but it was more than that: It had happened suddenly, but she was now acutely aware that she would most likely never see Rafi again. So what if his departure only confirmed that they were just having a good time? That was all she wanted, anyway. Rafi was sweet and handsome, but she barely knew him and, were she being completely honest, she couldn't see them spending the rest of their lives together. So why get upset over him leaving when he said he was going to all along? It was quite simple, so simple that Emmy suspected every woman on the planet instinctively understood the concept even when no man was able to wrap his brain around it: She didn't necessarily want him to stay, she just wanted him to *want* to stay. Was that really asking too much? And even though she would never, ever agree to go with him — truth be told, she could use a little alone time, and there was no denying she needed to catch up on work — couldn't he have had the decency to ask? A simple invitation to join him? Was that really so unreasonable?

He climbed out of bed and headed for the bathroom.

"I'm going to jump in the shower," he called, the door already closing. "I hope you know you're welcome to join me if you want."

Join what? The shower? The trip down south? The rest of his life as his beloved be-trothed?

This was exhausting. If she was going to make this kind of emotional investment in someone, he should at least be a proper boyfriend. But for a casual fling? She could drive herself crazy. The doubts were racing through her mind (*Just admit you're not cut out for this lifestyle, You're a monogamist at heart, Stop acting like an immature party girl,* and on and on).

Get it together, Emmy told herself as she

resolutely pulled on a pair of dependable cotton bikinis and one of her full-coverage, heavily padded, where-sex-goes-to-die bras. A navy pantsuit and white button-down shirt came next, and just as she heard the shower turn off, Emmy chose her classic loafers over the high-heeled pumps she'd been wearing for the last few weeks. By the time Rafi emerged, fully dressed in clean jeans and a blue shirt, Emmy was perched primly on the bed, flipping through her Filofax while trying to act aloof and preoccupied.

Rafi stood over her, pulled her hair into a ponytail, and kissed her neck. It was an intimate move, suggestive of people who had spent loads of time together, and for a moment Emmy was pleased. Pleased, that is, until Rafi released her hair and, after giving her a rather paternal kiss on the forehead, began to gather his watch and wallet and canvas backpack. He'd collected his things in just a minute and didn't seem bothered by the fact that Emmy appeared both silent and completely absorbed in her scheduling.

"I know you must have a lot of work to do, sweetheart, so I won't make this a long, sappy good-bye." He plucked his sunglasses from the night table and pushed them on top of his head.

"Mmm" was all Emmy managed. Was he

really going to just up and leave?

"Come here, give me a hug." He squeezed her arm to indicate she should stand up; when she obliged, she found herself in the middle of an embrace so lukewarm, so passionless, that it could have been shared with a distant grandfather or a close hairstylist. "Emmy, this was great. Really, really great."

"Uh-huh," she mumbled again. He either didn't notice or didn't care.

He followed this with another fatherly kiss and the obligatory hug, then headed to the door. "Safe flight tomorrow. I'll be thinking of you."

"You, too," she said automatically, with no feeling, although this did elicit from him a relieved smile, one that seemed to say, *Thank god you're not going to make this any more complicated than need be.*

A second later he was gone. It took Emmy only another minute or so to realize he hadn't bothered to ask for her e-mail address or phone number: She would never, ever see him again . . . and he clearly couldn't care less.

THE PERFECT-FOR-RIGHT-NOW RELATIONSHIP

The therapist's hands felt sensational working over her knotted shoulders, but even with the mood music and dimmed lighting and lavender aromatherapy oils, Leigh couldn't calm her mind. The month since she'd slept with Jesse had been torture, and for someone who was accustomed to obsessive thoughts and compulsive behaviors, well, that was saying a lot. There had not been a single second — literally, not one — that wasn't spent hashing and rehashing what had happened with Jesse, what was going to happen with Russell, or some twisted combination of the two. She'd been prepared to tell Russell everything immediately, but then she had a bit of time to think during her drive home from the Hamptons and had reconsidered. It wouldn't be fair to Russell or either of their parents to ruin everyone's Thanksgiving with some dramatic — and most likely relationship-ending — announcement. It had helped matters significantly when she'd received a voice mail from Jesse saying that he was leaving the following day for a holiday trip to Indonesia and wouldn't return until after the new year. It was almost like he was handing her a free pass on a silver platter, and although her conscience begged to be cleared, she decided she would bear the guilt and pretend that everything was fine until they'd all gotten through those horrible weeks of Thanksgiving, Christmas, and New Year's.

Somehow Leigh had made it through the last few weeks without having a complete nervous breakdown, but she was even more of a basket case than usual. With Emmy in Israel and Adriana in Brazil, she hadn't even had the opportunity to share with her friends what she'd done, although were she to be honest with herself, she was also relieved not to have to say it aloud. She'd even endured a particularly painful New Year's Eve party at one of Russell's colleague's apartments — a loft that was almost identical to Russell's, only this one was in SoHo — but when it came time to head back to work on January 2, she just couldn't do it. She called in sick that day and the next, an event so rare it warranted a suspicious phone call from Henry.

"Are you really sick, Eisner, or did something happen I should know about?" he had asked. She'd called to leave him a message on his voice mail at six in the morning, but he'd picked up on the second ring. Henry was a lifelong Sunday-night insomniac, so he'd taken to arriving at the office at four or five in the morning on Mondays, claiming those few isolated hours were his only decent work time the entire week. In her distress Leigh had forgotten this.

"What are you talking about?" Leigh asked with passably believable irritation. "Of course I'm actually sick. Why would you think otherwise?"

"Oh, I don't know, maybe because you haven't taken a sick day in all the years you've worked here, coupled with the fact that Jesse Chapman — fresh off the plane from Asia — left me three messages yesterday and another two this morning already. Just call me intuitive like that."

"What did he say?" Leigh asked. She knew in her heart that their professional relationship was essentially over, but she wanted the opportunity to present it to Henry herself, when she was ready.

Leigh could hear Henry sipping something and then chuckling. "He didn't say a goddamn thing. Claims he was just 'checking in,' and 'touching base' and 'saying hello,' which, coming from Mr. Chapman, may as well be skywriting for 'something is completely fucked and I'm trying to ascertain whether you know what it is or not.' "

Leigh inhaled, simultaneously impressed with Henry's perceptiveness and angry at Jesse's transparency. "Well, I can't speak for Jesse, but as far as I'm concerned, there's nothing to report. The manuscript is not yet where I want it to be, but it's no cause for concern," she said with a steadiness she didn't feel.

Henry paused for a moment, started to speak, and then changed his mind. "So that's your story and you're sticking to it, huh? All right. I don't buy it, but I'll accept it — for now. But the moment anything arises that puts our publication date in jeopardy, I want to know about it. I don't care what time of the day or night, whether it comes by FedEx or fucking carrier pigeon, I want to know. Okay?"

"Of course! Henry, you don't need to impress upon me how important this is, I promise. I swear I'm handling it. And I hate to cut this short, but it feels like I'm swallowing shards of glass right now."

"Glass, huh?"

Leigh nodded even though no one could see her. "Yeah, I'm guessing it's strep, so I probably won't be in tomorrow, either. But I have my laptop at home, and of course I'm always on my cell."

"Well, feel better. And I'm glad we had this little chat."

A shot of pain in her neck brought her back to the massage she'd scheduled right after hanging up with Henry. She flinched.

"Oh, sorry," the therapist said. "Was that too hard?"

"No, not at all," Leigh lied. She knew it was acceptable to provide feedback during a massage, that it was silly to pay a boatload of money and not enjoy it or, worse yet, to endure an hour's worth of pain, but no matter how often she was reassured of these facts, Leigh could not bring herself to say anything. Each time she swore to herself that she'd speak up, and each time she gritted her teeth through kneading that was too strong, music that was too loud, or a room that was too cold. She wondered if she was worried about hurting the masseuse's feelings. That would be ironic. No hesitation whatsoever in cheating on her fiancé, but better not tell the salaried stranger that you'd prefer a softer touch! Leigh shook her head in disgust.

"I am hurting you, aren't I?" the girl asked in response to Leigh's movement.

"Hurting is an understatement, actually.

It's more like getting pummeled by a professional boxer," Leigh said without thinking.

The girl began to apologize profusely. "Ohmigod, I had no idea. I'm so sorry. I can definitely be much gentler."

"No, no, I'm sorry. I, uh, didn't mean it like that. It just, um, it came out wrong. Everything's great," Leigh rushed to say. Why couldn't she control her own mouth?

The massage had seemed like a good idea that morning — if ever she'd needed to relax, it was now, and one of her authors had sent her a gift certificate for Christmas, so she didn't have to feel guilty about spending the money — but so far it had only served to provide a solitary, quiet chunk of time during which Leigh could do nothing but think.

She and Russell had plans to discuss the wedding over dinner that night, and Leigh could think of nothing she dreaded more.

"Your whole neck is knotted up pretty tight. Are you feeling a lot of stress lately?" the girl asked, working a muscle with her flattened palm in the same painful circular motion.

"Mmm," Leigh murmured noncommittally, praying the girl would intuit her disinterest in chatting.

"Yeah, I can tell. People always wonder

how we know where they're carrying their tension, and I'm always like, 'C'mon, guys, that's what we're trained for,' you know? Sure, anyone can rub your back and make it feel good, but it definitely takes a professional to locate those specific pressure points and smooth them out. So, what is it?" she asked. Her voice was low and not particularly grating, but the speed with which she talked made her sound anxious herself.

"What's what?" Leigh asked, annoyed that she was being forced to participate in this exchange.

"What's all your stress related to?"

For someone who had stopped seeing a shrink because she found it too revealing, Leigh was not thrilled with this line of questioning. Or any questioning, on anything, from anyone. And yet she was entirely unable to utter a few simple words, something along the lines of "I have a bit of a headache; would you mind if I just lie here quietly?" Instead, Leigh made up some inane story about tough deadlines at work and the pressure of planning the perfect Greenwich wedding. The girl clucked sympathetically. Leigh wondered what sort of reaction she might elicit were she to describe the real source of her tension, i.e., the fact that she had slept with one of her authors (and by "slept with," she really meant "had the best sex of her life in every imaginable position and variation over the course of ten mind-blowing hours") while still acting the part of loving and excited partner to her sweet, supportive, and totally clueless fiancé.

By the time the massage ended, Leigh felt slightly more anxious and significantly less relaxed. She pulled on her clothes — not even bothering to shower off the scented oils — and mentally tried to prepare herself to deal with the mess she had created. All she really wanted to do was return to her child-hood home, curl up under the blankets, and lose herself in some TiVo. She wanted it so bad she could feel it, and she was just about to drive Russell's car to her parents' when another image flashed into her mind. It, too, had a soft comforter and her favorite novels, but it included a panorama of both parents arriving home and attacking her with ques-tions. *Why are you here in the middle of the week? Where's Russell? How's work going? When are we going to choose the menu for the reception? What's happening with Jesse's book? Where are you going to register? Why do you look so miserable? Why? Where? When? Tell us, Leigh, tell us!* Her dull head-ache now had that special ice-pick quality to it, and she suddenly felt particularly gross with a layer of clammy leftover massage oil between her skin and her clothes.

She paid quickly and managed to stand her ground when asked to fill out a survey on her experience with the spa.

"You sure?" the receptionist asked, snapping her gum in quick, irritating bursts. "You get a fifteen-percent-off coupon for your next treatment."

"Thanks, but I'm in a rush," Leigh lied, almost smiling to herself (almost) when she calculated that probably half of what she said these days was completely untrue. She scrawled an unrecognizable signature on the gift certificate, handed over a twenty-five-percent tip in cash out of guilt for not being chattier with the therapist, and ducked out the front door before one more gum crack could drive her to murderous action.

Even with a heavy load of rush-hour traffic, the cab ride from the Upper East Side spa to TriBeCa felt like it took only thirty seconds. The cabbie was just dropping her off in front of Russell's building when her phone rang.

"Hey," Russell said when she clicked it open. He sounded different somehow, more distant, but Leigh told herself she was just imagining that.

"Hi! I'm just pulling up to your building

right now. Are you home?" Her own voice sounded forced and faux-cheery, but Russell didn't seem to notice.

"No, I'll be at least another hour, but I was hoping you'd wait for me. Just let yourself in and maybe order us some food? I can't wait to see you tonight."

"Me too," Leigh said and was relieved when she realized it wasn't a complete lie.

She'd just paid the driver and stepped out of the taxi when her phone rang again. She flipped it open without looking at it. "I forgot to ask, do you want sushi or Italian?" she said.

"I vote Italian," a female voice said with a laugh.

"Emmy! Are you calling from Israel? How are you?" Leigh didn't particularly feel like talking to anyone just then, but she couldn't just hang up on her best friend when they hadn't spoken in over a week.

"No, I just landed. I'm in a cab on my way back from JFK. What are you up to tonight? I was hoping I could drag you to dinner. I miss my friends!"

"I'm breaking up with Russell," Leigh said quietly, with absolutely no intonation. It took a second before she was even sure she had uttered the words, but Emmy's gasp confirmed it.

"What did you say? AT&T is shit. I don't think I heard —"

"Yes, you did. You heard me," Leigh said with more calmness than she'd felt in seventy-two hours. "I said I'm breaking up with Russell."

"Where are you?" Emmy demanded.

"Emmy, I'm fine. I appreciate your —"

"Where the fuck are you?" she screeched so loud Leigh had to move the phone away from her ear.

"I'm about to walk into his apartment. He's not home yet, but I'm ordering dinner for us and I'm going to do it then. Emmy, I know this must seem like it's out of nowhere, but —" Her voice cracked and a sob choked off her breath.

"I'll be right there. Listen to me, Leigh Eisner. I am on my way over there, okay?" Leigh heard the muffled sound of Emmy redirecting the cabbie to Russell's cross streets. "Are you still there? We're already through the tunnel and headed south on the FDR. I'll be there in ten, twelve minutes. Do you hear me?"

Leigh nodded.

"Leigh? Say something."

"I hear you," Leigh squeaked through a sob.

"Okay, don't move. Do. Not. Move. Understand? I'll be there momentarily."

Leigh heard Emmy hang up, but she couldn't bring herself to close her own phone. Why had she just said she was going to break up with Russell? It wasn't at all what she'd been thinking for the past couple of days, during her massage, on the ride back to the city. She'd merely reached the conclusion that she must be honest with him — at all costs — about Jesse. That even if it was only to selfishly assuage her own guilt, starting off a marriage based on cheating was probably not a brilliant idea, and Russell deserved to know the whole truth from the beginning. That said, she was also reasonably sure that Russell — with the proper reassurances — could be convinced to give her a second chance. It wouldn't have been pretty or enjoyable for either of them, but if she worked hard enough at assuring him that it was a complete fluke with Jesse (which it was) and would never happen again (not a lie), she figured they had a pretty decent chance of getting through this. What she hadn't even considered was that she might not *want* to get through this . . . until she'd blurted out those very words just moments before.

Leigh bought a cup of coffee from a tiny corner health-food shop with no proper half-and-half or fake sweeteners — where were all those goddamn Dunkin' Donuts when she needed one? — and retied her scarf tighter around her neck. She was about to walk into Russell's lobby when she heard Emmy's voice shouting behind her. She turned to see a cab screeching to a stop, a tan but panicked Emmy hanging out the back window.

Leigh stood and waited calmly in the doorway, watching as her friend threw three twenties at the driver, collected a few dollars' change, and dragged her rolling suitcase from the trunk.

"When did it get so fucking freezing?" Emmy hissed as she tried to yank the suitcase's handle up from its tucked position.

"About two seconds after you left," Leigh said, aware that she should help her friend but feeling no real inclination to do so. For the moment it felt perfectly fine to stand there and watch her own breath come out in hot streams against the frigid air. She was breaking up with Russell. Breaking up with Russell. Was she really going to up and end it, just like that? Call off the engagement, give back the ring, become un-affianced? Yes. Yes, she was.

"My god, this is uncivilized! Uninhabitable! Why do we choose to live like this?" Emmy kissed Leigh on the cheek. "Russell's not home, right? So we can go upstairs?"

Leigh held open the door and waved Emmy through. She used her key to summon the elevator that opened directly into Russell's full-floor loft, and both girls helped pull Emmy's suitcase on board. The panorama of stainless steel and black lacquer that greeted them when the elevator doors swept open was enough to shock Leigh back to the present; immediately upon seeing Russell's collection of metal sculptures and his decorator-chosen black-and-white prints, she felt the familiar feel of her fingernails digging into the flesh of her palms.

"Welcome!" Leigh sang with mock cheeriness. "Something about this place just warms the heart, doesn't it?"

Emmy left her suitcase by the door, tossed her down puffer coat over a dining room chair, and flopped awkwardly onto Russell's impossibly chic, rock-hard sofa. "I could name three dozen women off the top of my head who would kill to spend just one night in this apartment."

Leigh shot her a warning look.

"I'm just saying. . . ."

"You're right, of course. Which makes it all the more ironic that I'm not one of them." Her voice was quiet and serious, and for a moment Leigh wondered why she wasn't already crying.

Emmy patted a patch of couch next to her, but her hand ended up making a smacking noise. "Christ, that's hard," she muttered. "C'mere, sit down and tell me what's going on. I feel like this came out of nowhere."

Leigh walked toward Emmy but sat down on the Ligne Roset daybed opposite her. "It must seem that way, I guess. Hell, it sort of feels that way. But not if I'm going to be really honest with myself." Leigh felt her throat constrict and almost felt relieved that she was finally experiencing something resembling a normal reaction.

"What's going on? Have you two been fighting?"

"Fighting? No, of course not. Russell's as sweet and supportive as he's ever been. I don't know, I've just, well, I don't know. . . ."

"Ohmigod!" Emmy slapped her head. "How could I not have guessed? He *is* a man, after all. Russell's cheating on you, isn't he?"

Leigh could feel her eyes open wide, but she couldn't get any words out.

"*Oh. My. God.* That shit! Mr. I'm So Fucking Perfect is cheating on you? Leigh, sweetheart, unfortunately for both of us, I know exactly how you're feeling right now. Christ, I can't believe that he'd actually —"

"He's not cheating on me, Emmy. I'm

cheating on him."

That seemed to quiet everything down for a solid thirty seconds. Emmy looked as though she'd been struck, her face contorted with surprise as she struggled to process what she'd just heard.

"You're cheating on Russell?"

"Yes. Well, no. Not currently. But I did."

"With who? Whom. Whatever."

Leigh sighed. "It's not important. What matters now is that it's over, but I have to think it happened for a reason. People who are ecstatically happy in their relationships don't cheat."

Emmy held up her hand as if to ask for quiet. "It's not *important?*" she asked. "Leigh, darling, you're one of my two best friends on this planet. Not to make this entirely about me here, but come on! It's bad enough I had no idea you were sleeping with someone else while it was happening — and I recognize now's probably not the ideal time to be pissed at you for it — but to even suggest that you aren't going to tell me after the fact is absolutely ludicrous! I mean, do you really —"

"It was Jesse. Jesse Chapman."

Emmy threw up her hands in exasperation. "Jesus Christ, I don't know how she does it. It's like she has some sort of sixth sense for these things. Or maybe you just fuck enough people yourself and you can just *feel* when someone else is doing it, too. Un-fucking-believable. That girl is just unbelievable!"

"What are you talking about? Who is un-believable?"

The sound of Leigh's voice seemed to snap Emmy back to reality. "Oh, sorry. It's just that Adriana's been insisting for weeks now — maybe months — that you were sleeping with Jesse, and I insisted you weren't. Swore up, down, and sideways that it was the most ridiculous idea imaginable. I mean, you're engaged to Russell, for chrissake —"

Emmy stopped midsentence and clapped her hand over her mouth. "Sorry. Leigh, I'm so sorry, that came out all wrong."

Leigh shrugged. "Well, for the record, I'm not 'sleeping with' Jesse, and I never was. It happened exactly once, and it will never, ever happen again. So next time you talk to Adriana, you can tell her she was wrong."

Emmy's phone rang. The look on her face when she checked the caller ID confirmed it was Adriana.

"My god, does she have you wearing a wire?" Leigh said, shaking her head.

"That whole Latina intuition, so she claims." Emmy clicked off the phone and tucked it back in her purse. "So, at the risk

434

of sounding, uh, insensitive here, can I ask why you feel like you have to end everything with Russell? I mean, if Jesse was a onetime thing — and you want it that way — well, am I a completely horrible person for suggesting you just try to put it behind you?"

"It's not that simple."

"Does that mean you have feelings for Jesse?"

"No! Well, yes. Sort of. But Jesse actually has nothing to do with this. It's about Russell and me."

Emmy pulled a bottle of water from her bag, took a swig, and offered it to Leigh. Leigh shook her head no.

"I hear that," Emmy said carefully. "But I'm sure you've also considered that whole thing about not telling someone something hurtful just to unburden yourself. Like, if it's not going to help them to know, they're better off not knowing?"

Leigh had to remind herself to unclench her hands and try to lower her shoulders away from her ears. She didn't want to feel so annoyed with Emmy, but it was getting difficult to disguise. Obviously she had considered all of this, and obviously the situation was a great deal more complicated than Emmy presumed. Leigh certainly didn't feel compelled to — how did Emmy put it?

— *unburden* herself to Russell just because she'd screwed up and wanted forgiveness. If that were the case, she'd make the only rational decision possible and do exactly as Emmy had recommended: feel guilty for betraying her fiancé, swear to herself that it would never happen again, and move along. The problem came when she allowed herself to acknowledge that even though she probably could, she didn't *want* to move along.

She took a deep breath. "I'm not in love with Russell," she said.

"Oh, Leigh." Emmy jumped off the couch and made toward the daybed, but Leigh held up her hand.

"No. Please don't."

Emmy backed away and settled for resting her hand on Leigh's arm.

"Here's where I say something absolutely inane and ridiculously trite, like 'I *love* Russell, but I'm not *in love with* Russell,' right?" Leigh laughed and smeared a fat tear from her lower lashes to the side of her forehead. "My god, the whole situation is such a fucking mess. Who would've ever thought it was possible? The perfect one — Marcia, Marcia, Marcia! — agrees to marry a guy she doesn't love because everyone else loves him and she figures that, given enough time, she will, too. Then, rather than deal with her own self-created situation in a reasonably mature manner, she chooses to screw someone she's working with. A married someone! Thereby wrecking both career and love life in one tidy swoop. It would be funny if it weren't so pathetic."

"It's not pathetic," Emmy said automatically.

"I'm talking about myself in the third person. What's not pathetic about that?"

"Oh, honey." Emmy sighed. "I'm so sorry. I really had no idea it was this bad. None of us did. But you can't beat yourself up over something you don't feel. Russell's a great guy, and yes, he certainly seems like the perfect guy. But none of that matters if he's not the perfect guy for you."

Leigh nodded, "It just all happened so quickly! One minute we're taking romantic strolls in Union Square, and the next thing I know he's sliding a diamond onto my finger without ever even imagining the answer could be anything but yes. I just keep wondering when we ended up in such different places. I thought we were casually dating, having a good time, the perfect-for-right-now relationship. No end in sight, but not necessarily a great love affair, either. But engaged? To be *married*? Emmy, at the risk of sounding like the biggest moron alive — or the least perceptive one — I just didn't see it coming. I've spent every minute since then waiting to feel sure, to *know* that it's right, but I haven't, Em. I've never, ever felt that with Russell, and I think it's time to face the fact that I'm never going to."

Both girls froze at the sound of the elevator rising. Before either could say another word, they heard the doors open and Russell's footsteps make their way from the foyer to the kitchen, where the fridge quickly opened and shut again, and then he sauntered into the living room.

"Oh, hey Emmy. Sorry, I didn't know you were here," Russell said with a distracted look. Leigh could tell from the single fleeting glance he'd given her that Russell was not in the mood for company tonight. Well, that made two of them.

To her credit, Emmy didn't need any further hints. She jumped off the couch, and after kissing first Russell and then Leigh, she mumbled something about a mandatory work dinner and bounded out the door. She disappeared so fast Leigh didn't have a single minute to prepare what she was going to say. Or when. Or how.

"Hi," Leigh said shyly, studying Russell's face for any clue that he had overheard them. It was impossible, of course — they'd heard the elevator in the lobby and hadn't uttered a word as it had made its way upstairs — but she couldn't help hoping he'd caught a few slivers. How much easier all this would be if he had even the smallest clue what was coming.

"Hey. I hope I didn't interrupt you guys. She bolted pretty fast." He loosened his tie (the one her parents had bought him for his birthday last year), and then, as though deciding that it still wasn't enough breathing space, pulled it over his head and tossed it onto the Lucite coffee table.

"Yeah, well, you know Emmy, always on the run."

"Hmm. Did you order food?"

"Sorry, Emmy wanted to say hi on her way home from the airport, and we've been talking, just for a few minutes, and, well, I forgot. What do you want?" Leigh asked, grateful for something to do. She pulled out her phone and began scrolling through the numbers. "Sushi? Vietnamese? That place on Greenwich has great spring rolls."

"Leigh."

"Or we could just hit the diner if you want. A cheese omelet and well-done home fries? That could be really good right now."

"Leigh!" His volume stayed the same, but his voice was sharper, more insistent.

Her eyes shot up to meet his for the first time since he'd walked in. Russell never got annoyed with her, about anything. What if something happened at work today? Maybe he'd gotten in a fight with that associate producer who was always such a jerk. Or maybe the network had decided to change his time slot again? They'd been talking about tinkering with the schedule, and Russell was terrified he was going to get bumped out of prime time. Come to think of it, he had said earlier that day that he wanted to talk to her about something. What if, god forbid, something even more drastic had happened, and for some unknown, unpredictable, totally bizarre reason Russell had been fired? You couldn't very well go and break up with someone the same day they got fired, could you? Not if you had a shred of human decency, you couldn't — not even in the same month. Leigh shivered just thinking about it.

"Leigh, what's going on with you? You've been an absolute wreck for weeks on end, and I have absolutely no idea why."

"You didn't get fired?"

"What? What on earth are you talking about?"

"I thought you were going to tell me you got fired."

"Of course I didn't get fired. And I know we were supposed to go over all the wedding stuff tonight, but I think it's more important that we talk about you. What is it, Leigh?"

Well, it wasn't going to get any easier than that. He had literally gifted her with the most perfect opening imaginable. She took a deep breath, dug her fingernails into her palms again, and started talking.

"Russell, I know this is hard — it kills me even to say it — but I want to be straight with you." She stared at the floor, could feel him watching her. "I think we should take a break."

Well, okay, so that wasn't entirely truthful — a break implied a desire to work things out eventually — but at least she'd managed to get something out.

"A what?" Russell asked. Leigh looked up to see the unflappable Russell appearing completely confused, which unnerved her even more.

"I, um, I think we need to take some time. To think things over."

At this, Russell jumped off the couch and enveloped her in his arms. "Leigh, what are you talking about, 'take some time'? We're engaged to be *married,* sweetheart. We've got our whole lives ahead of us. Do you really want to wait to start all of that?"

Russell's hug was very much like what Leigh imagined it would feel like to get run over by a bus. Her lungs refused to fill with oxygen, and it was getting hard to ignore the pressure and flashes of light behind her eyes. But she knew she must persevere.

"Russell, I'm not sure I *want* us to get married," she said softly, as softly as she could say such cruel words.

Russell's silence was so complete that she would have wondered if he'd even heard her had he not pulled away and sat back down.

She sat next to him, close enough for intimacy but not so close that they were touching. "Russ, do you love me? Like, really, really love me? Love me so much you want to spend the rest of your life with me and me alone?"

He remained stoically silent.

"Do you?" she pressed, thinking — knowing — that the answer was surely no. If she'd suspected for so long that something wasn't right, he must have, too. She just needed to give him the chance to say it.

He took a deep breath and reached for her hand. He smiled. "Of course I love you that much, Leigh. That's why I asked you to marry me. You're my partner, my fiancée, my love. And I'm yours. I know it can be frightening sometimes when you realize you've found something this good, but Leigh, sweetheart, that's normal. I can't believe this is what's been worrying you all this time. Just a little case of cold feet. Poor baby, I'm sorry you kept that inside for so long."

He stopped long enough to hug her again, but this time Leigh pushed him away. His refusal to hear — to really listen — to what she was saying angered her: Was it really so impossible to fathom that she might not want to marry him?

"Russell, you're not listening to me. You know I love you, but I can't stop wondering if things didn't move so quickly with us because of circumstances, you know? You start dating someone at this age and they fit all the criteria of being smart and successful and attractive and everyone else is getting married and they're all asking you when you're going to settle down. And it just chugs right along. What might have been a great, fun, yearlong relationship when you're twenty-five all of a sudden starts to take on a whole new meaning at thirty, thirty-two. Then, before you know it, you're getting engaged and committing your life to someone you don't necessarily know all that well. Because 'it's time,' whatever that means. Christ, I'm not explaining this well. . . ."

Russell's gaze, just minutes before oozing

empathy and kindness, grew steely. "Actually, I think you're explaining yourself quite clearly."

"So you sort of understand what I'm saying?"

"You're saying that you think this is all wrong and has been for some time but you never had the nerve to tell me."

Now she wanted to tell Russell the whole truth, tell him all about Jesse and how happy and relaxed she felt when she was with him, how that single night of sex stayed more firmly planted in her mind than eighteen months' worth with Russell.

She was seconds away from blurting out the entire story when, thankfully, she stopped herself. What would be the point of telling him about Jesse? Was it really the charitable thing to do? Russell wouldn't have to take the rejection quite so personally if he could channel his energy into hating Leigh for her indiscretion. That didn't feel right, either. Why hurt him unnecessarily? But was it wrong to keep it from him, considering the conventional wisdom that it's noble to be completely honest and up-front? Confused and exhausted, she decided not to say anything. From the coldness of his last statement and the look in his eye, Russell didn't appear interested in much more talking. Why make everything harder than it had to be?

Suddenly he surprised her by grabbing her face and staring into her eyes.

"Look, Leigh, I know what you are feeling is nothing more than normal, natural cold feet. Why don't you take some time for yourself, you know, alone, like you suggested, and think about everything? Think it through."

Leigh sighed to herself. His pleading look was almost more unbearable than his anger. "Russ, I'm, uh . . . I'm —" *Say it,* she willed herself, *just pull the Band-Aid off quickly.* "I'm worried that will just prolong the inevitable. I think we should end things now."

Obviously this was true. She knew there was no point — no point whatsoever — in dragging this out, no matter how much less terrifying it might be to delay the unpleasantness. She knew beyond any doubt that things were permanently over, but hearing her own words was still downright shocking.

Russell stood up and walked toward the door. "Well," he said quietly, in that controlled voice of his that worked so well on-air. "I suppose there's nothing more to say. I love you, Leigh, and I always will, but I'd like you to leave."

These were the words that Leigh repeated

to herself as she rode home in the backseat of the first cab she'd ever hailed for herself when leaving his apartment. Almost as quickly as it had begun, her relationship with Russell was over, and gone with it was the anxiety she'd been harboring for months. She took a long, deep breath, and as the taxi flew up Sixth Avenue toward her building, she finally admitted to herself that, yes, she felt deeply sad about what had just transpired, but mostly she felt relief.

May Her Huge, Perky Boobs Give Her Back Pain By Thirty

"Emmy, I've been telling you this since the very first time you walked into my office. You have plenty of time."

"That's not what all the magazines out there say!" Emmy said and pointed toward the door. "Isn't it a mixed message to tell me that I've got all the time in the world and then stock your waiting room with a thousand articles that all tell me my ovaries are shriveling up?"

Dr. Kim sighed. She was a pretty Asian woman who looked at least fifteen years younger than her forty-two years, but this wasn't what bothered Emmy. The good doctor — who reassured Emmy at every single visit (and sometimes in between) that Emmy's childbearing years were still upon her — had herself birthed three perfect children, two boys and a girl, all before her thirty-first birthday. When Emmy repeatedly asked Dr. Kim how she'd juggled a husband, med

447

school, residency, and three children under the age of five, all while working four days a week and being on call every third night and every other weekend, the doctor just smiled, shrugged, and said, "You just do it. It seems impossible sometimes, but it always works out one way or another."

Emmy was lying spread-eagled on the exam table exactly one day before her thirtieth birthday, and she was determined to hear the heartening news again. "Tell me about your average patient," Emmy prompted, barely even noticing Dr. Kim's gloved finger inside her. She felt the pinch of the Pap smear Q-tip and held her breath to keep from moving.

"Emmy! You could tell it to me. I've told you a hundred times already."

"One more won't hurt."

Dr. Kim removed her finger and snapped off her glove. She sighed again. "I have approximately two hundred and fifty patients in my practice at this location. Of those women, the average age for first-time pregnancy is thirty-four. Which of course means that —"

"A whole bunch have to be even older than that," Emmy finished.

"Exactly. And while I don't want to misrepresent anything here — it's important you understand that this is the Upper East Side and probably the only place in the country, if not the world, where that statistic stands — the majority do not experience difficulty."

"So no pregnant patients in their twenties?" Emmy prompted.

Dr. Kim untied Emmy's robe and began to examine her left breast in a firm, circular motion. She stared at the wall as she did this, clearly concentrating. After finishing both sides, she pulled the robe closed again and placed a hand on Emmy's arm.

"Only a few," she said, looking at Emmy with concern.

"A few! Last time you said 'practically none.'"

"Only the very young wives of a few Mormon doctors from Utah doing their rotations at Mt. Sinai."

Emmy breathed a sigh of relief.

"Are you still happy with your pill?" Dr. Kim asked, making notations on Emmy's chart.

"It's fine." Emmy shrugged and sat up on the table, removing her feet from the sock-covered stirrups. "Certainly does work like a charm."

Dr. Kim laughed. "That is the point, isn't it? I'll leave you a new script for another six months' worth at the front desk, okay? We'll mail your test results within a week, but I don't foresee any problems at all. Everything looks perfectly healthy." She handed Emmy's chart to the nurse and, after making sure Emmy was covered, opened the door. "See you in six months. And sweetheart? Please relax. As your doctor, I'm telling you that there's absolutely nothing whatsoever to worry about."

Easy for you to say, with your three kids, Emmy thought as she smiled politely and nodded. *You, and Izzie, and all those other gynecologists with gaggles of children or sporting gigantic baby bumps themselves, telling me not to worry.* Izzie was due any moment now — she was already three days past her due date, in fact — but to her misery she hadn't felt a single contraction, nor dilated a fraction of a centimeter. Emmy had grudgingly agreed to wait until Izzie checked herself into the hospital to jump on a flight to Florida (Izzie insisted that first babies could be a week or even two weeks late, and it was stupid to rush down there until they were sure), but she couldn't stop thinking of her new nephew's impending arrival.

After dressing, Emmy jumped on the 4 train to Union Square. She figured on a brisk walk directly home to shower — something she always felt compelled to do after the K-Y-heavy exams — but as she exited the subway at Fourteenth and Broadway she found herself heading directly toward Leigh and Adriana's building. With Leigh's breakup only a week old and Adriana's new-found commitment to work, she figured at least one of them had to be home, sulking or writing or both, but the doorman shook his head.

"They did leave together, though," he said, checking his watch. "Probably an hour or so ago."

Emmy texted them both the same message: *WTF?? In your lobby. Where are you?* and received nearly simultaneous responses. Leigh's read *Shopping w/Adi for your 30th! Talk later;* Adriana's was a bit more concise: *If you want a bday present, go home.* Emmy sighed, thanked the girls' doorman, and began the slushy, freezing trudge to Perry Street. It was a cold, wet Friday evening in February, and Emmy was desperate for a shower, but she managed to avoid going home to her empty apartment for nearly two hours, as she found a reason to stop at nearly every block along Thirteenth: a hot coffee from Grey Dog on University; a long, adoring gaze at the puppies playing in the window at Wet Nose; an impromptu mani-cure and paraffin pedicure at Silk Day Spa,

451

where they were kind enough to take her without an appointment. No point in racing home only to sit by herself as the clock struck twelve and she kissed her twenties good-bye. She'd flat-out rejected the girls' offer of a fun night out — shot down suggestions for everything from an elegant dinner at Babbo (even though she was dying to try their mint pasta with the spicy lamb sausage) to a regressive night at Culture Club. It was only after weeks of pushing and prodding that Emmy finally agreed to show up the next afternoon for some sort of surprise birthday activity. Adriana and Leigh promised only that it wouldn't involve men of any kind, so she had grudgingly agreed. She planned to fill the hours between now and then with a bottle of wine and some quality self-pity. Perhaps, if she was feeling really motivated, she'd MaxDelivery herself some cupcakes.

By the time she reached her building and trudged up the five flights of stairs, she was drenched from head to toe: her hair from the freezing rain, her feet from the filthy slush, and her ladyparts from the overzealous application of medical-grade lube. There had been no birthday cards in her mailbox, and not a single package in the hallway outside her door. Nothing. She reminded herself that it was still only the day before, that if all else failed she could certainly rely on something from her mom and Izzie. She stripped just inside the doorway, tossing her wet clothes in a pile by the closet, and made a beeline for the bathroom. It was just as the hot water was fully soaking her hair that she heard her cell phone ring. Her home phone rang next, and then the cell again. She couldn't help but hope it was Rafi, that he'd tracked down her number somehow and was calling to apologize for being such an ass. Granted, it was unlikely that he'd found both her cell and home numbers, but who knew? He seemed resourceful enough, and besides, he was likely the only one of her recent men — *affairs* — who might even bother to find her. George had definitely moved on to his next undergraduate already, and there was no reason to believe Croc Dundee would ever be heard from again.

After towel-drying her hair and maneuvering her body next to the toilet so she could open the door, Emmy crossed the small studio and, kneeling down, naked, pulled a shopping bag out from under her bed. She carefully untied the grosgrain ribbon that secured the handles and gingerly removed the tissue-wrapped bundle from inside. Then, losing all patience, she tore the monogrammed foil sticker in half, bunched the tissue paper into a pile, and plunged her hands into the plushness of the single most expensive item she had ever owned. To call it a robe was a disservice to the luxurious softness of the four-ply cashmere, to its rich chocolate color and its elegantly simple monogrammed *E.* Robes were for covering up flannel pajamas or maintaining a modicum of decency between the locker room and the pool. But this? This was meant to drape sexily over every curve (or, in Emmy's case, to expertly accentuate what few curves there were), to feel as light as silk but as warm as down. It grazed the floor breezily as she walked, and the cinch-tie at the waist made her feel like a model. She was instantly flooded with relief. It had not been a mistake. She'd seen it a couple of weeks earlier in the window of SoHo's most expensive lingerie salon, a place where it was impossible to buy three inches of fabric for less than a few hundred dollars. Every bra, every panty, every pair of stockings in the store was more expensive than any dress she owned, which made the robe . . . well . . . a bigger chunk of her monthly rent than she cared to remember. How had she worked up the nerve even to enter the store? It remained a blur. All she knew was how good she looked wearing that robe in the plush salon dressing room with the heavy brocade curtains, her lips pursed and her right hip jutted out, standing sexily in the provided pair of stilettos. One look in the mirror tonight confirmed that nothing had changed in the weeks the robe had waited, virginal and wrapped, until her big birthday. Still in front of the mirror, Emmy combed her wet hair back into a chic chignon and bit her lips to make them swell. She slicked on a new sheer berry lip gloss from her makeup drawer and patted a bit onto her cheeks. *Not bad,* she thought with surprised pleasure. *Not bad for thirty at all.* Then, suddenly bored with the spontaneous makeover and ravenously hungry, she slid into a pair of snuggly sheepskin booties, retied the cashmere dream around her middle, and headed to the kitchen to make some soup.

The landline jangled again just as she plugged in her hot plate.

Private caller. Hmm.

"Hello?" she said, propping the phone between her ear and shoulder while she wrenched open a can of chicken noodle soup.

"Em? It's me."

No matter how many months went by, it felt like Duncan would always say "It's me," and Emmy would always know exactly who was speaking. A million thoughts flashed through her mind. He was calling to wish her a happy birthday . . . which meant he remembered her birthday . . . which meant he was thinking about her . . . which possibly meant he wasn't thinking about the cheerleader . . . unless, oh god, he was calling to give her news . . . news that had everything to do with the cheerleader . . . news that she was not prepared to hear, not tonight, not ever.

Reflexively she almost hung up, but something forced her to keep the phone to her ear. If she didn't say something soon she was going to ask him straight-out if he was engaged, so as a purely defensive maneuver she said the first thing that came to her mind.

"When did you make your number private?"

He laughed. His amused-but-not-totally-enamored Duncan laugh. "We don't talk for months on end and that's all you have to say?"

"Were you hoping for something else?"

"No, I guess not. Listen, I know you just got home and everything, but I was hoping I could come up?"

"Come up? To my apartment? You're here?"

"Yeah, I've, uh, been here awhile. At the copy shop across the street, waiting for you to get home. They're getting a little weirded out by me, I think, so it would be great if I could come in for a minute."

"So you've been just sitting there watching my apartment?" How odd to find something so creepy and so flattering at the same time.

Duncan laughed again. "Yeah, well, I called a few times before, right when you walked in, but you didn't pick up. I promise I won't stay long. I just want to talk to you face-to-face."

So he was engaged. That asshole! Probably thought he was doing something noble by coming all the way over here to tell her in person. And on the day before her birthday, which she was willing to bet any amount he had completely forgotten. He could take his face-to-face talk and shove it, as far as she was concerned, and without a moment's hesitation, Emmy told him as much.

"Emmy, wait, don't hang up. It's not like that. I just —"

"I'm pretty fucking sick of hearing what you want and don't want, Duncan. In fact, my life has been about a thousand times better without you in it, so why don't you run home now to your little pom-pom girlfriend and make her miserable. Because I'll tell you what: I'm not interested."

She slammed down the phone and felt a wave of tremendous satisfaction, which was instantly followed by a tremendous wave of panic. What had she just done?

Barely sixty seconds passed before she heard a knock at the door.

"Emmy? I obviously know you're there. Can you please open up? Just for one minute, I promise."

She knew she should be supremely pissed off that he'd used the key he'd never bothered to return, but part of her was downright curious: What could possibly be so important that Duncan — Mr. Indifference Personified — would resort to full-fledged stalking? She was also partly relieved; the Duncan she knew would never, ever make such an effort simply to announce his own engagement.

Not even bothering to kick off her furry slippers, Emmy opened the door and leaned against it. "What?" she asked without a smile. "What's so important?"

Winded from the five-flight climb, but significantly less than he used to be — the three or four times in five years he'd bothered to come to her place, that is — he looked pretty damn good, and she suspected the positive changes (thinner face, no deathly pallor, great haircut that hid the small bald spot) were the results of the cheerleader's hard work, not his own.

"Can I come in?" he asked with one of his specialty smiles, a grin that fell somewhere between flirtatious and bored.

Emmy backed against the door and waved her hand toward the apartment, making sure he saw her own supremely indifferent expression.

It took a couple of seconds to close the door and secure the lock, and when Emmy turned around again to face Duncan, he was staring at her with unabashed appreciation. Bordering on worship, were she to be honest with herself. And for possibly the very first time in Duncan's presence, she didn't feel the least bit self-conscious about her appearance.

"Jesus, Em, you look great," he said with more sincerity than she thought him capable of.

Emmy looked down at her robe, remembered the mini-makeover she'd performed after getting out of the shower, and secretly thanked the universe that he hadn't seen her a mere thirty minutes earlier.

"Thanks."

His eyes continued to move up and down her body, lingering appreciatively every few inches. "No, I mean like really, really great. The best you've ever looked. Whatever you're doing, it's definitely working for you," he said without a hint of irony.

Oh, you mean screwing my brains out with virtually every attractive stranger I meet? Buying sexy lingerie? Refusing to hate my body just because you did? Yes, shockingly, things are going well.

"Thanks, Duncan" was all she said.

He looked around the apartment. "Where's Otis?" he asked, his eyes fixed on the empty cage. "Did he finally . . ."

"Ha! I wish. Although I guess it's the next best thing."

Duncan stared at her questioningly.

"Adriana watched him during my last work trip — very grudgingly, I have to say — and she bitched about it for days. Then, out of nowhere, I get home, call her to say I'm on my way to pick him up, thank you so much for watching him, blah, blah, blah — literally, I've bought her a bottle of hundred-dollar wine as a thank-you and an apology — and she says he can stay for a while."

"Stay with her?"

"Yes! Can you imagine? She said they've bonded. That I was underappreciating Otis and that she's given him a new lease on life."

"To which you replied?"

"Like you even have to ask? I said she's absolutely right; I have underappreciated him, and it's true he and I have most definitely never bonded. That if she'd like him to stay for 'a while,' I could probably find it in my heart to allow it. That was eight weeks ago. I spoke to her this morning and the two of them were on their way to the 'birdie spa' — her words, not mine. I'm just holding my breath and praying it's not all a dream."

Duncan took off his overcoat and tossed it on a chair. He was still wearing a suit; he had come straight from work. He was carrying a plain brown shopping bag and Emmy couldn't help but wonder if this was a birthday present for her.

"Here, I got you something," he said when he saw her looking at it.

"You did?" Her voice sounded more hopeful than she would have liked. The bag was bulky when he handed it to her, heavy, and her first thought was that it must be some sort of photography book. Perhaps one of those photographic guides to great hotels, or a tour of one of the Caribbean islands they used to visit during Duncan's rare vacations.

Emmy eagerly pulled open the bag and was momentarily shocked to discover nothing more than a single ream of printer paper.

Duncan noticed Emmy's surprised expression and shrugged. "I sat in that damn shop for over an hour. I had to buy *something*."

"Uh-huh." So he hadn't remembered her birthday, or picked out his own gift for the very first time. This shouldn't have been surprising or disappointing, but for some reason, it was both.

"So, you're probably, uh, wondering why I'm here. . . ." He let his voice trail off, but Emmy didn't say a word. "I know that whole situation with Brianna wasn't easy for either of us, but that's, uh, over now, and I was hoping we could, uh, try to work through that."

Well. There it was. Emmy was so surprised she had to grab the counter for support. Her mind barely knew where to begin. He had just dropped three completely independent yet equally shocking bombs in a single sentence. First, there was that bit about calling the dramatic ending of their five-year relationship due to his own infidelity with a fitness trainer Emmy had bought him a "situation" — not to mention that disgusting little addition about it not being easy for him, either. Then there was the casual pronouncement that said "situation" was over, a detail he must have assumed Emmy knew, because how could she not be following the minutiae of his life? And last, the biggest one of all: Duncan was sitting in her apartment on a cold Friday night when he'd otherwise be out with his friends, nervously suggesting that they could "work through this." Emmy knew she was prone to exaggeration and flights of fancy — and of course further confirmation was needed — but this sounded to her like he was asking to get back together.

She had a million, trillion questions for him (Why did they break up? Whose idea was it? And, most important of all, why did he want to get back together with her?), but she refused to give him the satisfaction. Instead, she leaned back against the counter, crossed her arms, and peered at Duncan.

"Well, aren't you going to say anything?" he asked before jamming his pointer finger in his mouth and gnawing on a cuticle. *Number eight hundred eighteen of the things I don't miss,* Emmy thought.

"I'm not feeling so chatty tonight," Emmy said evenly, gazing at him.

He sighed as if to suggest this was all very difficult. "Em, look, I'm an idiot, okay? I know I fucked up, and I want to make it right. The whole Brianna thing — it was a glitch, a bump in the road, a totally meaningless thing that should've never happened in the first place. You and me, we're meant to be together. We both know it. So what do you say? I'm standing before you, hat in hand" — at this, he mimed pulling off a cap and holding it toward her — "begging you to come back to me."

He walked to her, wrapped his arms around her shoulders, and kissed her ever so softly on the lips. Emmy let herself be kissed, let him press his mouth to hers, and reveled in the familiarity and comfort of it. Duncan pulled away, and while gently brushing the hair back off her face, looked into her eyes and asked, "So? What do you say?"

Whether she'd admitted it or not, she'd waited ten months for this very moment, and here it was, and it felt every bit as incredible as she had envisioned. Emmy returned his gaze with her sweetest possible smile. "What do I say?" she asked coyly, flirtatiously. "I say I'm going to give myself the best thirtieth birthday present on earth and tell you — right here, right now, and for the last time ever — *to get the fuck out of my apartment.* That's what I say."

"You did *not!*" Adriana squealed, clapping her hands together.

"I did," Emmy said with a huge smile.

"Did not!"

"Did so. And I can't begin to tell you how good it felt."

Adriana hugged Emmy, pulled her as close

as their tiny table would allow. They were at Alice's Tea Cup on the Upper East Side, packed in with dozens, maybe hundreds of females of every imaginable age, rehashing Emmy's triumphant moment. "You so did the right thing."

"Um, yeah!" Emmy said with widened eyes. "Don't think for a second I'm doubting it. Do you believe that asshole had the nerve to show up at my apartment, on the eve of my thirtieth birthday, and ask me to take him back — all without ever bothering to apologize? He is loathsome."

"Always was." Adriana nodded until she noticed Emmy looking at her with a funny expression. "Oh, sweetheart, I didn't mean it like that. I was just agreeing that his actions were particularly repugnant this time." Good lord, these girls could be so sensitive!

An extra-perky adorable waitress approached their table. "Celebrating a special occasion today, ladies?" she asked.

Emmy snorted. "What gave it away? The crow's-feet or the three ringless wonders, out for afternoon tea, just like they will be in fifty years?"

"The three ringless wonders? That's a new one." Adriana rolled her eyes and glanced at Leigh, who sat, stone-faced, her bare left hand jammed under her thigh. Adriana felt bad; Emmy must not have known that Leigh had returned the ring to Russell the night before.

"Good, right? I just made that up right now. But it has a nice ring to it . . . ha! No pun intended!" Emmy cracked up.

"Sorry, I just figured since —" The waitress coughed and looked at her feet.

Adriana interrupted. "No, we're sorry. Actually, we *are* celebrating . . . this one's thirtieth birthday. And as you can see, we're struggling."

"Thirty? Really? You look great for thirty!" the girl said enthusiastically. She couldn't have been a day over twenty-four. "I can only hope I look so good then."

Thankfully, Leigh stepped in before Emmy could say anything truly nasty and said, "Yeah, she does, doesn't she? We're ready to order."

The waitress grinned while taking their orders and bounced off, convinced she'd just made someone's day.

"Bitch," Emmy hissed under her breath. "May her huge, perky boobs give her back pain by thirty."

Adriana slapped the table. "Did you see her sun damage? Please! That girl is going to look like a leathery hag when she turns thirty. Her boobs are the least of her problems."

"I don't know what you two were looking at, but I couldn't take my eyes off her hair," Leigh said.

"Her hair? What was wrong with her hair?" Emmy asked.

"Well, there is nothing wrong with it now, but you can just see she's going to be the thinning type. I sure wouldn't want to be thirty with a receding hairline and a thinned-out center part."

All three girls laughed.

"Yeah, well, you're right. . . . That was probably long overdue," Emmy said, picking up right where they'd left off before the unfortunate waitress incident. "It's just weird how everything unfolds, you know? I wanted nothing more than for Duncan to come back and declare his undying love for me, for us to run off into the sunset together, for him to realize what a horrible mistake he'd made, and then, the moment exactly that happens, all I want is for him to get hit by a bus. Is that normal?"

"Perfectly," Adriana said. "Don't you think, Leigh?" Adriana had tried to incorporate Leigh into the conversation earlier, but she hadn't said much of anything, had just sat there with a distracted smile and occasionally murmured a "hmm."

"Definitely," Leigh said now, turning to Adriana. "Our little girl is growing up! I think it's so —" The sound of Leigh's cell phone stopped her midsentence.

Adriana watched as she pulled it from her bag, checked the caller ID, and hit Ignore. "Jesse again?" she asked.

Leigh nodded. "You'd think he'd get the message by now. I haven't returned a single call since he got back from Indonesia."

"Yes, *querida?* And exactly what message is that?" Of course she couldn't be so blunt about it to her friends, but Adriana had been thrilled when Emmy had called with the news of Leigh's affair and subsequent breakup with Russell. Not that she didn't adore Russell — everyone adored Russell. But she adored Leigh more and wanted the very best for her. Now an affair? With a married man? Who also happened to be brilliant, volatile, and wildly inappropriate in myriad other ways? This was a wonderfully unexpected step in the right direction. If only Leigh could see it that way, too. . . .

"That what happened between us was a mistake, a onetime thing that happened months ago, for chrissake, and that we really don't need to talk about. I just don't understand why he has to make this harder than it is."

Emmy laughed. "Sweetheart, you can't blame the guy for recognizing that this is a little more complicated than that, can you? Does he know you ended things with Russell?"

Leigh's head whipped up. "Of course not," she said curtly. "What happened between Russell and me had nothing to do with Jesse."

Adriana snorted. The girl was delusional! When was she going to be able to just admit she was madly in love with the wrong guy? Adriana began to plot her next column; if her perfectly sane and rational friend could be so blind, other women must suffer as well. Perhaps she could call it "Deluded Thinking: A Primer." Or maybe "Why I Insist on Lying to Myself." Yes, that could work nicely.

Leigh glared at her. "What?"

"Do you really believe that, *querida?*"

"Yes, actually, I really do. Because it's true! Russell and I were" — she paused here, searching for the right words — "having problems long before I even met Jesse. I might concede — might — that what happened with Jesse helped open my eyes to what was going on with Russell, but even that's a stretch. I slept with Jesse because I was feeling lonely and probably a little bit scared of what was happening between Russell and me. It was a lapse in judgment during a particularly vulnerable time in my life. Nothing more, nothing less."

Emmy and Adriana exchanged looks.

"What? What are you two looking at each other for?"

Adriana was grateful when Emmy took the reins with her most soothing tone and diplomatic word choice. "We're not saying you don't think that's true, but . . . well . . . does that mean it has to be true for Jesse, too?"

"And it doesn't take a shrink to see that you look about a thousand times more relaxed than usual," Adriana chimed in.

Leigh rolled her eyes. "Look, you two, you know I love you both, but this is getting ridiculous! Regardless of how I feel — felt — about Jesse, you're both overlooking a rather important detail. Stay with me here, okay? Jesse. Chapman. Is. Married. Married, as in *committed for life to another woman.* Married, as in *sleeping with me makes him a liar and a cheater whom my best friends should not be encouraging me to pursue.* Married, as in —"

Adriana held up a hand. Nothing bothered her more than when Leigh went all preachy and puritanical on her. "All right, all right, we get it," she said.

A different server appeared, a man this time, carrying a tray of food.

"Oh, no! I hope we didn't scare off your colleague," Emmy said. "We were being sort of obnoxious."

The waiter looked at her strangely and began to auction off the food. "Lapsang Souchong Smoked Chicken Breast Salad with dressing on the side?" He placed it in front of Leigh. "And two Mad Hatters, with the scones and sandwiches at the same time, as requested. Your tea will be right out. Can I get you ladies anything else?"

"A husband? A baby? Some sort of life?" Emmy asked. "Any of those on the menu?"

He backed away from the table slowly, like she was a wild animal. "I, uh, I'll be back to check on you. Enjoy," he mumbled as he bolted.

"Christ, Emmy, get ahold of yourself. You're scaring people," Adriana admonished, although she secretly found the whole thing extremely entertaining.

Emmy sighed. "What else is new?"

"I've been doing a lot of thinking this past week," Leigh said, looking across the table at her friends. Adriana thought this inauspicious. Leigh's "thinking" almost always resulted in the type of decision that only made her unhappier. Adriana prepared herself for the sentence that would surely begin, "I'm thinking I should . . ."

"I'm thinking I should go back to school," she said quietly.

"What?" Adriana screeched. Where could this possibly be stemming from? School? "Why on earth would you do that?"

Leigh smiled. "Because I've always wanted to," she said.

"You have?" Emmy asked.

Leigh nodded. "For an MFA in creative writing. I wanted to go right after graduation — remember? — but my dad got me that assistant job at Brook Harris, and kept saying that no good editor — or writer for that matter — needed an advanced degree, that the best thing I could do for my career was to get started on it." She laughed bitterly. "What we both failed to consider was that this wasn't the career I wanted."

"But, Leigh, sweetheart, you're so good at it! Just seconds away from a huge promotion, working with a huge bestselling author —"

Leigh interrupted Emmy. "Worked with. Past tense."

Adriana sighed. Leigh could be so dramatic sometimes! "Just because you had sex with him does not mean you can't edit him, Leigh. If every single person refused to work with someone they'd slept with, the entire world economy would shut down."

"I agree," Leigh said. "We probably could've gotten over it. And god knows Henry wouldn't have cared, so long as that manuscript was in on time. I just meant it was past tense because I quit already. Yesterday."

"Stop it!" Emmy shouted. A group of middle-aged tourists turned to stare at them. "You're joking," she whispered.

"How come you didn't tell me yesterday, when we were shopping?" Adriana asked, gripping Leigh's arm. "Did you just forget to mention it?"

"I needed some time to process it. I told Henry that I wasn't in any rush, I'd stay as long as it took for a seamless transition, but that I was definitely leaving."

"Ohmigod," Emmy breathed.

"How did he take it?" Adriana asked. She she couldn't help being the teensiest bit upset that Leigh had upstaged her. After all, she had her own exciting news to announce.

"He was pretty surprised. Said he'd been getting bizarre calls from Jesse for weeks saying that he had done something — an unnamed something — that had probably made me uncomfortable, that it was entirely his fault, that it would never happen again, and apparently begged Henry not to hand him over to another editor."

"Well, that was nice of him. You don't think Henry knows, do you?" Emmy asked.

"No. From what he said, it sounds like he thinks Jesse came on to me in some way, made me uncomfortable, and I freaked. Figures that's why I don't want to work with him anymore, and he even tried to tell me that the occasional pervy author was part of the deal, a hazard of the trade or whatever." Leigh laughed ruefully and took a sip of tea. "I wonder what he'd think if he knew I practically dragged Jesse to bed?"

"*Querida,* I can't believe you actually quit your job! What's your game plan?"

"Guess what? For the first time in my entire life, I don't really know." Leigh refilled her teacup and didn't appear too concerned. "I want to take some time off, not rush into anything, maybe travel a little before hopefully starting school this fall. I haven't really figured it all out, but I'll probably have to sell my apartment and" — she paused for a minute and turned to Emmy — "find a roommate? No pressure, Em, I swear, but I know you hate your place and have been talking about moving forever, so no need to answer now, but maybe we could find a cute two-bedroom together somewhere?"

Leigh was ruining everything! Adriana had a whole plan. She had been so excited to tell Emmy about it, and now Leigh was screwing it all up. She tried to interject. "Well, guess what? I have something —"

"Ohmigod, are you kidding?" Emmy was practically shrieking. "I would love that. Love, love, love it. I can't stand that fucking studio for one more second. I'll move anywhere. Anywhere! My only requirement is an oven. And a stove. That should be manageable, right? Just say the word."

"Done!" Leigh said. "Let's start looking right away. I'm ready to move as soon as my place sells."

"Hellooooo? Do you two hear me? Hello!" Adriana said, a bit more peevishly than she intended. "I have something that might be of interest to you both."

The girls turned and looked at her expectantly.

"So, nothing's finalized yet — and I probably shouldn't even be saying anything — but I will most likely be moving to Los Angeles."

That silenced them. It was satisfying to watch Leigh gasp and Emmy's mouth drop open. *What's a girl got to do to get a little attention around here?* Adriana thought.

"What?"

"Why?"

"Is it Toby?"

"Are you moving in with him?"

"Do your parents know?"

"Is it definite?"

"Are you getting married?"

This was absolutely delicious, better even than she had hoped. She sighed dramatically. "Okay, okay, I'll tell you everything. Just calm down." By which she meant, of course, *Keep firing questions at me, I love it!* Happily, her friends obliged, and Adriana reveled in their curiosity until she got to utter the words she never thought she'd hear herself say, words that made her prouder and more excited than she could possibly have imagined.

"I have a job offer, and I plan to accept it," she said and sat back to relish her friends' reactions. It was so delicious springing exciting news on her unsuspecting friends. How else could you get them to pay attention?

"A what?" Leigh asked with a puzzled expression.

"What, exactly, do you mean by 'job'?" Emmy asked, looking equally confused.

"Oh, come on! What do you think I mean?" This was exasperating! Was it really so impossible to imagine her with a job just because she'd never kept one before? Puh-lease. The whole world worked; she was sure she could handle it, too.

"Okay, Adi, don't make us beg for it. Give us the rundown," Leigh said, leaning forward over the table.

Adriana took a deep, dramatic breath. So kill her for wanting to enjoy this! It wasn't every day Adriana de Souza was taken seriously. "Let's see, the CliffsNotes version is fairly straightforward. You already know about the *Marie Claire* column?"

Both girls nodded.

"Well, we were out to dinner the other night with some of Toby's colleagues at Paramount. He was bragging about my columns getting picked up — you should've seen it, he was absolutely adorable — and one of the women, a producer of some sort, started acting all interested. She kept asking all these questions about me, the columns, how *Marie Claire* found me, when the first one was getting published . . . and like a million others. I sort of thought she was just being polite, but she called the next day and told me that she was interested in — are you ready for this? — developing my ideas into a movie!"

"Ohmigod," Emmy breathed.

Leigh looked dumbstruck. "No way. No, no, no way!"

Adriana nodded happily. "Yes, yes, yes! I e-mailed her the samples I'd submitted to *Marie Claire* and she called back later that very same day. Said she wanted to preempt anyone else and start working on it before the first column actually gets published and, in her words, 'inevitably becomes a phenomenon.' She called me the next Candace Bushnell."

"Shut up!" her friends called out simultaneously.

"I'm completely serious."

Leigh leaned even closer; she was practically pressing her face against Adriana's. "So what does that mean? What will you do for her?"

"I didn't totally understand, either, but Toby said that the first step is to get an agent — he's recommending someone good — and then they'll negotiate a consulting contract on my behalf. The producer has a deal with Paramount and a trailer on their lot, and she's going to pair me with a screenwriter to work on developing a script. If everything goes through, I'll be moving in the next two months."

What she hadn't told her friends was that the producer was fine with her working from New York — had expected it, even — and that it was entirely her choice to move to LA.

It was just time for a change. Adriana had been in New York since the day she'd graduated, and she knew she'd move back sooner than later. If she didn't try living somewhere else now, it might never happen. Plus, the idea of getting even farther away from her parents and their meddling restrictions was immensely appealing.

"Adriana, that is so incredible. Incredible. Congratulations!" Leigh said as she pushed herself up from the table and went to hug her friend.

"Hey, what's wrong?" Adriana asked Emmy, who had begun tearing up.

"Sorry," she sniffled. "I really am so happy for you. I just can't believe you're going to move."

"*Querida!* You went first, remember? Culinary school in Cali? As if there aren't perfectly good schools on the East Coast. But you came back, and I will, too. Besides, I have something that might make you feel better."

"What?" Emmy asked. She said it petulantly, like a stubborn, curious child.

"I think you're really, really going to like it."

"What? Tell me! What?"

"Well, I was wondering if you wouldn't want to live in my apartment while I'm gone.

And" — she paused dramatically and turned to Leigh, who was just staring at her — "you, too, *querida*. I didn't realize you two were planning to live together, but what could be more perfect than my place? I spoke to my parents and they were thrilled about Emmy staying there, and I'm sure they'll love it even more if you'd both be there. Three bedrooms, rent-free, of course, with only two caveats: You have to send them their mail wherever they are once a week, and you have to deal with their occasional visit to New York. Which should be significantly less frequent since I won't be here. What do you both think?"

"Gee, I don't know," Leigh said. "Sounds like a shitty deal to me."

"Yeah, seriously. Fucking miserable. A free three-bedroom, its only responsibility a once-weekly trip to the post office. Christ, Adriana, how could you even suggest it?"

"Please, *querida!* The post office? Uch! We have an arrangement with UPS; they come to the apartment, pick up the mail bundle, package it, and ship it. You'll only need to collect it from the lobby mailbox," Adriana said in her best isn't-it-obvious voice.

Leigh slammed her hands against the table. "Holy shit, it just occurred to me. The penthouse means the top floor."

"Stating the obvious, Leigh," Adriana said.

"And the top floor means no one banging on the ceiling! Ohmigod!" she started to laugh and cry at the same time. "I don't think I've ever been so excited about anything in my entire life!"

Emmy made a dramatic show of raising her arms and staring at the ceiling. "Penthouse A, here we come!"

"And you, Adriana?" Leigh asked. "Where, my dear, are you going to live while Emmy and I sleep in blissful nonclomping silence? Do I sense some cohabitation in your immediate future?"

Adriana smiled. This might be the best part of all. "Well, Toby did ask me to move in with him," she said as the girls clapped, "and while things are going really well with us — surprisingly well, actually — I think that's even more reason not to jump into anything." She stopped, sipped her tea, and pretended to ponder something. "So . . . I'm going to take the money I'll earn from the consultant project and the columns and rent my very own little apartment in Venice Beach. Just a little studio, as close to the beach as possible. Near the farmers' market, I think."

Emmy turned to Leigh and sighed. "Leigh, do you believe it? Our little girl is growing up. Doing everything all on her own!"

Adriana held up her hands for silence. "Not so fast, *querida*. I do have one favor to ask of you, and it's a big one." She could feel herself tense up, praying that Emmy would say yes.

Emmy peered at her with curiosity. "A big one, huh? Bigger than Penthouse A? Hit me, Adi."

"I was hoping you might let me, uh, borrow Otis for the year? Oh, Emmy, I know he's your pet, and I know it's crazy to drag the poor thing across the country, but we've just bonded so much these past few weeks. In a weird way — and please don't laugh at me for this — I think of him as my good-luck charm. My life just sort of fell into place when he arrived. Would you mind terribly?" Adriana knew Emmy wouldn't mind — would in fact be ecstatic that she wanted to keep him — but there was no harm in letting Emmy think she was pulling one over on her, right? It was a small gift for a best friend.

"Hmm," Emmy murmured, pretending to mull this over. "I guess it would be okay. I mean, who am I to stand in the way of someone's good-luck charm? If you'd like to take Otis with you, then by all means, he's yours."

"To Otis," Leigh said, raising her teacup.

"To Emmy on her birthday. In the immortal words of our waitress, may everyone look so good at thirty!" Adriana added, holding her teacup aloft.

Emmy was the last to raise her cup and clink it with her friends'. "To the three ringless wonders. May we be every bit as wonderful but hopefully not so ringless in another thirty years."

"I'll toast to that!" Leigh said.

"Me, too," Adriana added, filled with excitement about everything that lay ahead. "Cheers, *queridas*. Cheers to us."

IT'D BE NAUSEATING
IF IT WEREN'T SO
GODDAMN CUTE

Three Months Later

"Emmy!" Leigh called from Adriana's old bedroom, which with the addition of her fluffy down comforter, a cluster of silver picture frames, and her favorite reading chair she had easily made her own. "The car's downstairs. We're going to be late!"

She heard her friend stomping back and forth between rooms, inevitably packing every item that wasn't nailed down. "Have you seen my Nano? Or my phone charger? I can't fucking find anything!"

Leigh zipped up her neatly packed carry-on roller and carefully placed the matching satchel on top of it. She ran through a mental checklist and, after satisfying herself that she hadn't forgotten anything, pulled her belongings into the hallway. She walked into Emmy's room — previously the de Souzas' guest room — went directly to her dresser, and plucked both Nano and phone charger

484

from the giant glass fishbowl Emmy used as a catchall. "Here. Throw these in your purse and let's go. We are *not* missing this flight!"

"Okay, okay," Emmy mumbled, yanking a brush through her hair. "This is an obscene hour to be awake, never mind actually moving. I'm doing the best I can."

It took another fifteen minutes to get Emmy out the door and ten more for the car to circle around the block, pick them up, and head to JFK. They were exactly thirty minutes behind Leigh's preferred schedule — just because the airlines suggested you should be there two hours beforehand didn't mean that two and a half wasn't better — and normally she'd be a wreck, but today she was too excited to let anything bother her. It had been almost three months since they'd last seen Adriana, sent her off with a blowout going-away dinner at the Waverly Inn with twenty-five of her nearest and dearest friends, and they were finally headed west for a visit.

Once Adriana moved, Emmy hadn't even bothered giving thirty days' notice on her apartment; she just paid two months' rent and moved out immediately. Leigh expected it would take some time to sell her place — after all, it had taken her over a year to find it — but the broker called two days after the first viewing to say they had an offer. She ended up selling it to the very first couple who saw the place (newly engaged, naturally, and giddy with excitement) at twelve percent more than she'd purchased it for a year earlier. Even less the broker's commission, Leigh earned enough on her initial investment to finance a few months' worth of doing absolutely, positively nothing — or at least nothing constructive — before she began school in September.

"So, do you think we'll go to the Ivy?" Emmy asked, cradling her Starbucks thermos between her hands. "I mean, I know it's hideously clichéd and trite and all that, but it *is* our evaluation brunch. I sort of think we have to go for it."

Despite the predawn hour, Emmy couldn't seem to stop talking.

"I don't know," Leigh said, hoping she wouldn't encourage her.

"Can you believe it's been a year since that first dinner at the Waverly Inn?" Emmy asked.

"I know. Crazy, isn't it? It feels like yesterday."

"Yesterday? You're fucking nuts. It feels more like a decade ago. This must have been the slowest year of my life. It's as though time just stood still. Like I'm living in this complete warped time freeze of —"

"Em, sweetheart, please don't take this the wrong way, but I need you to stop talking. Just until we get there," Leigh said.

Emmy held up a hand and nodded. "Enough said. No offense taken. I have no idea why I get like this. It's like exhaustion and this compulsive need to talk go hand in hand. The more tired I am, the chattier —"

"Please."

"Sorry. I'm sorry."

Leigh's phone rang. She got that flippy feeling in her stomach when she saw the caller ID. "Hi!" she breathed into the phone. "What are you doing up so early?"

"What would you say if I told you I set the alarm just so I could wish you a safe trip?" Jesse asked, sounding tired but happy.

"I'd say you were a giant liar and that you should tell me the real story."

He laughed and Leigh felt herself start to grin. Just the sound of his laugh was enough to make her feel giddy with excitement. "Well, in that case, you probably already know I've been up all night. Literally, just sitting here, waiting to call you."

"The up all night I'll believe, but try again on the waiting." She turned to see Emmy glaring at her while flapping her hands open and closed to imitate talking. Leigh smiled and blew her a silent kiss.

"All right, you got me. Up until three writing, then from three to six playing *Grand Theft Auto,* then coffee, then calling. More believable?" he asked.

"Much."

With any other man, she would've been horrified to discover a video-game addiction. It had even once been on her list of nonnegotiable deal-breakers (right there alongside excessive back hair and/or sweating, a penchant for bathroom humor, and any type of religious fundamentalism), but despite her ardent attempts at disapproval (mocking, eye-rolling, relentless teasing), she secretly found it adorable. And truth be told, she rather liked it when he let her choose the gangbangers' outfits at the beginning of each game. Was this love? She wasn't ready to say that yet, but damn, it had to be close.

"Are you in the car?" he asked.

Leigh sighed, picturing him stretched out under the covers, getting ready to sleep for a few hours before hitting up Estia's for his late-morning rounds. "Yeah. We're actually almost there, so I should go. I miss you."

"I miss you," Emmy whispered. "Oh, Jesse, baby, I miss you so much. How can I live without seeing you for an entire four days? Ohmigod, like two star-crossed lovers." Leigh reached over to poke her friend, but Emmy managed to flatten herself against the car door.

"What's she saying?" Jesse asked.

"Nothing at all." Leigh laughed. "I'll call you when we land, okay? Get some sleep." She resisted making a kissing sound into the phone for Emmy's benefit.

"My god, it'd be nauseating if it weren't so goddamn cute," Emmy said with a long, dramatic sigh.

It was nauseating, Leigh knew this, but she was too happy to care. Jesse had called incessantly for two straight months after "the incident," as they both now called it; he e-mailed, left messages with her assistant, texted her phone three, four, fives times a day. She screened him each and every time, not wanting to confuse her already screwed-up life any more. Just because it felt complicated didn't mean it was; regardless of how many times he called or apologized or tried to explain himself, the fact remained that Jesse was married. Period. She'd made a big enough mistake already just by sleeping with him; she didn't need to make everything worse by getting further involved.

Which worked, all said and done, until she decided to leave Brook Harris. She was still going into the office every day, but it was only to help transition her authors to their new editors. Henry had wisely taken Jesse on himself and, in that way that only an über-experienced editor can, had coaxed Jesse into cleaning up the writing without mortally offending him. When she read the galley, Leigh could only shake her head at its improvement: Jesse surely had another huge hit on his hands. Leigh had even managed to keep him mostly out of mind until the day he e-mailed her in all caps. It had no subject line and read, "MEET ME AT THE ASTOR PLACE STARBUCKS TONIGHT @ 7 P.M. I JUST WANT TEN MINUTES. AFTER THAT, I'LL LEAVE YOU ALONE IF YOU WISH. PLEASE COME. J."

Leigh did what any sane female faced with such an e-mail would do: deleted it to resist the temptation of replying, cleared her trash to resist the temptation of recalling it, and then called tech support to restore all her recently deleted e-mails. She briefly toyed with the idea of forwarding it to Adriana and Emmy for input and analysis, but then ultimately decided it would be a total waste of time; obviously, she would go.

By the time she arrived at Starbucks that night — a Monday, no less! — she was a wreck. Second-guessing herself like crazy, reminding herself what an absolute moron she was for even entertaining the idea of talking to Jesse, ex-lover and ex-author extraordinaire. What was the point? So she liked him — so what? There, she'd admitted it to herself. What did she want for that, some sort of prize? It only made it stupider and more masochistic to subject herself to such a meeting, one that would surely bring even more disappointment in an already less-than-stellar month. The fact that Jesse finally arrived, ten minutes late, flanked by an Asian girl so young she could be his daughter did not improve Leigh's outlook.

"Leigh," he said with a huge smile, holding his hand out to her. "I'm so glad you're here."

"Mmm," she replied, not standing up to greet either of them. Not that there was any need to stand — the smiling girl was pulling up a chair, and soon she and Jesse were both seated across from Leigh.

"Tuti, I'd like you to meet Leigh. Leigh, this is Tuti . . . my wife."

Leigh's eyes shot first to Jesse, who appeared not the least bit uncomfortable, and then back to the girl, who upon further inspection Leigh decided was probably even younger than she'd first thought, although not as pretty. Tuti had beautiful thick black hair, but it was cut in an awkward shape for her full face. "Oh dear god," Leigh said aloud before she could stop herself.

Tuti giggled sweetly, and Leigh saw that she had a significant overbite. Had this happened under any other circumstances, Leigh thought she would have found this girl adorable. Charming, even. But tonight? Like this? It was more than she could bear.

"Tuti, it's a pleasure to meet you. I've, uh —" She was automatically going to say "heard a lot about you," but it was too fraught with meaning. Instead, she said, "I hate to run, but I was just stopping by."

With this announcement, Tuti's face fell. "So soon?" she asked with a frown. "Okay, then I am going to get something to drink and leave you two alone. Leigh, Jesse? Something?"

Jesse patted her shoulder and shook his head no, and Tuti scampered off toward the counter.

"What were you thinking, bringing her here?" Leigh heard herself ask, as though her brain and mouth were no longer in contact. She popped three Nicorettes into her mouth and waited for the calm to wash over her. "No, don't answer that. I don't care what you were thinking. I just want to go."

She began to gather her things, but Jesse clamped his hand down over her arm.

"She's twenty-three and from Indonesia. Island of Bali, village of Ubud. I ended up there about a year after *Disenchantment* was published, went with a group of super-rich Europeans for a month-long party at someone's daddy's house. That was all well and good until one of them overdosed, and then the next day al Qaeda blew up that nightclub in Bali."

Leigh nodded. She remembered that.

"Needless to say, the party moved on, but something kept me there. I left Kuta, the city of the bombing, and headed inland, toward the mountains and the rice-paddy villages, where I'd read all of the artists and craftsmen and writers of Bali live. And sure enough, Ubud was just overflowing with them. The place was incredible! Every day was a festival of some sort, a huge, brightly colored celebration of the seasons or a holiday or a life event. And the people! My god, they were gorgeous. So welcoming, so open. Tuti's father and I became friends. He's only four years older than me, and he has her . . ." At this, Jesse shook his head. "He's a talented woodworker, more of an artisan really. We met one day when I went to his shop, and he invited me home for dinner. Beautiful family. To make a long story much, much shorter, I owe Tuti's father a great deal. He got me back on track with my life — in a lot of ways he saved it, I think — so I didn't really have a second thought when he asked me to marry Tuti."

Leigh wasn't sure where this story was headed, but she was fascinated — not to mention it now made perfect sense why the tabloids hadn't gotten hold of the story. Damned if she was going to show him that, though; instead, she took a sip of her coffee, tried to appear aloof, and said, "She's very sweet, Jesse. I can see why you married her." What she didn't say was *Why are you telling me this?*

Jesse laughed. "Leigh, I was being quite literal when I said I married Tuti because her father is very dear to me, and he asked me to. She was a child — still is — and I'm unspeakably fond of her, but we've never had a romantic relationship, and certainly never will."

"Ah, yes, well, that makes perfect sense." She didn't want to go the sarcastic route, but this whole situation was so confusing.

"After nine-eleven, the U.S. placed Indonesia on its short list of terrorist countries. So even though the island of Bali is ninety-eight percent Hindu — as opposed to the rest of the country, which is the same percentage Muslim — Tuti was denied a visa to so much as visit America. Her parents worked their entire lives to send her to the States for an education — as they did with her older brother — but the new political situation made it impossible. That's where I came in."

"You married her so she could get a visa?" Leigh asked, shocked. Didn't that only happen in the movies?

"I did."

Leigh could only shake her head in disbelief.

"Do you really find it that appalling?" Jesse asked. "This is why I didn't want to get into it before now."

"I don't think *appalling* is the word I'd use, but it's definitely . . . weird." Leigh peered at him, examined his face. "Didn't you ever want to get married one day to someone you actually love? Or was that not even a consideration?"

"I know this probably sounds strange to you, but to be perfectly honest, no, that was not a consideration. I'd recently come off this massively successful first book, and I was all caught up in the traveling and partying and women; marriage was the last thing on my mind. What was I really sacrificing by marrying Tuti in name only? She lives with three roommates in a walk-up on the Lower East Side. Goes to school at night, has a new boyfriend who seems like a nice kid. I take her out for lunch twice a month, and she loves bringing her laundry to my apartment because my cleaning lady does it for her. It's like having a niece, or a little sister. And it's never had any kind of negative impact on my life . . . until now."

Even now, three months later, Leigh could remember every word of what Jesse said next. How he'd been intrigued with Leigh from the moment they met in Henry's office; how much he grew to adore and respect her during the working Hamptons trips they'd shared; how he hadn't thought himself capable of caring about someone so much. He told her that he knew it was all happening so fast, but that he didn't want to waste any more of his life playing games or screwing around. She could take all the time she needed, especially in light of what had happened with Russell (Henry had told him everything), but he was committed to her and her only. Just tell him now if she felt the same way; if there was even the smallest chance she did, he would wait for her. Was there the smallest chance? She smiled now just remembering all of it.

The flight to Los Angeles was uneventful. As promised, Adriana was waiting for them at the baggage claim, chattering a mile a minute, filled with excitement and ideas about how the girls would spend their weekend.

"First and foremost, we shop," Adriana announced as she clicked open the doors to her brand-new, candy apple red BMW M3 convertible.

"Sweet car!" Emmy breathed, running her hand across its trunk.

Adriana smiled happily. "Isn't she hot? How can you live in California and not drive a convertible? It's a sacrilege. She's my 'independence gift' from my parents."

"You're joking," Leigh said, delighted that the three of them could fall right back into their familiar patterns.

"Not at all," Adriana sang. "They wanted to 'encourage' my decision to support myself — I'm paying entirely for my own apartment, by the way — so here she is. I mean, I could've rejected it on principle, but that just seems silly, doesn't it?"

The girls piled into the convertible and proceeded to work their way through lunch at the Ivy, store-hopping on Robertson so Emmy could pick up a pair of baby Uggs for her nephew, and a driving tour of Venice

Beach, Adriana's new neighborhood. Her studio was bright and modern, a clean, uncluttered space just two blocks to both the ocean and all the stores and restaurants on Main Street. Leigh couldn't remember feeling this happy, this *content,* for a long time, and as the girls sipped wine and dressed for dinner, the thought occurred to her that the anxiety-related heart palpitations and clammy hands and fingernails-in-the-palm digging were things of the past. The Nicorette was gone. She even slept most nights. It was almost impossible to imagine, but if she had to select a single word to describe her current emotional state, she might have even chosen *relaxed.*

Singing Shakira the entire car ride to West Hollywood, the girls were prepped and ready for a big night out. It only helped when Adriana pulled up to the valet at Koi and was given a rock star–worthy greeting, followed by a worshipful double cheek kiss and a "fucking gorgeous, Adriana!" by the otherwise obnoxious maître d'. They were immediately ushered past teeming heaps of sushi-seekers and sake-swiggers and deposited at one of the restaurant's best tables, a prime swatch of real estate that offered 360-degree views of the dining area and bar, and glimpses of the cocktail garden cum pa-

parazzi frenzy out front. A round of lychee martinis simply materialized, and within minutes the friends were in prime form.

"So, what's the plan?" Leigh asked Adriana, who had been approached and greeted by no fewer than three people in the last ten minutes.

"You're like a local celebrity," Emmy said to Adriana, shaking her head. "Not that I'm remotely surprised, but still . . ."

Adriana flashed her perfect teeth and performed her sexy hair-flick move to what Leigh would swear were audible groans from nearby tables. "*Querida,* please, I'm blushing!"

"Yeah, right," Emmy said. "Our shy, fragile flower, just waiting to bloom."

"Okay, so maybe not so shy," Adriana concurred. "And as for our plan, well, we aren't committed to anything. We could meet up with Toby later, or" — Adriana smiled devilishly again, clearly indicating which choice would be her preference — "we could head to Vine and meet up with some of those guys from Endeavor. One of them has a sick house and always throws great pool parties. . . ."

"What's this I hear? A new love interest, perhaps? What about Toby?" Leigh asked, popping a piece of salmon sashimi in her mouth.

"What about Toby?" Adriana said, the up-to-no-good smile back again. "He's lovely, as always. But that's not to say there aren't many more lovelies out there. . . ."

"Does he know?" Emmy asked.

Adriana nodded. "He's wonderful, sweet, even fun sometimes. I told him I'd love to keep seeing him on a nonexclusive basis if he was okay with that, and he was. Can you really expect a girl in a brand-new city with so many delicious treats to choose only one? It's inhumane!"

"So, as far as our pact goes . . . ," Emmy said, letting her words trail off.

"Yes, that *is* why we're out here, isn't it? It's been exactly one year since the agreement, and we're supposed to evaluate this weekend. Declare a winner," Leigh said.

Adriana waved her hand dismissively. "The pact? Please. I'm so over it."

Emmy laughed. "So are you admitting defeat?"

"Absolutely, one hundred percent, not for a single second," Adriana said, sipping her martini and delicately licking her lips. "Admittedly, there's no ring" — she wagged her left hand, fingers spread — "but there could have been. And still can be, from Toby or anyone else. I might be thirty in a sea of gorgeous twentysomethings, but the more time

I spend here, the more obvious it becomes: They're amateurs. They're little girls. They don't know the first thing about seducing or keeping a man. We're women . . . in every sense of the word."

The waiter appeared at their table and began to uncork a bottle of Dom Pérignon. "We didn't order that," Leigh said, looking to her friends for confirmation.

"It's from the gentlemen sitting at the end of the bar," he replied, the festive pop of the cork punctuating his words.

All three girls swiveled immediately to look.

"They're cute!" Leigh said in the way committed girls do the world over. *They're totally fine . . . for you. I won't be partaking because I'm madly in love with someone so much better. . . .*

"Way too preppy," Adriana said automatically, her eagle eyes taking in the four men.

"We don't have to sleep with them, but we do have to invite them over for a drink," Leigh said in her most reasonable voice.

"Please, we don't owe them anything but a thank-you smile and a little wave," Adriana said, performing both with a flourish as she spoke.

Neither girl noticed that Emmy's face was beet red, that she was fidgeting with her hands and refusing to look back at the bar.

"You okay?" Leigh asked, wondering if Emmy was having a Duncan-related regret, or worse, if they were his friends. They looked like East Coast prep-school guys, not at all like native Californians, and as Leigh watched Emmy grow more and more uncomfortable, she was sure she had hit on something. "Are those friends of Duncan's?" she asked.

Emmy shook her head no. "I'm so humiliated. My god, I never thought I'd see him again. What happens abroad stays abroad, right? Or what doesn't happen . . ."

"What is she talking about?" Adriana asked Leigh.

Leigh shrugged; damned if she knew.

"Is one of them a card-carrying member of the Tour de Whore? Or perhaps more than one?" Adriana asked with a wicked smile.

"God, I wish," Emmy sighed. "One of them — the guy in the striped collared shirt — is Paul. I can't believe he recognizes me. This is so embarrassing. What am I supposed to do?"

"Who's Paul?" Leigh asked, scanning her brain to recall the names of Emmy's conquests from the past year. "The Israeli?"

"Croc Dundee?" Adriana asked.

"The guy on the beach in Bonaire?"

"Someone else entirely we haven't heard of and are therefore going to torture you for?"

"No!" Emmy hissed, looking very distressed. "I met Paul at the Costes in Paris, the first trip I took after the tour began. He's the one I threw myself at, who completely rejected me. Had to go to his ex-girlfriend's party. Any of this ringing a bell?"

Both girls nodded. "That was a year ago," Leah said. "I'm sure he doesn't even remember you inviting him to your room, just the great conversation you had."

"Uh-huh, keep telling her your lies," Adriana said.

"It doesn't look like you have much choice," Leigh whispered. "He's coming over here. Three o'clock. Two. One . . ."

"Emmy?" he said, sounding endearingly nervous. "I'm not sure if you remember, but we met in Paris, at the worst hotel on earth. Paul? Paul Wyckoff?"

"Hi!" Emmy said with the perfect amount of enthusiasm. "Thanks for the champagne. These are my friends Leigh and Adriana. This is Paul."

Everyone shook hands and smiled and made a minute or two of small talk before Paul dropped two back-to-back conversational bombs. It turned out that although Paul was in LA for the week to visit his newly born niece, he'd actually moved to New York six months earlier and was living in a great apartment on the Upper East Side. As if that wasn't enough to digest, he managed to mention how upset he'd been when Emmy never responded to the note he'd left for her, how he was sorry for just ditching her like that, but he'd been hoping to hear from her so he could make it up to her.

"Note? What note?" Emmy asked, all pretense of playing it cool totally gone.

"How easily we forget!" Paul laughed, and Emmy thought she might have to stand up and nibble on his lips then and there. "The one where I wrote this whole apology for leaving so abruptly, and I gave you all my contact information and basically begged you to get in touch. I left it with the front desk at the Costes when I checked out the next . . ." His voice drifted off and he smiled as he realized what had happened. "You never got that, did you?"

Emmy shook her head. "Sure didn't," she said cheerfully. This was, quite possibly, the best news she'd heard in an entire year.

Paul sighed. "I should've known better." He turned to the girls and, addressing Leigh and Adriana, asked if he might interrupt their dinner and steal their friend for a drink outside in the garden.

"She's all yours," Leigh said, waving her friend off, thrilled to see Emmy so happy.

"Only for a few minutes!" Adriana called after them. "We have plans after dinner." Adriana turned to Leigh and shook her finger admonishingly. "Don't make it so easy for him," she reprimanded.

When Emmy returned twenty minutes later, she was flushed with excitement.

"So, how was it?" Leigh asked. "Judging by your face right now, I'm guessing it wasn't utterly humiliating."

Emmy laughed. "Not for me, at least. He said he had to work up the nerve to send over the champagne tonight because he was still embarrassed that I never called him. Can you believe it?"

"Unbelievable," Leigh said, shaking her head. "And he lives in New York now? Are you kidding me?"

Emmy grinned happily, but there was barely a chance to celebrate. A minute later, Paul came back to the girls' table. "Hey, I hate to do this again," he said with a sheepish smile, "but I've got to run."

Emmy was so stunned that it prevented her from saying what she was thinking, namely, that Paul could take his whole *Oh, I'm so sorry you never got my note* act and shove it. Just minutes earlier she'd been going through a mental checklist of what she needed to do before she went home with him that very night (write down Adriana's address so she could get home the following morning, borrow an extra Tampax or two from Leigh, double-check that she was wearing the cute camisole she thought she was), and now she was about to be left . . . again.

"Going to another ex's party?" Adriana asked sweetly.

"Actually, I'm, uh . . . Christ, it sounds stupid."

Bring it on, Emmy thought to herself. *Between the three of us, we've heard every stupid excuse in the book.*

Paul checked his watch before jamming his hands into his pockets. He cleared his throat. "I'm doing the night shift for my brother and sister-in-law, and it starts right about now, so . . ."

"The night shift?" Emmy asked.

"Yeah, it's only their fourth night at home after leaving the hospital and they're sort of freaked out. Tired, too. I, uh, had some extra vacation time and figured I'm pretty good at staying up late, so I volunteered to take care of the baby at night." He shook his head. "She's a handful."

Leigh and Adriana shot each other a look. This guy may as well have had THE FUTURE FATHER OF EMMY'S CHILDREN tattooed across his forehead.

"Oh, how sweet!" Emmy cooed, all anger and disappointment immediately forgotten. "Does your sister-in-law pump and then leave it for you in bottles? Is the baby good? I bet she's a little colicky if she's up all night. My sister just had a baby, too, and he's a little scoundrel."

"Yeah, she's having a rough time with the nursing — said it's the hardest thing she's ever done — so it's a combination of breast milk and bottles right now. But the baby — Stella, that's her name — is really good. She's just so new, you know? She's up every two hours."

"Awww," Emmy cooed, gazing at Paul with unabashed adoration. "She sounds adorable."

"Yeah, so I better run." He paused and appeared to think about something. "Hey, so no pressure whatsoever — I know you're here with your friends and all — but it'd be great to have some company if —"

Emmy didn't wait for him to finish. "I'd love to," she interrupted him. "I'm practically an expert now, and I can see you're in dire need of help."

Paul smiled, and even Adriana thought he looked absolutely delicious. "Excellent! I'm going to grab my coat and say good-bye to my friends. Meet you by the door in a couple of minutes?"

Emmy nodded and watched as he walked back toward the bar.

"You're not *really* going, are you?" Adriana asked in such a way that indicated she already knew the answer was *Of course not.* "He can't expect to run into you and have you follow him around like a puppy."

Emmy took a long pull on her martini, set it down carefully, and smiled at Adriana. "I suppose I should *woof* right now."

"Emmy!" Adriana started to say, "Have I taught you nothing about —"

She held up a hand, and Leigh found herself silently cheering her on. "Stop being the rules Nazi, Adriana. Save it for your younger, more inexperienced fans. We" — she motioned around the table and smiled hugely at her best friends — "are all experts now. And we did it the old-fashioned way."

Adriana opened her mouth to argue, but appeared to reconsider. "All right," she said with an understanding nod. "I'll buy that."

"To us," Leigh said, her glass aloft.

The girls clinked and sipped and smiled. It might be the end of the pact, but somehow, they all knew it: The good stuff was just beginning.

ACKNOWLEDGMENTS

Thanks first and foremost to Marysue Rucci, who is so much more than the world's best editor; to Sloan Harris for talking me down from every ledge in town; and to David Rosenthal for cracking me up, time after time, always knowing when it's most needed (and least appropriate). Thank you to the unparalleled team at Simon & Schuster, especially Aileen Boyle, Tracey Guest, Victoria Meyer, Katie Grinch, Leah Wasielewski, Jackie Seow, and Ginny Smith. I owe JoAnna Kremer, copy editor extraordinaire, a huge debt for making it look like I know more than the most rudimentary rules of grammar. Special gratitude to Melissa Perello for the crash course in all things chef-related. To Deborah Schneider, Vivienne Schuster, Betsy Robbins, Lynne Drew, Claire Bord, Helen Johnstone, Dave Patane, Kyle White, Stephen Frank, Judith Hirsch, and Cathy Gleason, thanks for all the much-appreciated advice and guidance in your many areas of expertise.

Thank you a million times over to my girlfriends, whose stories I've stolen shamelessly: Audey Kent, Victoria Stein, Helen Coster, Alli Kirshner, Julie Hootkin, Laura Dave, Megan Deem, and Gretchen Bylow. To the Cohens — Allison, Dave, Jackie, and Mel — for welcoming me into the family with open arms and lots of wine. Mom, Dad, and Dana — thanks for being funnier and more sarcastic than me, for reminding me of it every day, and for returning my endless bitching and complaining with support and understanding . . . I love you all so much. Most of all, I want to thank Mike, who endured countless "hypothetical" conversations about how "my characters" should get engaged, and still managed to surprise me with the perfect real-life proposal. From the first panic attack to the very last line edit, you helped this book (and this writer) in more ways than I'll ever admit.

ABOUT THE AUTHOR

Lauren Weisberger is the author of *The Devil Wears Prada,* which spent more than a year on the *New York Times* hardcover and paperback bestseller lists. The film version starring Meryl Streep and Anne Hathaway won a Golden Globe Award and grossed over $300 million worldwide. Her second novel, *Everyone Worth Knowing,* was also a *New York Times* bestseller. She lives in New York with her husband.